ECONOMIC ANALYSIS FOR BUSINESS DECISIONS

NEW EDITION

I0647226

For

M.B.A. & P.G.D.B.M. (Semester - I)

As Per New Syllabus, Effective from June 2013

Dr. Mukund Mahajan
Ph.D

NIRALI ™
PRAKASHAN
ADVANCEMENT OF KNOWLEDGE

N2959

Economic Analysis for Business Decision

Second Edition	:	**July 2016**
©	:	**Author**

Published By :
NIRALI PRAKASHAN
Abhyudaya Pragati, 1312, Shivaji Nagar
Off J.M. Road, PUNE – 411005
Tel - (020) 25512336/37/39, Fax - (020) 25511379
Email : niralipune@pragationline.com

➢ DISTRIBUTION CENTRES

PUNE

Nirali Prakashan : 119, Budhwar Peth, Jogeshwari Mandir Lane, Pune 411002, Maharashtra
Tel : (020) 2445 2044, 66022708, Fax : (020) 2445 1538
Email : bookorder@pragationline.com, niralilocal@pragationline.com

Nirali Prakashan : S. No. 28/27, Dhyari, Near Pari Company, Pune 411041
Tel : (020) 24690204 Fax : (020) 24690316
Email : dhyari@pragationline.com, bookorder@pragationline.com

MUMBAI

Nirali Prakashan : 385, S.V.P. Road, Rasdhara Co-op. Hsg. Society Ltd.,
Girgaum, Mumbai 400004, Maharashtra
Tel : (022) 2385 6339 / 2386 9976, Fax : (022) 2386 9976
Email : niralimumbai@pragationline.com

➢ DISTRIBUTION BRANCHES

JALGAON

Nirali Prakashan : 34, V. V. Golani Market, Navi Peth, Jalgaon 425001,
Maharashtra, Tel : (0257) 222 0395, Mob : 94234 91860

KOLHAPUR

Nirali Prakashan : New Mahadvar Road, Kedar Plaza, 1st Floor Opp. IDBI Bank
Kolhapur 416 012, Maharashtra. Mob : 9850046155

NAGPUR

Pratibha Book Distributors : Above Maratha Mandir, Shop No. 3, First Floor,
Rani Jhanshi Square, Sitabuldi, Nagpur 440012, Maharashtra
Tel : (0712) 254 7129

DELHI

Nirali Prakashan : 4593/21, Basement, Aggarwal Lane 15, Ansari Road, Daryaganj
Near Times of India Building, New Delhi 110002 Mob : 08505972553

BENGALURU

Pragati Book House : House No. 1, Sanjeevappa Lane, Avenue Road Cross,
Opp. Rice Church, Bengaluru – 560002.
Tel : (080) 64513344, 64513355,Mob : 9880582331, 9845021552
Email:bharatsavla@yahoo.com

CHENNAI

Pragati Books : 9/1, Montieth Road, Behind Taas Mahal, Egmore,
Chennai 600008 Tamil Nadu, Tel : (044) 6518 3535,
Mob : 94440 01782 / 98450 21552 / 98805 82331,
Email : bharatsavla@yahoo.com

niralipune@pragationline.com | www.pragationline.com

Also find us on [f] www.facebook.com/niralibooks

Preface ...

According to the Revised Syllabus of the University of Pune, beginning academic year 2013-14, for MBA and PGDBM, **Economic Analysis for Business Decisions** has been prescribed for Semester – I. The complexities of business practices and decisions have increased tremendously, especially due to the intensity of global competion and advances made by Information and Communication Technology. However, Economics being the basic discipline for all management courses, a clear understanding of the basic economic theories cannot be replaced. Economic theorisation involves an academic rigour and conceptualisation of the basics involved in the economic life of a modern society. Whatever practices of business are followed by business firms have to be tested on the touchstone of economic concepts. This is because practices may differ over a period of time and from place to place, but the theoretical foundation remains unchanged and hence the basic relationships among different variables have to satisfy basic economic criteria to judge the lastingness and equitability of business practice.

Basic concepts of Economics have to be studied at the management studies level because students who have graduated in science, engineering, medicine and such other non-commerce-non-economics streams need an exposure to these basics in economics. Most of the management decisions need a proper understanding of micro economics. But macro analysis cannot be totally eschewed as foreign trade, public finance, national income accounting etc. are very much a concern of modern business. Money market and capital market are by far the most important such concerns of business firms.

Demand analysis, demand forecasting, market categories and equilibria alternatives for determinateness of solutions are an important part of micro economic analysis. Similarly, determinants of demand, costs, profitability are of critical importance for business leaders. Several concepts of public finance and financial markets need to be properly grasped for arriving at crucial decisions in policy formulations at the firm/industry levels.

Like all my books, the present one, I am sure, would prove to be user-friendly. This combination of lucidity of diction and soundness of logical analytical method is a verily a tight-rope walking. But a non-compromising approach cannot escape this. I am confident that the teachers and students alike will find this book useful. Suggestions for improvement are always welcome.

I am grateful to my long-time friend and publisher, Shri. Dineshbhai Furia for encouraging me to keep writing. Shri. Jigneshbhai Furia and Shri. Amol Mahabal are my young friends, but for whose priceless assistance and insistence, this book would not have seen the light of the day. I am also thankful to Mr. Ramesh Zunjare for his excellent type-setting work. Many other friends from Nirali Prakashan have contributed their mite in bringing out this book. I am equally thankful to all of them.

6/4, Rambaug Colony,
Navi Peth, L.B. Shastri Road,
Pune – 411 030
August 1, 2013

- Dr. Mukund Mahajan

☆☆☆

Syllabus ...

ECONOMIC ANALYSIS FOR BUSINESS DECISIONS
M.B.A. (Sem. I : Course Code 102) AND
P.G.D.B.M. (Sem. I : Course Code 103)

1. **Basic Concepts of Economics**

   Introduction to Economics, Basic Economic Problems, Circular Flow of Economic Activity, Nature of the firm - Rationale, Objective of maximizing firm value as present value of all future profits, Maximizing, Satisficing, Optimizing, Principal agent problem, Accounting Profit and Economic Profit, Role of profit in Market System, Adam Smith and Invisible Hand.

2. **Demand Analysis and Forecasting**

   Determinants of Market Demand at Firm and Industry level - Elasticity of Demand - Market Demand Equation - Use of Multiple Regression for Estimating demand - Case study on Estimating Industry Demand (Formulating equation and solving with the aid of software expected)

   Demand and Supply

   Market Equilibrium - Pricing under perfect competition, Monopolistic competition, Case study on pricing under monopolistic competition, Oligopoly - Product differentiation and Price discrimination; Price - Output decision in multi-plant and multi-product firms.

3. **Cost Concepts**

   Cost Concept, Opportunity Cost, Marginal, Incremental and Sunk Costs, Cost Volume Profit Analysis, Breakeven Point, Case Study on Marginal costs.

   Risk Analysis and Decision Making

   Concept of risk, Expected value computation, Risk management through Insurance, diversification, Hedging, Decision Tree Analysis, Case Study on Decision Tree Technique.

4. **Money and Capital Markets in India**

   Role and Functions of Money Markets, Composition of Money Market, Money Market Instruments, Reserve Bank of India - Functions, Regulatory Role of RBI w.r.t. Currency, Credit and Balance of Payment, Open Market Operations.

   Role and Functions of Capital Markets, Composition of Capital market, Stock Exchanges in India, Role of SEBI, understanding of stock market quotations in financial press expected.

5. **Public Finance Infrastructure**

   Familiarity with important Terms/Agencies/Approaches/Practices related to National Income (such as GDP, PPP, Growth Rate), Foreign Trade (such as GATT, WTO) and Union Budget (such as Revenue Account, Capital Account, Revenue Deficit, Fiscal Deficit, Plan and Non-plan expenditure) is expected.

   Understanding of Summarized budget for the current financial year is required (knowledge of detailed budget provisions not required).

☆☆☆

Contents ...`

☆☆☆

Lets go with...

CHAPTER

1

BASIC CONCEPTS OF ECONOMICS

❧ SYNOPSIS ❦

1.1 Introduction to Economics

According to the traditional approach, the study of Economics was divided into four main divisions viz. Consumption, Production, Exchange and Distribution. The modern approach is different. The study of economics is now usually divided into two parts : (a) Micro economics (Price Theory), and (b) Macro economics (Income Theory).

It has become an accepted practice these days to approach economic theory either via micro analysis or macro analysis. These terms micro economics and macro economics - were coined by Prof. Ragnar Frisch during the 'twenties'. Today, we hardly observe any modern treatise on economic analysis which does not deal with this popular distinction between micro economics and macro economics.

Historically, Economics started its march as a science, along macro lines only. In the latter half of the middle-ages, economic thinkers advocated expansion of trade for the prosperity of people and nations. These thinkers, referred to as *mercantilists*, viewed the economy as a whole and advocated on optimum employment of the economy's resources as an objective. Adam Smith's *Wealth of Nations*, published in 1776, was the first treatise to discuss the automatic working of the market mechanism. Adam Smith paved the way of classical theorisation which was mainly micro-analytical in its approach. However, Malthus (1766 - 1834) among the classical writers and Karl Marx (1818-1883) among the later writers had shown great vision in macro analytical approach. But again, due to the efficient and smooth functioning of the economies of developed countries, the Neo-classical economists shifted emphasis onto micro-analysis. Dr. Alfred Marshall perfected the micro approach, though his 'Principles' did contain discussion of macro-economic variables. It was only after the Great Depression that the limitations of micro-economic solutions to macro-level problems became evident. Lord John Maynard Keynes was the first to present (in 1936) a comprehensive macro-economic theory. The years which followed saw the development of both micro and macro economics on the lines of two separate approaches.

1.1.1 Micro Economics

(A) Meaning of Micro Economics :

As pointed out by Lerner, *"Micro economics consists of looking at the economy through a microscope, as it were, to see how the millions of cells in the body economic - the individuals or households as consumers, and the individuals or firms as producers-play their part in the working of the whole economic organism"*. The economy can be compared to a living organism. In this organism, hundreds and thousands of individuals acting as consumers or producers are like the blood cells in our body. The blood cells can be studied through microscope only. In the same way, the economic behaviour of individual consumers and producers as small groups of persons engaged in an economic activity can be studied through micro economics only. For example, an individual consumer faces a problem of distributing his income on various commodities which he can buy within the limited range of his income. He wants to do this with a view to maximising his personal satisfaction. This is a micro level problem and the equilibrium of an individual consumer forms a part of micro economics. An individual producer faces similar problem of equilibrium when he tries to maximise his profits by adjusting his own production to the share of market demand available to him. In an industry there can be many firms, each independently taking decision of production, but still sharing a common interest with other firms in the same industry. The equilibrium of the firm and the equilibrium of an industry are matters at the micro level even though the groups concerned are sometimes very small and sometimes relatively large. What is important to remember is the fact that micro economics does not go beyond this and cannot study the equilibrium of the entire economy as a whole or the supply of goods and services at the level of the economy as a whole. This is beyond the scope of micro economics.

Important Definitions of Micro Economics :

(a) **K. E. Boulding :** *"Micro economics is the study of particular firms, particular households, individual prices, wages, incomes, individual industries, particular commodities."*

(b) **Ackley :** *"Micro economics deals with the division of total output among industries, products, firms and the allocation of resources among competing groups. It considers problems of income distribution. Its interest is in relative prices of particular goods and services."*

(c) **McConnel :** *"Micro economics is concerned with specific economic units and detailed consideration of the behaviour of these individual units."*

(B) Nature of Micro Economics :

(1) Allocation of Resources : Micro economic analysis explains the allocation of resources assuming that the total resources are given. It tries to explain the proportion in which various goods and services will be produced. Under conditions of perfect competition, the function of resource allocation is performed by the price mechanism. So, micro economic analysis has to consider the price determination of different goods and services under different market conditions. Just as commodities are bought and sold at the market, the resources or the factors of production are also bought and sold at the market. The study of rent, wages, interest and profits, therefore, becomes a subject matter of micro economics.

(2) Optimum Allocation of Resources : While studying the price-determination, it is not enough to study how prices of various commodities and factors are determined. A more important problem is one of ensuring an optimum allocation of resources. Micro economics aims at studying the way in which such an optimum use of available resources can be ensured. Whatever is produced in the best possible manner should also be consumed in the best possible way. These are the problems of production and distribution and are concerned with equilibrium of the producer and equilibrium of the consumer. The various laws governing the process of production and consumption as well as the conditions and constraints experienced in these fields are matters of study in macro economics.

(3) Welfare Economics : Efficiency of production and consumption, as noted earlier, are concerned with welfare economics. In the words of the well-known American economist Professor A. P. Lerner, *"In micro economics, we are more concerned with the avoidance or elimination of waste or inefficiency arising from the fact that production is not organised in the most efficient manner. Such an efficiency means that it is possible, by rearranging the different ways in which products are being produced and consumed, to get more of something that is scarce without giving up any part of any-other scarce item, or to replace something by something else that is preferred. The micro economic theory spells out the conditions of efficiency (so as to eliminate all kinds of inefficiency), and suggest how they could be achieved. These conditions (called "pareto-optimal" conditions) can be of the greatest help in raising the standard of living of the population".*

(C) Features of Micro Economics :

(a) Nature of Micro Economics : Micro economics is the study of the behaviour of the individual units, in specific, consumers, firms and factors of production.

(b) Methodological Approach : Micro economics has an 'individualistic' approach. It is an inquiry as to how an 'individual' person maximises satisfaction or how a 'particular' firm maximises profits or how a 'particular' family adjusts its expenditure to its income.

(c) Economic Variables : Micro economics is concerned with the behaviour of micro-variables or micro-quantities, for instance, individual demand, individual supply, individual industry, particular commodity prices and so on. As Prof. Ackley observes that, micro economics deals with the division of total output among individual industries, scarce resource allocation among the various competing users, the motive of each one being optimisation – satisfaction or profit. Thus, it deals with individual incomes and output.

(d) View-point : Micro economics intensively studies the economy by splitting it or slicing it in various components. It is also said that micro economics is like studying **a tree** and not the whole of forest. It is a study of the economy by worm's eye-view, i.e. getting information of some very specific component of our economic system.

(e) Scope of Study : The micro economics is price and value theory, the theory of the household, the firm and the industry, production and welfare theory. In other words, it deals mainly with pricing and distribution. It deals with the theory of commodity pricing, factor pricing and theory of economic welfare.

(f) Price Theory : Micro economics is also referred to as Price or Value Theory as prices are the core of micro economics.

(g) Assumptions : Micro economics deals with 'particular'. In this dynamic world, to derive laws in economics based on individual experience is far too difficult. To hold the laws good, generally the laws in Micro economics are based on certain assumptions. They generally carry a phrase, "other things being equal ...." Only on the fulfillment of these conditions can the law of micro economics hold good.

(h) Classical Support : Traditional or classical approach was micro analysis. In fact, they believed that the conclusions of micro analysis can be extended to deal with macroeconomic problems.   In other words, all classical theories are based on assumptions with which micro economics is explained. Thus, the greatest exponents of micro economics are classical writers.

(i) Types : Micro economics is of three types :

    (i) Micro-static which deals with the relationship between different micro-variables at a 'given' time under conditions of equilibrium.

    (ii) Comparative Micro-static : It is an analysis which 'compares' the equilibrium positions of the relationship between micro-variables at different points of time.

    (iii) Micro-dynamics : It refers to the process which explains the transition from one equilibrium to another.

(j) **Difference in Outlook :** Some sort of 'aggregation' is studied in micro economics also. However, the 'aggregate' nature is different in micro than macro analysis. For instance, 'market' (demand by all the buyers) is a topic of micro economics. But, 'market' is for an individual commodity and not for all goods together. In this way, the aggregation in 'micro' analysis is still an individualistic approach.

(k) **Tools of Study :** Micro economics is studied with the help of an indispensable tool namely 'Marginal' Analysis.

(l) **Laws of Micro Economics :** Examples of certain basic and important principles are Law of Demand, Law of Diminishing Marginal Utility, Law of Equi-marginal Utility. Laws of Returns explaining behaviour of the firms, theories of rent, wages, interest and profit or theory of distribution. All these are explaining a consumer's or a producer's behaviour.

As **Prof. Boulding** describes it, both micro and macroeconomic analyses confine themselves to the study of economic variables, though their approaches are different. Micro and Macro approach, both have their own significance to the study of economic problem. There is no watertight compartment to their distinctions. For instance, while studying a country, then district in it is a microanalysis and a country is macro study. But when studying world economics, that particular country is a microeconomic approach.

(D) Scope of Micro Economics :

According to **Prof. Boulding,** *"Micro economics is the study of particular firm, particular household, individual price, wage, income, industry and particular commodity".*

In the words of **Leftwitch,** *"Micro economics is concerned with the economic activities of economic units as consumers, resource-owners and business firms".*

(1) **Analysis of Economic Constituents :** Micro economics, as the foregoing definitions point out, is the analysis of economy's constituent elements - households, firms, industries and sectors (e.g. agricultural sector, industrial sector etc.) As the name 'micro' (meaning small) itself suggests, it is not aggregative, but elective. It tries to explain the behaviour of individual consumer or the smallest unit of consumption, i.e. the household and individual producer or the smallest unit of production, i.e. the firm. The decisions regarding production and consumption taken by these producers and consumers when add up to market supply and market demand respectively, micro economics seeks to explain the working of the market for individual commodities. Just as there is a market for commodities, there is a market for each individual factor of production. These two markets are not independent of each other. Because the factors of production earn in the factor-market and spend in the product market, any change in the former gem reflected in changes in the latter. On the assumption of the consumer's objectives of satisfaction-maximisation, micro economics studies the conditions of equilibrium of the consumer. Similarly, on the basis of the assumption of profit-maximisation, macro economics seeks to explain the equilibrium of the producer i.e. the firm and then the industry.

(2) Economic Decisions : Through the interplay of the forces of demand and supply, prices of commodities like tea, coffee, sugar, cloth, launderer's services etc. are determined. As a result of the interplay of these forces, therefore, decisions regarding 'what to produce' and 'how much to produce' are taken. Guided by the profit-motive, producers try to produce things in the most economical way and this answers the question 'how to produce'. This whole process is the subject matter for micro economics.

(3) Study of the Factor Market : Along with the product market, the study of the factor market is also undertaken by micro economics. When it studies rent, profits, wages and interest, it seeks to answer the question, 'For whom to produce'.

The fact of scarcity of resources makes it imperative to ensure that resources are used in the best way, by avoiding all wastes. To repeat what **Prof. A. P. Lerner** has said, *"In micro economics, we are more concerned with the avoidance or elimination of waste, or with inefficiency arising from the fact that production is not organised in the most efficient manner. The micro economic theory spells out the conditions of efficiency (so as to eliminate all kinds of inefficiency), and suggests how they could be achieved. These conditions (called 'Pareto-optimal' conditions) can be of the greatest help in raising the standard of living of the population".*

(4) Study of Economic Decisions : It will thus be clear that of the six basic problems the economy viz. what commodities are produced and in what quantities; how are the commodities produced; how is the output shared; are production and distribution carried out in the most efficient manner, fall within the purview of micro economics.

It would be necessary to remember that, inspite of demarcation of limits of micro economics; its subject matter does have links with the subject matter of macro economics. When, for instance, the equilibrium of a firm or an industry or that of a household is disturbed, the disturbance has repercussions on the entire economy. Or, again, the process of readjustment to a new equilibrium affects the entire economy. In fact, micro economics studies, in detail, all the inter-relations of various sectors of the economy and their actions and reactions upon each other. The study, thus, rightly represents a micro economic view of the system. The following chart outlines the scope of micro economics.

(E) Importance of Micro Economics :

From the historical point of view, micro economic analysis was developed first. But, after the Great Depression and especially after the publication of Keynes' thesis, which brought about a Revolution in economics, micro economic analysis was subjected to severe criticism. Thereafter, most of economists focused their attention mainly on the differentiation between micro economic analysis, and the development of macro economic analysis. But inspite of the rapid development of macro economic analysis during recent times, micro economic analysis has maintained its position. It is still regarded as an important part of economic analysis. The theoretical and practical importance of micro economics can be summarised as follows :

(1) Allocation of Resources : Micro economic analysis can explain the allocation of resources under conditions of perfect competition or in a free enterprise economy. Micro economic analysis can explain why there is an increase in the production of some commodities and why there is a fall in the production of other commodities. It is as good as explaining the structure of the economy.

(2) The Distribution of National Income : The distribution of national income and the forces at work in bringing about this distribution can be explained with the help of micro economic analysis.

(3) Consideration of Welfare : The maximisation of social welfare can be brought about if there is perfect competition in the market. But normally, such a competition does not exist. The greater the deviation from perfect competition, the greater will be the reduction in social welfare. Another great hurdle in the maximisation of social welfare is the existence of externalities when the action of one brings in profit to someone else or puts him to loss for no fault of his, social welfare is endangered. All this can be studied with the help of the micro economics.

(4) Importance in the Applied Field of Economics : Micro economic analysis becomes very handy and useful in the field of applied economics such as international trade and public finance. Micro economic analysis can be used to find out the gains from international trade, the incidence of taxes, the impact of taxes on various commodities, and so on. Even the distribution of gains from international trade can be found out with the help of the concept of the elasticity of demand, and the demand and supply analysis.

(5) The Terminology and Tools of Economic Analysis : All the terminology and various tools used in economic analysis are a valuable contribution of micro economics to the development of economics. The terms which are to be used in any scientific analysis must have a precise connotation. Various terms such as demand, supply, production, price, cost and several others have been constantly used in micro economic analysis and have now acquired an exact and specific meaning. This has made the logical development of modern economics easy and has imparted precision to it. Similarly concepts like margin, opportunity cost, elasticity, etc. have become very handy and useful in modern economic analysis.

(F) Limitations of Micro Economics :

Micro economic analysis was subjected to very severe criticism. The main reason for this was the refusal to recognise the limitations of this analysis, mainly by classical economists and others who upheld this analysis. We have already seen the different ways in which micro economic analysis is useful. Now, let us see its main limitations.

(1) Inadequate Analysis : Micro economic analysis always thinks of individual factors of production or individual consumers or producers, etc., whereas macro economic analysis thinks in terms of aggregates and averages. The statement or conclusion which may hold good or may be true on individual levels, may not be so on aggregate levels. For example, saving is a virtue on the individual level. But, if the entire society follows this principle, the effective demand is reduced. Then, employment will be reduced and this will result in reducing national income, as shown by Lord Keynes. Similarly, it may be possible for an individual employer to lower the wage rate and provide employment for a larger number of labourers. But if all the employers decide to reduce wages, there will be a fall in effective demand, which may lead to a reduction in the national income itself, and will create unemployment. Thus, the conclusions which emerge from micro economic analysis should be accepted only after putting them to macro economic tests.

(2) Micro Economic Results are always Based on Certain Assumptions : Micro economic results or conclusions are always based on certain assumptions. For example, other things being equal under the conditions of perfect competition, etc. are the normal assumptions. These other things are never equal, or the assumption of perfect competition is never true in practice. The conclusions of this analysis are expected to provide solutions to various day-to-day problems. So, it is necessary to bear in mind that these limitations, which are inherent in micro economic analysis are imposed by these assumptions.

(3) Micro Economic Analysis Falls Short of Expectations : The aggregative analysis or the overall approach to any economic problem is beyond the reach of micro economic analysis, because it studies the economy in parts and not as a whole. But, the economy always functions as a whole. So, this analysis falls short of expectations.

(4) Inadequate Scope : Some of the problems faced by an economy are just beyond the scope of micro economics. For example, public finance or the monetary policy, etc., cannot be studied with the help of micro economics. But at the same time, it is true that some macro economic problems become more intelligible because of micro economic analysis. For example, the behaviour of an individual consumer is studied in micro economics, but, it becomes useful in determining the propensity to consume which is a macro variable.

1.1.2 Macro Economics

(A) Meaning and Definitions of Macro Economics :

In recent years increasing attention has been given to the analysis of the economic system as a whole. This is Macro economics.

- In the opinion of **R. G. D. Allen**, *"the term 'macro economics' applies to the study of relations between broad economic aggregates".*

- **Prof. Kenneth E. Boulding** puts it, *"Macro economics deals not with individual quantities as such, but with aggregates of these quantities, not with individual incomes but with the national income; not with individual prices but with the price level; not with individual outputs but with the national output".*

  It, thus, deals not with one family but all the families taken together; not with one firm but all the firms in an economy. Hence, macro economics deals with the great averages and aggregates of the system rather than with particular units in it.

- **Ackley** defines macro economics as, *"the study of the forces or factors that determine the levels of aggregate production, employment and prices in an economy and their rates of change over time".*

These various definitions imply that macro economics is that branch of economic analysis which studies the behaviour of not one particular unit, but of all the units combined together. It is the study of 'Aggregates' and hence can be called as 'Aggregate Economics'.

It is the study of the working of the economic system as a whole. It studies the behaviours of macro-quantities and macro-variables. Macro economics splits up the economy into sectors or lumps for the purpose of study, hence it is also called the 'Method of lumping'.

(B) Nature of Macro Economics :

(1) Macro economics deals with the functioning of the economy as a whole. Macro-analysis conceives of equilibrium between demand and supply in the economy as a whole.

(2) Among other things, macro economics seeks to explain how the economy's total output of goods and services, the price level of goods and services and the total employment of resources are demanded.

(3) Macro economics also seeks to investigative into the causes responsible for initiating changes in total output, aggregate employment and the general price level.

As mentioned above the Keynessian economists had developed macro economics to "full bloom" by the sixties. Its field of study is vast.

(C) Scope of Macro Economics :

The following chart will illustrate the scope of macro economics.

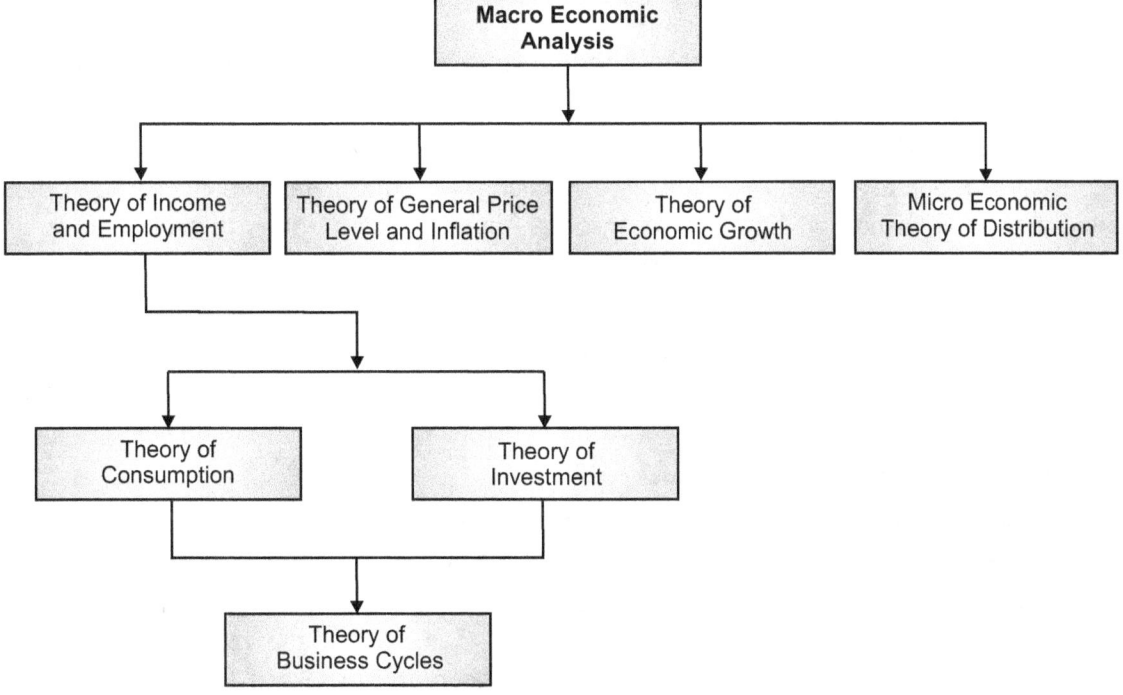

Fig. 1.1 : Scope of Macro Economics

The subject-matter of macro economics is :

(i)   It deals with theory of income, output of employment.

(ii) Theory of trade cycle is a part and parcel of macro economics study.

(iii) Changes in prices leading to inflation, deflation or reflation.

(iv) In detail it deals with the theory of Economic Growth.

(v)   Macro Theory of Distribution.

(D) Special Features of Macro Economics :

The main characteristics / features of macro economics are as follows :

(1) Nature : Macro economics is the study of the behaviour of the economy as a whole. Macro analysis conceives of equilibrium between demand and supply in the economy as a whole.

(2) Aggregative Approach : Macro economics is aggregative in their methodological approach. Macro economics has been developed to describe the typical nature of aggregate economic behaviour. It studies the overall averages and aggregates of the system.

(3) Economic Variables : Macro economics is concerned with the behaviour of macro variables or macro quantities such as aggregate demand, general price level, aggregate supply, total consumption, total expenditure etc. Thus, macro economics concentrates on variables like the aggregate volume of output of an economy, total employment and total investment.

(4) Area of Problems : Macro economics pertains to the problems of the size of national income, economic growth and the general price level, employment level etc.

(5) Income Theory : Macro economics is also referred to as the 'Income Theory' in economics. The reason is that when there is change in aggregate demand or any other aggregate, it is linked with the level of income. Thus, in macro analysis, income, and not price, is the link between demand and supply.

(6) Assumptions : Macro economics is a more realistic approach, as the theories in it are based on few assumptions. In this approach full employment is not assumed. We study the determinants of full employment and see how the fullest possible employment can be attained.

(E) Importance of Macro Economics :

(1) Brought many a Paradox to Light : Macro economics is of a comparatively recent origin. Its real development took place after 1935-1936. Perhaps, the thesis of Lord Keynes synthesized macro economic theories for the first time. This clarified the functioning of the capitalistic system. The study of macro economics pointed out the fallacies involved in applying the micro economic conclusions to macro economic problems and as pointed out earlier, brought many a paradox to light.

(2) Gives Complete Picture of the Economy as a Whole : Macro economic analysis gives a complete picture of the economy as a whole. This makes it more important and handy in the context of the economic policy. The macro-approach to economic problems is more useful in determining the policy regarding business cycles, inflation and deflation, public finances, international trade etc.

(3) Increase in Utility of Economics : Many of the micro economic models are based on several assumptions which may be essential, but the conclusions derived from these assumptions are far from reality and may be true only under ideal conditions. So these are not very useful in practice. This was the general belief. But because of the progress made by macro economics, it became possible to find out answers or solutions to several problems which were to be faced in our day-to-day life. Many macro economic conclusions could be tested with the help of surveys. So, micro economics has high potentialities to guide the economy as a whole in the day-to-day business of life. That is why, it can be said that macro economics has increased the utility of economics.

(4) Used for Development of Micro Economics : Macro economics can be used for the development of micro economics. For example, the Law of Diminishing Utility is a very important law in micro economics. This law is based on the observation of the reactions of innumerable persons. Thus, the observations and conclusions, on a macro economic level can be used for furthering the development of micro economics.

(5) Study of Factors of Production : Various factors of an economy are studied independently in micro economics as one single unit. But, when all these factors come together, they may function or behave differently. For the study of this, macro economics is more suitable.

(F) Limitations of Macro Economics :

So far, we have seen the importance of macro economics in a nut-shell. Because of the close relationship of macro economic problems and because of the guidance which it can give the government for determining the economic policy, the development of macro economics during the last few years has been very rapid. Similarly, its popularity has increased. Because of the continuously increasing interdependence of social life, increasing social responsibilities of the government in the economic field, increasing importance of the economic policy and broadening of the field of economic planning, the growing importance of macro economics is inevitable. But while accepting this importance of macro economics, one has to note its limitations also. These limitations are as follows :

(1) No Specific Conclusions : Macro economic conclusions are always expressed in terms of averages or aggregates. In doing so, it is necessary to aggregate individual experiences. Similarly, individual experiences are to be generalised. It is not possible to neglect the importance of individual experiences; so, one has to be very careful while generalising them. As has been often stated earlier, what holds good on an individual level may not hold good on a general level. For example, an individual depositor may withdraw his deposit from the bank at any time, but if all the depositors go and withdraw their deposits at one and the same time, the bank may fail. So the aggregates and averages are to be interpreted with caution.

(2) Needs Elaborate Analysis : It is always necessary to add and find out the aggregates of individual units. This can be done when all the units are similar or identical, otherwise this aggregate does not have any meaning. As **Prof. K. E. Boulding** has pointed out : 6 apples + 7 apples = 13 apples is meaningful; 6 apples + 7 sweet berries = 13 fruits may also convey some meaning, but 6 apples + 7 buildings has no meaning. So, by taking totals like the last one, macro economics may not lead you anywhere. Therefore, one has to be very careful while taking and interpreting aggregates in macro economics.

(3) Smaller Influence on all Economic Fields : All macro economic trends do not have a similar influence on all economic fields. For example, an increase in the general price level affects different social groups differently. Some are adversely affected, while others are benefitted.

(4) Needs careful attention of Macro Economic Classification : Macro economic variables are important from the point of policy, but at times, their analysis or classification is more important. For example, the national income has increased by 20% or the prices have gone up by 10% has no meaning beyond a particular limit. It will be more important to know the changes in the income of particular groups in society or two know the change in prices of luxuries, necessities, etc.

(5) Deceptive Concepts : While using these macro economic concepts for the determination of economic policies, one has to be very careful because many times these concepts are deceptive. For example, if the average depth of water in river bed is said to be 3 feet, and taking this as a guide if a person not knowing swimming, attempts to cross the river on foot is likely to be drowned. This may be the case of several macro economic conclusions. For example, even if the price level is stable, you cannot positively say that rationing and price control is not necessary. Because it is possible that the prices of agricultural commodities might have increased and by chance the prices of manufactured commodities might have decreased, thus leaving the price level unaffected. But under these circumstances, price control in both these fields will be required.

(G) Micro Economics Vs. Macro Economics :

(1) Individual Vs. Aggregate : The word **'Micro'** is derived from the Greek word **'Mikros'** which means **'Small'**. Thus, micro economics is the study of economic activities of individuals and small group of individuals.

The word **'Macro'** is derived from the Greek word **'Makros'** which means '**Large**'. Macro economics is the study of aggregates and averages. It is the study of the economic system as a whole.

Thus, micro economics is an Individualistic approach to the study of economic theory, whereas macroeconomic is Aggregative Economics.

(2) Price Theory Vs. Income Theory : The basis of micro economics is the 'price mechanism'. It studies price theory with the help of two economic forces in the market, namely, demand and supply forces. These forces help to determine the equilibrium price in the market.

The basis of macro economics is 'income mechanism'. It studies national income and its impact on output and employment in the economy. The national income (or national output) is determined by aggregate demand and aggregate supply.

(3) Partial Vs. General Equilibrium : Micro economics is based on the partial equilibrium analysis. It helps to explain the equilibrium conditions of an individual, a firm or an industry.

(4) Static Vs. Dynamic : Micro economics is considered as a static analysis. Macro economics is considered as a dynamic and changing analysis.

(5) Scope of Study : Micro economics has prices at its core of subject-matter. Thus, its field of study extends to : (a) Theory of product pricing with its two constituents namely theory of consumer's behaviours and theory of production, (b) Theory of factor pricing namely theories on rent, wages, interest and profit, (c) Theory of economic welfare.

The field of macro economics analysis circles around income theory. Its areas of interest are : (a) Theory of income, output and employment with its two constituents viz. theory of consumption function and theory of investment function, (b) Theory of trade cycle, (c) Theory of prices i.e. theories of inflation, deflation and reflation, (d) Theory of economic growth, (e) Macro theory of distribution.

(6) Exponents : Prof. Marshall's *magnum opus*, "Principles of Economics " (1890) dealt in detail with micro economics.

John Maynard Keynes' celebrated work, "General Theory of Employment, Interest and Money" (1936) is an outstanding example of macro economics.

(7) Objectives : The main objectives of micro economics are to maximise utility (demand side) and maximise profits at minimum cost of production (supply side).

The main objectives of macro economics are full employment, economic growth, price stability and favourable balance of payments.

(8) Slicing Vs. Lumping Method : Micro economics splits up the whole economy into small individual units and studies each unit in detail. Hence, it is also referred to as study by 'slicing' method.

Macro economics studies the economic behaviour in its totality. It divides the economy into sectors (or lumps) for study. Hence, it is referred to as 'Lumping' method.

Micro economics is study of the economy by worm's eye-view. On the other hand, macro economics is study of the economy by bird's eye-view.

(9) Importance : The study of micro economics is important for resource utilisation, taking business decisions and for social welfare.

The study of macro economics is important for the formulation of economic policies for the whole nation, for analysing trade cycles etc.

(10) Assumptions : Micro economics is based on different assumptions concerned with rational behaviour of individuals. The assumptions on which the laws are based are too many and make the study unrealistic. Macro economics bases its assumptions on such variables as the aggregate volume of the output of the economy. The theories of macro economics are more realistic as they are based on much less assumptions.

(11) Difference in outlook : Micro economics deals not only with individual units in the economic system. It deals with some sort of aggregates also. However, the 'aggregates' dealt in micro economics and in macro are altogether different. For instance, it may study an industry which comprises of a large number of firms. But, it is homogenous 'aggregates' in micro economics. On the other hand, aggregates in macro economics is of heterogneous in character.

(12) Variables and Quantities : Micro economics deals with micro variables and micro quantities, for instance, it studies individual demand, individual supply, particular firm or a particular industry, family income, prices of a particular commodity etc.

In macro economics, the study is of macro variables and macro quantities, for instance, aggregate demand, aggregate supply, total output, total consumption, national income, general price level etc.

From the above distinction, it leads us to conclude that micro and macro economics are two clear, rigid and distinct approaches to the study of economics. However, the distinction is not too rigid. What is micro economics in one situation may be macro in another situation.

The two approaches may seem to be competitive in approach but at the bottom they are complementary to each other. In fact, the two approaches are interdependent on each other. They must be integrated judiciously in a manner for the complete functioning of the economic system. For example, the cost of production of a particular firm is not determined by the demand for factors by that firm alone (micro) but by the demand of the entire economy (macro). Similarly, the sales of a firm are not influenced by the price of its product, but by the purchasing power of the society.

To isolate any economic phenomenon and call it as self-determined is difficult. The study of macro economics is important as it deals with aggregative variables such as national income and national output. In the same way, micro economics study is significant as national income is ultimately the result of the decisions of millions of business firms and individuals.

Micro economics contributes to macro economics and macro economics contributes to micro economics. For instance, the theory of investment is field of micro economics. It is derived from the behaviour of individual entrepreneur who is guided by returns on capital and rate of interest. However, this theory applies not only to the individual entrepreneur but to the economy as a whole. Thus, macro economics derives its functions from micro economics.

In the same way, micro economics depends upon macro economics. For example, theory of interest in micro economics is influenced by macro economic aggregates. Rate of interest is influenced by liquidity preference of the people on one side and by the supply of money on the other side. Both the components are of macro economics.

Both the approaches deal with different subjects but there is a good deal of interdependence between them. Thus, the two approaches are not mutually exclusive and must be properly integrated for fruitful results.

In the words of Prof. Samuelson, "there is no opposition between micro and macro economics. Both are absolutely vital. You are less than half-educated if you understand the one while being ignorant of the other".

1.2 Basic Economic Problems

The world is at work because of the existence of wants. Wants are the beginning of economics. Human beings are born with wants, continue to live with wants and perhaps die with wants. Moreover, these wants are unlimited. Had they been limited, the economic problem would not have arisen at all. On one hand, wants are unlimited and on the other, the means available to satisfy them are always limited.

Normally, any society or economy has three types of resources :

(1) Land, forests, minerals etc., which are supplied by Nature or are known as the free gifts of nature and are generally referred to in economics by the term 'Land'.

(2) Human resources are called 'Labour' in economics. This includes the physical and mental energies and also the inherited and acquired qualities of human beings.

(3) There are various tools and implements produced by human beings which are for the production of consumers' goods. All such produced means of production are called 'Capital' in economics.

These three are generally referred to as 'factors of production', in economics. The person who brings all these three factors of production, together and actually starts production is called the 'entrepreneur' and is referred to as the fourth factor of production.

All these factors of production 'are used by human beings to satisfy their wants, and are termed as means to satisfy wants.' These means which can be used for satisfying human wants are always limited. Because of the limited nature of means and unlimited nature of wants, economic problems arise. It is said that, this is the basic reason for the creation of economic problems. But as a matter of fact limitedness is not the sufficient reason for the creation of economic problems. In fact, 'scarcity' is the fundamental theme of economics.

Scarcity and limitedness are two different things. Scarcity is the result of circumstances. For example, the supply of air is limited but not scarce. But because of particular circumstances, if it becomes scarce, it may create an economic problem. So, when a person is made to forgo something in order to obtain something else, we say that there is scarcity. This is the real characteristic of scarcity. Scarce resources have alternative uses. When we decide to use these resources for a particular purpose, we have to forgo the rest of the purposes. This is called *opportunity cost*. Thus, the basic problems in economics spring up from these **two sets** of things : one is the **scarcity of resources** to satisfy human wants and the other is the possibility of **using these resources alternatively**.

In this attempt to satisfy unlimited wants with scarce resources with alternative uses, the following six fundamental problems arise. Every economy has to face and solve these problems. These six fundamental economic problems which we have already considered under the *scope of Economics,* can be summarised as follows :

(1) Optimum Allocation of Available Resources : Are the available resources in any country *fully* and optimally *utilised* or not? Or, are some of the resources kept idle? This problem is created mainly because of the scarcity of resources. As they are scarce, they need to be utilised fully. This problem is discussed in the analysis of business cycles and in the *Keynesian Analysis of Employment.*

(2) Extent and Composition of Production : *Which commodities are produced and in what quantities*, is another question. This problem arises because of the scarcity of resources. This is because under the conditions of full employment, you cannot increase the output of any one commodity without reducing the output of another commodity. That is why, it is essential to ensure proper allocation of available resources. Under conditions of perfect competition, the proper allocation of resources is done by the price mechanism. This aspect is studied in the *Theory of Value.*

(3) Choice of Technology : The methods and *techniques used to get the required production* is the third problem. There are various methods and techniques of producing a commodity. When these methods and techniques change, there is also a corresponding change in the proportion of factors of production. In view of this, the methods and techniques assume significance. This forms the subject matter of the *Theory of Production.*

(4) Distribution of Produced Goods and Services : *How* the produced *goods* and *services* are shared by the population of a country or how they are distributed is the fourth problem. This is studied in the Theory of Distribution.

(5) Efficient Utilisation of Available Resources : How are the available resources utilised? By applying the test of *maximum efficiency* to the problems studied under (2), (3) and (4) above, the optimum pattern of production and distribution is determined. This is studied by *Economics of Welfare.*

(6) Productive Capacity of the Economy : *Whether the capacity* of the economy to produce goods and services is *growing or is static ?* This capacity is called the productivity of the economy. In order to satisfy more and more wants of the people and improve the standard of living, it is necessary that the productivity of the economy grows. This productivity of the economy as a whole grows fast in the case of some economies, while in the case of others it grows slowly, and in the case of some it does not grow at all, and the economy remains stagnant. All this is studied in the *Theories of Economic Growth*.

These six are the basic Economic problems. The efforts to solve these basic problems show the scope of economics. As already noted

As already noted, the study of economics is broadly divided into two parts; one is Micro economics and the other is Macro economics. These two terms were first used by Prof. Frisch of the Oslo University in 1933. From these two approaches, it is possible to understand the way in which the study of economics is divided into two parts and how these two approaches together address to the basic economic problems. The theories mentioned against each basic problem, indicate the vastness of the scope of Economic Theory.

1.3 Circular Flow of Economic Activity

The process in which national income and expenditure of an economy flow in a circular manner continuously through time is referred to as circular flow of income and expenditure.

The different constituents of national income and expenditure viz. exports, imports, taxes, government saving, investment, etc. are depicted in the diagram in the form of currents and cross-currents. It is drawn in such a manner that any time N.I. = N.E. (National Income equals National Expenditure).

Illustration of Two-sector Economy :

Suppose, in the economy there are only two sectors i.e. 'household and firm' sector. All the factors of production (land, labour, capital) are owned by household sector. For the productive services of the factors, they get paid and this constitutes their **income** but it is firms' **expenditure**.

Firms' sector is one which is consisting of producers of products. Under household sector, consumers purchase the goods and make payment to the firms' sector. This is now income of firms' sector and expenditure of household sector.

Fig. 1.2 shows, circular flow of income and expenditure in a model of two sectors – Firms' and Household.

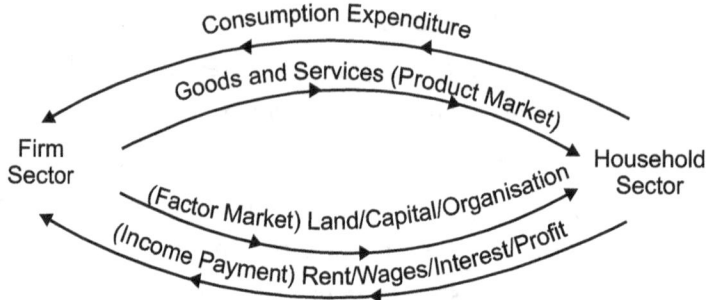

Fig. 1.2 : Circular Flow of Income and Expenditure (Two-sector Model)

Fig. 1.2 shows Product Market is in upper circular part and factor market is in lower circular part. In product market, household sector purchases goods and services from Firms' sector. On the other hand in factor market, household sector receive income from Firms' sector for providing services.

Therefore, household sector purchase goods and services produced by firms' sector and make payments to them for goods and services. The firms' sector makes payments to Household sector for their services in the form of rent to land, wages to labour, interest to capital, and profit to organisation. Hence, payments or expenditure move in circular manner as marked by arrows (in outer circle).

Take the inner circle, goods and services flow from Firms' sector to household sector in the product market. Services flow from household sector to Firms' sector in factor market.

Thus, income payments flow in opposite direction to flow of goods and services. Both flows together form GNP (Gross National Product) = GNI (Gross National Income). The diagram also shows how aggregate income and aggregate expenditure are always equal.

1.4 Nature of Firm – Rationale – Objective of Maximising Firm Value as Present Value of All Future Profits, Maximising, Satisfying, Optimising, Principal Agent Problem

(A) Nature of Firm – Rationale :

Production with the profit motive is modern concept in the sense that it has become dominant only after the industrial revolution. Before the industrial revolution, most of the economies of the world were agricultural economies. The profit motive was always a secondary motive in an agricultural economy. But in modern times the profit motive became the only dominant motive of production. A firm is a unit of production where production is done with the sole aim of profit maximisation.

Definitions of a Firm :

For the sake of understanding this concept of the firm, let us study some definitions of the firm given by eminent economists.

(1) *"The firm may be defined as an independently administered business unit.* — **Hanson**

(2) *"A firm is a centre of control where the decisions about what to produce and how to produce are taken."*

(3) *"A firm is a business unit which hires productive resources for the purpose of producing goods and services."*

(4) *"A firm is an independent organisation whose destiny is determined by the magnitude of the aggregate pay off and in which the aggregate pay off depends directly on its performance and especially on the production and sale of services or goods."*

— Harvey Leibenstein

From the above definitions, it will be seen that there is a substantial difference in all these definitions and still in their own way they describe the firm correctly. This is so because these definitions are by various economists, who were writing at different times and places. Every economist has given prominence to the questions which were more important for him or for his country or when he was writing, and so if we study the various features of firm as revealed by these definitions, the concept will be more clear. The following features of a firm emerges from these definitions :

(1) It is a centre where decisions about what, where, how and how much to produce are taken.

(2) It is a centre where the means of production are hired or purchased and used for production.

(3) It is a centre, where the success of production is reviewed in its entire context and decisions are taken.

(4) It is a centre, where the means of production are collected, the production is done, and the sale and distribution of production is also effected.

(5) It is a centre where all the decisions about production are taken. These include decisions regarding the distribution of the product, advertising, sale and those regarding facing competition also.

From the above features of a firm, it will be clear that a firm has to perform several functions simultaneously – i.e. to produce a commodity, to sell and distribute the commodity, to advertise the commodity and to perform all those things which will be required to survive competition. On top of this, the firm is expected to make as much profits as possible. Theoretically speaking, a firm is expected to organise all the factors of production in the most profitable manner. If one studies the structure and functions of modern firm the above definitions will appear to be too simple, because in modern times the firm is expected to perform so many other functions.

Formerly, the entrepreneur was taken to be an independent factor of production. Even today the entrepreneur is no doubt a very important factor of production but it has become so highly indispensable that it is very difficult to separate it from the production unit of the firm because ultimately the will to produce is provided by the entrepreneur. The mere presence of all the factors of production and a market does not guarantee production. The will to produce is very important and it cannot be separated from the entrepreneur. Thus the entrepreneur becomes inseparable from the firm.

The Firm as a Producing Unit :

The firm is the smallest unit of decision making on the side of production and supply. In the words of **Prof. Lipsey,** *"The firm is defined as the unit that uses factors of production to produce commodities that it then sells either to other firms, to households or to the central authorities (meaning government, public agencies etc.). The firm is thus the unit that makes the decisions regarding the employment of factors of production and the output of commodities."*

How much to buy is decided by the households. In keeping with preferences of the consumers, the firms decide how much to produce, how to produce etc. Through advertisements, a firm may try to increase its sales, but the decisions to buy belong to the buyers. The decisions regarding choice of techniques and quantity of a commodity are taken by the firm. The firm is assumed to take consistent decisions in relation to the choices open to it. The internal problems regarding the process of decision-making i.e. who reaches decisions, how are they reached etc. are ignored. We take firm as a single smallest possible unit. It is taken as our item of behaviour on the supply side just as the household is taken as our item of behaviour on the demand side.

Again, just as the household is assumed to seek satisfaction maximisation, the firm is assumed to seek maximisation of its profits.

The firm may be a proprietorship firm or a partnership firm or a multi-national corporation. That it is a unit of decision-making is our criterion. Therefore, for an economist, Tata Engineering and Locomotive Company Ltd. is a firm, Bharat Heavy Electrical Ltd. (BHEL) is a firm and some *Rambharose Bhel-pure* vendor is also a firm. Again, what form of business organisation should be chosen or how decisions should be taken are subjects to be discussed by business organisation and management experts. An economist assumes that the firm is internally properly organised and is capable of taking decisions.

The Firm and the Industry :

For understating the difference between a firm and an industry, it would be advisable to understand the nature of a competitive industry. A competitive industry has three basic characteristics : (a) Large number of firms; (b) Homogeneous product; and (c) Freedom of entry.

In a competitive industry, there is a large number of firms so that the action of a single firm has no effect on the price and output of the whole industry. Every firm therefore enjoys the freedom to increase or decrease its output substantially by taking the price of the product as given. Secondly, every firm in a purely competitive industry must be making a product which is accepted by customers as being identical with that made by all the other producers in the industry. This is known as the 'condition of homogeneity'. This ensures that all firms have to charge the same price. The buyers, of course, are to decide that the product is the same. The buyers should not find any real or imaginary differences between the products sold by any two pairs of firms. Finally, there should be no barriers to the entry of new firms (or exit of old firm) to (or from) the industry.

We considered competitive industry because we wanted to contrast such an industry with a monopoly. Under monopoly, there is only one firm producing a product. Entry into the industry is not free; because if entry of an additional firm is allowed, it no longer remains a monopoly. Thus, under monopoly, the firm is the industry or the distinction between the firm and the industry disappears under conditions of monopoly.

Between these two extremes, we get a wide range of market structures where there are more than one firm producing the same product. Strictly speaking, all firms producing the same i. e. homogeneous product make an industry and whatever all such firms supply becomes the supply of the industry. In practice, however, we speak of the cotton textile industry, though all cotton textile units do not produce identical textile products. Though the sugar produced by sugar factories might have different grades of quality, we speak of one sugar industry. Similarly, we speak of the automobile industry, steel industry, cement industry and so on.

It should, therefore, be clear that all firms, producing a given product, together make an industry.

The Firm and the Plant :

A plant is a technical. unit of a given capacity of output. For example, we speak of a sugar plant. What is it ? It is nothing but an assembly of several machines, linked together (not necessarily physically but by processes also) capable of producing a given quantity of sugar per day.

For example, a weighing system which weighs the sugarcane, the conveyor system that takes the cane for crushing, the crushing machinery, and the machinery for removing impurities and so on, until finally sugar is filled in gunny bags. This entire assembly of machines makes a plant. This whole plant taken together is capable of producing a given quantity of one product -sugar. A plant thus produces any one product, obviously in cooperation with other factors of production. A sugar plant will produce sugar in co-operation with workers, managers, technicians etc. and after the necessary amounts of raw material, other chemicals and fuel are supplied to it.

The firm, on the other hand, is an economic unit. The decisions are taken by the firm. What quality of sugar is to be produced, how much of it be produced, to which market it should be sold and from which farmers the sugarcane should be purchased etc. are decisions to be taken by the firm.

It is not necessary that a firm has only one plant. Thus, for example, a sugar factory (i.e. a firm engaged in the production of sugar) may have a sugar plant; an alcohol plant (i.e. a distillery), a cattle-feed plant (producing cattle feed out of bagasse) - all under one management. When we say one management, we are implying one firm though there are various plants. It is also possible that a plant supplies goods to more than one firm. The difference, basically, is that between a technical unit and an economic unit.

One last ward about a firm, we speak of the producer or the 'entrepreneur'. Whenever we speak of a producer or an entrepreneur we imply a firm that takes decisions. Internally the decisions might be taken by a group of directors, managers or a sole proprietor – our unit on the supply side is the firm.

We said that the smallest unit of production where business decisions are taken is the firm. Let us spell out these business decisions that a firm is called upon to take.

(1) Production Decisions : The firm has to decide what to produce. It means that the firm has to decide which product or products or services or which brands of commodities it would produce and supply to the market. The decision is important for the survival and prosperity of the firm and it is expected that the firm will take the right decision since it aims at profit maximisation.

(2) Price Decisions : The process of production is not complete until the product reaches the doorsteps of the consumer. This involves the considerations of price at which the product is offered for sale. The lower limit to the price is set by the cost of production. But there might be occasions when the producer will have to sell the product even at a loss, by covering just variable costs. For earning maximum profits the firm may like to fix a high price. Competition may force the firm to obtain only normal profits.

(3) Quantity Decisions : Along with what to produce, the firm has to decide how much to produce. This requires demand forecasts and demand, in part, depends upon the price decisions of the firm.

(4) Technological Decisions : As noted earlier, another fundamental problem regarding production is how to produce ? Every firm, at its own level, has to face this problem. This problem requires the firm to take a decision regarding the choice of technique.

(5) Organisational Decisions : When all the above decisions, which are closely interlinked, are taken, the firm has to decide upon the form of organisation with all legal implications. Should the firm be organised as a partnership firm ? Or should it be organised as a joint stock company ? As you are aware, there are many other forms of organisation also. The form to be chosen depends upon scale of operation, market to be served, capital required, and so on.

(6) Locational Decisions : Where should the plant be located ? This is a locational decision. Some factories have got to be located near the source of raw materials while others have to be located near the market. After considering all the pros and cons, the firm has to decide the location of the unit.

The foregoing discussion of business decisions already suggests the interdependence of these decisions. The quantity to be produced is, on the one hand, related to the demand estimates and, on the other hand, it is related to the price (as suggested by the law of supply). Price decision depends upon the quantity to be produced and the technique to be adopted. This is why all these decision are required to be taken simultaneously. This brief reference to the business decisions would also underline the place of issues like scale of production, demand forecasting, behaviour of costs and equilibrium of the firm in our study of micro economics.

(B) Objective of Maximising Firm Value as Present Value of All Future Profits :

Profit Maximisation : What is the motivation of a firm ? In other words, what is it that a firm tries to achieve and what is it that drives the firm into activity? The traditional theory of the firm has provided an answer in terms of profit maximisation. Traditional theory has a parallel explanation of the demand and the supply sides. On the demand side, the smallest unit is the household and all consumption decisions are taken at the level of the household. The objective of the consumer, i.e. the consumer-household, is maximisation of satisfaction. In the same way, the smallest unit on the supply-side is the firm. The objective of the firm is **maximisation of profits**. Profit maximisation thus becomes the motivation of a firm.

This is how traditionally a business firm is regarded. It is viewed as an economic entity with a basic objective of maximising profits. The level of output and the combination of inputs are so chosen as to maximise profits in the given conditions of factor costs and product-price. In other words, a firm takes into account the price of the product ruling at the market and decides to produce that amount of the product which will fetch maximum profits for the firm. This can be ensured by equalising marginal revenue and marginal cost. The equality of MR and MC then becomes the condition of equilibrium i.e. the position which the firm would not like to disturb. Why ? Because it ensures maximum profits which is the sole objective of the firm. This condition, originally devised for a purely competitive market, was extended to other market categories as well.

The maximising theory thus becomes the traditional theory of the firm. Why was profit-maximisation taken as the sole objective in this traditional approach ? The following points can be mentioned by way of justification of the motivational hypothesis.

(1) Motive Force of a Capitalist Society : Just as coercive power is the motive force in an authoritarian system, profit-seeking is the motive force in a capitalistic system. In fact, every producer of goods and services works for profit. Profit not only provides the incentive but guarantees efficiency and ensures proper allocation of resources. In a market economy, therefore, profit motive does occupy a key position.

(2) Determinate Solution : What level of output should a firm aim at ? The answer is : that level which guarantees maximum profits. To the question, this becomes the single determinate solution. When we consider other objectives, we shall see that they do not provide such a determinate solution.

(3) Proprietorship Firms : In the eighteenth and the nineteenth centuries, proprietorship firms dominated the business field. The modern complexities of organisation were absent. These firms very clearly aimed at profits and mostly maximum short-run profits.

(4) Assumption of Competition : The classical economists assumed perfect competition. Under perfect competition, a firm can get only normal profits in the long-run the maximising condition of equating MR with MC is the only situation where a firm can function. In all other situations the firm closes down.

(5) Simplified Model : Model-building is an important tool of analysis and unless some of the less important variables are 'frozen' by simplifying assumptions, one cannot build a model. A simplified model would lead to conclusions which can subsequently be modified in the light of circumstances obtaining in a region, at a time.

(6) Rationality Assumption : Man is assumed to be a rational animal and the profit-motive can logically be adapted to this basic assumption.

Thus, on the basis of the profit maximisation motive, the classical economists constructed the theory of the firm. This theory provides an answer to how a firm adjusts its supply to market conditions, how it fixes the price under conditions of imperfect competition and how resources are combined to produce the desired output. It also explains how product variation and selling costs can serve the objective under conditions of monopolistic competition.

(C) Maximising, Satisfying, Optimising, Principal Agent Problem :

(1) Maximising : Prof. William J. Baumol has argued that maximisation of sales rather than of profits is the ultimate objective of the firm and that sales maximisation is the most valid assumption about the behavior of the firm. Empirical evidence, in his opinion, strongly supports his hypothesis.

Prof. Baumol concedes that sales maximisation cannot be irrespective of cost considerations. In fact, he even concedes the possible conflict between sales maximisation and profit maximisation. He therefore argues that, in practice, businessmen normally promote sales subject to the limitation that costs incurred are fully covered. He says, "Once this minimum profit level is achieved, sales rather than profits become the overriding goal". The objective, in his opinion can 'usefully be characterised, approximately, as *sales maximisation subject to minimum profit constraint'*. He believes that this objective is not too far from the truth. "So long as profits are high enough to keep stock-holders satisfied and contribute adequately to the financing of company growth, management will bend its efforts to the augmentation of sales revenues rather than to further increase in profits", Baumol states. Rationality, in his view, consists in pursuing the accepted ends efficiently and consistently.

(2) Satisfying : The first major revision of the traditional approach actually came from Herbert Simon. His approach is known as the Satisfying Theory. Simon believes that instead of hunting for the best possible alternative, a firm might be content with a policy that secures for itself a satisfactory level of profit. He says, "He (the entrepreneur) must expect the firm's goals to be not maximising profits, but attaining a certain level or rate of profit, holding a certain share of the market or a certain level of sales. Firms would try to 'satisfy' rather than to maximise".

The Satisfying Theory has several commendable features :
  (i)   This theory deals not with the equilibrium alone but also with the method of achieving it.
  (ii) In this model, the aspiration level does not remain static. It rather changes with changing circumstances.
  (iii) When actual performance of the firm falls short of the desired level, search behaviour is induced. This search may result in a way of reaching the desired level. But, more importantly, it may bring down the aspiration level itself, if the original level is found unattainable.
  (iv) The principle of satisfying is more convenient in as much as it can include multiple objectives within the fold of the firm. (v) Each of the objectives can enter as a constraint and how many of these objectives are satisfied and to what extent can be the touch-stones for judging the performance of the firm.

The following observations by critics are worth noting :
  (i)   Evidence shows that aspirations tend to adjust themselves to the maximum attainable and then the distinction between the satisfying theory and the maximising theory disappears.
  (ii) When multiple objectives are under consideration and a conflict arises the best one is chosen. Again it becomes a maximising theory.
  (iii) In a world of competition, the satisfying firms would lag behind the maximising firms and hence they (the former) will be tempted to accept the maximising objective.

The merit of Simon's theory is that it provides a behaviourial analysis conducive to a dynamic treatment. In fact, Baumol's theorem is an extension and a refinement of Simon's thesis where Baumol selects two three objectives suggested by Simon, viz. a certain level of sales and that of profits.

(3) Optimising : The ultimate aim of every individual is satisfaction. Therefore, several economists like **Prof. Benjamin Higgins, Melvin Reder** and **Tibor Scitovsky** have sought to replace the profit maximisation motive by the more general notion of utility maximisation or *preference function maximisation,* i.e. optimisation. These economists point out that profit maximisation does not necessarily mean satisfaction or utility maximisation. If we view an entrepreneur as a person interested in maximising his satisfaction, money profits become a means of fetching material well-being. In other words, a larger profit may allow him more comforts and luxuries. But it would involve harder work, neglect of health and a orifice of other joys which can be availed of by playing or listening to music or engaging in a hobby. Satisfaction can also be derived reducing the entrepreneurial activity and by availing of more, leisure. The leisure or what Hicks calls 'quiet life is an essential ingredient of an individual's welfare. But the more the work put in, the less would be the leisure available to the entrepreneur.

A. Papandreou argues that a firm's objectives grow out of interactions among the various participants in its activities, is interaction produces a general preference. Scitovsky's argument spells out the approach : a business executive may choose to maximise profits and forgo leisure, or to choose total leisure and forgo profits, or may decide on some combination of both. The motivational hypothesis of the firm can thus be derived from its reference levels. The preference for leisure can be incorporated into the analysis of an entrepreneur who is supposed to maximise satisfaction. The theory can be represented as an ordinal measure. That is, one can show that one alternative is better than the second one.

Contrary to classical assumption of profit maximisation, the approach to profits based upon observations of the behaviour of the firms, we find various objectives persued by firms. Earning profits is of course an important basic goal; however, the extent of profit expected obviously varies according to the degree of competition, the nature of the product, size of the firm and so on. Each firm has to decide its own objectives from the set of various objectives suggested by various economists. Thus, each firm has its own utility function which consists of its own preferences for profits and for other objectives. By striking a balance amongst various objectives, a firm tries to optimise its utility by achieving the best combination of profit and other objectives.

(4) Principal Agent Problem : The principal-agent problem refers to the situation when the managers pursue their goals such as high salaries, power, prestige, perquisites even at the cost of the owners (i.e., their principals). The shareholders want to maximise their profits or present value of the net worth of their companies, managers who pursue their own goals, often take decisions which are contrary to the interests of their owners.

Principal agent problem is generally fenced in large corporations whose ownership is separated from management.

1.5 Accounting Profit and Economic Profit

Let us take an example to understand the difference between the economic concept of profit and the accounting concept of profit. Suppose an individual starts at his residence the business of repairing scooters. At the end of the year, he gets a total revenue of ₹ 15,000/-. Out of this, let us say, he spent ₹ 5,000/- on the wages of his helper, tools and spare parts, etc. What remains is a sum of ₹ 10,000/-. Apparently, one would be tempted to conclude that this is his profit. But it is not so. The place that is available to him might have saved him a sum of, say, ₹ 3,000/-. In other words, the place of work might have an opportunity cost. His own transfer earnings may be say ₹ 6,000/-. Had he borrowed the money capital, the interest would have been say ₹ 1,000/-. Besides, a provision will have to be made for the wear and tear of the tools and instruments; i.e. a certain amount will have to be deducted for depreciation. Thus calculated, the total costs would be (i) Helper's wages, spares etc. : ₹ 5,000/- + (ii) Rent : ₹ 3,00/- + (iii) Entrepreneur's management wages : ₹ 6,000/- + iv) Interest : ₹ 1,000/- + (v) Depreciation : ₹ 500/-. This takes the total cost equal to ₹ 15,500/- against the total revenue of 15,000/- showing a net loss of ₹ 500/-.

The loss in the above example does not become apparent because the entrepreneur uses some of the factors owned by himself and therefore the remunerations to these are not actually paid. It should be obvious from the above example that these difficulties may not arise in respect of large industrial units. In such units, ownership is with the shareholders while the management is entrusted to the salaried managers. Thus, most of the costs enter the account books and the accounting and economic concepts of costs in such cases come closer.

According to the financial accounting principles, the assets of a concern have claims from two sides : from the owners and from the lenders. Therefore, in any business unit,

Assets = Liabilities + Proprietorship.

Therefore,   Assets – Liabilities = Proprietorship or the net worth.

The balance-sheet of any concern shows, during a given period, the total liabilities and the net worth after these are deducted. Similarly, the profit and loss account or the income statement shows the changes in the balance sheet of the unit from the beginning of the year and those at the end of the year is the net income or profit. The funds statement is based on this profit and loss statement. This statement indicates the financial standing of the business concern. The funds statement shows the amount of cash available and how it has been invested.

While preparing all these statements, the accountant has to include items, the truth about which can be tested. But in doing so, many difficulties arise. For example, while preparing the balance-sheet, the cost of the asset that is taken is the one at which the asset was purchased. The current value of the asset is not considered. Similarly the changes in the value of money are ignored. It is also incorrect as is done in financial accounts, to calculate net profits by deducting from the total revenue of year the total costs incurred during that year.

The economic concept of net profit will have to be altogether different. In the valuation of any asset, the economist is guided by the concept of opportunity cost. For example, the accounting method will take into account the original price of a machine; but in the economic concept, the replacement cost of the machine would be used. For valuation of the machine, further alternatives would be to take the price of a similar machine, if the same is not available; or to consider the total expected return of the machine and from that calculate the present worth of the machine. We are familiar with the various cost concepts that can be used and how these concepts are different in the economic theory and the accounting practice. Thus, the differences in the profit concepts arise out of the differences in cost concepts. The modern method used for valuation is based on the cash-flow technique.

It will also be necessary to remember that the sum total of all the individual machines added together will not be the correct value of the total establishment. This is because the goodwill enjoyed by the concern will also have to be included in its total worth. This is how the economic and the accounting approaches differ and make measurement of profit more complicated.

1.6 Role of Profit in Market System

Profits refer to the net revenue or the difference between total sales and total costs. Profits play a very crucial role in a market system.

(1) Prime Motivation for Producers : In a market system, what is often called the price mechanism' (or market mechanism) decides automatically 'what' is to be produced, 'how' things will be produced and 'for whom' they will be produced. The consumers demand what they are willing and able to buy. But who is to produce and supply these goods ? The answer is 'the producers'. How do they produce ? By combining or pooling together the necessary resources in the most efficient way. Why should they do it ? Guided by their own self-interest, the producers do everything possible to earn *profits*. Profit motive triggers the forces in the product and factor markets in motion, so that equilibrium in both markets is achieved simultaneously. As Prof. Samuelson has put it : "Life a master using carrots and kicks to coax a donkey forward, the market system deals out profits and losses to get *How*, *What* and *For Whom* decided."

(2) Risk and Uncertainty-Bearing : The most important role of profit, according to mainstream economists is that it serves as a reward to entrepreneurs for bearing risks and uncertainty. According to the well-known American economist **F. B. Hawley** profit is the reward for risk and responsibilities of the entrepreneur concerned. According to **Frank H. Knight**, who made the role of profit in relation to risk-bearing very clear. He views risks in business as inherent and classifies them in two types : Those risks which can be statistically estimated and can be insured are **Insurable Risks** and they are of two types : (a) Risks to property due to earthquakes, floods, riots, fire etc.; (b) Risks of dishonesty like theft, burglary, robbery etc. By paying certain premium these risks can be insured and the premia can be treated as costs. Risks which cannot be insured, according to **Knight**, are the responsibility of the entrepreneur. *Profits, by covering such non-insurable risks, are an important incentive that prompts an entrepreneur to undertake production.* **The non-insurable risks** are :

(a) **Competition Risks :** Competition risks arising out of entry of new rivals or introduction by existing rivals of new methods / techniques of production.

(b) **Technical Risks :** Technical risks arise when newly installed machinery becomes out-dated due to technological progress.

(c) **Risks of Government Policies :** Risks of government policies arise through changes in government policies affecting business like taxation and public expenditure policies, import-export policies, labour laws, financial policies etc.

(d) **Business Cycle Risks** : Business cycle risks arise due to economic fluctuations or cycles of prosperity and depression, which are a characteristics feature of a market economy.

(3) Innovations : According to **Prof. Schumpeter**, profits arise because the entrepreneurs introduce innovations. In other words, profits prompt entrepreneurs to undertake innovations which, in turn, lead to economic progress. Innovation refers to any purposeful change which fetches profits when successful. Development of new products, new production functions, new modes of marketing, improvements in existing techniques etc. are forms of innovation. In a static society supernormal profits disappear. A hunt for excess profits makes the entrepreneurs to adopt innovations. This makes the economy dynamic and paves the way for economic progress.

(4) Measure of Performance : Profit is viewed and often used as a measure of performance in a market economy. A higher level of profitability acts as an indication that the business is being run successfully and effectively. There are, of course, other indicators too, but profit is a direct and universally intelligible measure of a firm's performance. Profit, as a measure, has several advantages : (i) It can be used as a single criterion for evaluating any proposed course of action. (ii) It facilitates a quantitative analysis of alternative proposals by directly relating benefits to costs for comparison. (iii) Where diverse and dissimilar products, processes or functions are carried out under one management, performance of each such centre can be judged by applying the measure of profit. (iv) As such, decentralisation and delegation of responsibilities becomes possible. (v) For shareholders or general public, it acts as single broad measure of performance.

(5) Covering Costs of Staying in Business : Profit, according to **Peter Drucker**, serves another important purpose : as a premium to cover the costs of staying in business. Such costs are necessary to tide over the contingencies of replacement, obsolescence, and some such risks. Unless adequate profits are generated, provisions for such costs cannot be made. After all, continued existence and a sound footing in the chosen field of business enjoy good – will amongst the people.

(6) Ensuring Supply of Future Capital : In a competitive world, corporates are concerned about making satisfactory provision for the future. Usual practice is creating various funds, besides depreciation, like reserve fund, sustainability fund, sinking fund etc. Contributions to such funds are made through undistributed profits (or retained profits). This can be called direct provision for future supply of capital. Indirectly, profit can serve as an inducement to future investors. The firm may thus be able to attract domestic / external capital in the forms of stock, bonds, time-bounds deposits, and that too, at lower rates of interest.

Market Mechanism :

Market Mechanism or Price Mechanism is a way of solving the economic problems. An economy having market mechanism is also referred to as a market driven economy or a capitalist economy, or a free enterprise economy. In such an economy, the 'invisible hand of market mechanism brings about optimum allocation of resources through the operation of price system. Usually, when there is a shortage of supply against demand of a commodity, price of that commodity tends to rise. Then, resources also will tend to be reallocated by the producers to the production of that commodity. Since production is profit-oriented, and profit depends on price, resources will tend to move from low price sectors to high price sectors. In this way, demand and supply in different sectors will be adjusted and scarcity is dealt with. Dealing with scarcity and allocation of resources is the main economic problem, which is thus automatically solved through price mechanism or market mechanism in a market economy.

In a market-driven economy, the **Market Mechanism** with its competitive price system serves automatically to solve the three most important basic economic problems : What to produce, How to produce and For whom to produce.

In the product market, consumers' preferences get reflected through the expenses they are willing to incur. Every rupee spent by the consumer is a like as vote cast in favour of a good he opts for. Decisions of firms to supply interact with consumer demand decisions in the product market. The problem of 'What' is thus resolved. The answer to 'For whom' is provided by the interaction of demand for and supply of inputs, in the Factor Market. Owners of inputs are households and they 'expect' certain rate of remuneration while firms offer certain rates of the same. Interactions between these two determine wages; rent, interest rates. These, in turn, decide the share of each factor in the national product.

The third problem resolved by the market mechanism is 'how to produce'. Competition among firms forces each firm to reduce the price of its product. For this, every firm tries to improve its productive efficiency and this solves the problems 'how'. In short, a market economy, a system of markets, prices, incentives, profits and losses works automatically to address the basic economic problems of composition of production (what to produce), the best technology to produce or allocation of resources (how to produce) and distribution of total product (for whom to produce). Firms seek to produce goods yielding highest profits, by adopting techniques that minimises costs. When consumers spend their earnings arising out of their ownership of labour, land and capital on goods and services of their choice, the question 'for whom' finds an answer.

"Invisible Conductor of the Economic Orchestra." – **T.J.B. Hoff**

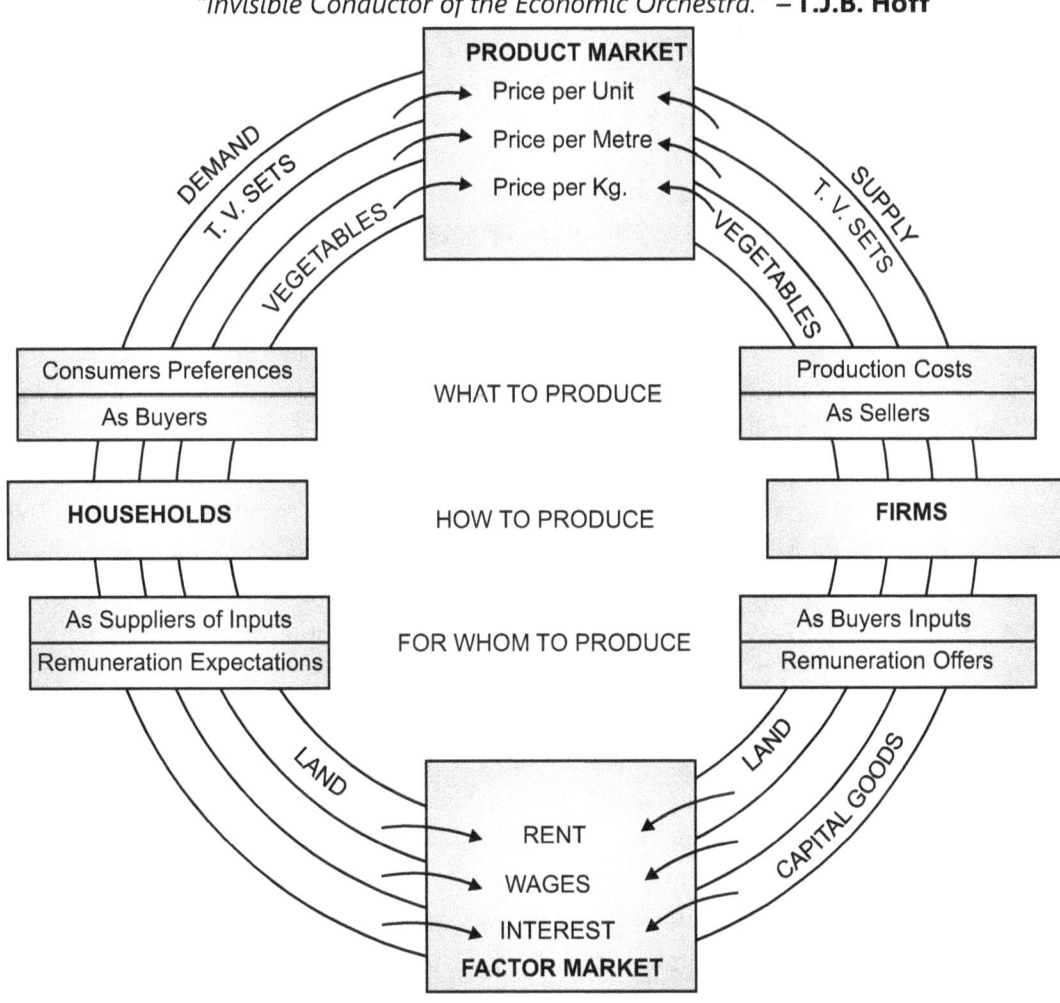

Fig. 1.3 : Market Mechanism

1.7 Adam Smith and the Invisible Hand

Of the six basic economic problems faced by a modern economy, three are more fundamental and so 'more important' as we may call them. These three have been faced by humanity right from the beginning of human civilisation. In the primitive civilisation, it was 'custom' that decided what, how and for whom to produce. These customs varied from habitation to habitation and time to time. The *Jajmani* systems in northern India or the Balutedari in Maharashtra are historical examples of custom which ruled economic activity of individual members of the society.

The process of decline of feudalism which started with *Magna Carta* (1215) i.e. the famous charter of liberty and political rights obtained from King John of England to the onset of Industrial revolution (middle of 18th century), gradually gave way to social structures based on individual freedom, equality and other values characteristic of a democratic society. This process got reflected in the economic organisation variously called 'private enterprise system' or 'private property capitalism' or just 'capitalism'. Alongwith political freedoms, the economic freedoms of individuals like freedom to acquire property, freedom of enterprise, free choice of consumption, freedom of exchange etc. were accepted as most desirable parametres of a democratic or free society. During the heyday of capitalism, the doctrine of *laissez-faire* or the policy of complete non-intervention by the Government, in economic activities of people, ruled as the most sacrosanct value. All classical economists, who assumed full employment and perfect competition, upheld this doctrine of non-interference.

During the second half of the 19th century, Karl Marx (1818 - 1883) challenged the hypotheses of free enterprise economists and provided a socialist model of economic organization based on his philosophy (Marxism) of 'dictatorship of the proletariat'. Soviet Russia, after the 1917 October Revolution, adopted **command economy** as an economic system designed to address the basic economic problems. In a command economy, all decisions about production and distribution are taken and enforced by the Government through the agency of a planning body and individuals and firms are to follow the dictates of the plan. Soviet Russia, East European countries, China and some other Latin American and Asian countries adopted this model with modifications as felt necessary.

North American and European industrial countries (and Japan) experienced a rapid economic development mainly through freedom of enterprise. However, due to the influence of Marx and Keynes and many other thinkers and also owing to practical experience, Government intervention and participation in economic activities went on increasing, in the Western developed countries. In almost all countries in North America and West Europe, a steadily increasing role of the State was witnessed since the beginning of the late 19th century. The economies therefore came to be known as mixed economies, having a co-existence of a public sector and a private sector.

However, since the nineteen eighties, and especially after the disintegration of the socialist bloc of countries, the trends in America and Europe are reverting back to the conservative approach of 'that Government is best which governs the least'. This explains why people have come to re-invent Adam Smith and his *invisible hand*.

Foundation of Modern Economics :

Adam Smith's treatise *'The Wealth of Nations (1776)'* is viewed as the foundation of modern economic theorisation. Smith observed the functioning of the market mechanism and was 'thrilled' to find that thousands of producers, traders and transporters, workers and artisans, consumers and money-lenders are working independently, without any co-ordinating authority and without any plan. And still there was no chaos. Instead, an 'order' got settled. This automatically equilibrating system not only works but it has survived for decades. Read what Smith himself says :

"Every individual endeavours to employ his capital so that its produce may be of greatest value. He generally neither intends to promote the public interest, nor knows how much he is promoting it. He intends only his own security, only his own gain. And he is in this led by an **invisible hand** *to promote an end which was no part of his intention. By pursuing his own interest he frequently promotes that of society more effectually than when he really intends to promote it."*   **– The Wealth of Nations (1776)**

What Smith means is that –

(i)   Every individual, when left to himself, pursues his own self-interest.

(ii) As an owner of resource/s, he tries to maximise his gain or return.

(iii) He does not intend to promote public interest, though unconsciously he does contribute to it.

(iv) All individuals in the society, freely following their self-interest, do promote maximum public good, guided by an *invisible hand*.

(v)   Leaving individuals fully free to follow their own self-interest is a more effective way of achieving maximisation of social benefit than any intentional effort at maximising it.

Smith's invisible hand doctrine represents a concept that explains how an orderly outcome gets established through the free play of the market mechanism. In short, invisible hand is nothing but the automatism of the market mechanism.

Visible Failures of Invisible Hand :

Over two centuries of the post-Smith world has witnessed a number of limitations and failures of the market mechanism. Prof. Samuelson has highlighted two of the most important failures : Market Imperfections and Externalities.

(1) Market Imperfections : Smith himself has accepted that the virtues of the market mechanism can be realised only when the checks and balances of perfect competition obtain. Perfect completion ensures normal profits, prices based on average costs, full employment of productive resources and an optimum allocation of resources. But perfect competition has never existed. As such, varying degrees of imperfections creep into the market. Imperfections lead to monopolistic profits, underemployment, and inflation, disparities in income and wealth and exploitation of the weaker sections of the society.

(2) Externalities : Prof. Pigou was perhaps the first influential economist to point out the divergence between private and social costs and benefits. Externalities focus on the same issues. Externalities are spillover effects of an uncontrolled market economy. An industrial unit polluting air or water does not pay for water or air purification. A firm undertaking plantation creates a healthy environment that benefits the citizens around who do not pay for the benefit. Such cases lie outside the purview of the invisible hand where the government has to step in (a) *Provision of public goods* like national defense, law and order or provision of safe drinking water are such cases which cannot be left to the market mechanism. (b) *On grounds of equity*, the state may provide mid-day meals to students or free medical aid to the economically weaker sections, whom the invisible hand would never touch. (c) *Economic fluctuations* or *Business cycles* which are a characteristic features of a free enterprise economy cause hardship to the society in the form of unemployment, inflation and business instability, stabilisation then becomes a governmental function.

The new converts to the cult of invisible hand will have to take in their stride such limitations which tend to multiply with growing complexities of a modern economy.

Questions for Discussion

1. What is Micro Economics ? State its Features, Scope and Importance.

2. What is Macro Economics ? State its Features, Scope and Importance.

3. Describe the Basic Problems of an Economy.

4. Explain the Circular Flow of Economic Activity.

5. Explain the Concept of Accounting Profit and Economic Profit.

6. State the Role of Profit in Market System.

7. Explain : Adam Smith and Invisible Hand.

8. Write short notes on :

    (A) An Approach to Economics.

    (B) Nature of Firm - Rationale

    (C) Objectives of Maximising Firm Value.

    (D) Micro Economics Vs. Macro Economics.

Lets go with...

CHAPTER

2

DEMAND ANALYSIS AND FORECASTING

2.1 Demand

(A) Concept and Definitions of Demand :

The theory of demand is concerned with the economic activities of a consumer. In other words, theory of consumption rests on the foundation of demand analysis. The process through which a consumer can get the goods and services he wants to consume is known as demand.

(1) According to **Professor Hibdon**, *"Demand means the various quantities of a good that would be purchased per time period at different prices in a given market"*. Demand, from economic point of view thus requires three things :

(a) The price of a commodity,

(b) The quantity of the commodity that a consumer or; consumers are willing to buy during a period of time, and

(c) A given period of time.

(2) Benham's definition of demand is well-known. According to him, *"The demand for anything at a given price is the quantity of it which will be bought per unit of time at that price"*.

(B) Characteristics of Demand :

The concept of demand as reflected in the above definitions, can be clarified along the following characteristics of demand :

(1) Desire and Demand : For demand to come into existence, the consumer must have the desire to buy the commodity. But only desire is not enough. He must also have the ability to buy the commodity. The desire may spring from need. Millions of people in a country like India have hundreds of needs but they cannot be converted into demand because the people do not have the capacity to buy the goods which they need. It is, therefore, to be clearly understood that desire by itself cannot make demand. Secondly, it is not necessary that people demand whatever they need. It is common knowledge that people need, from the point of view of health, milk, a balanced diet or medicines; but people demand less nutritious food or tobacco or liquor. This they do because their desires prompt them to do so. It should, therefore, be very clear that need, desire and demand are different things and neither need nor desire can be called demand but only the desire backed by ability to buy becomes demand.

(2) Price and Demand : Demand in economics is always at a price. Without a specific mention of price, the amount demanded has no meaning. If you ask a consumer how much he would buy of a commodity, he will have no answer. It is, therefore, necessary to specify not only the commodity in quantity but also the price of the commodity for the consumer to tell us exactly how much of the commodity he is willing to buy.

(3) Reference to a Period of Time : The quantity of a commodity demanded necessarily refers to some period of time. Thus, one may demand 10 kilograms of sugar per month or 3 kilograms of edible oil per month or 4 shirts per year and so on. The change in the period of time obviously results in a change in the quantity demanded also. It must also be remembered that the quantity a consumer demands satisfies his requirement for a period of time; but the price of the commodity in question does not remain stable in that period. Therefore, the price to be specified refers to a particular point of time. This is why Benham has used the phrase *"per unit of time"*.

(C) The Law of Demand :

It is our common experience that we demand more of a commodity when its price falls and, conversely, we buy less of a commodity when its price rises. The law of demand is based on this common experience.

As noted above, there are so many determinants of demand. However, the theoretical purpose of demand analysis is to explain the behaviour of market price, the allocation of resources and the distribution of income. In this matter, price-demand relationship is important. Besides, to simplify the analysis of demand, price-demand relationship can be studied in isolation. The law demand, therefore, singles out price-demand relationship and holds all other determinants of demand as given and constant. When all other determinants of demand, except the price, are thus frozen, we can study the relationship between the one determinants i.e. price and demand.

(a) The Law of Demand States, *"Other things remaining the same, a rise in the price of a commodity leads to contraction of demand for it and a fall in the price leads to expansion of demand for it."* Some statements of the law of demand are as follows :

(b) According to Professor Samuelson, *"Law of demand states that people will buy more at a lower price and buy less at a higher price, other things remaining the same."*

(c) *"According to the law of demand"*, as Fergusson has put it *"the quantity demanded varies inversely with price"*. (This is why changes in demand due to price changes are known as variations in demand).

Assumptions of the Law of Demand :

According to **Professor Stigler** and **Boulding**, the main assumptions of the law are :

(1) No change in tastes and preferences of the consumers has taken place;

(2) Consumers' income remains the same. Marshall insisted on money income remaining unchanged, but Milton Friedman rightly assumes that the real income of the consumers remains constant;

(3) The price of the commodities related to the commodity concerned remain unchanged; and

(4) There is no change in the wealth of the consumers.

Demand Schedule and Demand Curve :

The price-demand relationship as expressed-by the Law of demand can be shown arithmetically. For this purpose, we can prepare a demand schedule. The Law can also be shown graphically by drawing a demand curve. The demand schedule indicates the various quantities a consumer is willing to buy at various prices. Table 2.1 is such an imaginary demand schedule. When the price of sugar is ₹ 40.00 per kg., the consumer, for example, demands one kg. of sugar. When the price falls to ₹ 38.00, he demands 1.5 kg. In this way, the demand goes on increasing as the price goes on falling.

Table 2.1 : Demand Schedule

Price (₹)	Demand for Sugar (kg.)
40.00	1.0
38.00	1.5
36.00	2.5
34.00	4.0
32.00	5.5
30.00	7.0

On the basis of such a demand schedule, assuming that the price and quantity demanded are divisible upto a very small fraction, we can plot the points on a graph and get a curve which is known as the demand curve. In economics, price is conventionally taken on the Y-axis and the demand or supply on X-axis.

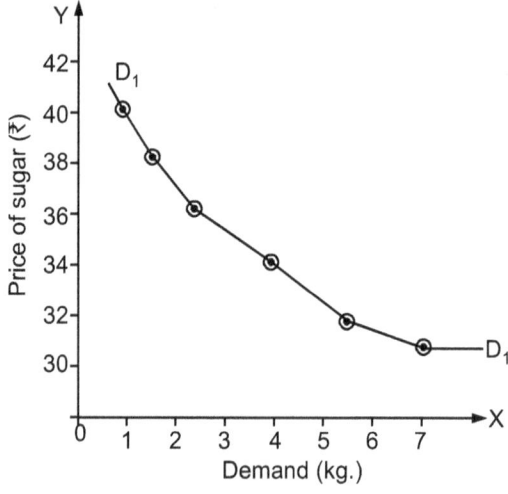

Fig. 2.1 : Demand Curve

Fig. 2.1 shows the Demand Curve (D_1 D_1). The figure shows that at ₹ 40, 1 kg of sugar is demanded, at ₹ 38, 1.5 kg of sugar is demanded, at ₹ 36, 2.5 kg of sugar is demanded, at ₹ 34, 4 kg of sugar is demanded, at ₹ 32, 5.5 kg of sugar is demanded and at ₹ 30, 7 kg of sugar is demanded. This shows that when the price of the sugar is high (i.e., ₹ 40, ₹ 38 and

₹ 36), less quantity of sugar is demanded (i.e.; 1 kg, 1.5 kg and 2.5 kg) and when the prices of sugar get reduced (i.e.; ₹ 34, ₹ 32 and ₹ 30) the demand for sugar goes on increasing (i.e. 4 kg, 5.5 kg and 7 kg). This shows an inverse relationship between the price of the sugar and quantity of sugar demanded. i.e., when the prices of sugar are high, less quantity of sugar is demanded, and when the prices of sugar are low, more quantity of sugar is demanded.

In this way, the demand schedule and demand curve illustrate the price-demand relationship. The demand curve or the demand schedule does not indicate the relationship of demand with other factors we noted earlier as the determinants of demand.

But why does demand respond to changes in price in this way ? The demand schedule and the demand curve underline the inverse relation between price and demand. But why is this relationship inverse ? In other words, why does the demand increase when there is a fall in the price ? Let us examine this question.

Fundamental Characteristics of the Law of Demand :

We can now summarise fundamental characteristics of Law of demand (or demand curve) as follows:

(1) **Inverse Relationship :** The price-demand relationship is inverse as stated above.

(2) **Demand as a Function of Price :** Demand is viewed here as a function of price. This means that price is an independent variable and demand is a dependent variable. In other words, the law of demand considers the effect of price on demand but not vice versa.

(3) **Static Assumption :** The demand curve shows the price-demand relationship at a given time. If the time changes the responses of demand to a change in price may also change.

(4) **Other Things Remain the Same :** Except the price, all other factors influencing the demand are assumed to be constant. The effect of other factors on the demand curve can be shown by drawing a new demand curve. This phenomenon is known as *'shift in the demand curve'*.

Exceptions to the Law of Demand :

The price-demand relationship as expressed by the law of demand is normally experienced in practice. But at times, the consumer is found to act contrary to the normal behaviour expressed by the law of demand. It is, therefore, necessary to examine such situations to find out whether there are any exceptions to the law.

(1) **Expectations of the Consumers :** When the consumers expect a further fall in the price, they tend to postpone their purchases. This causes a fall in demand. In the same way, when the price is rising and a further rise in the price is expected, the demand will actually extend. These situations indicate a direct and not an inverse relationship between price and

demand. This, strictly speaking, is not an exception to the law of demand because an intention of the consumer is to buy more when the price is less. The consumer behaviour's, which appears to be contrary to the law, is only a temporary phase prompted by the expectations though basically guided by the same intention underlying the law of demand.

(2) Goods of Distinction : Some goods are in demand only because they are costly, as their possession indicates a position of distinction. The American economist Veblen was the first to point out this type of exceptional behaviour on the part of the consumers. According to Veblen, the demand for articles of distinction like diamonds, jewellery etc., is more as their price rises. This is because a rich man's desire for distinction is satisfied better when articles of distinction are high-priced and the poorer man cannot buy them. Conversely, the demand for such articles will fall if they become cheap. Such a situation is contrary to the assumption of rationality and as such it can be treated as a limitation.

(3) Giffen's Paradox : Sir Robert Giffen found that during the 19th century famine, in Ireland, people were so poor that they spent major part of their income on potatoes which were the cheapest food available, and spent a small amount on meat. When potatoes became cheaper, people could save some of their expenditure on potatoes. This amount they could spend on meat and, therefore, they could do with a smaller amount of potatoes. Thus, a fall in the price resulted in a fall in demand for potatoes. This is contrary to the law of demand and such a situation arises as a result of income effect and in respect of inferior goods. A situation like this is known as Giffen's paradox.

(4) Ignorance on the Part of the Consumers : Many times the consumers judge the quality by the price of the product. When a product becomes cheaper, it may be considered inferior and, therefore, it would be demanded in lesser quantities. A rise in the price of the same commodity may be constructed as betterment of quality and the demand may therefore go up. Benham has given an example of a book which was sold out only when its price was revised upwards. This can also be said to be a limiting case because, in economics, we assume that man is rational and is capable of judging the product independently of the price.

(D) Individual and Market Demand :

Market demand is the sum total of the quantities demanded by all the consumers at the market, at given price. Table 2.2 illustrates this point. Suppose A, B, C and D are the only four consumers in the market. Their individual demands are given in their individual demand schedules. If we add together quantities demanded by all the four consumers at each price, we get the market demand at that price. For example, at ₹ 10 per kg. A demands 1.0 kg. of sugar, while B, C and D demand 2.0 kg., 0.5 kg. and 3.5 kg. respectively. Together A, B, C and D demand 7 kgs. This therefore is the market demand when price is ₹ 10 per kg. Thus, by adding together the individual quantities demanded at all prices, we get a market demand schedule. In table 2.2, columns 1 and 6 read together can be called the market demand schedule.

Table 2.2 : Individual and Market Demand Schedule

Price	Demand (kg.)				Market demand
(₹)	A	B	C	D	(kg.)
Column - 1	Column - 2	Column - 3	Column - 4	Column - 5	Column - 6
10.00	1.0	2.0	0.5	3.5	7.00
9.50	1.5	2.5	1.0	4.0	9.00
9.00	2.0	3.0	1.5	4.5	11.00
8.50	3.0	4.0	2.0	5.0	14.00
8.00	4.0	5.0	3.0	6.0	18.00
7.50	5.5	6.5	4.0	7.0	23.00
7.00	6.5	7.5	5.0	8.0	27.00

(E) Consumer Demand :

Consumer Demand for a product consists of two elements, i.e. (1) Individual Demand, and (2) Market Demand.

Individual Demand refers to the quantity of a good a consumer would buy at a given price during a given period of time. It is single consuming entity's demand.

Market Demand for a product, on the other hand, refers to the total demand for the product of all the buyers taken together, during a given period at a given price.

(F) Market Demand Equation :

The above table 2.2 shows how market demand for a product can be obtained by horizontally adding the quantities demanded at each price, i.e. columns (1) and (6) put together give us market demand for the product. Therefore, if the demand of the ith individual is

$$Q_i = f_i (P),$$

Market demand can be expressed as :

$$Q = \sum_{i=1}^{n} f_i (P) = f (P) \ (i = 1, 2, 3, 4 \ ....n).$$

Alternatively, market demand, can be estimated by the following formula :

$$Q = P \times Q_i \times C_n$$

Where,   Q = Market or industry demand (Total quantity demanded)

P = Price during the period under consideration

Q_i = Quantity demanded by an Average Consumer

C_n = Total number of consumers in the market

Industry demand can also be estimated by using the same formula provided the total demand refers to the total products produced by *all the firms in the industry*. For example, the market for Maruti cars is for cars produced by one firm i.e. Maruti Suzuki. But the market for Four Wheeler Automobile industry covers all the firms supplying these products.

2.1.1 Determinants of Market Demand at Firm and Industry Level

In the definition of demand, we have made a reference to price and unit of time. The demand, price relationship is of central importance in the study of the market. Further, it does not mean that demand is determined by price alone. In fact, there are various factors on which the market demand and individual demand for a product depends. These factors are known as determinants of demand. They can be summarised as follows:

(1) Price of the Product : The quantity of the product demanded by the consumer depends on the price of the product. If the price rises, demand falls and vice versa. More about this relationship we shall take up when we go to the law of demand.

(2) Income and Income Distribution : The demand for a product also depends upon the income of the consumer. The consumer would buy more of a commodity at the same price if his income increases. Normally, therefore, an increase in the income leads to an increase in the demand for all commodities. There are some exceptions to this normal rule and they are referred to as inferior goods. In case of inferior goods, demand for them falls with increase in income. When we consider market demand for a product i.e. demand of a group of consumers, the distribution of income also becomes an important factor. In a society where income disparities are high, the handful of rich would demand a wide range of luxury goods while the poor will be tied down to bare necessaries. If income distribution is less uneven and the gap between rich and poor is narrow, the basket of goods and services demanded by such a society would be different from the one demanded by the former group of consumers with high income disparities.

(3) The Number and Prices of Substitutes : Demand for a commodity depends upon the number of substitutes available to the commodity. In case of cold drinks, for example, there are many substitutes and when one of them disappears from the market, its demand is shared by the rest of the cold drinks. As a result, each individual drink experiences an increase in demand. As against this, *gur* (or jaggery) is the only substitute for sugar and if it disappears from the market, the demand for sugar may experience an increase which would be much higher than the increase experienced in case of anyone cold drink. Thus the larger the number of substitutes, the smaller is the effect on demand for a single member of the family of the substitutes. Conversely, if the number of substitutes is limited, the effect of a change in the number of substitutes on demand is large.

The prices of substitutes also influence the demand for the product under consideration. Thus, when the price of *gur* rises, the demand for sugar will rise, though the price of sugar itself is unchanged.

(4) Consumers Preferences, Tastes and Needs : A consumer demands a commodity because it satisfies his want. The demand for the commodity, therefore, will depend upon the intensity of his want. A consumer has a scale of preferences during a given period of time. Over time, if the scale of preferences changes, the demand will also change. Needs of the consumer influence the intensity of their wants. Once a need is satisfied, his want of that commodity goes down on the scale of preference, making room for some other want which now becomes more intense. Demand also depends upon the tastes of the consumers. The demand for cassettes of Classical music and the demand for cassettes or CDs of film songs are examples in point.

(5) The Number of Consumers : When market demand for a commodity is under consideration, the number of consumers in the market becomes a relevant factor. The number of consumers depends upon:

(a) **Size of the Population :** Larger the size, greater the number of consumers and higher will be the demand at each price.

(b) **Structure of Population :** A change in the structure of population also results in a change in the demand. For instance, if the proportion of adults increases and that of children below five years of age decreases, the demand for children's clothes will decrease and that for garments for adults will increase.

(c) **Transport and Communication :** Facilities of transport and communication serve to expand the market and cause an increase in the demand for a product.

(6) Expectations of the Consumers : If the consumers expect a further fall in the price, the initial fall in the price will not be followed by a rise in demand. Instead, demand will contract as a result of a fall in price, because consumers are expecting further fall in prices.

(7) Advertisement : Advertisements create demand for a product by informing the consumer that the commodity being advertised is available at the market. Advertisement also persuades the consumer to buy the commodity concerned by bringing to his notice several qualities of the product.

(8) Other Facilities : While selling a commodity, the sellers offer a number of facilities like Hire Purchase or Warranty or Post-sales service or free home delivery etc. to the consumer. These facilities also influence demand for the product concerned.

2.2 Elasticity of Demand

(A) Elasticity of Demand :

In our statement of the law of demand, we saw that there is an inverse relationship between price of the product and the demand for it. The law of demand is however a qualitative statement of the relationship between the price of the commodity and its quantity demanded by the consumer. Actually, it is not enough to know that a fall in price would lead to an extension of demand. The business firm, for example, would like to know how much more it would be able to sell if it reduces the price of its product by a given amount. In other words, the law of demand itself does not imply any quantitative aspect. This is because of the fact that there is no quantitative unit relationship between price and demand. For example, a 10% fall in the price of goods may result in a 10% increase in the quantity demanded; but, in case of some other commodity, it is possible that a 10% reduction in price may lead to a 25 or even 50% increase in demand. It is, therefore, desirable to know the quantitative relationship between change in price and change in demand. This task can be performed with the help of the concept of elasticity of demand. This concept was introduced by economists like Cournot and Mill; but was developed by **Dr. Alfred Marshall**. Elasticity of demand can be defined as the *extent to which the quantity demanded of a commodity changes in response to a given change in price*. In other words, elasticity of demand is the capacity of the demand to expand or contract in response to a given changes in price.

(B) Concept of Elasticity :

As developed by Marshall, the concept of elasticity was applied to price elasticity. But later on, the concept was made more inclusive. Elasticity of demand is a concept of judging the responsiveness of demand. As we noted earlier, changes in demand can be caused by several factors which determine demand for a commodity. Obviously, demand is responsive to each of these factors i.e. quantity demanded of a product would respond to each of these factors. But all the factors are not equally important from the point of view of either theoretical analysis or practical policies. For example, take *tastes* of the consumers. This is an exogenous factor and there is no point in measuring the responsiveness of demand to this factor - though in practice this factor is important. Efforts, therefore, are made to measure the responsiveness of demand to changes in certain important factors like price, income, prices of related products, sales promotion etc.

Let us consider price as a factor for understanding the concept of elasticity. While considering the responsiveness of the quantity demanded to changes in price, we may wish to make some such statement: *'The demand for sugar was more responsive to price changes twenty years ago than it is today or 'the demand for milk responds more to price changes than does the demand for tea'*. It is thus clear that the degree of responsiveness of quantity demanded to price changes varies from product to product. Elasticity of demand indicates the degree of responsiveness of quantity demanded to changes in market price. This then becomes the concept of price elasticity of demand. Likewise, we can speak of income elasticity of demand or cross elasticity of demand.

(C) Price Elasticity of Demand :

Dr. Marshall has defined the price elasticity of demand as follows: *"The elasticity (or responsiveness) of demand in market is great or small according to the amount demanded increases much or little for a given rise in the price"*. Because Marshall has made a specific reference to price change, he is obviously referring to the price elasticity of demand. We can therefore define price elasticity of demand as the *degree of responsiveness of demand for a commodity to a change in price.*

As we saw earlier, Marshall was the first economist to give a clear formulation of price elasticity of demand. Expressed in more accurate mathematical terms, price elasticity of demand is the *ratio of proportionate change in the quantity demanded of a commodity to a given proportionate change in its price*. Alternatively, it is the *ratio of a relative change in quantity to a relative change in price*. If E_p stands for price elasticity, then,

$$E_p = \frac{\text{Percentage change in demand}}{\text{Percentage change in price}}$$

Let us suppose that the percentages are as follows :

The price falls by 1%; and the demand increases by 3%. Because the price falls, the change in price can be shown by $-$ 1%. Thus, $E_p = \frac{3\%}{-1\%} = -3$. Alternatively, if the price rises by 1%, the quantity demanded may fall by 3% and the equation would be $E_p = \frac{-3\%}{1\%} = -3$. It would therefore be important to remember that due to the inverse relationship between price and quantity demanded either the numerator or the denominator will be negative. As such E_p will always be a negative quantity. Because it is always negative, the minus sign is generally omitted.

Types of Price Elasticity of Demand :

(1) Perfectly Elastic Demand : Perfect elasticity refers to that situation where the slightest rise in price causes the quantity demanded of the commodity to fall to zero; and conversely the slightest fall in price causes an infinite increase in the quantity demanded of the commodity. The demand thus is hypersensitive and the elasticity of demand is infinity. As such, this is an extreme case of elasticity which is very rarely to be found in practice but is of great theoretical importance. In terms of our formula, a 5% increase in demand with no fall in price will give us the equation :

$$E_p = \frac{5}{0} = \infty$$

Thus, infinite elasticity of demand means that the firm can sell any amount of commodity at the ruling price, but if the price is increased by 1 paisa, the demand will come down to zero.

(2) Perfectly Inelastic Demand : It refers to a situation where the demand is unaffected even after a substantial change in price. In other words, any amount of rise or fall in price might have taken place, but the quantity demanded of the commodity remains unchanged. The demand, in such a case, has no responsiveness to a price changes and therefore the elasticity of demand is said to be zero. Like perfectly elastic demand, examples of perfectly inelastic demand also are rarely found in real life. This concept also is theoretically very valuable.

If we suppose that price changes by 50% but change in demand is zero, then :

$$E_p = \frac{0}{50} = 0$$

(3) **Highly Elastic Demand :** When a small proportionate change in the price of a commodity is accompanied by a large proportionate change in its quantity demanded, we get a case of relatively elastic or highly elastic demand. In other words, highly elastic demand is one where a small proportionate fall in price leads to a sizeable proportionate increase in demand and vice versa. For example, if a 40% increase in demand is the outcome of 20% fall in price then :

$$E_p = \frac{40}{20} = 2$$

(4) **Inelastic Demand :** When a large proportionate change in the price of a commodity is followed by a small proportionate change in its quantity demanded, we can say that the demand is inelastic. In other words, inelastic demand is one where a large proportionate fall in price is followed by a small proportionate rise in demand and vice versa. For example, if the demand for a product, increases by 5% following a 10% rise in price, then :

$$E_p = \frac{5}{10} = 0.5$$

(5) **Unit Elasticity of Demand :** This is the situation where proportionate change in price is accompanied by an equal proportionate change in the quantity demanded. For example, let us say, a 20% increase in price leads to a 20% fall in demand. Then :

$$E_p = \frac{20}{20} = 1$$

Such a demand is said to be just elastic or the elasticity is said to be equal to unity.

In short, the five types of price elasticity of demand can be summarised, thus :

$$E_p = \infty, E_p = 0, E_p > 1, E_p < 1, E_p = 1.$$

Determinants of Price Elasticity of Demand :

Price elasticity of demand seeks to measure the exact responsiveness of demand to changes in price. The responsiveness or sensitiveness of demand to price is not the same in respect of changes in price. This precisely is the reason why we try to measure elasticity. The responsiveness or the elasticity of the demand for commodity will be more or less depending upon a wide variety of factors influencing the elasticity of demand. These factors are :

(1) **Degree of Necessity :** We know that commodities are classified as necessaries, comforts and luxuries. Other things being equal, the demand for necessaries is less elastic than the demand for comforts and luxuries. Why it is so is not difficult to explain. Necessaries are goods which must be bought whatever the price and so the demand for them is inelastic. On the other hand, if the price of luxury articles rises, a consumer can do either by buying less of it or by not buying it at all. This is the reason why we find that prices of necessaries can be raised without much loss of the market.

(2)   The Proportion of Consumer's Income Spent on the Commodity : The demand for a commodity on which the consumer spends only a small proportion of his income is inelastic. For example, the demand for match-boxes will not change even when its price rises by 100%. This is because the proportion of one's income spent on match-boxes is insignificant.

(3)   Habits : Wants are habit-forming and the demand for a commodity to which a consumer is accustomed is generally inelastic. For example, a person who is accustomed to a particular brand of coffee will not reduce his demand even when there is a rise in its price. In the long-run, if the price continues to rise, the consumer may turn to substitutes or may try to do with a smaller quantity of coffee.

(4)   Existence of Substitute : Commodities which have a number of substitutes face an elastic demand. In such cases, a small rise in the price of a commodity induces the consumer to turn to substitutes, assuming that their prices have not changed. Conversely, a fall in the prices of a commodity induce consumers to buy this commodity rather than its substitute.

(5)   Number of Uses of the Commodity : A commodity which can be put to several uses, also has an elastic demand. Take the case of electricity. A fall in the price of electricity would induce the consumer to use electricity for air-cooling, cooking, water-heating, besides using it as a source of energy for agriculture, industries etc. When the price rises, electricity will be used only for essential purposes. The demand thus can be adjusted to price changes and, therefore, becomes elastic.

(6)   Durable Goods : The demand for durable goods is more elastic because when a rise takes place in their prices, the consumption can be postponed and when a fall is there in their price, one can buy goods in anticipation of future demand. When furniture prices rise, one can postpone its purchase and, conversely, when the present price is low, one can buy furniture for future use.

(7)   Time : As we have noted earlier, the demand for a commodity always refers to a period of time. The time period can be a day, a week, a month or several years. The elasticity of demand, therefore, depends upon the length of time allowed. The longer the period of time allowed, the more elastic will the demand become and the shorter the period of time, the more inelastic is likely to be the demand. This happens because :

(a)   The consumers are unable to change their habits in the short period but when a longer period is allowed, they can change their habits and make the demand more elastic.

(b)   The consumers can postpone the demand for a while even when the price of commodity has fallen, in anticipation of a further fall in price.

(c) The demand may not change because the goods already purchased by the consumers are durable.

(d) A fourth cause can be added in the form of time required in the development of substitutes. For example, a rise in the price of cooking (LP) gas may not immediately result in the fall for its demand. In the long-run, however, the production of solar cookers or microwave ovens or bio-gas plants may become widespread and may provide a viable substitute to the cooking (LP) gas.

(8) Range of Prices : The elasticity of demand is also influenced by the range of prices at which the commodities are sold. Very high-priced commodities are purchased only by the very rich. Therefore, a slight change in price does not cause any change in demand. The demand for such products, thus, is inelastic. Similarly, the very low-priced commodities also face an inelastic demand. The reason being that those who wanted to buy cheap commodities are already buying them and a fall in their prices does not lead to any sizeable increase in the demand for them. We can therefore conclude that at very high and very low prices, demand is inelastic though it becomes elastic at moderate prices.

Methods of Measuring Price Elasticity of Demand :

The importance of the concept of elasticity lies in its measurability. Let us, therefore, try to understand various methods of measuring price elasticity of demand.

(1) Point Method : Besides the method of measuring elasticity in terms of percentage changes in price and demand, there are three more methods devised by the economists. One of them is known as point method. This method has been suggested by Dr. Marshall. According to this method, we take a straight line demand curve joining two axes and measure elasticity between two points on the demand curve which are assumed to be infinitely close to each other. Basically, this is a graphical method but the calculations can be made algebraically, as under : If E_p is the price elasticity, P is the price, ΔP is a slight change in price, Q is the quantity of the commodity demanded and ΔQ is a slight change in demand, then price elasticity can be calculated by the formula :

$$E_p = -\frac{\frac{\Delta Q}{Q}}{\frac{\Delta P}{P}}$$

Example : When the price of any commodity 'X' falls from 51 paise to 50 paise per unit, the demand for the commodity increases from 100 units to 101 units. What would be the price elasticity of demand ?

In this example, ΔP is 1 and ΔQ is also 1. According to our formula, therefore

$$E_p = -\frac{\frac{1}{100}}{-\frac{1}{51}} = +\frac{51}{100} = 0.51$$

The demand in this example is inelastic because the elasticity is positive but less than 1.

(2)   Arc Method : Instead of taking 2 points on the demand curve very close to each other, if we take an arc or a small part of the demand curve the method becomes arc method. This method enables us to take sizeable changes in demand and price into account because in practice slight changes are difficult to find.

This method also can be used with the help of an algebraic formula.

Let us suppose P_1 is the initial price, P_2 is the new price, Q_1 is the initial quantity demanded and Q_2 is the new demand. If E_p stands for price elasticity, the formula for finding out E_p will be :

$$E_p = -\frac{\dfrac{Q_1 - Q_2}{Q_1 + Q_2}}{2} + \frac{\dfrac{P_1 - P_2}{P_1 + P_2}}{2}$$

$$= -\frac{\dfrac{Q_1 - Q_2}{Q_1 + Q_2}}{\dfrac{P_1 - P_2}{P_1 + P_2}}$$

Example : The demand for a commodity increases from 5 units to 15 units after a fall in price from ₹ 9 to ₹ 8 per unit. What will be the price elasticity in this case ?

Solution : According to our formula.

$$E_p = -\frac{\left(\dfrac{5-15}{5+15}\right)}{\left(\dfrac{9-8}{9+8}\right)} = \frac{\left(-\dfrac{10}{20}\right)}{\left(-\dfrac{1}{17}\right)}$$

$$= \frac{1}{2} \times \frac{17}{1} = 8.5$$

E_p is 8.5 and the demand is highly elastic.

(3)   Total Revenue or Total Expenditure Method : Elasticity of demand can also be measured with the help of total revenue of the form or total expenditure of the consumer on the product concerned. If a slight fall in the price leads to a sizeable increase in demand; it will cause an increase in total revenue. The demand in this case will be highly elastic. If, on the other hand there is a fall in the total revenue because a fall in price does not lead to an equivalent increase in quantity demanded, it would be inelastic and will be shown by a fall in total revenue. Since the proportionate change is known as a case of unit elasticity, in terms of total revenue, we shall find that total revenue remains constant as price and demand changes. Table 2.3 illustrates this method.

Table 2.3 : Total Revenue Method of Measuring Elasticity

Price (₹)	Weekly demand (units)	Total revenue of the firm (₹)	Elasticity of demand
9	50	450 ⎫	
8	150	1,200 ⎪	
7	200	1,400 ⎬	Highly Elastic, $E_p > 1$
6	300	1,800 ⎭	
5	360	1,800 ⎫	
4	450	1,800 ⎬	Elastic, $E_p = 1$
3	550	1,650 ⎫	
2	700	1,400 ⎬	Inelastic, $E_p < 1$
1	900	900 ⎭	

(4) **Does slope of the curve indicate Elasticity ?** The slope of the demand curve is thought to show elasticity of demand. Does the demand curve indicate the elasticity of demand ? The slopes of two demand curves will broadly indicate which demand is relatively more elastic or less elastic if the two curves are drawn to the same scale. But strictly speaking, elasticity of demand is different at two different points on the same curve when the demand curve is a straight line. Therefore, the slope of the demand curve does not indicate elasticity of demand. However, in the three cases of (i) perfectly inelastic demand, (ii) perfectly elastic demand, and (iii) unit elasticity of demand, the demand curves indicate elasticity. Figures (2.2, 2.3 and 2.4) will illustrate this point.

Let us consider Fig. 2.2 first.

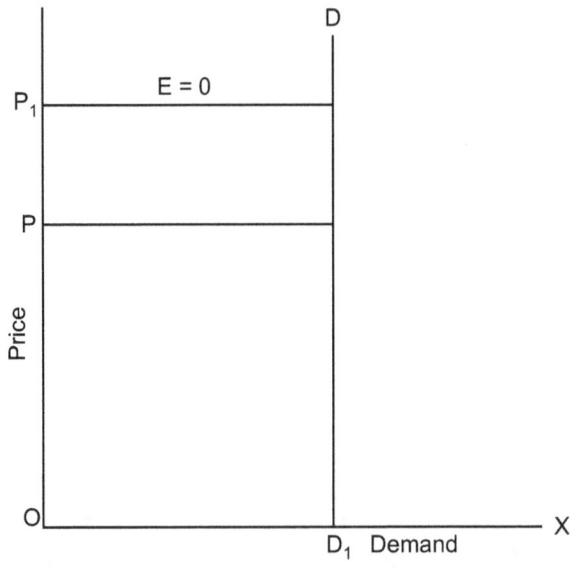

Fig. 2.2 : Perfectly Inelastic Demand

The straight line demand curve DD_1 is parallel to Y-axis. This is an example of perfectly inelastic demand. Whether the price is OP or OP_1 (or any other price which is less or more than OP), the quantity demanded does not change. It is constant at OD_1 in the diagram. Here $E_p = 0$. Fig. 2.3 shows unit elasticity of demand. This demand curve is a rectangular hyperbola. The rectangular hyperbola is a curve where the product of the 'X' and Y' coordinates is constant at all points on the curve. For example, in the diagram $RP \times RQ = SP_1 \times SQ_1$. In other words, when we take any point on this curve and draw a perpendicular to Y-axis, we are actually indicating a price. When we draw a perpendicular to the X-axis from the same point, we are indicating the corresponding quantity demanded. Price $\times$ quantity is nothing but total expenditure of the consumer or the total revenue of the producer. When the total revenue is constant, the elasticity of demand is unity or $E_p = 1$. This is why the demand curve of this type shows unit elasticity of demand.

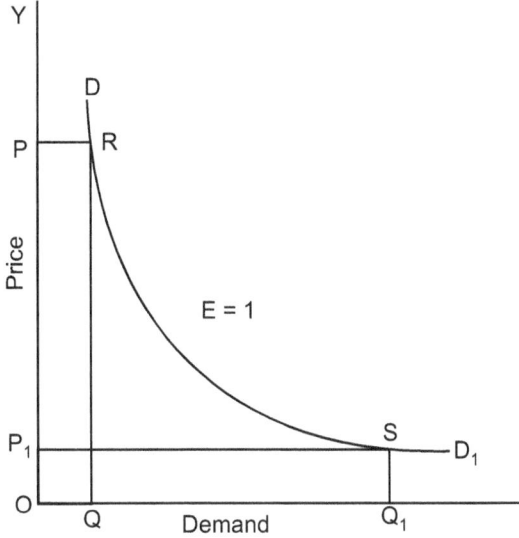

Fig. 2.3 : Unit Elasticity of Demand

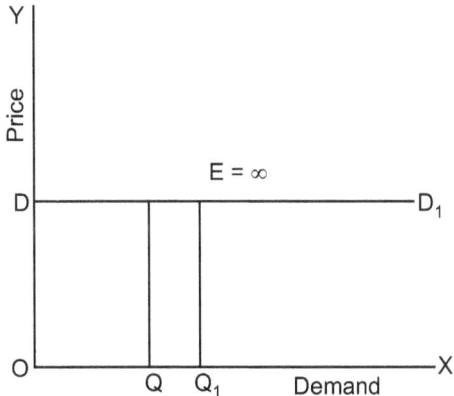

Fig. 2.4 : Perfectly Elastic Demand

Fig. 2.4 shows a straight line demand curve parallel to X-axis. The diagram shows that at the ruling price OD, any amount of the commodity can be sold. This is a case of perfectly elastic demand or $E_p = \infty$.

Significance or Importance of the Concept of Price Elasticity of Demand :

The concept of elasticity of demand plays a very important role in theoretical discussions in economics. A more remarkable point about this concept is that it serves as a very important guide for policy formulations in a number of areas.

(1) Pricing under Imperfect Competition : When production is carried out under conditions of imperfect competition i.e. under conditions of oligopoly or monopoly or monopolistic competition, the individual producer has to take into account the elasticity of demand for his product. While fixing the price of the product or effecting a change in the existing price, if demand for the product is inelastic, one can profitably raise the price. Similarly, when elasticity of demand is different in different markets, the monopolist can follow a policy of price-discrimination i.e. charging different prices for the same product at different markets.

(2) Policy Formulations by the Government : The concept of elasticity of demand is of immense practical importance in various policies formulated and followed by the Government. In import policy, for example, if the government bans the import of a product the demand for which is inelastic, there are chances of the product being smuggled into the country. In fiscal policy, if the finance minister imposes a tax on a product the demand for which is inelastic, the expected revenue accrual is certain. On the other hand, if the demand is elastic and the product is taxed, the expected tax revenue may not be realised because of the fact that consumers will purchase less of the product following a rise in the price caused by taxation. In the same way, elasticity considerations are helpful to the Government in the formulation of agricultural policy, industrial policy, monetary policy and developmental planning.

(3) Resource Prices : The concept of elasticity of demand plays an important role in the fixation of a resource price or reward for factors of production in a market economy. For example, if the demand for labour in a particular industry is inelastic because the job is to be carried out manually and mechanisation is not possible, the trade unions can press for a wage-rise and would actually get their demands approved. The demand for labour here is inelastic. Land rents in urban areas are high because land is demanded for various uses like commercial, residential or industrial uses. The demand becomes inelastic because there is no substitute to land.

(4) Terms of Trade : When two countries exchange their commodities in the field of international trade, the rates at which these commodities are exchanged are known as *terms of trade*. For example, if India and Bangladesh are exchanging tea and jute, the rate of exchange will be based upon the elasticity of demand for jute in India and elasticity of demand for tea in Bangladesh. If India's demand for jute is relatively more elastic, terms of trade will be in India's favour.

(5) Rate of Exchange : In practice, international trade is carried out in terms of foreign exchange. Therefore, whatever we said in respect of terms of trade can be applied to rate of exchange also. For example, the rate of exchange between dollars and rupees will have to be fixed after taking into account the elasticity of our demand for import from America and the elasticity of American demand for goods exported from India.

(6) Public Utilities : Public utilities like supply of drinking water or production and supply of electricity or road transport etc. are owned and operated by the Government because they involve highly inelastic demand. Take the case of drinking water. People cannot do without water and will have to use water, whatever the charges levied by the supplier. This is why local authorities take over the responsibility of water supply as public utility.

(D) Income Elasticity of Demand :

As indicated in the beginning, we can now switch over to another determinant of demand viz. income and consider elasticity of demand by holding all other determinants, including price, constant. Income elasticity of demand for a product shows the extent to which a consumer's demand for that product changes consequent upon a change in his income. Income elasticity of demand can be defined as the *ratio of proportionate change in the quantity demanded of the commodity to a given proportionate change in income of the consumer*. The formulae for measuring income elasticity of demand can be stated, thus :

Measurement of Income Elasticity of Demand :

Formula 1 :

$$Ey = \frac{\text{Proportionate change in quantity demanded}}{\text{Proportionate change in consumer's income}}$$

Example : A 20% rise in income causes a 30% increase in demand for a product 'X', what will be the income elasticity of demand for 'X' ?

Solution : According to formula mentioned above :

$$Ey = \frac{30}{20} = 1.5$$

Formula 2 : A second formula which is mathematically more rational is suggested as under :

$$Ey = \frac{Q_2 - Q_1}{Q_2 + Q_1} \div \frac{Y_2 - Y_1}{Y_2 + Y_1}$$

In this formula, Q_1 is the initial consumer expenditure on any commodity 'X' (which represents the demand for the product 'X') and Q_2 is the new expenditure on the same commodity after a change in income. Y_1 denotes initial income and Y_2 stands for changed or new income.

Example : A consumer spends ₹ 200 per month on sugar when his income is ₹ 10,000 per month. When his income increases to ₹ 12,000 per month, he spends ₹ 400 on sugar. What will be the income elasticity of demand for sugar in this case ?

Solution : According to the above formula :

$$E_y = \frac{400 - 200}{400 + 200} \div \frac{12,000 - 10,000}{12,000 + 10,000}$$

$$= \frac{200}{600} \div \frac{2,000}{22,000}$$

$$= \frac{1}{3} \times \frac{22,000}{2,000}$$

$$= \frac{1}{3} \times \frac{11}{1} = \frac{11}{3} = 3.67$$

Income elasticity of demand in this case is 3.67.

Types of Income Elasticity of Demand :

According to the value of income elasticity of demand, we can classify income elasticity into the following five types :

(1) Negative Income Elasticity : When the demand for a product decreases as income increases and conversely when demand for a product increases as there is fall in income, the income elasticity of demand is negative. The demand for inferior goods is of this type.

(2) Zero Income Elasticity : When a change in income has no effect upon the quantity demanded of a product, the income elasticity of demand would be zero. Demand for salt is an example of this type.

(3) Unit Income Elasticity : Income elasticity of demand will be equal to unity (i.e. 1) when demand for the product increases in the same proportion in which income increases. Unit elasticity of demand is considered to be a dividing line between necessaries and comforts. In other words, the income elasticity of demand for necessaries will be less than unity : while the income elasticity of the demand for comforts will be more than unity. Both these cases are noted below.

(4) Low Income Elasticity of Demand : When the income elasticity of demand for a product is positive i.e. greater than zero, but less than one, we say that the income elasticity of that demand is relatively less. Such a variety of relatively less income elasticity or income-inelasticity of demand suggests that the commodity concerned must be a necessary. This is because as income increases the percentage of income spent on necessaries goes on diminishing, according to Engel's Law of family expenditure.

(5) High Income Elasticity : As opposed to the above category, we get high income elasticity of demand for products which satisfy the consumers' comforts and luxuries. In other words, the income elasticity of demand for articles of comforts and luxuries is greater than unity.

The income elasticity for different products differs widely. Income elasticity of demand tends to be very high in respect of luxury articles like gold, jewellery, precious stones, paintings, cars etc. As against this, income elasticity of demand is very low in respect of commodities like salt, vanaspati, matches, kerosene, washing soap etc. Besides the type of a commodity i.e. whether it is a necessary or comfort or luxury, the proportion of a consumer's income spent on the commodity is also a major factor influencing income elasticity of demand.

Uses or Importance of Income Elasticity of Demand :

The concept of income elasticity of demand is useful in many areas of economic policy-formulations as well as analysis of various situations.

(1) **Economic Development :** In case of economic development, when national income is increasing, we can find out how much will be the increase in the demand for a given product, by considering the income elasticity of demand for that product.

(2) **Economic Fluctuations :** Economic fluctuations are a characteristic feature of a capitalistic economy. Phases of prosperity and depression alternate in such an economy. The concept of income elasticity can be a very useful guide in finding out what products would be demanded during the phase of prosperity. Similarly, during the phase of depression, certain necessaries will continue to be demanded. As noted above, necessaries are commodities with very low income elasticities.

(3) **Economic Planning :** The concept of income elasticity of demand is of great help to the planners who are planning for the economy as a whole. When economic development is being planned, the planners have to set targets of production in terms of physical quantities for various sectors of the economy. With the help of income elasticity, the planners can estimate the possible increase in demand for the product, as a result of the targeted rate of growth of the economy. This would make the physical targets more realistic and would serve to maintain physical balances - a difficult task for the planners.

(4) **Demand Forecasting :** Firms are required to forecast the demand for their product. With the help of statistical information regarding trends in growth of income as well as changes of distribution of income, the firm can forecast the demand for its product by using income elasticity of demand for that product as a guide.

(5) **Foreign Trade :** In the area of foreign trade, a country needs to take into account the income elasticity of demand for its imports as well as exports. A country exporting agricultural products and articles of necessity faces an income-inelastic demand, compared to a country which is exporting articles of luxury. This difference influences terms of trade. Income elasticity of demand serves as a guide in the matter of balance of payments disequilibrium also. For example, India has been an exporter of jute, tea, coffee, and spices; but the demand for all these commodities is income-inelastic. The rate of growth of India's

exports therefore has remained relatively low. As against this, India's demand for imports like electronics, machinery, consumer durable etc. is income-elastic. Consequently, the rate of growth of India's imports has remained high. Thus we have been facing the problem of an increasing trade deficit in India during the last few years.

The list of areas where income elasticity of demand is useful can be increased further by mentioning public finance, labour policy, industrial policy, etc. where the concept is useful.

(E) Cross Elasticity of Demand :

In practice, commodities are seldom independent of one another. Among the wide range of products that we see at the market, we find that most of these goods are related on the basis of the relationship, we can group these products either as substitutes or as complements or as a third group of goods which are neutral. In the context of the relationship between goods, the concept of cross elasticity of demand can be used. Cross elasticity of demand may be defined as the *ratio of proportionate change of quantity demanded of commodity 'X' to a given proportionate change in price of the related commodity 'Y'*. With the help of formula, similar to the one we noted earlier, we can say :

$$E_c = \frac{\text{Percentage change in quantity demanded of 'X'}}{\text{Percentage change in the price of 'Y'}}$$

If we assume the two commodities X and Y are substitutes of each other and that the price of Y rises but that of X remains constant, the quantity demanded of X will increase because the consumers will now substitute X for Y, since Y has become costlier. Conversely, if the price of Y falls leaving the price of X unchanged, the quantity demanded of X will decrease because the consumers will now substitute Y for X since Y has become cheaper than before.

Cross elasticity can also be measured by another formula as given below :

$$E_c = \frac{\dfrac{QX_2 - QX_1}{QX_2 + QX_1}}{\dfrac{PY_2 - PY_1}{PY_2 + PY_1}}$$

In this formula, QX_2 is the new demand for X, QX_1 is the original demand for X; PY_2 is the new price of Y and PY_1 is the original price of Y.

If X and Y are perfect substitute for each other, the cross elasticity of demand will be infinity. It means that the slightest rise in the price of Y will cause an almost infinite rise in the demand for X and the slightest fall in the price of Y will reduce the demand for X to almost zero. If, on the other hand, two goods are no substitutes at all, the cross elasticity of demand will be zero. A change in the price of one commodity will not affect the quantity demanded of the other commodity. It will thus be clear that the cross elasticity of demand for substitutes varies between zero and infinity.

If the relationship between X and Y is that of complementarily, the cross elasticity in such a case will be negative. A rise in the price of Y will mean not only a decrease in the quantity demanded of Y but also a decrease in the quantity demanded of X because both are demanded together. For example, ball-point pens and refills are complementary goods. When the price of refills rises, it causes a fall in the demand for refills as well as for ball-point pens, because both are demanded together.

Commodities X and Y will be perfect substitutes only when they are totally identical. In that case, they will not be two different commodities at all. Therefore, in practice, infinite cross elasticity of demand cannot be found. In practice, the cross elasticity of a demand can thus be positive, zero or negative. The cross elasticity is positive when X and Y are good substitutes (and almost infinity when X and Y are almost perfect substitutes). It is zero when X and Y are not related to each other or do not possess any substitutability : they are independent of each other. It is negative when X and Y are complementary goods. In the first case, a rise in the price of Y (price of X remaining constant) will cause an increase in the quantity demanded of X. In the second case, a rise or fall in the price of Y (price of X remaining unchanged) does not affect the quantity demanded of X at all. In the third case, a rise in the price of Y (the price of X remaining unchanged) will cause a decrease in the quantity demanded of X

Example : Because the price of Y increases from ₹ 10 to ₹ 12 per kg., the sales of a firm producing commodity Y rise to 220 kg from 200 kg. per week. Find out the cross elasticity and state the relationship between commodities X and Y.

Solution :

$$E_c = \cfrac{\cfrac{220 - 200}{220 + 200}}{\cfrac{12 - 10}{12 + 10}} = \cfrac{\cfrac{20}{420}}{\cfrac{2}{22}}$$

$$= \cfrac{\cfrac{1}{21}}{\cfrac{1}{11}} = \cfrac{1}{21} \times \cfrac{11}{1}$$

$$= 0.52$$

The cross elasticity of demand is 0.52 and X and Y are substitutes.

Uses of the Concept : Perfect substitutes are seldom found in practice. Perfect complementarity is equally rare. But, broadly speaking, there is a complementarity or competition i.e. substitutability among several commodities. Under such circumstances, the entrepreneur can judge the effect of his pricing policy on the quantities demanded of the products of others and vise versa on the basis of the cross elasticity of demand.

Distinguishing Price, Income and Cross Elasticity of Demand :

The law of demand tells us that consumers will respond to a price decline by buying more of a product. But the degree of responsiveness of the consumer demand may vary considerably from product to product, as noted above. Economists measure how responsive, or sensitive, consumers are to a change in the price of a product by the concept of the price elasticity of demand. When a given change in price causes substantial change in demand, we say the demand is price-elastic.

Income of the consumer is another important factor influencing demand for a product. That is, given the prices of all goods and services in the market, a change in consumer incomes will give rise to a change in the purchases of products. The concept of income-elasticity of demand measures the change in the quantity of a product demanded as a result of the change in consumer income. In other words, income elasticity of demand shows how responsive the demand for a product is to a change in consumer income.

While income elasticity measures the effect of a change in consumer incomes upon the purchase of a product and price elasticity measures the effect of a change in a product's price upon the quantity demanded of that product, cross elasticity of demand measures the responsiveness of demand for one product to a change in the price of some other product. When two products, say X and Y. are related to each other, a change in the price of Y will cause a change in the quantity demanded of product X. When consumers income and the prices of all other goods are constant, the concept of cross elasticity of demand measures the effect of a change in the price of product Y upon the quantity demanded of product X.

It will thus be clear that *(i) price elasticity measures the effect of a change in the price of Y on the demand for Y; (ii) cross elasticity measures the effect of a change in the price of Y on the demand for X; while (iii) income elasticity measures the effect of a change in consumer's income on the demand for X or Y or Z or any other product; other things being given.*

We have seen that the quantity of a commodity demanded at the market during a given period of time is determined not only by the price of that commodity but also by prices of related goods, tastes of the consumers, incomes of the consumers and so on. Obviously, a change in any of these factors will lead to a change in demand. When we relate the change in demand to a change in price, we are holding the other determinants constant. By the same logic, as we shall see in detail a little later, we can allow some other determinant like income to vary and hold all other factors including price constant. For the present, let us consider, the price-demand relationship.

2.3 Forecasting of Demand

A forecast is a prediction about a future event which is most likely to happen under given conditions. In a world full of uncertainties, formation of some view about the future is inevitable. Therefore, firms try to forecast the likely demand for their products. Predictions of future demand for a firm's product or products are known as demand forecasts. Forecasting as an important function of management came in vogue after the great depression and became more common after the second world-war. Demand forecasts are important because huge resources are involved in the modern large-scale production. It has come to be reckoned as an important function of management.

(A) Demand Estimation and Demand Forecasting :

With the geographical widening of the market and with a global competition in the fields of durable consumer goods and producer's goods, demand estimation is becoming increasingly more and more important. For a firm catering to a local or regional market, it is possible to arrive at a broad estimate of demand for the firm's product. However, for a wider market which, in many cases, has become a global market, demand estimation has become very important. Demand estimates, though they refer to the existing demand for the product, have to keep in view a time-frame. The demand estimation thus becomes a short-term demand forecast. As such, the purposes of short-term forecasts discussed under the heading' Short-term and Long-term Forecasts' become the *objectives of demand estimation*.

Forecasts are made for a future period. But for the purpose of estimating demand, one has to rely on past experience to check the reliability of the current demand estimates. The forecasts for past and present periods are called *ex-post forecasts*. Generally, they are carried out for testing the credibility of the forecasting method/model which the firm wants to use for genuine forecasts, i.e. forecasts for a future period.

Besides, they also serve to throw some light on the current year plan and the need of a revision of the budget for the current year. Another important purpose demand estimation serves is to test and prevalidate the variables to be included in the demand function of the firm. These variables may, and do, differ from firm to firm. Hence, the need for this exercise.

Methods of Demand Estimation :

For demand estimation, the following three methods are used :

(1) Consumer's Interviews : Consumers are interviewed with regard to their consumption habits. Interviews can be on census basis or on sample basis when the number is very large. Here, past and present consumers are interviewed, through surveys, so as to obtain relevant information regarding all variables (like income, tastes of consumers, substitutes etc.) useful for estimating the demand function.

(2) Market Experiments Method : Actual shops can be opened in selected localities and the response of consumers can be judged. Alternatively, using simulation technique, one can provide token money to a set of consumers who can shop around in a simulated market. Then, consumer reactions to quality, packaging, price and changes in these variables are observed. Obviously, actual experiments are more reliable.

(3) Regression Method : This method, more commonly used, involves four steps : (i) Identifying variables influencing demand for our product, (ii) Collecting historical data, (iii) Selecting appropriate form for the function, and (iv) Estimating the function.

All of these methods are used for demand forecasting also; and demand forecasting is the more important and challenging task facing any business. Therefore, all the above-mentioned methods, alongwith other methods, are discussed in detail, under *demand forecasting*. The details include need, objectives, criteria, uses, limitations etc. for providing an insight into the topic of discussion.

(B) Necessity of Forecasting Demand :

Forecasting of demand by some technique or the other is highly essential. An entrepreneur can forecast on the basis of hunch or intuition or personal judgement. Alternatively he can employ more definite methods which can bring down demand forecasts in measurable terms. Forecasts based on personal judgement or common sense are a game of guesswork. It is true that mature and experienced entrepreneurs do get a feel of the market and are perhaps successful because they have some sort of a sixth sense in foreseeing the future demand. However, we cannot adopt this type of forecasting in an organised and measurable way on the mass level. Basically there are two main reasons why forecasting should be taken as a serious function of the management : (1) It is a part of business management, and (2) Any systematic plan or forecast is better than no plan at all.

An organised forecasting system may not be necessary as long as the concerned firms are small and their operations are simple. The estimates of demand in case of small firms can safely be left to the guess-work and foresight of the entrepreneurs themselves. But as a business unit grows in size, in complexity and in diversity of its products and processes, forecasting becomes a specialised and a separate function of management. The necessity of forecasting can be summarised as follows :

(1) Achievement of Planned Objectives : Every firm aims at certain pre-determined objectives. For attainment of these objectives, the firm needs a reasonably accurate forecast of trends in the economy in general, and of its sales income in particular.

(2) Preparing a Budget : Every firm has to prepare a well conceived budget incorporating costs of production and expected earnings. The expectations of earnings must be backed by a forecast of annual sales and prices. Such a budget enables the firm to control its costs and to reduce the area of avoidable risks. Such a systematic exercise is also better than personal judgement of the entrepreneur as a guide to business.

(3) Stabilisation of Production and Employment : Market demand fluctuates due to seasonal, cyclical and erratic changes in the situation but the level of production cannot be changed every now and then. If an annual forecast of demand is ready, a plan of production can be prepared for the whole year and seasonal variations can be met by depletion or replenishment of stocks. This policy would also enable the firm to maintain a stable labour force. Such a stable labour force is essential because one cannot recruit and retrench workers at will, following variations in market conditions.

(4) Future Expansion : Every firm has to think in terms of its plans of expansion in future. Such a long-term plan has to be based upon forecasts of demand.

(5) Long-term Investment Programmes : Expansion plans for the future, necessitate a long-term programme of investment as well as a plant of future recruitment. For example, a firm has to consider various alternatives of raising funds as well as alternatives of deploying these funds. Similarly, future requirement of personnel must be anticipated so as to evolve satisfactory programmes of training and apprenticeship.

(6) Sales Budgeting : Demand forecasting is crucial for sales budgeting. It determines production and inventory plans, the level of costs and the level of employment. Sales budgets are also useful in computing standard costs, in establishing profit goals and in preparation of capital budgets, future cash flows and sources of funds. Sales forecasts and sales budget act as regulators of a firm's operations and serve to improve the quality of business decisions.

(7) Control of Inventories : A satisfactory method of control of raw materials semi-finished products, finished goods, spare parts and work-in-process must depend upon a satisfactory estimate of future requirements and availability of all these as well as their estimated prices. The use of standard costing for the purposes of setting prices and controlling costs depends upon a satisfactory forecast of demand. Thus forecasting can be of great help in introducing business discipline and scientific management.

(C) Short-term and Long-term Forecasts :

Sometimes a distinction is drawn between short-term and long-term forecasts, mainly because the purposes of these two types of forecasts are different.

(1) Purposes of short-term Forecasts : A firm has to prepare a short-term forecast for a number of purposes : (i) *Production policy* is one such immediate purpose. Because a firm has to prepare a short-term plan of production which needs short-term forecasts so as to avoid either underproduction or over-production (ii) For a realistic price policy the firm has to prepare a short-term demand forecast. (iii) *Cost-effectiveness* is an important consideration in management. This can be introduced with the help of demand forecasts. (iv) Securing short-term credit becomes possible if the requirements of such credit are at least approximately available. On the basis of demand forecasts the firm can tap various sources of credit in advance and thus save time as well as expenses which are likely to be wasted in an eleventh hour effort at securing credit. (v) *Distribution channels* can be arranged in anticipation of future demand if the forecasts of the demand are available .

(2) Purpose of Long-term Forecasts : Long-term forecasts serve several purposes : (i) *A plan of expansion* is usually prepared for a long-term by a firm. Such a plan involves expansion of existing plant, diversification of production and training and apprenticeship programme for workers. Long-term forecasts for this purpose are necessary. (ii) *Raising of capital* for future expansion is another important purpose. Long-term demand forecasts spell out the needs of capital and accordingly a plan of raising funds from various sources can be formulated. (iii) *Man-power planning* can also be stated as an independent purpose of long-term forecasts.

(D) Nature and Scope of Demand Forecasting :

Savage and small have served a warning in respect of demand forecasting; because they fear that demand forecasting is likely to be construed to mean many things. Similarly it is possible to use a demand forecast in a number of ways. It is therefore necessary, in their opinion, to outline the nature and the scope of demand forecasting. In the opinion of these authors, consideration of the following factors is important as they demarcate the scope of demand forecasting.

(1) Time-frame : A firm has to be certain about the time-frame for which it needs a forecast. In this context every firm has to first decide upon the period of time. Whether the firm chooses a 3 year period or 5 year period or still longer period is important, because the conveniences and inconveniences of the methods of demand forecasting to be used by the firm depending upon the timeframe .

(a) Short-term Forecasts : Normally, a period of one year is considered to be short-term for demand-forecasting. Short-term forecasts can be reasonably accurate because internal policies of the firm (like sales promotion) or external policies (like tax policies of the government) do not change during such a short period. Short-term forecasts can be based on current experiences and opinions of the people who know.

(b) Long-term Forecasts : When a new plant is to be erected or an existing one is to be expanded, a firm needs to take into account a period ranging from 5 to 10 years. Such forecasts have to depend upon statistical methods and more elaborate exercises of demand forecasting.

(c) Secular Forecast : Secular demand forecasts refer to still longer period where secular factors, influencing demand become more relevant. These include factors like population growth, economic development, changes in the direction and composition of international trade or political developments in the country and so on. Thus, the decision regarding the time-frame for the forecast occupies an important place in demand-forecasting.

(2) Level of Forecasts : Demand forecasts can be prepared on various levels.

(a) Level of the Economy : Entrepreneurs can have their own forecasts based upon total national output or gross national product, the indices of which can be available to them.

(b) Level of the Industries : At the level of industries, demand forecasts are usually prepared by business associations like chambers of commerce and industries. Forecasts regarding prospects of an industry and future demand for the product of an industry can be formulated on the basis of market surveys, past trends in demand and other statistical methods. Industry level forecasts are useful to every member firm because every firm can compare its own position vis-a-vis the position of the Industry.

(c) Level of a Firm : On the level of a firm one prepares demand forecasts from the point of view of an individual firm. It is this level of forecast which occupies an important place in microeconomic analysis.

(3) General and Specific Forecasts : Many times demand forecasts are prepared in general for all the products of a firm. Such forecasts have their own uses. However, a firm needs a more detailed information regarding an extent or demand in a particular region or the quantum of demand for each individual product. This requires specific forecast. Too many details may blur the overall picture and just an over-all picture based on general forecast is of little use to the firm. This fact must be remembered while preparing general as well as specific forecasts.

(4) Established Products and New Products : Forecasting demand for established products must be placed on different footing, since these products are already being produced. Knowledge of the current level of the demand for these products and present competition in this field can be an advantage to the firm for using statistical methods of demand-forecasting. This is not possible in respect of new products. So, for forecasting the demand for new products, one has to use different methods and face different problems.

(5) Classification of Products : While preparing demand forecasts, it is necessary to classify the products concerned into capital goods, consumer goods, and durable consumer goods, because each of these classes of goods faces a different type of demand. The demand for capital goods is a derived demand and faces severe fluctuations. The demand for durable consumer goods can be postponed and therefore falls suddenly during depression. The demand for consumer goods is related to the income of the people. With an increase in income, the demand for consumer goods increases, but a fall in consumer's income is not immediately followed by a decrease in demand in the same proportion.

(6) Special Factors : Each demand forecast has to take into account, special factors relating to every product and the market for every product, the nature of competition, the extent of uncertainty, unforeseen risks, and possibilities of forecasts going wrong are some of these special factors. These factors influence the demand differently, at different places and at different times. Similarly there are product-wise differences in the combinations of such special factors entering into demand forecasts. For example, a change in fashion is a special factor that enters into the demand forecast for readymade garments. Intense competition is a factor to be considered by producers of cosmetics, while weather forecasts are an important factor for producers of umbrellas, rain-coats and aircoolers.

(E) Criteria for a Good Method of Demand Forecasting :

There are various methods of demand-forecasting. Out of these alternative methods available to a firm, it has to choose the best method. Which method would be the best ? For answering this question we can outline the following criteria, which would serve as parameters for testing the various methods of demand forecasting.

(1) Plausibility : The method of demand forecasting should be intelligible to the executives who are going to use it. At the same time they should feel confident that the technique used by a method will be helpful to them in formulating a particular forecast.

(2) Simplicity : Various mathematical and economic models can be used with an advantage but they are highly sophisticated and complex. Majority of these models therefore are not acceptable to small and medium-sized firms. Such models may be used by national and multinational corporations because they can afford to have special cells for demand-forecasting. Majority of the managements however require a method which is simple and easy to understand.

(3) Economy : Techniques of demand forecasting involve costs. These costs must be weighed against returns. A method yielding high level of accruals but involving huge amount of costs may not be acceptable simply on grounds of costs. In areas where accuracy is likely to bring in huge profits, however, the high costs of forecasting may prove to be worth their while. Economy would therefore suggest a balancing of costs involved and benefits expected.

(4) Accuracy : Every firm expects its forecasting to be as accurate as possible. By accuracy, we mean closeness to reality. Some check of accuracy of past performance against the present happening and the present forecast against future predictions is highly desirable. Accuracy can be increased by finding out deviations after every forecast. We must however remember the fact that precision would involve higher costs and would go against the criterion of economy.

(5) Availability : The criterion of availability refers to the timely availability of the forecast as well as availability of adequate and uptodate statistical data for the preparation of the forecast. To what extent is a forecast meaningful depends upon the statistical data used by the forecaster. At the same time, if the forecaster tries to collect too much of data and spends a lot of time in arriving at the forecasts, the forecasts are likely to be meaningless for decision-making. They would reach the management too late.

(6) Durability : The criterion of durability is important because a forecast prepared by incurring sizeable costs must last over a reasonable period of time. Forecasts which are based on stability of the underlying variables measured in the past and which are simple in nature are likely to be more durable.

(7) Flexibility : A forecast should be flexible and not rigid because an element of uncertainty is always associated with business plans. A set of variables whose coefficients can be adjusted from time to time for meeting the changing conditions can prove to be a more practical way of imparting flexibility to a method of demand-forecasting.

(8) Consistency : Consistency implies that a firm's forecasts should be consistent with the forecasts at the level of the industry or on the national level. For example, a forecast indicating buoyant demand for one's product would be inconsistent if the national level forecast is that of imminent depression and unemployment.

2.3.1 Methods of Forecasting Demand for Established Products

Over the past few years various techniques of forecasting demand with respect to either the economy as a whole, or an industry or an individual firm have been evolved. As noted above, a forecaster has to choose one or more techniques by testing them against the criteria we have discussed. In many organisations more than one technique is employed with varying degrees of sophistication. Fundamentally, there are two approaches open to the forecasting of demand : One is to obtain information directly without any particular reference to the various forces which determine the demand, and the other is to estimate the effects on the curve of change in the various determinants taken singly or in combination. Because the first approach is more relevant to our course, we will concentrate on that and avoid going into the complexities and mathematical difficulties involved in the second approach, by making a brief reference to it.

Much economic forecasting is concerned with estimating changes in general business conditions because forecasts of general business conditions help us to prepare the forecasts of the sales of a particular industry or a particular firm.

On the national level the GNP or the total flow on final goods and services is usually calculated from the point of view of forecasting. This may be considered as measure of aggregate demand. Thus, on the basis of national income statistics, we can forecast changes in general business conditions. A detailed study of national income statistics may enable a forecaster to get an insight into the movement of private consumption expenditure, government expenditure, savings and so on. This type of information regarding macro-variables is helpful in preparing micro-level forecasts. This is why we made a brief reference to them. Macro level forecasts are used in national economic planning. We are concerned with micro-level forecasts here. So, let us now turn to such forecasting techniques.

Forecasts prepared on the level of the firm can be divided into two types : One can be called 'interview and survey approach' which depends upon market research, survey, etc. for trying to get a feel of the intentions of the consumers by interviewing them. Secondly, 'projecting past experience' can be the other approach, for getting an insight into the future. The first type is more useful for short-term forecasts while the second one is more useful in long-term forecasts.

(A) Interview and Survey Approach :

A direct way of demand-forecasting is to get this information regarding future plans of expenditure of the consumers either from the consumers themselves or from those who have some knowledge of the consumers' intentions. The interview and survey approach, thus, tries to find out the intentions of the consumers, with the help of which one can get a fairly dependable estimate of future demand. This approach consists of the following methods.

(1) Buyers' Interviews or Survey of Buyers' Intentions : The most direct approach is to go out and ask the prospective buyers, or existing buyers of our product, to indicate their demand schedule for our product. This method of forecasting is based upon obtaining the opinions of the consumers and, therefore, it is also known as opinion polling approach. This method is useful when the producer and-the consumer come into direct contact or where the major share in one's market demand is that of a handful of big customers.

For example, if a firm sells 85% of its output to 20 big buyers and remaining 15% is sold to 500 small buyers, then it should not be difficult to contact these 20 big buyers.

Alternatively, when buyers and sellers do not have a direct contact, buyers can be contacted by mail or a limited number of buyers can be contacted personally and interviewed by using statistical sampling methods.

Limitations :

In respect of industrial purchases where a big firm is selling raw materials or spare parts etc. to other firms on a large scale and on a regular basis, this method is of great help. However, a firm dealing with individual consumers cannot depend upon this method because the method has the following limitations :

(a) The buyers or consumers, many times, are not able to tell even broadly how much of a product they are likely to demand in future.

(b) When they do tell, possibly, what they tell us is their desire and not their plan of purchase.

(c) This method proves to be costly where the number of buyers is very large.

(2) Sales Force Polling : Those firms which have a sales staff can take advantage of their services. Experienced salesman who have technical background and have undergone some training in conducting interviews can perform this task satisfactorily. In the absence of a large number of salesmen and sales representatives, a firm can rely on dealers in different areas and forecasts made by the dealers, then, can be added together. Many times, the sales manager, production manager etc. sit together to finalise the forecasts from the estimates received from the dealers. That is why this method is also known as 'collective opinion method'.

Advantages :

(a) It is a very simple method and does not involve any statistical complexities.

(b) These forecasts are based upon information received from sellers or those who are closely connected with sales. As such these forecasts are likely to be very close to realities.

(c) This method is also used for forecasting demand for new products.

Limitations :

(a) This method is entirely subjective and therefore is likely to carry the biases of the sellers or salesmen into the estimates they report back.

(b) This method is useful in the short-run only.

(c) The job of the salesmen is to sell the product. As such they are not expected to have even a broad idea about the state of economy or likely changes in this state in future nor are they trained in the specialised function of forecasting.

(3) Consumer Field Surveys : When the number of customers is very large and the product is a standardised one, this method is used on the basis of sample surveys. Because it is not possible to contact millions of consumers, recourse is taken to sample surveying. Besides, a complete enumeration for knowing the intentions of all consumers involves a tremendous expenditure in terms of money as well as time. The method of statistical sample surveys removes these inconveniences and helps collect the necessary information in reasonable period of time and at reasonable costs. Due to the progress made by the statistical techniques and with the help of the theory of probability, it is possible now to use sample surveys profitably for getting a reasonably accurate demand forecast.

Limitations :

Whatever the progress made by the technique of sample surveys, such surveys are subject to the following limitations :

(a) Deficiency in the Collection of Information : The success of a sample survey depends upon the responses of the informants. If the informants furnish information freely and honestly, the results can be realistic. Much depends upon the skill of the investigator. If the investigator fails to elicit proper information, the survey becomes defective. One remedy to remove this deficiency is to prepare the questionnaire carefully. The questionnaire thus can contain checks and counter-checks. It can help us to corroborate the information given by the informants. One can also elicit information in a round-about way where informants find direct questions inconvenient. Improvements in the interview techniques may also enable the investigator to remove these deficiencies.

(b) Mistakes in Surveys : The surveys may contain the following mistakes :

(i) Faulty selection of samples : The sample selection has got to be on random basis. Only then can each member of the population to be surveyed stand a chance of being selected. Many times this is not strictly followed.

(ii) Shortcomings of sample surveys : The sample may be random but still it cannot be comparable to complete enumeration nor can it be called representative. A larger sample reduces -the error but raises the cost of the survey.

*(iii) **Creation of information that does not exist** :* Howsoever one may try to avoid mistakes, one basic difficulty remains : The informant's answers to questions should be in the right spirit. If the informant is not cooperative and tries to escape by giving some replies or the other, then misinformation might be collected. For example, in the field survey for a new product when a consumer says that he will not buy it; and the field investigator takes it seriously, field forecast will go wrong. This is because the consumer does buy new products either on the recommendations of his friends or after experiencing for himself.

(4) Panel of Experts : Demand forecasting can be assigned as a specialised job to a panel of experts. These experts might be the employees of the firm or may be outsiders i.e. experts from some other firm or employees of some consultancy agency.

The success of this method depends upon how the panel of experts prepares the forecasts. If the forecasts are based upon the hunches or the common sense of the panel of experts, possibilities are that the forecasts would be biased. It is therefore necessary to know the assumptions, the circumstances and the logic of reasoning adopted by the panel of experts before finally accepting the conclusions drawn by the panel. Otherwise this method would amount to buying at a high price, what any businessman would tell us just by common sense.

(i) The need for a careful examination of the forecasts by the firm, and (ii) a control over costs are the limitations of this method.

(5) Delphi Method : This method tries to arrive at a consensus by questioning a group of experts, repeatedly, until the responses appear to converge on one line. It is also possible to get disagreement but the causes of disagreement are supplied with responses of others to previous questionnaires coming from different respondents. The leader of the group, or co-ordinator, gives these responses of others alongwith reasons. The experts to whom these previous questionnaire-responses (with reasons) are given are requested to give their reactions. In exchanging opinions among experts, the names of earlier respondents are not exposed. This avoids 'bandwagon effect' or 'ego involvements' in publicly announced opinions. The co-ordinator then arrives at a consensus or common opinion of the group or panel of experts, to serve as a forecast.

Advantages :

(a) Since anonymity is throughout maintained, experts can express their views candidly.

(b) It enables to obtain the opinions of several experts simultaneously without actually inviting them together for a conference. This saves time as well as money.

(c) Another advantage is that a large number (at times, a few hundreds) of experts with diverse specialisations in areas like industrial policy, science and technology, administration, economics, accountancy, financial management, marketing management, etc. can be simultaneously approached. This brings in a balanced view.

Limitations :

(a) The method assumes that the experts identified are rich in their own expertise, experience and knowledge. This may not always be possible for all firms, big and small.

(b) The method also relies heavily on the group leader or co-ordinator who is expected to be objective in judgement, able to conceptualise issues for discussion and competent to analyse and draw inferences. Such co-ordinators may not be easily available or to get them may be huge expenses.

(6) Forecasts based on Composite Management Opinion : In some firms it is customary to use opinions of senior management executives as forecasts. The task of assessing the opinions of senior executives is usually assigned to a small committee or the general manager.

Limitations :

This method has the advantage of saving time, low cost and avoidance of complicated statistical methods. However, even after granting that the experience of management and the executives' opinions are important, they cannot be accepted as objective forecasts, because they do contain an element of subjectivity.

(B) Projecting Past Experience as a Method of Forecasting :

In the first approach, we considered various methods of forecasting demand on the basis of knowing buyers' intentions. In the second approach of projecting past experience into the future, the following methods may be noted :

(1) Correlation Analysis : Some variables are dependent on other variables and are called *dependent variables*; while others which are independent are known as *independent variables*. For example, demand is a dependent variable, and income, an independent variable. Correlation analysis establishes the relationship between such variables. If past correlation is assumed to remain constant in future also, we can take into account the future estimates of an independent variable and prepare demand forecasts on that basis. This is simple correlation. One can use multiple correlations where more than one independent variable is involved.

Limitations :

(a) The assumption here is that the correlation between two variables will continue in future also. This assumes that the forces responsible for the correlation will continue to operate in the future as well. This might not happen. For example, the number of students and the demand for benches are correlated. But the same correlation may not exist in future if students are prepared to pay higher fees and the colleges provide chairs and tables. Thus, if the forces behind the correlation change, the forecasts may go wrong.

   (b) Correlation between variables does not necessarily mean that there is a casual connection between the two variables. Thus, in a given year, the income of the consumers may increase and in the same year the sales of long-play records may also increase. Mathematically, the two variables will have a *positive correlation*. But will it be wise to conclude, without further analysis, that increase in income always leads to increase in the sales of long-play records ?

   (c) Even when a casual relation exists between the two variables, it is not safe to assume that the same relationship will exist in future as well.

In short, forecasts based on correlation need some modifications based on the analysis of the forces of demand, casual connections and such other factors, before using them for decision-making.

(2) Regression Analysis (Use of Multiple Regression for Estimating Demands) : For the estimation of demand, the statistical method most frequently used is the one known as regression analysis. A detailed discussion of the technique is beyond the scope of this book. Let us consider only the outline of the method.

The first step is to specify the variables which are likely to influence demand. The second step is to obtain accurate estimates of these variables. The third and final step is to specify the form of the equation. The most common form is a linear relationship like the one given below; (A linear functional relationship is one which can be represented on a graph by a straight line) :

$$D = a + bP + cY + dA$$

where D stands for quantity demanded, P represents the price, Y stands for the disposable income and A for advertising expenditure.

The linear demand function is commonly used because many demand functions are approximately linear. The least squares method can be used for estimating the parameters a, b, c, and d and regression coefficients, for linear equations.

Limitations :

   (a) Besides the three variables considered above, there are many others which influence demand.

   (b) These variables themselves are highly interrelated, with the result that they interact on each other and are determined simultaneously.

   (c) Dynamism in real life raises a doubt whether the same relationship will hold good in future also.

If handled by professionals, this method improves reliability of forecasts.

(3) Projection of Trends into Future : On the assumption that a dependent variable which was influenced by an independent variable in the past will continue to do so in the future, forecasts can be made on the basis of statistics of past performance.

Trends which can be recognised easily can also be projected easily in the future. Such trends are rare in practice, but for understanding the method, let us assume that, the trends are easy to recognise. For example, if demand has been 90,100, 110,120 in the past four years, it will be 130, 140 and so on in the years to come.

In practice, trends cannot be established so easily. Various techniques may therefore be used for establishing trends. The term 'trend' refers to the long-run growth or decline in a series. Trends are found out and projected into the future without looking into the causes of past movements and relationships. The basic assumption is that tomorrow would more or less be like today.

When the sequence of numbers is not so simple as noted in the above example, 'time series' technique can be used. A firm, which has been in existence for some time, normally, has enough data regarding sales pertaining to different time periods. For example, if you take quarterly periods on X-axis and average sales on Y-axis, you can get a graph showing time-series. This can be projected in future.

Table 2.4 : Moving Average

Year	Sales (thousand of units)	3 – Yearly moving area
1	36	–
2	64	60
3	80	84
4	108	90
5	82	100
6	110	107
7	129	–

Another technique for establishing trends is the use of moving averages. The accompanying table (Table 2.4) shows how moving average can be calculated. Once an average demand curve is drawn, its slope helps us draw a trend curve for using in demand forecasting.

Limitations :

(a) Cyclical variations can be used for correcting trends. But when would a trade cycle will turn remains unknown.

(b) Another limitation is the occurrence of unpredictable events like wars, earthquakes etc.

Yet another technique is known as *exponential smoothing*. It is a popular technique for short-run forecasts. It is based on giving different weightages to past forecasts, in a way that emphasizes recent forecasts. This is because recent past is more relevant for future then is the distant past.

For example, consider this formula :

New Forecast = Last Period's Forecast + a (Last Period's Actual Demand – Last Period's Forecast)

In this formula, a is weight or smoothing constant, which is taken in the scale $0 - 1$ (i.e. $0 < a < 1$). Last period's forecast may be an average of earlier four, five or six periods. That could also be calculated by the moving average method. To smooth out the forecast, 'a' is used as a constant and this formula gives the desired forecast.

The advantages of this technique are :

(i)   It is easy to use and efficiently handled by computers;

(ii) This too is a moving average type; but it does not require much of the past data;

(iii) Actually tried by banks, manufacturing companies etc., it is found to be useful and practical.

2.4 Market Equilibrium – Pricing under Perfect Competition

2.4.1 Features of Perfect Competition

(1) Perfect Knowledge of the Market : The buyers and sellers should have a perfect knowledge of the market. This is the first necessary condition of perfect competition. Every buyer knows what price every seller is ready to accept and every seller knows what price every buyer is willing to offer. This knowledge guarantees uniform price throughout the market. Because there is perfect knowledge of the market, no seller will accept a price lower than that ruling in the market; nor will any buyer offer a price higher than the market price.

(2) Absence of Transport Costs : Another assumption of perfect competition is the absence of transport costs - or else, free transport facilities have to be assumed. In the absence of this assumption, the production costs of firms producing at two different centres will differ and, therefore, prices will be different. Different prices are an indication of market imperfection. That is why this assumption is important.

(3) Free Entry and Free Exit for Firms : In perfect competition there should be a complete   freedom for firms to enter or exit the industry at their choice. It implies that, free entry would allow pumping of new blood in the industry. As such, there shall be many firms in the industry. Each firm shall be small in size and producing a small fraction of the total output. Likewise, if some firms are incurring losses, they can exit from the industry. In perfect competition there can be no monopolistic control on the market, there is a fair competition. The firms that can supply at the ruling price enter the industry, while others which are inefficient and who cannot supply at the prevailing price are incurring losses. They exit the market.

(4) Perfect Knowledge of the Market : In perfect competition, there is an existence of perfect knowledge on part of the buyers and sellers about market conditions. In perfect competition there is no necessity of incurring any expenditure and advertisement due to perfect knowledge. The sellers too have perfect information about potential sales at various price-levels. In short, both the buyers and sellers have perfect knowledge of the price. At this 'price', total demand is equal to total supply and this price is known as 'market-clearing price'.

(5) No Transport Cost : A perfectly competitive market assumes the non-existence of transport   costs. The assumption is on the basis of reasoning that the various firms are so close to each other that there are no transport costs. The assumption of no transport costs is because the goods are considered homogeneous, only when they happen to be in the same place. If the goods are at a different place, the two goods are not homogeneous because their prices differ due to transport costs. Since in perfect competition existence of uniform price is essential, there cannot exist transport costs.

(6) Perfect Mobility of Factors of Production : The smooth functioning of perfect competition necessitates perfect mobility of factors of production. The factors of production should be free to move into any industry which they consider profitable for themselves. The existence of perfect mobility of factors is essential for fulfilling the first condition of perfect competition i.e. large number of sellers in the market.

(7) No Government Interference : In perfect competition, it is necessary to have non-existence of any artificial restrictions on the demand, supply, prices of commodities and factors of production in the market. There must be no governmental fixation of the prices of goods and factors of production. There must be no artificial controls on demand of goods through governmental rationing.

2.4.2 Price and Output Determination under Perfect Competition
(A) Short-run Equilibrium of a Firm :

When market is perfectly competitive, an individual firm cannot influence the market price because of the existence of a large number of firms, homogeneous products and free entry and exit of firms. What an individual firm can, however, do is to take the price determined at the market as *'given'* and adjust its own supply according to that price. At the ruling price, the firm can sell any amount of its product. In other words, the demand faced by a firm in the competitive market is perfectly elastic. A firm can sell infinite number of units at the ruling price; but its sales will fall to zero with a slight increase in price. The average revenue curve of a firm, therefore, is parallel to the X-axis. Fig. 2.5 illustrates the short-run equilibrium of a firm, by assuming the market price as given.

The left half of figure 2.5 illustrates the demand and supply curves of the industry, while the right half of figure shows the cost and revenue curves of an imaginary firm. It is important to note that the Y-axis in both figures are drawn to the same scale, but X-axis are drawn to different scales since the industry's demand and supply are larger quantities than a firm's demand and supply. Let us begin with D D_1 as the industry Demand Curve and S S_1 as the industry Supply Curve. Demand and supply are in equilibrium at the point E. Therefore, QE will be the market price. A straight line, drawn parallel to the X-axis from point E, cuts the Y-axis of the right portion of the diagram at point P and proceeds further to the right. From the point of view of the firm, as the price OP is going to be constant, this very line becomes the AR curve for the firm. This AR curve is parallel to the X-axis and hence, AR and MR are the same. AC and MC are the average and marginal cost curves of the firm. The MC curve cuts the AR = MR curve from below at point M. Therefore, at OK level of output, the firm is in equilibrium. At this price, AR curve is below the AC curve. The line KM extended upwards cuts the AC curve at point N. Therefore, KN or OS is the average cost. OP is the price and OS is the average cost, so PS is the loss per unit of output. The total loss is shown by the dotted area PSNM. But since MR = MC and the MC curve cuts the MR curve at point M from below, this is the minimum loss under the given cost and revenue conditions. It should be remembered here that when it is not possible for a firm to earn profits, the firm will incur losses and will try to minimise its losses. The conditions that ensure maximum profits also ensure minimum losses. Therefore, in this example, the firm attains equilibrium at the OK level of output, in spite of the fact that it is making a loss.

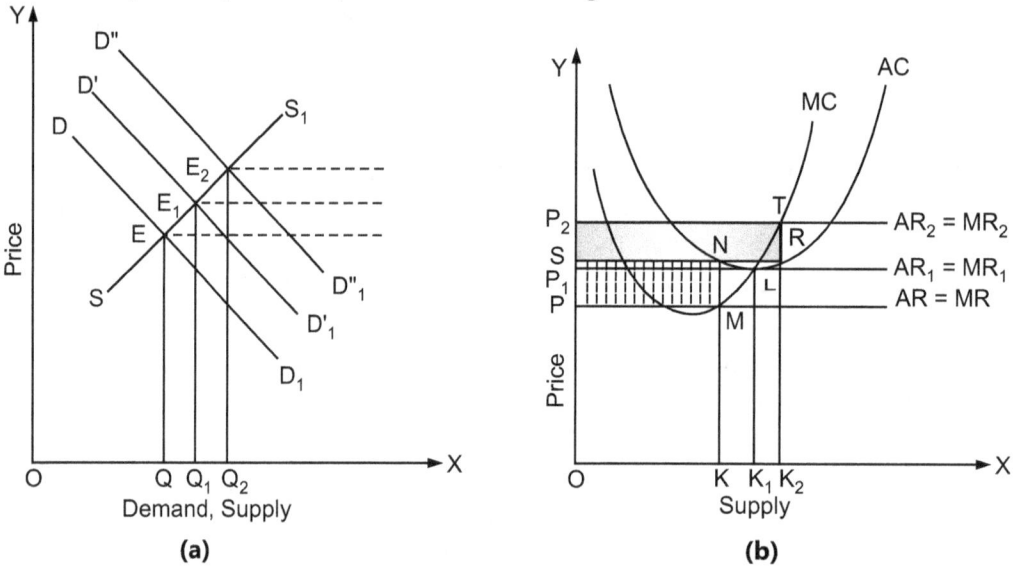

Fig. 2.5 : Market Price and Short-run Equilibrium of a Firm

The second possibility is that the industry demand curve may be at a position shown by $D' D'_1$. The market price would then be $Q_1 E_1$. For the firm (the right half of the figure) the price would be OP_1, giving $AR_1 = MR_1$ as the firm's average and marginal revenue curves. AR = MR curve touches the AC curve at point L. Since L on the AC curve, is closest to the X-axis, MC cuts AC through this point only. Therefore, point L marks the equality of MR and MC, and OK_1 is the equilibrium output of the firm. At this output, OP_1 is the price and OP_1 is also the average cost. The rectangle $OP_1 LK_1$ is the total revenue and also the total cost of the firm. The firm will, therefore, earn only a normal profit which is included in the average cost. Thus, in this case, there will neither be supernormal profits nor losses to the firm.

The third possibility of a short-run equilibrium is that the industry demand curve may be shown by $D'' D''_1$. The market price will then be $Q_2 E_2$. The straight line drawn from E_2 and parallel to X-axis gives $AR_2 = MR_2$ as the firm's revenue curve. The MC curve cuts the MR_2 curve from below at point T. Therefore, point T ensures the condition of equality between MR and MC and gives OK_2 as the equilibrium level of output. At this level of output, OS or $K_2 R$ is the average cost and OP_2 is the price. The shaded area $SP_2 TR$ represents the supernormal profit earned by the firm.

Under competitive conditions, the equality of MR and MC and the fact that the MC curve cuts the MR curve from below are the two usual conditions of equilibrium of a firm which explain the short-run equilibrium of a firm. In the short-run, when a firm attains equilibrium, under perfect competition, there are three possibilities regarding profits : the firm may run into a loss, it may make only normal profit, or it may earn a supernormal profit.

(B) Short-run Equilibrium and Cost Differences

The fixed factors cannot be changed in the short-run though variable factors can be changed. In considering a short period, therefore, can we assume identical cost conditions for all the firms in an industry ? A little thought will show that three possibilities have to be considered : (a) all the factors of production employed by all the firms may be homogeneous; (b) the entrepreneurs may be heterogeneous but all other factors may be homogeneous; and (c) all factors may be heterogeneous. These different possibilities entail differences in cost conditions of different firms. An analysis of these three situations is, therefore, necessary to understand the equilibrium of a firm.

(1) **Equilibrium when all factors are homogeneous :** When all the factors of production employed by a firm, are homogeneous, all the firms in industry will have identical cost curves. If we consider the firm in Fig. 2.5 as one such firm, the cost curves of all other firms in the industry will also be the same as depicted in the right portion of Fig. 2.5.

Let us consider the possibilities of equilibrium on the basis of the right portion of Fig. 2.5. If the market price is OP_2, all firms in the industry will earn supernormal profits and the profit of each firm will be as shown in the area SP_2 TR. These supernormal profits will attract new firms towards the industry. Therefore, every firm will attain its equilibrium, in the short-run. But since the number of firms in the industry is not stable, the industry, in this case, will not be in equilibrium. In other words, 'full equilibrium' will not be established.

When the market price is OP_1, the average revenue curve of every firm in the industry will be AR_1 = MR_1. As already shown, point L will indicate the equilibrium of a firm and OK_1 will be the equilibrium output of every firm. At this level of output, every firm earns normal profits. The existing firms will, therefore, leave that industry, nor will new firms be attracted towards this have no desire to leave the industry. As such, 'full equilibrium' will be established, where all the firms as well as the industry as a whole, will have attained equilibrium.

The third possibility can be that the market price is OP and every firm is making a loss equal to the dotted area PSNM. Since that is the minimum loss under the circumstances, all the firms are in short-run equilibrium. But because they are making losses, it is possible that some firms leave the industry. Therefore, the number of firms in the industry will be unstable and consequently the industry will not be in equilibrium. Full equilibrium, therefore, is not possible.

In the long-run, no firm will remain in the industry if it incurs losses. But in the short-run, a firm may continue to produce so long as its variable costs are at least covered, because, in any case, it will have to bear the fixed costs even when the level of output is zero. It will, thus, pay the firm to produce if at least the variable costs are met. If, however, the loss exceeds the fixed costs (i.e., the variable costs are not met), it will be prudent for the firm to stop production. This is because, if the firm stops production it will have to bear only the fixed costs; which will be less than the loss involved in continuing production.

Summary : Under conditions of perfect competition, in the short-run, both the firm and the industry will be in equilibrium only if the price is equal to the average cost of every firm and every firm in the industry earns only normal profits. But that the industry has just adequate number of firms which brings about a price that is equal to the average cost of every firm, is an accident. This possibility will, therefore, be rare. If a price settles at a higher level, all the firms will earn abnormal profits. A price lower than this will entail losses for all the firms. In either case, the firms will be in equilibrium; but not the *industry*. In these two cases, *full equilibrium i.e. equilibrium of both the firm and industry is not possible.*

(2) Equilibrium when entrepreneurs are heterogeneous but all other factors are homogeneous : When all factors except the entrepreneurs are homogeneous, all the entrepreneurs will have to pay the same remunerations to the factors of production they employ. But since the entrepreneurs are heterogeneous, their efficiency will be different. Therefore, efficient entrepreneurs will be able to produce at a lower cost as compared to the inefficient ones. Thus, though all the firms are producing the same product and are selling it at the same price, their costs of production, and hence, their cost curves, will be different.

Under these circumstances the firm having the most efficient entrepreneur will find himself in a condition similar to the one at the price OP_2 in figure 2.5. It will be able to earn a profit as shown by the shaded area. Other firms, headed by less efficient entrepreneurs, may earn just normal profit like in Fig. 2.5 when price is OP_1. There might be yet other firms working under even less efficient entrepreneurs. These firms will be in positions shown in Fig. 2.6.

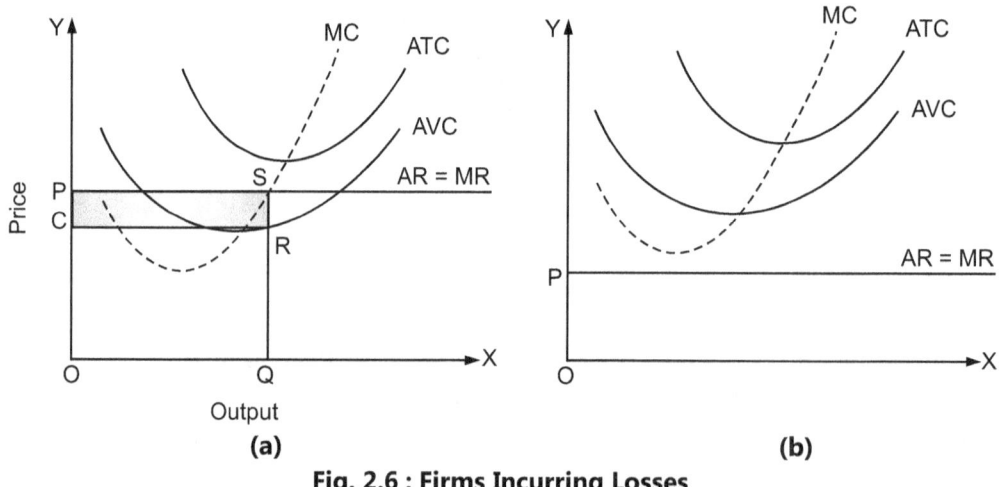

Fig. 2.6 : Firms Incurring Losses

The firm whose cost curves are represented in Fig. 2.6 (a) is incurring a loss as the whole of its ATC (average total unit cost) curve lies above the AR = MR curve. But its AVC (average variable cost) curve is, in part, below the AR = MR curve. Therefore, its equilibrium will be given by the usual condition that MC equals MR and the MC curve cuts the MR curve from below. The firm will be in equilibrium at OQ level of output where it will earn a sum of rectangle PCRS over and above the total variable cost. The firm can thus cover all variable costs plus a part of the fixed costs. Since the loss involved is less than fixed costs, the firm will be in short-run equilibrium.

The least fortunate firms which have the most inefficient entrepreneurs will be in a position as depicted in Fig. 2.6 (b). These firms have their variable cost curves lying entirely above the AR = MR curve. The firms are not able to cover even their variable costs or their losses will be greater than their fixed costs. It would then be better for them to close down.

Summary : Under conditions of perfect competition, in the short-run, when entrepreneurs are heterogeneous and all other factors are homogeneous, differences in the capabilities of the entrepreneurs will cause cost differences between firms. These cost differences with a uniform price would create a situation where : (i) some firms will earn supernormal profits; (ii) some firms will earn normal profits; (iii) some firm will incur losses but will be able to cover their variable costs; while (iv) some firms may not even be able to cover their variable costs - such firms will close down. The firms falling in the first three categories will attain their short-run equilibrium by equating their marginal revenues with their marginal costs. The industry, however, will not be in equilibrium as some of the firms are closing down. Thus, 'full equilibrium' will not be possible.

(3) Equilibrium when all factors are heterogeneous : If all the factors of production are heterogeneous, the differences in costs between firms will be even larger than where only entrepreneurs differ in efficiency. The same kind of situation as described in (2) above will be obtained. The cost differences will however be larger than in situation (2). The firms which have all efficient factors can produce at the lowest per unit cost and earn the largest amount of profit. At the other extreme may be the firms having all inefficient factors and incurring losses. It is not necessary, that the inefficient firms may not earn a profit. What is certain is the difference in profits arising out of the difference in costs. Between these two extremes will lie firms having more or less efficient factors and making more or less profits or losses.

Summary : Under perfect competition, in the short-run, when the firms have heterogeneous factors, those firms which cannot cover even the variable costs will close down. All other firms will attain an equilibrium position by equating their marginal costs with their marginal revenue. By doing so, they will either be maximising their profits or be minimising their looses. But since the number of firms in the industry is not stable, the industry will not be in equilibrium, or a 'full equilibrium' will not be possible.

(C) Long-run Equilibrium of the Firm and Industry :

In the long-run, all factors are variable. Therefore, all the costs of a firm are variable. It is possible to change the plant and adjust the capacity according to the requirements of production. Similarly, the exit and the entry of firms is possible.

For long-run equilibrium as well, the equality of MR and MC is necessary. Under perfect competition, since MR = AR, in equilibrium also, MC is equal to AR. This means that under conditions of perfect competition, in equilibrium, marginal cost and price are equal. But in the long-run, the price must be equal to average cost as well. This is because a price higher than average cost would mean supernormal profits (as normal profits are included in the average cost). If competing firms are earning supernormal profits, new firms will enter the industry in the long-run. Similarly, if the firms are incurring losses, an exodus of firms will set in, and in the long-run, the number of firms which remains in the industry will be just enough to produce that output which can be sold at the market only at a normal profit. The exit of firms causes a reduction in market supply and a rise in market price. When this happens, the losses of firms which remain in the industry disappear. On the other hand, the entry of new firms causes an increase in the market supply and a lowering of the price. New firms continue entering until the supernormal profits are totally competed away and all the firms earn only normal profits. Thus, in the long-run, the equality of price and average cost becomes a necessary condition for equilibrium. In other words, the condition for long-run equilibrium of a firm under perfect competition is price AR = MR = AC = MC.

(1) **Equilibrium when all factors of production are homogeneous :** It is necessary to consider long-run cost curves while analysing the long-run equilibrium of a firm. We shall have to consider the three possibilities of availability of factors of production, in the long-run, as we had done in the context of short-run equilibrium.

When all the factors of production are homogeneous, they earn the same remuneration; cost curves of all firms in the industry are identical; the entry and exit of firms is free; all firms earn only normal profits. The state of equilibrium of all firms will be as shown in Fig. 2.7 (b). The long-run average cost curve (LAC) of a firm touches the AR = MR curve, at point S. Since point S is nearest to the X-axis from the LAC curve, the long-run, marginal cost curve (LMC) cuts the LAC curve at point S only. Point S therefore, marks the equality of AR, MR, AC and MC. The firm attains long-run equilibrium at OQ level of output, and at OP price. Since the average cost is also OP, the firm earns only normal profits. Any profit higher than this, would attract new firms and any profit lower than this, would cause an exit of existing firms. Since the cost curves of all firms are identical, all firms will earn only normal profits.

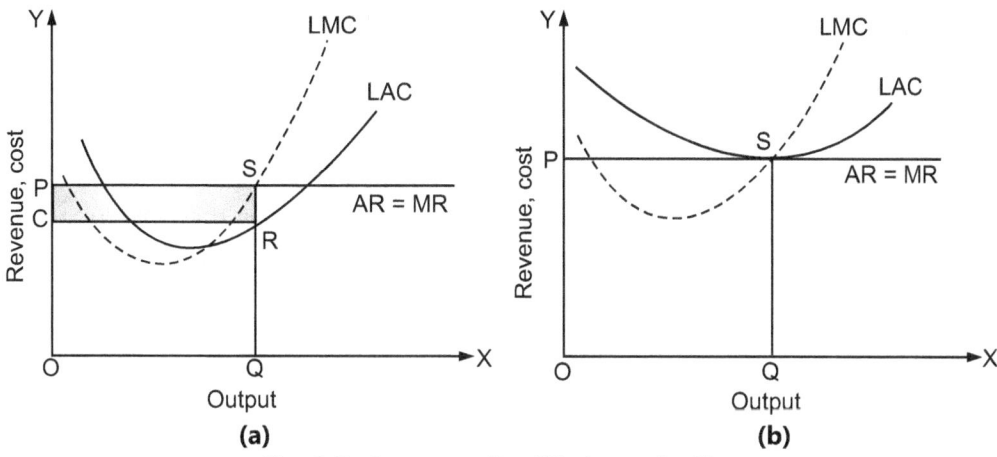

Fig. 2.7 : Long-run Equilibrium of a Firm

Summary : Under conditions of perfect competition, in the long-run, when factors of production employed by all the firms are homogeneous, all the firms as well as the industry will be in equilibrium. For every firm, the condition of MR = MC = AR (price) = AC will be satisfied. It is obvious that full equilibrium will be established.

It will be clear that only in the situation described above, every firm will be producing at the lowest average cost. In other words, when : (i) all factors of production are homogeneous; (ii) all factors of production are perfectly mobile; (iii) there is perfect competition in the factor market; and consequently, (iv) the cost curves of all firms in an industry are identical, every firm will attain its optimum size.

(2) Equilibrium when entrepreneurs are heterogeneous while all other factors are homogeneous : When entrepreneurs are heterogeneous, in spite of the homogeneity of all other factors, some firms will be able to produce at lower costs than the others. This would result in cost differences between the firms and even in the long-run, some firms may earn supernormal profits.

Let us consider, for instance, Fig. 2.7 (a). This represents the equilibrium of a firm headed by an efficient entrepreneur. This firm reaps a supernormal profit, equal to rectangle PCRS, even in the long-run. On the other hand, the firm in Fig. 2.7 (b), only earns normal profit, though, the average revenue of both the firms is the same, because the cost of production of this [Fig. 2.7 (b)] firm is higher. This latter firm, can be called a *marginal firm* because a slight reduction in its (normal) profit will make it leave the industry. The firm represented by cost curves in Fig. 2.7 (a), is *an intra-marginal firm*. It can earn supernormal profit. It is, of course, possible that an equally efficient firm may enter the industry, drive away the inefficient firm [Fig. 2.7 (b)] and compete away the profit of the efficient intra-marginal firm [Fig. 2.7 (a)]. In this case, all firms will earn only normal profits. But then, the heterogeneity of entrepreneurs as we assumed, no longer remains and all factors become homogeneous. Therefore, if entrepreneurs are heterogeneous and they remain heterogeneous even in the long-run, then even in the long-run, firms headed by relatively more efficient entrepreneurs can earn supernormal profits.

Summary : Under conditions of perfect competition when entrepreneurs are hetero-geneous and all other factors are homogeneous, full equilibrium is unlikely even in the long-run. Though all the individual firms will be in equilibrium and no firms will be running into losses, some firms will be earning abnormal profits. Therefore, new firms will be attracted towards the industry and as such, the number of firms in the industry will not be stable. Thus the industry under these conditions will not be in equilibrium even in the long-run.

(3) Equilibrium when all factors are heterogeneous : When all factors are heterogeneous, the least efficient firm will be the marginal firm and it will earn a normal profit. On the other hand, the most efficient of the intra-marginal firms, one will earn supernormal profits. Other firms will earn profits to a greater or less extent depending upon their efficiency.

2.4.3 Equilibrium under Perfect Competition / Equilibrium Output of a Perfectly Competitive Industry

The demand curve of a competitive industry can be explained in a simple way. Each firm in the industry faces a particular demand at a given price. Quantities demanded at a price by buyers from all the firms in the industry, added together will be *industry demand* for the product at that price. If we take different prices and add up the corresponding quantities demanded by buyers from all the firms, we can find out the industry demand schedule and the industry demand curve. The industry demand curve, you will find, slopes downwards from left to right.

For getting the industry supply curve, let us assume that in the short-run, both the industry and the firm are in equilibrium. When all factors are homogeneous, this would mean that all the firms are producing at the minimum average cost [see equilibrium as shown by point L when price is OP_1 in Fig. 2.5 (b)]. Under such condition, when a firm tries to increase its supply, it can do so along the Short-run Marginal Cost curve. This curve, slopes upwards to the right. Since all firms have identical cost conditions, the SMC curves of all firms will be upward-sloping. As the industry supply curve is the horizontal sum of SMC curves of all firms, the industry supply curve also will slope upwards to the right.

However, in the long-run, when the price changes, there will be possibilities of losses or abnormal profits. The number of firms in the industry will change. Under identical cost conditions, all firms will be of optimum size. By adding together the optimum output of all firms at a given price, we can get the industry supply. If we obtain the industry supply in this way at various prices, we can get the supply curve of the industry. If the industry is subject to increasing costs, the industry supply curve will be upward-sloping. If the industry is subject to constant costs, the supply curve will be horizontal and parallel to X-axis. Finally, if the production of the industry is under decreasing costs, the long-run supply curve of the industry will slope downwards from left to right. Thus, to sum up, the short-run supply curve of the competitive industry will always be upward-sloping, but the long-run supply curve may be upward-sloping, downward-sloping or parallel to the X-axis depending upon the cost conditions of the industry.

(A) Equilibrium of Demand and Supply :

By considering the nature of the demand and supply curves of a competitive industry, we can describe the equilibrium between demand and supply under conditions of perfect competition. In discussing equilibrium, we stated that the market price will be determined by the intersection of demand and supply curves, when these curves are given. Let us discuss the equilibrium between demand and supply with the help of Fig. 2.8. DD_1 is the demand curve and SS_1 is the supply curve; both intersecting at point E. Perpendiculars from point E to X and Y-axis meet the axis in points Q and P respectively. At price OP, demand and supply are brought into equilibrium. At this price the industry demand, and also the supply, is OQ. Thus, the price OP brings the demand and supply into equilibrium. Equilibrium in the market implies a situation depending on and satisfying the existing conditions of demand and supply. In addition, it also implies a situation of rest, or absence of change, over a period of time. This means that the state of equilibrium will last as long as demand and supply conditions remain unchanged. If the demand and supply conditions remain unchanged and yet, the equilibrium is disturbed, it will be restored. As shown in the figure, if the price rises to OP_1, demand will be OQ_1 and supply will be OQ_2. As supply exceeds demand, every firm will try to sell off its output by reducing its price. Thus, competition among the firms will bring down the market price to OP. If the price falls further to say, OP_2 (Fig. 2.8) supply will be OQ_1, and demand OQ_2 at this price. Because demand exceeds supply buyers will bid a higher price to ensure their possession of the product. Thus, competition among buyers will take the price upto OP. At OP, a higher price, supply would expand, demand would contract and the two would again be in equilibrium. The equilibrium supply would again be OQ and the demand would also be OQ. Thus the equilibrium when disturbed is restored.

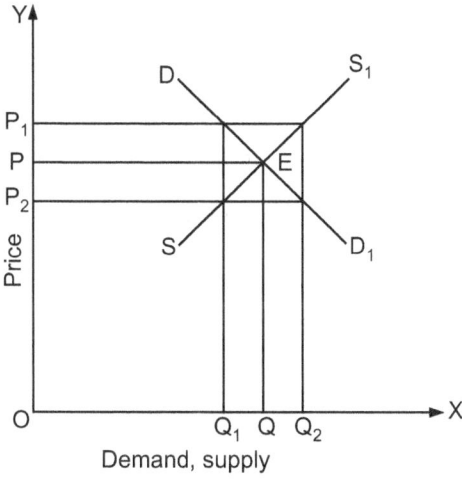

Fig. 2.8 : Equilibrium of Demand and Supply

2.5 Monopolistic Competition – Pricing under Monopolistic Competition

(A) Imperfect Competition and Monopolistic Competition :

We have so far discussed perfect competition and monopoly as two extremes. Though these two extremes are theoretically important, in practice, they do not actually exist. What one may accost in practice may, at best be approximations to perfect competition and monopoly in the form we discussed above. But when competition is not perfect, the situation can be called as one of imperfect competition. A very large number of sellers, homogeneity of product and perfect knowledge of the market are basic conditions of perfect competition. These conditions together ensure that no firm will have control over price, buyers will have no preferences regarding sellers and a single uniform price is established in the market. In the absence of these conditions, the market becomes imperfect. Imperfect competition can further be classified into monopolistic competition, oligopoly and duopoly.

Monopolistic competition refers to a market situation where there are many firms selling differentiated products. The following features will fully explain the nature of monopolistic competition and how it differs from both perfect competition as well as monopoly.

2.5.1 Characteristic Features of Monopolistic Competition

Monopolistic Competition is characterised by the following features :

(1) Existence of a Number of Firms : An important condition of monopolistic competition is the existence of many firms. Though the number of firms in the industry is less than that under perfect competition, the number has to be large enough to allow a healthy competition among the firms. Under monopolistic competition, the supply of even the largest firm is small in relation to the market supply. Usually, there are many small firms under monopolistic competition. Monopolistic competition is usually found in those fields of production where there are no special advantages of large scale production and where capital requirement is not very large and the decisions of one firm have no effect on other firms.

(2) Product Differentiation : Product differentiation is another significant feature of monopolistic competition. Products of different firms are not homogeneous as under perfect competition. On the contrary, every firm tries to impress upon the consumers the *'differentness'*, and thereby, the superiority of its own product. Basically, the product may be the same, but even so, every firm attempts to differentiate its own product from the product of its rival firms. Thus, the situation is one in which there are many products in the market which are close substitutes of one another; but the product of every firm is different from that of every other firm. Therefore, there is competition among the various products (which are similar but not the same) and simultaneously every firm enjoys 'monopoly' in the field of its own product. The markets of toothpastes, tooth-brushes, toilet and washing soaps, face powders, other cosmetics, and many more products which we use every day are of this type. There is competition among the producers; but at the same time there is monopoly with regard to each *'brand'*. That is why, the situation is termed as *monopolistic competition.*

A product can be differentiated in many ways : (a) Differentiation may be based upon some characteristics of the product itself. Such differences may arise due to patented features, trade marks, trade names, peculiarities of packing, etc. Differences may also be qualitative, arising out of differences in workmanship, design, colour, style, etc. (b) Differentiation may arise due to conditions surrounding the sale of the product. For example, differentiation can be introduced by providing hire-purchase facilities, or by giving a guarantee for a particular period or by guaranteeing free after-sale services for a given period, or by agreeing to accept the return of the product or by providing home-delivery, etc.

(3) Easy Entry and Exist : The third characteristic feature of monopolistic competition is free entry and free exit of firms. As stated above, when the requirements of capital are not very large, new firms can easily enter the field of production. Similarly, the exit of firms is also unrestricted. The number of firms in the market being very large, entry and exit of firms does not have any significant effect on the market supply.

(4) Multiplicity of Prices : Due to factor-immobilities, or transport costs or ignorance of market, a single uniform price cannot be established in the market characterised by monopolistic competition. On the contrary, similar products which are differentiated by brand names and advertisements are sold at different prices. Every producer enjoys the freedom to price his own product; this freedom is within certain limits. Every producer has his own price-policy. Under perfect competition, this freedom is not available to an individual firm.

(5) Elastic Demand : The Average Revenue Curve of a firm under monopolistic competition is not parallel to the X-axis as it is under conditions of perfect competition. Because, the products of all firms are not identical, buyers can have preferences. So it is not possible for a firm to sell an infinite amount of the product at the ruling price as it is assumed to happen under perfect competition. Therefore, under monopolistic competition, the Average Revenue Curve of a firm is not parallel to the X-axis as it is under perfect competition. Under monopoly, the Average Revenue Curve of the firm is steep because there are no close substitutes for the product. Under monopolistic competition, on the other hand, a firm's product does have close substitutes, and therefore, the Average Revenue Curve cannot be steep. Thus, the AR curve faced by a firm under monopolistic competition is shallow indicating a highly elastic demand. Therefore, if a firm reduces the price of its product while prices of rival products are unchanged, there would a sizeable increase in the sales of the firm.

Thus, the market form with characteristics noted above, contains elements of both monopoly as well as competition; and so it is called *monopolistic competition*. As already noted, commodities like toothpastes, soaps, cigarettes etc., are produced under conditions of monopolistic competition.

2.5.2 Price and Output Determination under Monopolistic Competition (Equilibrium under Monopolistic Competition)

The equilibrium of a firm under monopolistic competition has significance from the practical point of view. As we have noted earlier, there is an overwhelming majority of cases in reality, who are producing under conditions of monopolistic competition. We have already noted the assumptions of monopolistic competition. Monopolistic competition has elements of both monopoly and competition. Therefore the average revenue curve or the demand curve faced by a firm in monopolistic competition is neither as steep as it is under monopoly nor is it parallel to the X-axis as it is under perfect competition. The product under monopolistic competition is not homogeneous. Product differentiation is a distinctive feature, of monopolistic competition. Therefore, a firm cannot sell an infinite amount of its product at the ruling price. This is possible for a firm only under perfect competition. This is why the average revenue curve of a firm under monopolistic competition cannot be parallel to the X axis like that of a firm producing under perfect competition. On the other hand, the average revenue curve of monopoly firm is steep because the demand is inelastic as the product has no close substitute. This too is not possible under conditions of monopolistic competition. We know that in monopolistic competition, there are close substitutes to the product of any individual firm. The demand faced by a firm i.e. the AR curve of a firm under monopolistic competition will be flatter than that of a monopoly firm. Thus, under conditions of monopolistic competition the AR of a firm will slope downwards from left to right but will be flatter compared to the AR curve of a monopolist. Thus, because the demand is highly elastic, a little reduction in price by a firm causes a great increase in its sales, prices of other firms being unchanged.

The elasticity of demand for the product of firm under monopolistic competition depends upon the following considerations :

(1) How far is the product of a firm differentiated from the products of other firms and how deep-rooted is the preference of the buyers for the product concerned. The greater the degree of the product differentiation, the less elastic will be the demand for the product. Similarly, the more deep-rooted are preferences of buyers for a product, the less elastic will be the demand. Thus, if products are similar, the buyer can switch over to other products easily and the demand will be elastic. Similarly if the preference for a particular brand (say for toothpaste) is not firmly rooted, the buyer may switch over easily to another brand and the demand for it will then be more elastic.

(2) The elasticity of demand also depends upon the total number of firms in the market. The larger the number of firms, the more elastic will be the demand for the product of any single firm. This is because the larger the number of firms, the larger is the number of close substitutes to a firm's product.

Many a time, the demand curve is flat, indicating elastic demand over a certain range and becomes steep as the price falls further. In such a case, the demand curve gets a kink. But normally, the demand curve is a continuous one. In order to make our analysis simple it is desirable to draw a continuous demand curve.

The AR and the MR curves of a firm under monopolistic competition are downward-sloping.

(A) Cost Curves of a Firm under Monopolistic Competition :

As monopoly firm is the only firm in the market, its cost curves can be assumed to be given. But under monopolistic competition, there is a large number of firms. It may happen that all firms are employing more or less similar factors and paying them at almost the same rate. But even then, due to product differentiation and the internal economies available to the firms, their cost curves are inevitably different. The relationship between AC and MC is however the same or the usual one.

(B) Short-run Equilibrium of the Firm :

It is essential to note the difference between the short period and the long period, from the point of view of profit. A firm can earn abnormal profits in the short-run with the help of product differentiation and variation. But this profit is difficult to retain in the long-run. There is a great deal of competition from other firms and every firm is trying to attract buyers by impressing upon them the superiority of its own product. Therefore, supernormal profits are impossible in the long-run under monopolistic competition. In the short-run, however, supernormal profits can be earned by a firm as rival firms do not get enough time to produce a close substitute. Similarly, the entry of new firms into the market is not possible in the short-run.

We know that maximisation of money profits is the objective of any firm. The equality of MR and MC therefore, becomes the condition of equilibrium. The price corresponding to the equilibrium level of output becomes the price charged by the firm concerned.

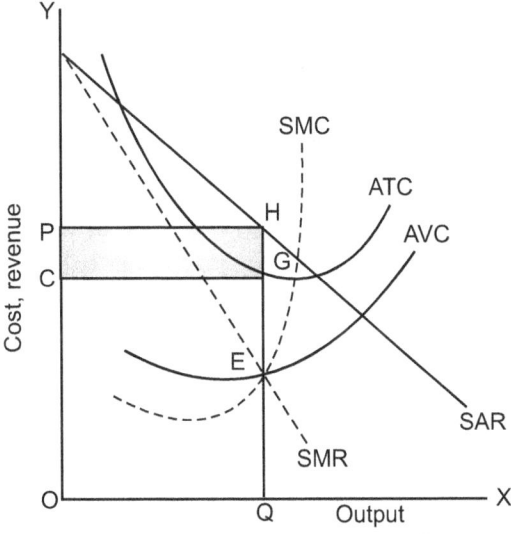

Fig. 2.9 : Short Period Equilibrium – Monopolistic Competition

Fig. 2.9 shows the short period equilibrium of a firm under monopolistic competition. SAR and SMR are the short period average and marginal revenue curves respectively. SMC is the short period marginal cost curve. ATC is the average total cost curve and AVC is the average variable cost curve. The equilibrium output OQ is given by the point E which is the point of intersection of SMR and SMC. OP is short period price. PCGH is total supernormal profit earned by the firm. This is the maximum profit under the conditions of cost and revenue given here.

Fig. 2.9 represents the cost and revenue conditions of one firm. The figure is just one example of equilibrium. We can conclude that under similar conditions, a firm can earn abnormal profits. There are many firms in the market and every firm faces a different set of revenue and cost curves. We cannot, however conclude that all firms, earn supernormal profits in the short period because one firm is earning them. It is possible that old and established firms are in a position to charge a higher price and internal economies are also available to them and so they are earning supernormal profits. It may be noted that new firms can earn only normal profits or may run into losses in the short-run. Fig. 2.9 represents the equilibrium of some firms; the equilibrium positions of some other firms will be as shown in Fig. 2.10 they may be earning just normal profits.

(C) Long-run Equilibrium of the Firm :

Under monopolistic competition, as under perfect competition, the entry of new firms and the exit of old firms are free. Therefore, a full equilibrium is not possible in the short period. Though individual firms may attain equilibrium in the short period, the *group* of firms will not be in equilibrium. For 'full equilibrium' it is necessary that the total supply of all the firms should be sold at the ruling price and the number of firms should be stable.

The first condition referred to above i.e., the sale at the market of the total supply of all the firms at the ruling price, is similar to the equilibrium of demand and supply under perfectly competitive market. In monopolistic competition, though a single uniform price is not established, as under perfect competition, there is a general level of prices. For example, in every range of prices, many brands of cigarettes are available. If a particular brand of toilet soap is available at ₹ 20.00, between the range of ₹ 20.00 and ₹ 30.00 many more brands of soap are available. This enables us to speak of a particular level of prices ruling at the market. From this we can think of a general level of AR curves of all the firms. Every firm under such circumstances will try to fix its price and output at a level where MR = MC, on the assumption that its action will have no effect on the price policies of other firms. The sum of individual supplies of all firms in such equilibrium gives us the total supply of the group or the market. If this supply equals market demand for all the firms' products taken together at the current level of prices, the *group* will be in equilibrium. If the total supply of all the firms exceeds the market demand, the ruling level of prices will start falling and the AR curves will shift towards the point of origin. Obviously, the MR curve will also shift. The new MR curve and the long period MC curve will interest to give the equilibrium output and corresponding equilibrium price of the firm. This new supply will be less than the earlier supply. On the contrary, if the market demands for all the firm's products increases, the AR and MR curves will shift to the right and away from the point of origin. The equilibrium of market demand and supply will ultimately be established and every firm will equate its long period marginal cost with its marginal revenue.

The second condition for long period equilibrium is that the number of firms in the market should stabilise. In the short period, if the existing firms are earning supernormal profits, new firms will be attracted towards the market in the long period. The long period prices will, therefore, be lower. At the same time, the demand for factors of production will have increased since more firms have now entered the field and are demanding the same factors of productions. This will lead to an increase in the average and marginal costs of all the firms. This increase in costs and decrease in prices will wipe away the supernormal profits, which the firms could earn in the short period. At the same time, the firms that were running into losses in the short-run, will leave the field in the long-run. Therefore, in the long period, under monopolistic competition, every firm will earn only normal profits.

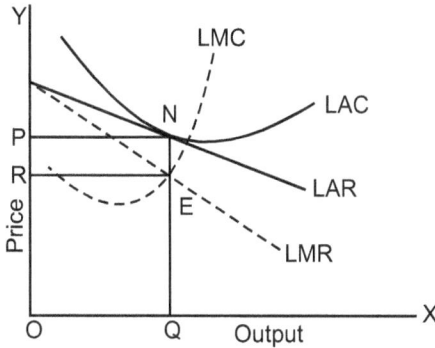

Fig. 2.10 : Long-run Equilibrium

The long-run equilibrium of a firm under monopolistic competition is shown in Fig. 2.10. LMR and LAR are the long period marginal revenue and long period average revenue curves respectively. Similarly, LAC and LMC are the long period average and marginal cost curves respectively. Point E indicates the intersection of the LMR and the LMC curves. OQ is the equilibrium output and OR is the price. Point N shows the equality of the long-run average cost and long-run average revenue because the LAR is tangent to the LAC at point N. Therefore, price (OP) is equal to the average cost and the firm earns only a normal profit. Thus, the long period equilibrium of a firm in monopolistic competition is similar to the long period equilibrium of a firm under perfect competition. But this equilibrium under monopolistic competition is different from the long period competitive equilibrium of a firm in two respects :

(1) Under perfect competition, a firm's average revenue curve is parallel to the X-axis and it touches the average cost curve in the latter lowest point i.e., the point which is nearest to the X-axis. On the other hand, the AR curve of a firm under monopolistic competition in the long-run is tangent to the AC curve before it reaches its lowest point. This is because the AR curve is downward sloping and the AC curve is U shaped. The long-run supply of a firm under monopolistic competition is therefore, less than the supply of a competitive firm. It should also be obvious that the firm under monopolistic competition, in spite of its earning normal profits, does not attain its optimum size.

(2) Under perfect competition in the long-run, the price is equal to average cost as well as marginal cost. This happens in competitive conditions because the equality of AR and AC takes place at the point of lowest per unit cost and the MC curve also passes through this point. Under monopolistic competition, however, the average revenue equals the average cost before the latter reaches its minimum or while the average cost is still decreasing. The MC curve however, cuts the AC curve at the latter's lowest point as usual. Therefore, the price under monopolistic competition, in the long-run equilibrium, is equal to the average cost but is more than the marginal cost.

2.6 Oligopoly – Product Differentiation and Price Discrimination

Another form of imperfect competition is oligopoly or competition among a few. This type of market does not have only one producer as under monopoly nor does it have a very large number of sellers as under monopolistic competition. This is a market of a few or a limited number of sellers. The Word 'Oligopoly' is derived from two Greek words: 'Oligoi' meaning a 'a few' and 'pollien' meaning 'to sell'. Thus, the meaning of the word itself explains what an oligopolistic market is like.

(A) Features of Oligopoly :

The characteristics of an oligopolistic market are as under :

(1) Small Number of Sellers / Producers : Small number of sellers or producers is a basic characteristic of oligopoly. Oligopoly comes into existence when a few firms dominate the market of a commodity. Generally speaking, when we refer to the big three or the big six producers we mean that a major portion of the market supply of the product concerned is under the control of these big producers. Such a market comes under the oligopolistic category of markets even if the remaining twenty or twenty five per cent of the market supply is shared by a number of small firms.

When a number of firms producing for a market is small, every firm has a significant share of market supply. As such, the actions and policies of any firm will have repercussions on other firms. hence, while trying to improve its own position in the market, every firm has to consider the probable reactions on and of its rivals. The possible reactions of rival firms have to be taken into consideration while formulating policies regarding product price, advertising outlays, product quality and design and so on. This type of clear-cut mutual interdependence is a special feature of oligopoly. Such interdependence is absent in "*perfect or monopolistic competition*", because the number of firms is large. The monopolist on the other hand, has no rivals and so interdependence is ruled out, by definition. However, under oligopoly, because of the small number of firms, the actions of one firm exercise direct influence upon other firms. In all probability, it is possible to identify the firm that has caused such repercussions and it can be expected that the affected firms react accordingly.

(2) Product Differentiation not a Necessary Condition : Product differentiation is possible under oligopoly, but it may not always be done. Generally, oligopolists produce more or less standardised products. Generally, Oligopolist firms producing raw materials or semifinished products offer almost uniform products to the buyers. For example, the production of iron and steel, copper or cement is dominated by a few firms and the products are more or less uniform. On the other hand, oligopolistic industries producing consumer goods offer differentiated products. For example, scooters tyres, cars, radio-sets and many other durable consumer goods in India are produced under oligopolistic conditions and the products are definitely differentiated.

(3) Control over Price Circumscribed by Mutual Interdependence : Under oligopoly every firm is free to price its product; but this freedom is closely circumscribed by the mutual interdependence of firms which, as noted earlier, is a special feature of oligopoly. A firm can attract customers of rival firms to itself by lowering the price of its product. But, the rival firms losing their customers will retaliate by further lowering the prices of their products. This will result in competitive price cutting also known as price-war. Ultimately, all the firms in the industry will suffer losses. On the contrary, if a firm raises its price, it will lose its customers and the rival firms will gain by sticking to their existing prices. Price-raising would thus result in pricing oneself out of the market. Thus, under oligopoly, though every firm is free to fix its price, there is a general tendency to adhere to the existing prices.

An alternative to price war or pricing oneself out of the market is to reach collusive agreement regarding pricing of products. Because the number of firms in the market is small. The group can agree to raise or reduce prices together. Once such agreement is reached, the group as a whole can control the market price as a monopolist does.

(4) Barriers to Entry : In oligopolistic industries, obstacles to entry are formidable. Entry of new firms is prevented by ownership of crucial patents or ownership of vital raw materials. Many times technological conditions are such that production is economic only on a large scale. A new firm therefore will have to start production on a large scale from the very outset. It is not possible to make a modest beginning and expanding gradually as the firm gets established. As such, the scale of production also may make entry of a new firm difficult. Also, the existing firms enjoy advantages such as reputation of their brand names, long established distribution channels, goodwill of customers etc., and any new firm desirous of entering the field will have to consider these factors which make entry difficult. However, entry of new firms is not impossible as it is under monopoly; it is only difficult.

(5) Advertising and Sales Promotion : Large amounts of money are usually spent on advertising and sales promotion under oligopoly. However, the nature of an advertisement and the expenditure on it, depends on whether the products are differentiated or not. If products are differentiated, every firm would spend large sums of money on advertising. This would be done to convince the consumers that its product is superior to those of its rivals. This would be competitive advertising. On the other hand, when products are standardised, advertising is not competitive. Usually, some amount of expense is incurred on advertisements, but the purpose of advertising is to keep the firm in the public's eye. This is because the users of the products are themselves industrialists and skilled businessmen who know the quality of the product and who are not likely to be carried away by the claims of the advertisements. For instance, the users know the quality of steel produced by the Tatas, Mysore and Hindustan Steel Ltd. and consequently advertising for them is scarce. But there is a great deal of competitive advertising for consumer products like tooth-pastes, hair-oils and creams etc.

Quality competition attains great importance when products are differentiated under conditions of oligopoly. Therefore, oligopolist firms spend large sums of money on research and design as well as on packing, colour and so on.

(B) The Basis of Oligopoly :

Why does an oligopolistic market exist ? The obvious answer is *'because entry of new firms is difficult'*. Thus, the factors that make entry of new firms difficult act as the basis of oligopoly. These factors are as under :

(1) Patented techniques of production and control over the supply of raw material provide a cost advantage to the existing firm. This cost advantage acts as an obstacle to the entry of new firms.

(2) If the products are differentiated, the buyers develop preferences and may have cultivated the habits of using a particular brand of product. This established habit of the buyers gives an advantage to the existing firms and acts as a deterrent to the new firms.

(3) The production techniques, in some cases, are such as to take the optimum size of the firm to a very high level of production. Thus, if a commodity is to be produced at the lowest average cost, the scale of production is required to be large. This requires a large capital investment which new firms may not dare to risk.

(4) Existing firms which enjoy one or more of the above mentioned advantages may themselves create artificial barriers to the entry of new firms.

(5) As a part of the industrial policy, the government may make it compulsory for the new firms to obtain a licence before starting production. The procedure of the industrial licensing, if it is cumbersome and lengthy, may itself create an obstacle to the entry of new firms.

2.6.1 Price under Oligopoly

Unlike the other market structures discussed so far, oligopoly presents a special situation where building up a single price theory is difficult. The difficulties involved can be summarised as under :

(1) Oligopoly includes several market situations like two-three big firms dominating or all 10-15 firms competing, product-differentiation and standardisation, firms acting in collusion or cut-throat competition, strong barriers to entry or weak barriers to exit, and so on. As a result, one single solution, and that too determinate, becomes difficult.

(2) Demand curve itself is not determinate. It can be a straight horizontal line or can be downward-sloping or can have a kink. This is because the reactions of consumers and rival producers to one's own price changes are unpredictable. In fact, different possibilities may give different demand curves.

(3) Specific assumption regarding the behaviour of the firms are also difficult to make. The variety of objectives of a firm hold good most strongly in oligopoly situations and therefore specific assumption about a single objective (e.g. Profit-maximisation) becomes difficult.

(4) Finally, perfect or monopolistic competition requires a theory of mass behaviour while monopoly calls for the theory of individual behaviour and both these are possible. In case of oligopoly, however, we have a third situation, viz., group behaviour, for which one single theory is not possible.

(A) Oligopoly Pricing :

Under oligopoly, without product differentiation, there would be two possibilities : Either the firms will coalesce (i.e. come together) and fix a single *monopoly price* or they will indulge in a price war and allow the price to fall to the level of a *competitive price*. The larger the number of firms in the market, the more difficult will it be to reach an agreement and the greater the chances of price to be a competitive price. In that case, the firm will in the short-run face an indeterminate situation, but in the long-run, it will earn only normal profits and will reach an equilibrium like that of a competitive firm.

With product differentiation also, there are the same two possibilities noted above. However, because of brand-names, each firm has its own customers. Therefore, in the short-run the firms may get more freedom to raise or reduce their prices without losing their customers. In the long-run, however, they will have to count the possibility of their rivals' reactions. Accordingly, the long-run oligopoly equilibrium will be like that under monopolistic competition.

When the number of firms is small, they can come together and fix a price that maximises the profits of the entire group. Such an arrangement however will not last long because (i) every firm would like to have its own pricing freedom, (ii) the government's anti-monopoly legislation may be evoked, or (iii) new firms can enter the market.

Therefore the possibility of price leadership, wherever possible, appears more tenable. One dominant firm will fix a price (like the monopolist) and try to maximise its own profits. Other smaller firms will pick up that price and adjust their supply to maximise their own profits.

(B) Price Rigidity :

One of the characteristic features of oligopoly is price-rigidity. By whatever way, once the price is fixed, it tends to remain fixed or constant, inspite of changes in demand and cost conditions. Why prices tend to be rigid ?

1. Because the demand curve (i.e. response of customers to price changes) is indeterminate, a firm sticks to a price that has been established.

2. A new price would mean a new sales promotion drive, explanation of why price was raised etc. and still there is uncertainty.

3. Existing price must have come through phases of negotiations, conflicts, compromises and rival strategies etc. A change in price may initiate a chain of actions and reactions again.

4. In the event of a fall in demand, firms would spend more upon advertisements and sales promotion rather than cut the price.

5. The price could be already very low to prevent entry of a new firm.

In modern times, oligopolistic firms try to avoid price-competition by (i) intensifying technological competition, (ii) seeking maximum productive efficiency through technological advance, (iii) ensuring survival via technical superiority, and by (iv) depending upon their R and D for long-run profits.

More about Equilibrium under Oligopoly :

Oligopoly, as we have already noted, is a market structure in which a small number of large firms producing either homogeneous or differentiated products dominate an industry. A characteristic feature of oligopoly is that any change in the output or price of one firm almost always provokes retaliation from other producers. This reaction can take many forms. All the firms may come together to form a cartel or they may openly or tacitly accept the price leadership of the largest firm or firms may enter into non-price competition or a situation of price rigidities may prevail. Producers of differentiated products in oligopoly are actually free to set their own prices. But experience shows that they try to maintain *status quo*. This is so because a price-cut initiated by any one firm can trigger off a chain of reactions. A price-cut once introduced is not reversible. A price-war may start. Ultimately all stand to lose. Under such circumstances non-price competition on the basis of quality design, service, sales-promotion etc. is preferred to a price competition. Oligopoly prices therefore are found to be rigid.

(C) Kinked Demand Curve (Sweezy's) Model :

Various models have been suggested to demonstrate the equilibrium and price-and-output determination under oligopoly. Prof. Paul Sweezy's model is perhaps the most popular one and hence we shall consider that one model only. This model provides an explanation of price-rigidity, i.e. why price is not changed. The individual oligopolist sees the situation somewhat like this. If he raises the price his rivals would not follow suit and hence he is likely to lose his customers to his rivals. But if he reduces his price, others would do the same thing quickly. As a result, at a price higher than the customary one, demand is seen to be highly elastic; while at a price lower than the ruling one, the demand is seen to be highly inelastic. See figure given here. In this diagram, DD_1 is the demand curve which is more elastic in the portion DP_1 and less elastic in the portion P_1D_1.

The equilibrium condition is the profit maximising condition i.e. MR = MC. Note that the DD_1 curve is the AR curve. The marginal revenue curve (MR) is discontinuous between points H and R. It is this gap HR that explains price-rigidity. According to the usual condition MC = MR, we can find out the profit maximising output. Marginal cost curves like MC, MC_1 cut the discontinuous portion HR of the MR curve so as to give the same equilibrium output OQ. The price therefore remains unchanged at OP though costs rise or fall.

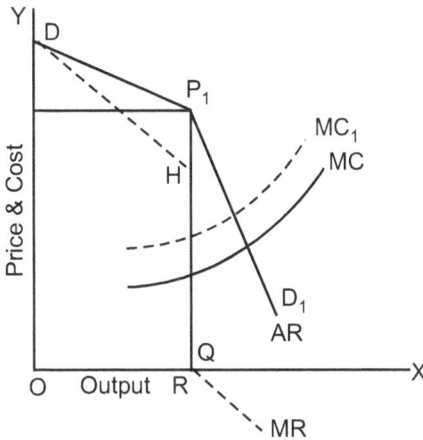

Fig. 2.11 : Oligopoly Equilibrium – Kinked Demand Curve Model

If the second option of a cartel is chosen by the oligopolists, and if it is a perfect cartel, the price would be determined by the joint MC and MR curves of all firms taken together. All the firms would then adjust their individual supplies to the cartel price as given. Some firms may earn profits and others may earn only normal profits. Due to such differences in profitability, cartels do not last long. At times, therefore, profits are pooled together and are then distributed But this arrangement also cannot satisfy all.

Price Leadership is another possibility when there is one big or established firm, it sets the price and others accept that price for adjusting their supplies. If the product is homogeneous, one price may get fixed. If products are differentiated, a range a prices may move together. Thus, for example, cigarettes, bathing soaps washing soaps, electric fans, etc. are produced in oligopolistic conditions, in India, and a particular grade of the product is priced between a certain price-range. A change in the price is usually effected by the price-leader and others follow suit.

To conclude, therefore, we can say that oligopoly is more common but since it can take various forms, a single model cannot explain its price and output equilibrium. Non-price competition makes things more complex. Rivals use advertising quality changes, in packing other services accompanying the product etc. as non-price competition. A single determinate economic explanation as a guide to policy is therefore not possible though broadly one can describe how output and pricing policies are determined by the oligopolists. The models discussed above at best, provide some alternatives available to them.

2.6.2 Price Discrimination

We assumed in our discussion of monopoly pricing that the monopolist charges only one price. But, the monopolist can charge different prices from different customers because he alone controls the price. If the monopolist discriminates between customers, the act is called price discrimination and such a monopoly is called a *discriminating monopoly*.

Price discrimination can take various forms :

(a) **Personal Discrimination :** Personal discrimination means selling goods or services at different prices to different persons. For example, professionals like doctors, lawyers, etc. charge different fees from different persons.

(b) **Place Discrimination :** Place discrimination means charging different prices for the same product at different places. For example, selling a product very cheap in the international market and charging a high price for the same product in the domestic market is a case of place discrimination.

(c) **Use Discrimination :** Use discrimination means charging different prices for different uses of the same product or service. For instance, electricity is supplied to agriculture at a lower rate than that supplied to industries.

Degrees of Price Discrimination :

Since price discrimination or charging different prices from different consumers depends upon the seller's ability to divide the consumers or the markets; we can think of different possibilities. Our basic assumptions, are noted above under the heading 'when is price-discrimination possible ?' Under such circumstances favourable to the monopolist, discri-mination, according to economists, is possible at various degrees. Let us consider them.

(1) First Degree Discrimination : If and when a seller can know the price each customer is willing to pay, he charges the same price and leaves no consumer's surplus for the buyer. The seller, in other words, sets the price at the highest level where all those who are willing to buy atleast one unit of the product buy atleast one unit each. The seller thus extracts all the consumer's surplus of all buyers who buy the first unit of the product. Then, by lowering the price, he sells second unit each to extract consumer's surplus on the second unit. This procedure would continue and at lower prices, new entrant would buy their first unit, old ones would buy second or third unit, and so on. Lowest price would equate MR with MC and this entire consumer's surplus would be extracted by the monopolist. Mrs. Joan Robinson refers to the type as 'perfect discrimination'. The case of a doctor charging the highest fee from the richest patient and the lowest from the poorest patient comes close to such first degree discrimination. This type would however be rarely, if at all, found in practice.

(2) **Second Degree Discrimination :** A larger size of the market rules out the possibility of perfect discrimination. Second degree discrimination can be adopted by the monopolist – a method also known as *block pricing method*. Here the monopolist divides his potential buyers into blocks like (i) the richest, (ii) the middle class, and (iii) the poor. The highest price would be charged to the rich. A little lower to the middle class and the lowest to the poor. This type of second degree discrimination is possible when –

   (a)   the number of customers is large and price-rationing is possible;

   (b)   the demand curve for all buyers is identical; and

   (c)   it is possible to charge a single rate to a large number of consumers.

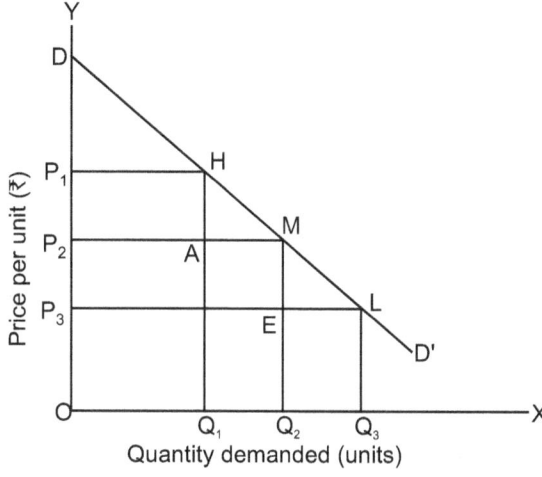

Fig. 2.12 : Price Discrimination – Second Degree

In this Fig. 2.12, demand is measured along X-axis and price along Y-axis. The monopolist charges OP_1 – the highest price for OQ_1 units; a lower price OP_2 for Q_1Q_2 units; and the lowest price OP_3 for Q_2Q_3 units. His Total Revenue (TR) = ($OP_1 \times OQ_1$) + ($OP_2 \times Q_1Q_2$) + ($OP_3 \times Q_2Q_3$). Please note that in this second degree discrimination, the entire consumer's surplus is *not* extracted by the monopolist. Thus, according to our figure, those paying the highest price OP_1 can still enjoy DP_1H amount of consumer's surplus. Similarly, the middle and the lowest block consumers are able to retain HAM and MEL amounts of consumer's surplus, respectively. Of course, a major portion of the surplus satisfaction is extracted by the seller.

The possibility of dividing the consumers into various blocks for the purpose of discrimination can be used in public interest when the monopoly is with the Government or is subjected to strict Government control when allowed to remain in private sector and with permission to discriminate. Differential rates can be and are charged for lower and higher consumption of electricity, residential and commercial uses of water, power etc. Banks discriminate between priority and non-priority sectors, concessional rates are charged for D-zone areas by a number of service providers. Many such examples can be cited which aim at maximising social welfare.

(3) **Third Degree Discrimination :** In the case, the monopolistic sets different prices at different markets which have market demand curves exhibiting different elasticities. Monopolists and/or oligopolists often face this sort of situation. In fact, businessmen, big and small, can monopolise a particular market and act as one of many competitors at another market. Whatever follows under 'When is Price Discrimination Profitable ?' is a case of third degree discrimination which is common and, therefore, discussed in detail. When one refers to discrimination, this degree is what one has in mind.

When is Price-Discrimination Possible ?

Price discrimination is possible under the following circumstances :

(1) **Market Imperfections :** Price discrimination is possible under conditions of imperfection in the market which may arise in any of the following ways :

(a) **Ignorance of the Market :** This means that the buyers at one place are ignorant of the price being charged for the same product, at another place. The monopolist can then take advantage of this ignorance and sell his product at different prices at different places.

(b) **Want of Rational behaviour :** Many times, the decisions of the buyers are not rational. They may be guided by some other considerations or they may have certain misconceptions and prejudices. For example, a higher price is often regarded as a symbol of better quality and the buyers buy a dearer product rather than a cheaper one because they think that the costly product must be superior in quality. This gives the monopolist an opportunity to discriminate and charge different prices.

(c) **Monopoly :** Market imperfections lead to the emergence of monopoly and control over price is not possible without monopoly power. Therefore, we do not find price discrimination in a perfectly competitive market.

(2) **Differences in Elasticity of Demand :** The very fact that different prices can be charged means that the slopes of the demand curves are different. Because the firm is one, the cost curves are the same. But to have different prices, equilibrium points must be different. Thus, the points of equilibrium will be different only when revenue curves are different. This means that the market is divided into two or more parts and in each sub-market, the shapes of revenue curves are different or the elasticities of demand are different. This fact enables the monopolist to charge a higher price where the demand is inelastic and a lower price where the demand is elastic.

(3) Geographical or Artificial Division of the Market : Market segmentation is necessary to charge different prices. This division should however, be a perfect one. Otherwise, if the buyers can buy the product in the market where price is low and sell it where the price is high, the same price will ultimately be established in both the markets. The market is divided by factors like transport costs, tariffs, legal restrictions, etc. The monopolist can practice discrimination only when the market is divided into different divisions or groups.

(4) Nature of the Product : Sometimes discrimination is possible due to the nature of the commodity. For instance, a caterer having two restaurants - one in the midst of the city and the other away from the city can charge different prices for a cup of tea at these two places. He can do so because a cup of tea is required to be served hot and it is impossible for anybody to purchase a number of cups of tea in the city and sell it again outside the city. In case of services, this fact is more accentuated. Because coconuts are chap in the city, they can be purchased and transported to a suburb. But a doctor's or a priest's service cannot be purchased at a lower price in the city and carried to a suburb. The residents of distant localities have to purchase these services at whatever prices they are available. In such conditions discrimination becomes possible.

When is Price-Discrimination Profitable ?

The profitability of price discrimination depends upon how the discriminating monopoly attains its equilibrium. Even under a discriminating monopoly, the condition of equilibrium is the same i.e. equality of MR and MC and the intersection of the MR curve by the MC curve from below. Here, however, instead of one, two markets have to be considered because charging two prices means separating the two markets. In both markets, equality of MR with MC is necessary for equilibrium.

Assumptions of Price Discrimination :

Our discussion of equilibrium under discriminating monopoly : is based on following assumptions (i) that there is perfect competition among the buyers in both the markets; and (ii) that the buyers in the two markets cannot contact each other.

To examine the profitability of price discrimination, let us consider the two possibilities : (a) When elasticity of demand in both the markets is the same; and (b) When the elasticities of demand in the two markets are different or not the same.

(a) When elasticity of demand is the same : If elasticity of demand in both the markets is the same at all prices, the slope of the average revenue curves in both the markets will be the same throughout the length of the AR curves. Therefore, in spite of the fact that the two markets are different, price discrimination will not be profitable since the demand curves are exactly the same.

(b) When elasticities of demand are different : When elasticities of demand in both the markets are different, monopolist can charge a high price where demand is more inelastic and he can charge a low price and allow the sales to increase where the demand is more elastic. Reduction in supply to the market where demand in inelastic results in increasing total revenue. We know that when e < 1, a fall in price results in contraction of total revenue and a rise in price leads to an expansion of total revenue. On the contrary, where e > 1, a fall-in price leads to an increase in total revenue. Therefore, it will be profitable for the monopolist to reduce his supply in the market where demand is inelastic, so that the price can rise. The same supply can be diverted to the other market where demand is elastic. Thus, it will result in a fall in the price and an increase in the total revenue. This policy will cause an increase in total revenue in both the markets. The act of diverting supply from one market to the ether will continue until the marginal revenues in both the markets are equal.

Fig. 2.13 shows the equilibrium of a firm under discriminating monopoly. All three dia-grams are drawn to the same scale and therefore, the slopes of the demand curves can be compared for purposes of elasticities of demand. The elasticities in market (a), [Fig. 2.13 (a)] and in market (b) [Fig. 2.13 (b)l, are different. This is clear from the slopes of the AR curves in the diagrams. Market (a) has an inelastic demand and market (b) has an elastic demand. The curve MR_3 in Fig. 2.13 (c) is the sum of MR_1 [Fig. 2.13 (a) and MR_2 [Fig. 2.13 (b)]. OS is the total supply. The marginal revenues (MR_2 and MR_2) in both markets are equal at OM level. At the same level, MR_1 and MR_2 (which together are equal to MR_3) are equal to MC in Fig. 2.13 (c). Point E in Fig. 2.13 (c) is therefore the point of equilibrium and the dotted line passing through E and running parallel to the X-axis, intersects MR_2 and MR_1 to give us the equilibrium output in both the markets. In market (a), equilibrium output will be OQ and in market (b), equilibrium output will be OR. These two, i.e., OQ + OR together are equal to OS, the total supply of the monopoly firm. The price in market (a) is OP_1 while the price is market (b) is OP_2. It is clear that because of inelastic demand the price in market (a) is higher. A relatively elastic demand in market (b) calls for a lower price. The shaded area in Fig. 2.13 (c) represents the total profits of the monopolist.

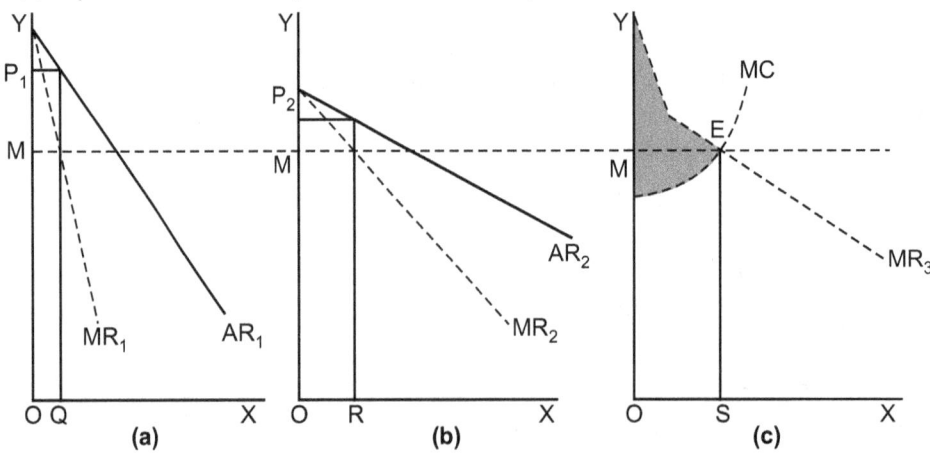

Fig. 2.13 : Equilibrium under Discriminating Monopoly

Price Discrimination and Social Interest :

As price discrimination is perverse to the society's interest, it is usually criticised on the ground that an inelastic demand creates a situation where the consumer is likely to be exploited by the monopolist. But price discrimination is not always harmful. In the following cases, price discrimination may be beneficial to the society : (i) The total output with price discrimination is greater than that with a single price. The increased output is to advantage of the society. (ii) It is possible that a market is being served which in the absence of price discrimination would not have been served. For instance, a country can compete effectively with other countries in the international market if it sells a given product at a higher price in the domestic market. This can be justified within limits of given circumstances. (iii) When total costs cannot be covered with a single price, price discrimination is helpful. For example, the cost involved in the manufacturing and distribution of postcards is higher per unit than the price of the postcard. But the post office can afford to sell the postcard cheap because other postal charges are higher and so they compensate for losses arising from the cheap sale of postcards. Thus, unless the circumstances in which price discrimination is practised are examined - carefully, it is not possible to pass a judgement regarding its harmfulness to the society.

2.7 Price – Output Determination in Multi-product and Multi-plant Firms

(A) Price Output Determination in Multi-Product Firm :

So far we saw how price and output of a commodity get determined under different market categories. However, all these cases were based on the assumption that the firms concerned are producing a single homogeneous product. In practice, we find that most firms are producing more than one product. Even the firms specialising in one product (e.g. four-wheeled automobiles) produce different models of varying sizes and comforts. They need to be treated as different products. Most of the white goods like refrigerators, T.V. sets, mobile phones, laptops, washing machines, air conditioners etc. are produced in differentiated models and the consumers view them as different products. They are substitutes for each other. Many times, products which are not related to each other are produced by the same firm. All such firms have the following characteristics :

(1) Products produced by the same firm are viewed by the consumers as different products; and

(2) Therefore the markets to which they cater can be separated.

The issue of pricing under these conditions becomes one of multi-product pricing or production pricing.

The conditions of equilibrium are the same as we saw in respect of various market categories. However, in this case, the demand curve for each product is different. And being produced by one organisation under common and interchangeable production facilities, they share common costs and therefore marginal costs and average costs remain inseparable. In other words, the different products produced by one firm have their own independent AR and MR curves but they share a common AC and MC curves.

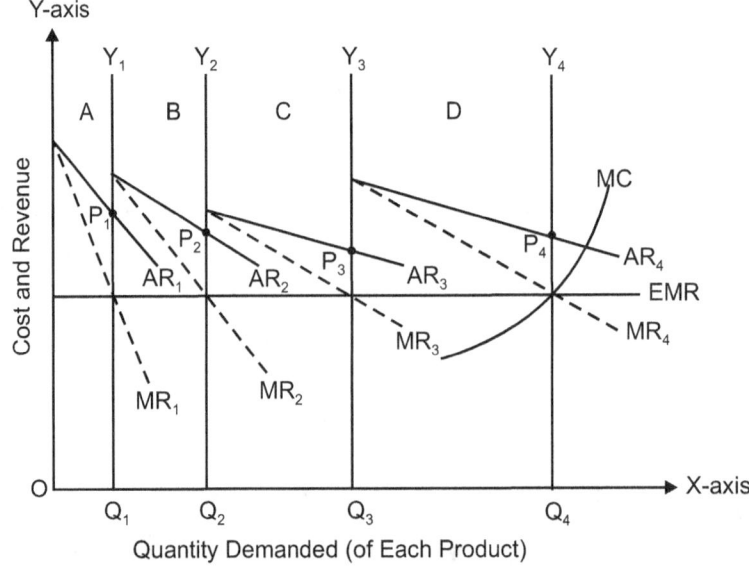

Fig. 2.14 : Price Output Determination in Multi-product Firm

Let us suppose the firm under consideration is producing four products A, B, C and D. Each product has its own AR and MR curves. The AR represents demand curve and when all AR curves are drawn to the same scale; their slopes can show differences in price elasticities of demand. A steep AR curve is indicative of the monopoly power. While the flatter the AR curve the greater the elastic-extreme case being that of perfect competion where AR is parallel to X-axis, indicating perfect elasticity.

In Fig. 2.14, A, B, C and D are four segments depicting AR and MR curves for the four products A, B, C and D. Note that for product B, Q_1Y_1 is taken as Y-axis, for product C, Q_2Y_2 becomes the Y-axis and so on. Point Q_1, Q_2 etc. act as points of origin respectively. Similarly, AR_1 and MR_1 are the AR and MR curves of product 'A', AR_2 and MR_2 are revenue curves of product 'B' and so on. Do not forget the property of MR : it bisects the horizontal distance between AR and Y-axis. Also, the AR curves are shown to have different slopes, indicating different elasticities of demand, without which markets cannot be separated. (see the discussion of discriminating monopoly for details). A and B are markets where the firm near-monopoly or oligopoly with very few competitors. C and D are products the markets for which are more and more competitive, oligopoly with little more rivals and/or monopolistic competition. But the points Q_1 or Q_2 etc. are obtained only after going through the following exercise.

The profit-maximisation condition is the same : MR = MC. We must therefore find out the points where this condition can be satisfied in each segment of the market. The marginal cost of all four products taken together is shown by the curves MC. The marginal revenues (MRs) for products A, B, C and D are added together horizontally to get the aggregate MR curve. (For simplification, it is not shown in the Fig. 2.14). Let us suppose, this aggregate MR cuts the factory MC curve at point C. From this point of intersection, we draw a line parallel to X-axis. EMR (Equal Marginal Revenue) is such a line. The points of intersection of EMR and MR_1, MR_2 etc. would give us the points of equality of MR and MC. These points give us the equilibrium output of each product. Thus, from the first point of intersection, when we draw a perpendicular to the X-axis, it meets the axis at point Q_1. When the straight line starting form Q_1 is extended to meet AR_1 we get point P_1. Thus for product 'A' the output gets determined as OQ_1 and the price-fetching maximum profit would be Q_1P_1. In the same way, the equilibrium level of output for product 'B' would be Q_1Q_2 and the price chargeable would be Q_2P_2. For 'C' the output Q_2Q_3 and price Q_3P_3 is determined. Finally, for 'D' the price Q_4P_4 will be charged and Q_3Q_4 output will be produced. Please mark that steepness of AR means greater monopoly power resulting in smaller quantity of output produced and higher price charged by the producer firm. Thus, profits from producing each product are maximised and therefore, taken together, the overall profit earned by the firm is maximised.

(B) Price and Output Determination in Multi-Plant Firm :

Just as many of the modern firms produce multiple products, many firms produce a single product and sell it at a uniform price but production is carried out at multiple plants. Firms producing washing machines, refrigerators, automobiles etc. produce the same model at different plants located in different countries / regions. Since they use different technologies or local labour and material, their costs (AC and MC) vary from plant to plant. But they face a uniform demand function. How do such firms decide upon the price ? Again, a decision regarding total output and allocation of individual plantwise output is also to be taken.

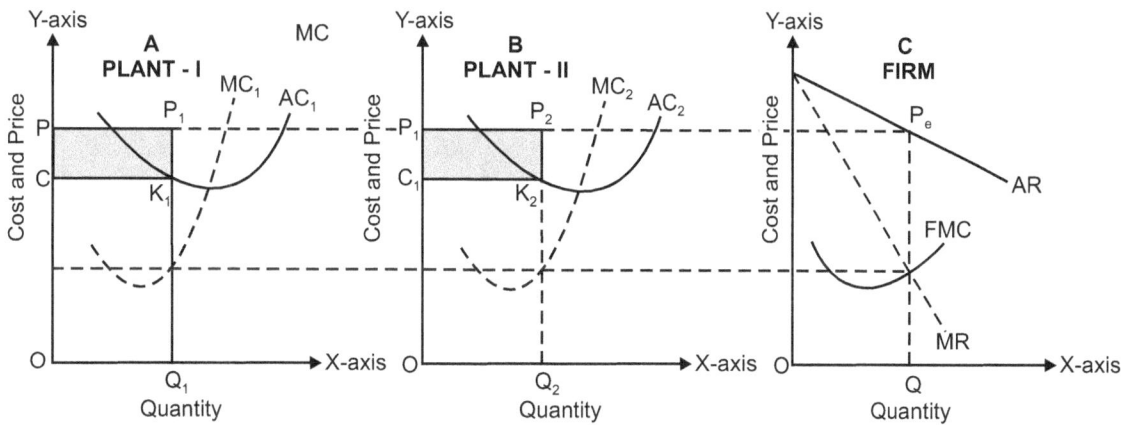

Fig. 2.15 : Price and Output Determination in Multi-plant Firm

Uniform demand function gets reflected in a uniform or a single AR curve. Cost curves are different. In Fig. 2.15, Plant - I and Plant – II have different cost curves, as shown in parts A and B of the figure. Part C shows the demand function faced by the firm. FMC is the firm's marginal cost curve obtained by horizontally adding together MC_1 and MC_2. The interestion of FMC and MR gives us the equilibrium output of OQ. From point Q when a perpendicular is drawn to meet AR in P_e i.e. equilibrium price, we get OP or QP_e as the price determined. From P_e we have drawn a perpendicular to Y-axis to get the price fixed for both plants. From the point of intersection of FMC and MR, similar perpendicular is drawn to meet Y-axis. This line gives us common MR for all plants. Thus, point of intersection of this horizontal MR and MC, of Plant - I gives us OQ_1 output allocated to Plant - I. Similarly OQ_2 output can be allocated to Plant - II. Note that $OQ_1 + OQ_2 = OQ$. The profit is given by finding out the excess of price over average cost multiplied by the quantity produced and supplied. Therefore K_1P_1 in Plant - I and K_2P_2 in Plant - II are such profits per unit to be multiplied by quantities of the product. Thus, PCK_1P_1 represents total profit earned by Plant - I and $P_1C_1K_2P_2$ is the profit earned by Plant – II. When these two quantities representing maximum profits for individual plants we get the firm's profit, which is maximum. Similar geometrical model can be constructed for more than two plants as well.

Questions for Discussion

1. What is Demand ? State its Characteristics.
2. Explain Law of Demand. State the Assumptions and Exceptions of Law of Demand.
3. State the Determinants of Market Demand at Firm and Industry Level.
4. What is Elasticity of Demand ? State its Types.
5. Explain the Types and Determinants of Price Elasticity of Demand.
6. What is Income Elasticity of Demand ? State its Types.
7. Explain Pricing under Perfect Competition.
8. Explain Pricing under Monopolistic Competition.
9. Explain Price and Output Decision in Multi-plant and Multi-product Firms.
10. Write short notes on :
    (A) Market Demand Equation.
    (B) Use of Multiple Regression for Estimating Demand.
    (C) Oligopoly.
    (D) Product Differentiation.
    (E) Price Discrimination.

Lets go with...

CHAPTER

3

COST CONCEPTS

3.1 Cost Concept

Clarity of cost concepts is important in the theory as well as in the practice of a firm. For one thing, whatever be the objective of a firm, it is necessary to ascertain that it is not incurring losses. Besides, is firm a required to take decisions like expansion, adding new products, marketing of old products etc. It is, therefore, necessary to have a clear idea of different cost concepts.

Prof. Joel Dean mentions the following purposes of taking into account various cost concepts and cost distinctions :

(1) Clearing the Fallacies in the Traditional Outlook : In traditional thinking, actual costs or costs recorded in the account books of a firm are believed to be only important costs. In fact, they are no more than the recorded history of moneys expended by the firm. They are useful for legal as well as auditing purposes; but for decision making, more logical and appropriate cost-concepts must be taken into consideration.

(2) To Provide a Proper Perspective to Costs : The cost concepts and distinctions we are presently going to discuss enable us to examine the practical problems in their proper perspective.

(3) Analysis of Accounting Costs : Many times it is necessary to analyse accounting costs into proper classes for a better understanding of a given problem. This can be done with the help of different cost concepts.

(4) Forecasting and Policy Making : For forecasting and taking policy decisions regarding the size of the plant, the level of output, the nature of advertising, etc. it is necessary to consider various cost distinctions.

We saw the effects of changes in proportions of factor combinations on average and marginal physical product. Factors of production are required to be purchased. In other words, resources are scarce and their prices are determined at the factor market. Firms buy these factors at a price. Thus, employing factors of production involves cost. Production in economics means creation of utilities. Utilities can be created by changing form, place etc. Creation of utilities requires participation of factors of production. Because every additional equal unit of input causes different quantities of marginal output, as shown by the law of variable proportions and returns to scale, cost per unit of output also differs from level to level of output. Let us go into the details of how costs change with changes in the level of output. For this purpose, we shall have to consider certain relevant cost concepts.

3.2 Opportunity Cost, Marginal Cost, Incremental Cost and Sunk Costs

(A) Total Cost :

Total cost represents cost of production, plus selling and distribution expenses.

Thus, Total Cost = Cost of Production (+) Selling and Distribution Expenses

(B) Opportunity Cost and Actual or Outlay Costs :

The following cost distinction is based on an economic versus accounting view of costs. Actual costs refer to the costs actually incurred in money terms. Such costs are recorded in the books of accounts of a firm. On the other hand, opportunity costs are defined as an *earning from the next best use of a factor forgone by employing it in its present use.* Since the best utilisation of resources is an objective of all economic activities, this concept is very important in economic theory.

A simple example will make the concept of opportunity cost clear. Let us suppose that a piece of land is being used to grow sugarcane. Is it the best use of that piece of land ? What is the 'real' cost of growing sugarcane ? The concept of opportunity cost can answer these questions. If sugarcane is not grown on that piece, what are the alternatives ? In order of expected income, let us say, the alternative crops are wheat, cotton and jowar. Next best use, then, is growing wheat. Whatever income wheat might have earned on that piece of land is forgone by using the land for sugarcane. The foregone earnings of wheat represent the opportunity cost of growing sugarcane. Sugarcane growing is desirable so long as sugarcane fetches more earnings than wheat. Only then sugarcane growing would be considered the best use of land. Actual cost of growing sugarcane, on the other hand, is the sum-total of the costs of seed, fertilisers, water, labour and so on. The example clearly distinguishes opportunity cost from actual cost and also indicates the possibility that producing something that seems to be profitable on the basis of actual costs may be unprofitable on the criterion of opportunity cost.

Practical Importance of the Concept of Opportunity Cost :

(a) **Measuring Profitability :** Many times opportunity cost is a more rational basis for measuring profitability. For example, suppose a weaving mill has its own spinning section. For finding out the profitability of the weaving section, it is not proper to calculate the actual cost of cotton etc. Had the firm sold yarn in the market, the price thus fetched, should be taken as a cost for the weaving section. This is the only right method of finding out the profitability of the weaving section.

(b) **Important Long-run Decisions :** It is the opportunity cost that is important in any long-run decisions. For example, while choosing between an independent business and a service, after graduation, the salary in the service should be taken as an opportunity cost for finding out the profitability of the business. To take another example, the cost of college education is not just the sum-total of expenses of books, tuition fees, etc. The salary foregone of a full-time employment is the real cost (i.e. opportunity cost) of college education. These two examples show how, in the long-term decision making, opportunity cost is an important concept.

(c) **Importance in the Capital Budget :** Opportunity cost is an important guide while framing the capital budget. For example, for hiring a shop-space in the central place of a city, a businessman is required to pay ₹ 2,00,000. The interest on this amount is not a proper measure of the cost. He could run a shop in another locality where no 'pugree' is required and utilize this amount as 'capital' for his business. The earnings of this second shop, which are foregone, should be taken as the cost of having a shop in the central locality. This is the opportunity cost.

(d) Alternatives Available to the Firm : Actual cost is based on what the firm is actually producing. Various alternative uses of the resources of the firm and selection of the most profitable out of them is possible only on the basis of opportunity cost.

Measurement of Opportunity Costs :

Where factors are actually paid, the problem is not difficult. But where the entrepreneur uses his own factors like his own house, his own land etc., because no payment is required to be made, the opportunity cost is likely to be considered zero. This is obviously wrong. Whatever remuneration a factor might have fetched if rented out should be taken as the opportunity cost of the factor, under such circumstances.

(C) Incremental Cost and Sunk Costs :

Conceptually, marginal cost and incremental cost are closely related. But the distinction between the two needs to be underlined. Marginal cost refers to the cost of the marginal unit of output, as we have discussed in detail, elsewhere in this book. Incremental cost, on the other hand, refers to the total additional cost associated with the marginal batch of output. Marginal cost is a theoretical concept used for analysing situations, problems and decisions. In practice, however, marginal cost cannot be measured due to indivisibility of inputs. Thus, for producing one more shirt how many machines, how many workers etc. Would be needed ? Men and machines are indivisible. In the long-run, in practice, firms increase their quantity of output by employing more men, installing more machines, purchasing more materials. This results in additional output for which additional cost was incurred. These additional costs are incremental costs.

(D) Average and Marginal Costs :

Marginal cost is the addition made to the total cost by the production of one more unit of output. In the words of Dooley, "*marginal cost is the change in total cost associated with a change in output*". Therefore, the fall in total cost caused by producing one unit less than before would be an alternative way of finding out the marginal cost. The average cost, on the other hand, is total cost divided by the total number of units produced. We saw that total costs can be divided into fixed and variable costs. Total fixed costs divided by the number of units produced gives us *average fixed cost*; while total variable costs divided by the number of units produced gives us *average variable cost*. Because fixed costs plus variable costs are equal to total costs, the sum of total costs divided by the total number of units produced is also known as *average total unit cost*. All these cost concepts are going to be very important in the cost analysis of a firm we are going to take up presently.

3.2.1 Classification and Analysis of Costs

(1) **Historical Cost :** These are the costs which are ascertained after these have been incurred.

(2) **Estimated Cost :** Estimated cost is a reasonable assessment of what a cost "will be".

(3) **Standard Cost :** Standard cost is a planned cost for a unit of product or service rendered.

(4) **Marginal Cost :** Marginal cost is the cost incurred by a company for the additional output.

(5) **Incremental Cost :** Incremental cost measures the addition to unit cost which results from an addition to output. It is generally expressed as a cost per unit.

(6) **Opportunity Cost :** Opportunity cost is the sacrifice involved in accepting the alternative under consideration.

(7) **Replacement Cost :** It is the cost of replacing an existing asset.

(8) **Sunk Cost :** These are the historical costs which have already been incurred or sunk in the past.

(9) **Relevant Cost :** These are the costs which have a bearing on the decisions under the consideration of the management.

(10) **Manufacturing Cost :** It is the cost of operating the manufacturing department of the organisation.

(11) **Administration Cost :** It is the cost for formulating the policy, directing the organisation and controlling the operations.

(12) **Selling and Distribution Cost :** Selling cost is the cost of stimulating demand. Distribution cost is cost by distributing the product.

(13) **Research and Development Costs :** These costs are incurred to discover new ideas, processes, products by experiment.

(14) **Pre-production Costs :** These costs are incurred when a new product is introduced.

(15) **Fixed Cost :** It is that portion of the total cost which remains constant irrespective of output upto the capacity limit.

(16) **Variable Cost :** It is a cost which changes according to the changes in output.

(17) **Semi-variable Cost :** These costs vary in some degree with volume but not in direct or same proportion.

(18) **Engineered Cost :** These are the costs which vary directly with the level of production.

(19) Discretionary Cost : These are the costs that arise from periodic appropriate decisions that directly reflect top management policies.

(20) Controllable Costs : It is the cost which can be influenced by the action of a specific member of an organisation.

(21) Non-controllable Costs : It is the cost which cannot be influenced by the action of a specific member of an organisation.

(22) Conversion Cost : It is the cost of converting new material into finished goods.

(23) Common Costs: Common costs are the costs which are incurred collectively for a number of costs centres and required to be suitably apportioned to the individual cost centres.

(24) Traceable Cost : These are the costs which can be easily identified with cost unit or cost centres.

(25) Joint Cost : Joints costs are the costs of two or more manufactured goods of significant sales values that are produced by a single process and are not identifiable to individual products upto a certain state of production known as the "split-off point".

(26) Avoidable Costs : The cost which can be avoided under the present conditions is an avoidable costs.

(27) Unavoidable Costs : The cost which cannot be avoided under the present conditions is an unavoidable cost.

(28) Total Cost : It represents cost of production plus selling and distribution expenses.

3.3 Cost Volume Profit (CPV) Analysis

Cost Volume Profit (CVP) Analysis shows relationship between expenses (costs), revenues (sales) and net income (net profit). CVP analysis furnishes a picture of profit at various levels of activity.

Objectives of Cost Volume Profit (CVP) Analysis :

(1) To help in setting up flexible budgets which indicate costs and profits at various levels of activity.

(2) To assist in performance evaluation for purpose of control.

(3) To assist in formulating pricing policies particularly in period of recession.

(4) To ascertain profit for a desired volume of sales.

(5) To forecast profits fairly and accurately.

(6) To determine variable cost per unit at various levels of output.

(7)   To ascertain the impact of increase or decrease in fixed costs.

(8)   To ascertain sales at break-even points in units and value.

(9)   To evaluate the effect of reduction or increase in price or price differentials in different markets.

(10) To know the amount of overhead costs which would be charged to product at different levels of operation.

3.4 Break-even Point

3.4.1 Concept of Break-even Point

Analysis of costs helps us in understanding the various considerations involved in the calculation of the total cost of production. The analysis also throws light on the cost output relationship and the level of output at which average cost would be minimum. However, minimisation of costs is not the goal of the firm. In fact, the conventional objective of a firm is to maximise profits. Economic theory, as we noted in the beginning, follows the course of model building and in the interest of building a model of a firm in equilibrium, the theory is keen on getting a single determinate answer. However, in practice, as noted earlier, the firms can have various objectives. In keeping with the objective chosen by a firm, it would try to reach that level of output which conforms to the dictates of such an objective.

Whatever the objective of the firm, profitability has got to be understood because profits are the reward of enterprise and no firm would continue to operate if it does not generate profits. Obviously, cost alone would not be a sufficient guide for deciding upon the size of the firm, i.e., the level of output at which the firm would like to stabilise its production. The other variable which is necessary for this decision is the revenue which is the value of output produced and sold at the ruling market price. Then only we are able to find out the amount of total profit which is equal to Total Revenue (TR) minus Total Cost (TC).

Minimisation of cost or optimisation of output refers to the optimum level of output which is given by the lowest average cost of production. But this is not the objective of the firm and even from the theoretical point of view; maximum profit coincides with minimum average cost only under conditions of perfect competition and in the long-run. There too, the firm earns only normal profits and not maximum profits. Therefore, it is necessary to find out whether the firm is making profits, at what level of output it starts making profits and whether, in the given circumstances, it is possible to make profits. As such, in practice, the firm has to go into the details of cost and revenue analysis for the following reasons :

(1') Maximum Profits is not necessarily the objective of a firm, in practice;

(2) Even if it is so, it does not coincide with the minimum average cost;

(3) Whatever level of profit is aimed at, it cannot be achieved immediately when a firm starts production, in actual practice;

(4) In reality, firms start production at a loss, in anticipation of future profits;

(5) For planning its production, a firm is better equipped if it can know beforehand the level of output at which total cost and total revenue would be equal.

All these considerations underline the importance of the break-even analysis, i.e., the analysis showing the range of no-profit production and profitable production. This analysis is an important tool which is used to study the relationship between total cost and total revenue and find out total profits and losses over the entire range of output contemplated by a firm. The cost-output and the price-output relationships which indicate the total costs and total revenue respectively, when shown graphically, can be either linear or non-linear. Let us examine both these types of revenue and cost functions.

3.4.2 Break-even Point with Linear Functions

When the cost and revenue functions are linear, the resultant curves would, in fact not be curves but straight lines. Figure 3.1 illustrates the break-even point with linear cost and revenue functions. In this figure, the level of output is measured along the X-axis; while cost and revenue measured in Rupees is shown along the Y-axis. The cost and revenue functions in this diagram are based on the assumptions that the total fixed cost is fixed at OS throughout the level of output under consideration; and the variable cost varies at a constant rate of ₹ OS per unit produced, as the level of output increases. Let us say that the constant rate of increase in the variable cost is ₹ K per unit. The short-run linear cost function therefore would read as follows :

$$TC = OS + K \times Q$$

In the same way, assuming that the product of the firm can be sold at the market at a price of ₹ P per unit, the linear revenue function would read as

$$TR = P \times Q$$

The firm can now collect and put together the data regarding its total fixed cost (TFC), total variable cost (TVC) and total cost (TC), as well as total revenue (TR) alongwith the increasing levels of output in a tabular form. By plotting the points on graph, the cost and revenue functions, as shown in figure 3.1 can be obtained. In this diagram, TFC is the line showing total fixed cost at ₹ OS for the given level of output, which is parallel to the X-axis because the fixed cost is the same throughout at various levels of output in the given range shown in the diagram. The line TVC shows the variable cost increasing at a constant rate and therefore, with a slope of ΔQ / ΔVC which is equal to 1 / K. The line TC is obtained by vertically adding together the TFC and TVC at each of the points on the X-axis, i.e., at various levels of output. For example, at the level of output OQ, total fixed cost QR + total variable cost QN gives us the total cost QT. The straight line TR shows the total revenue as obtained by multiplying the quantity at each point on the X-axis by the price per unit (i.e., Q × P). The line TR intersects the line TC at point T where the output is OQ. Therefore, point T is the break-even point which corresponds to the OQ level of output. Thus the break-even point shows that the firm's total cost (TC) equals its total revenue (TR), at OQ level of output. At all other levels of output below the level OQ, TC is more than TR. The difference between these two lines up to the point T indicates TC – TR and therefore, shows a loss which is called Operating Loss. Beyond this level of output, i.e., after crossing the point T. Total revenue TR exceeds total cost TC. The distance between TR and TC after crossing OQ level of output, therefore, shows a profit known as Operating Profit. It therefore, follows that, in the given cost and revenue conditions in our example, the firm must produce at least OQ units of output to make its total cost and total revenue breakeven.

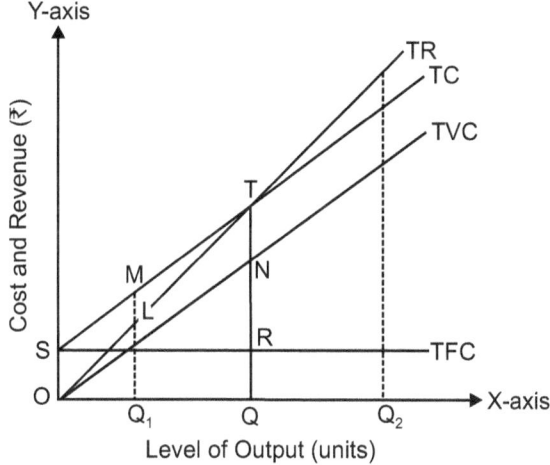

Fig. 3.1 : Break-even Point with Linear Functions

It is necessary to remember that the linear functions, as shown and discussed above, are subject to an *important limitation*. This limitation stems from the fact that the break-even analysis based on linear functions is really based upon the assumptions that the cost and revenue functions are linear. When they are linear, the Total Cost and Total Revenue functions are straight lines and, as such, they intersect each other at only one point (point T in Fig. 3.1). As a result, the whole range of output is divided into two parts : the first part of unprofitable operation, up to the break-even point, and the second part of profitable operation, after crossing the break-even point. In reality, these functions are hardly linear and more often than not, they are non-linear, due to the changing price and cost conditions. The result is that the average variable cost (AVC) and price vary with a change in output. It may, therefore, happen that the total cost or TC is increasing at an *increasing* rate while the total revenue or TR is increasing at a *decreasing* rate. As a result, over a certain range of output in the beginning, TC exceeds TR. This is very logical and understandable because at the starting point of production, total revenue is zero because the output is yet to be produced and sold at the market. But the total cost (OS) has already been incurred in the form of fixed cost. Variable cost however would start varying with the output as actual production starts and progresses towards higher and higher levels.

3.4.3 Break-even Point with Non-linear Functions

The aforesaid considerations bring us to the more important part of break-even analysis which is reflected in non-linear functions. The following diagram (Fig. 3.2) shows non-linear cost and revenue functions. In this diagram, the straight line TFC represents the total fixed cost which remains constant at OS level throughout the range we have taken under consideration (since we are discussing short - run cost curves). TC is the total cost curve which is obtained by adding together the total fixed and the total variable costs, i.e., the vertical distance between the X-axis and the TFC plus the vertical distance between the TFC and the TC. It follows that by deducting TFC from TC or by measuring the vertical distance between TFC and TC, we get the total variable cost. For example, in Fig. 3.2, when the level of output is OQ_3 total fixed cost is Q_3P (which is equal to OS) and total variable cost is PN and when these two are vertically added together ($Q_3P + PN$) we get Q_3N as the total cost. The curve TR shows the total proceeds from a sale which is known as 'total revenue' or 'TR' at different levels of output given the market price. TR – TC = TP which means total profits can be obtained by deducting the total cost from total revenue. Thus, at OQ_3 level of output Q_3R is the total revenue and Q_3N is the total cost, therefore, $Q_3R – Q_3N = NR$ is the total profit.

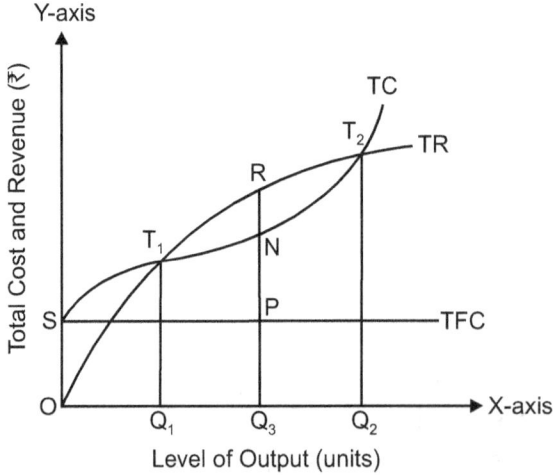

Fig. 3.2 : Break-even Point with Non-linear Function

In this diagram, (Fig. 3.2), we find that TC and TR curves are intersecting each other at two points, viz., T_1 and T_2. At both these points TR = TC. Since the point of intersection of TR and TC curves shows the break-even point, we get two break-even points in this case. T_1 is the lower break-even point and T_2 is the upper break-even point. The lower break- even point indicates the end of the range of output causing losses and the beginning of the range of the output yielding profits. The upper break-even point, on the other hand, indicates the end of profit-yielding range of output and the beginning of the range causing losses. All levels of output which are lower than OQ_1 are causing a loss and this loss is measured by the vertical distance between TC and TR curves. Similarly, all levels of output higher than OQ_2 would cause a loss as measured by the vertical distance between TC and TR at each level of output. It should therefore be clear that :

(1) At all levels below the lower break-even point as well as at all levels higher than the upper break-even point the firm is making an operational loss;

(2) At all levels of output between OQ_1 and OQ_2 or over the range between the two break-even points,the firm is earning an operational profit.

It follows that the firm's profitable range of output lies between OQ_1 and OQ_2 units of output. Since the vertical distance between the TR and TC curves over this range indicates total profits, OQ_3 level of output would be the profit-maximising output. This is because NR is the longest vertical straight line that can be drawn between the two curves.

Since the break-even analysis is a tool of practical importance, the analyst should first pre-test the actual behaviour of the cost and revenue functions and verify whether they are linear or non-linear. After ascertaining the constant or variable rate of change, one can draw the functions by imputing the actual values.

3.4.4 Applications of Break-even Analysis in Decision-making

The break-even chart is useful for empirically applying the same for determining the cost functions. Nowadays, the break-even analysis is widely used by company executives as a tool. Let us turn our attention to the usefulness of break - even analysis.

(1) Profit Projections : The empirical short-run profit function is a relatively stable because changes in costs are followed by changes in selling prices. Secondly, in adverse conditions efficiency demands a control over costs and this sort of earnestness compensates for the uncontrollable elements of costs.

(2) Passive Selling Costs : Under the competitive conditions of the present business environment, selling price and selling efforts are *not* normally adjusted to frequent changes in the short term demand for the firm's product. As such, the assumptions of constant selling price and passive selling cost proves to be more realistic and useful for short - run estimations.

(3) Expense Control : The intense competitions among firms makes it imperative for every firm to remain cost-effective. For a stricter control over costs, break-even analysis is useful. Of course, it is necessary to remember that all costs are not controllable; but there are controllable components which can be kept under limit.

While judging the usefulness of the break-even analysis, it is necessary to note that the break even analysis, in practice, does not concentrate on a single break-even point. It rather provides a flexible set of cost-projections and revenue predictions under the expected future conditions relevant for this analysis.

3.4.5 Limitations of Break-even Analysis

Besides the *first* limitation of break-even analysis noted above, there are few more limitations which need our attention. The *second* limitation is regarding the determination of the firm's cost curve. The cost function is difficult to establish in a static form. *Thirdly*, cost data are the by-product of the needs of financial accounting and as such follow rigid conventions in this regard. As a result, imputed costs are likely to be excluded; valuations and cost-allocations are arbitrary and for the timing of semi-investment expenditures, there is scope for discretion. *Fourthly*, the inclusion of selling costs impares the usefulness and accuracy of the estimate of total cost. This is because a high co-relation between output and selling cost does not necessarily mean a stable functional relationship. Again, selling cost have a long-run effect also and part of the selling costs needs to be allocated to long-run costs. Finally, when a firm has various plans, the estimation of costs becomes very difficult.

3.5 Risk Analysis and Decision-making

3.5.1 Concept of Risk

In a dynamic world in which we live, uncertainty about the future events is something like a hanging sword over our heads. Still we live a life that is enjoyable, at times tolerable, at times thrilling and at times challenging. Prof. Julian Simon has very lucidly compared a case of insurance to a case of gambling for explaining our ways of dealing with risks. When we insure our house or car or a business establishment, we pay a premium to the insurance company for shouldering the risk, on our behalf. As against this, someone who gambles in a casino, pays the casino for shifting the risk to him. How is it that in one case a man pays for transferring the risk on to the insurance company and in another he pays for 'buying' a risk ? There is no contradiction. In the first case, we want to avoid risk that is avoidable and in the other case, we want to accept the risk not only because it is thrilling but also because the reward for facing risk is sizeable.

What is risk then ? And how does it differ from uncertainty ? Insurable uncertainty is risk and non-insurable risk is uncertainty. This is easily said than understood. In any business, the most certain thing is the uncertainty of the future outcome of one's decisions. By keeping everything uncertain, one cannot carry on business for the simple reason that liquidity or safety of the business must be guarded and, at the same time, profitability must also be ensured, since profitability is the goal of a firm. The way out, therefore, is : wherever desirable and possible, minimise or avoid uncertainty and whatever it is unavoidable, accept it and prove your spirit of enterprise. Some types of uncertainty can be insured against, because those types can be forseen and measured by using quantitative techniques.

Let us therefore make the distinction between Risk and Uncertainty very clear : (a) In the first instance, risk is uncertainty to the extent it is measurable; (b) in case of risk, the probabilities of outcomes of a decision can be judged in advance at the time of making the decisions; and (c) the event that emerges as an outcome is often repetitive in nature, i.e., you can find out its frequency distribution. In other words, uncertainty is the unforseen possibility of a loss or a crisis in future. As against this, risk is the possibility of a loss or danger, occurring in future, that can be foreseen.

Physical risk, on account of accidents resulting in damage to property and equipment, risks in transit in case of import and export trade, transportation risks etc. are examples of risks; while the risks of emergence of a substitute, the risk of technology being obsolete or the risk arising out of cyclical fluctuations in demand are unforeseen and are matters of uncertainty.

In business, there are several factors affecting the degree of certainty or uncertainty involved in the cost and revenue forecasts adopted for the evaluation of various proposals. Some of the questions involving uncertainty in their answers are :

(a) What will be the total demand for the product proposed, in future ?

(b) Will the company be able to obtain the share in the market that is expressed as the anticipated share in the project proposal ?

(c) In a world of rapidly changing technology, to what extent will the demand for the product be affected due to new technological developments ?

(d) In what direction will the material costs in future change : upwards or downwards and to what extent ?

(e) Will our capital asset proposed to be acquired become obsolete or outdated and, if yes, to what extent ?

3.5.2 Expected Value Computation

Expected value is a concept employed in statistical analysis. It is a weighted average approach that involves multiplying each possible outcome in a situation with its probability to arrive at the expected outcome.

Computation of Expected Value :

(1) Familiarise yourself with situation at hand. Before enumerating the possible outcomes and probabilities make sure to have an overall grasp of the situation in which an outcome is generated.

(2) Enumerate all of the possible outcomes. It helps to make a list of all the possible outcomes in the given situation.

(3) Determine the probability of each outcome.

(4) Calculate the expected value. The expected value is calculated using the outcomes and their probabilities.

(5) Understand the implications of the expected value calculation.

3.5.3 Risk Management through Insurance, Diversification, Hedging

(1) Risk Management through Insurance : 'Insurance' means indemnity or protection against risk of loss. 'Insurance' is a popular means in business to protect from uncertainties.

"Insurance is a co-operative device to spread the loss caused by a particular risk over a number of persons, who are exposed to it and who agree to insure themselves against the risk.

Insurance is like a sort of provision which a wise man makes against unfortunate happenings.

Features/Characteristics of Insurance :

(a) Insurance' is a contract between Insurer and Insured.

(b) Insurance is a contract of 'Indemnity'.

(c) The contract is embodied in a document. This document is known as a policy.

(d) The amount paid by insured to insurer as a consideration is known as 'Premium'.

Importance / Role of Insurance :

(a) **Safe Business Operations :** Insurance protects and safeguards the interest of individuals and businessmen in their business operations. It gives them safety and creates confidence in their minds. This, indirectly, brings expansion of business activities.

(b) **Diversification of Risks :** Insurance results in diversification of risk among specialised professional agencies called Insurance Companies.

(c) **Security :** Insurance creates a sense of security and confidence among all sections of the society.

(d) **Promotes Rate of Savings :** Insurance promotes rate of savings and investment and leads to capital formation in an economy.

(e) **Better Security for Loans :** Insurance provides better security for loans and advances offered by banks.

(f) **Expansion of Commercial Activities :** Insurance brings safety in storage and transportation and this lead to expansion of commercial activities.

(g) **Healthy Investment Climate in the Country :** Insurance creates proper investment climate in the country.

(h) **Accelerating the Industrialisation Process :** Insurance it accelerates the process of industrialisation in the country.

(2) Risk Management through Diversification : In finance, diversification means reducing risks by investing in variety of assets.

Diversification is a corporate strategy to increase sales volume for new products and new markets. Diversification can be expanding into a new segment of an industry that the business is already in, or investing in a promising business outside the scope of the existing business to reduce the business uncertainties.

(3) Hedging : A hedge is an investment position intended to offset potential losses / gains that may be incurred by a companion investment.

A hedge can be constructed from many types of financial instruments including stocks, exchange-traded funds, insurance, forward contracts, swaps, options, many types of over the counter and derivative products and future contracts.

3.5.4 Decision Tree Analysis

Another important tool of analysing uncertain events likely to occur in future but base upon our present decisions is preparing a decision tree. It indicates the sequence of events mapped in the form resembling branches of a tree.

Many uncertain likelihoods pose of problem of judging and assessing. However, it is always better to put things on paper and then weight the various options likely to emerge. For example, consider the choices a student faces. Let us suppose that he is considering two options : taking a degree in management or a degree in law. Fig. 3.3 considers these two options and expected events sequentially. If you go through all the branches of the tree you will realise the various alternatives available, choices to be made and consequences that are likely to follow. You will also realise that if the analysis of the student's problem is made like this, it enables him to arrive at a decision in a systematic and rational manner.

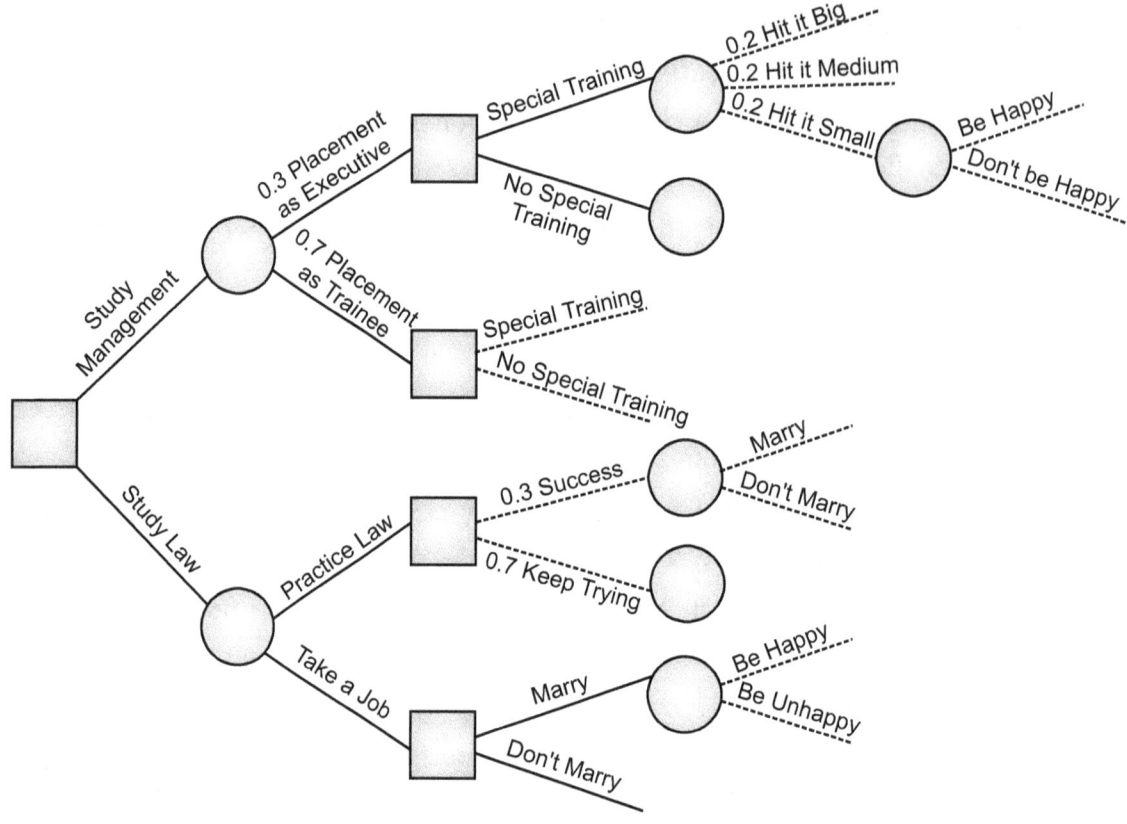

Fig. 3.3 : The Decision Tree

A firm, let us suppose, faces three projects, i.e. 3 branches. Each branch will have 3 branches of high, medium and low demand. Each of these will have a corresponding probability multiplier (0.3, 0.7 etc. shown in Fig. 3.3). From the data of cash flows and probabilities, we can get present value of expected returns in each of these cases. By calculating profitability index we can rank the proposals in order of profitability.

Key Steps in Constructing a Decision Tree :

(1) **Identify the Alternatives :** When a proposal is received, proposals regarding alternatives can be summoned from other departments, or from R and D or from the market analysis department etc.

(2) **Prepare a Layout :** Once the alternatives involved in the investment decision become clear, the structural layout of the decision tree can be formulated.

(3) **Obtain Necessary Data :** For finding out the estimates of alternative cash flows the probabilities thereof, a great deal of statistical data are required to be collected from a number of sources.

(4) **Evaluate the Alternatives :** Alternatives which are desirable should be taken up for evaluation and then one can proceed to apply criteria for evaluating each alternative.

(5) **Identify the Proposal and the Alternatives :** First the proposal should be exactly defined and then the alternatives also should be carefully drawn; and understood in terms of fund requirements and sources available.

(6) **Display the Decision Tree** : The graphic display of the decision tree has to be prepared. Each alternative is assigned a probability. This is called branching of probabilities.

(7) **Find Expected Values :** The PVS of cash flows are then to be ascertained; and then find the expected values of future returns.

(8) **Take the Decision :** On the basis of profitability indices, one can take the decision.

Decision-making under conditions of risk and uncertainty is becoming increasingly of vital importance. On the one hand, the cost of business risk is growing. New set of environmental regulations, judicial attitudes, ever-changing nature of technology and a global competition have increased the cost of business risk. This is because of the fact that losses cannot be recovered from product prices due to competition. Nor can risk insurance be available for a wide variety of risks. Business risks rooted in a variety of variables like prices, volume of sales, advertising effectiveness, intensity of competition, raw material costs, manufacturing costs, energy costs, rates of inflation, etc. can hardly be insured against. They then attain the nature of uncertainties. On the other hand, the shareholders and other stakeholders are understandably not fully prepared to bear the uncertainty. They may be risk-averse or risk-neutral or risk-preferred. The investment decision under such circumstances becomes still more difficult.

We noted a number of ways for risk and uncertainty adjustment. The extent of risk can be measured with the help of (i) standard deviation, (ii) coefficient of variation, and (iii) a combination of decision tree and standard deviation. Still some critical variables from the point of view of the project under consideration remain exposed to uncertainty. For this purpose, sensitivity analysis is undertaken to judge how far the variables (like wages, prices, etc. noted above) important for a particular decision are sensitive to uncertainty and risk. The values of these variables may change or even new variables may creep in. The possibilities of such happenings are considered in such an analysis. Sensitivity analysis indicates critical variables and assumptions, shows where the management's efforts should be focused and identifies the areas where more attention should be paid, even after the project is sanctioned.

It is, therefore, advisable to build a risk management capability by (i) creating awareness of the company's interest throughout the organisation, (ii) instituting a built-in structure of risk management, and (iii) generating an alertness regarding new pressures coming in with fresh uncertainties and risks. After all, the management of risk and uncertainties has got to be a collective endeavour.

Questions for Discussion

1. Explain : (a) Opportunity Cost, (b) Marginal Cost, (c) Incremental Cost, (d) Sunk Cost.

2. What is Cost Volume Profit Analysis ?

3. Explain the Concept of Break Even Point.

4. Explain Risk Management through Insurance, Diversification and Hedging.

5. Explain : Decision Tree Analysis.

6. Explain the Classification and Analysis of Costs.

7. Write short notes on :

    (A) Cost Concept.

    (B) Concept of Risk.

    (C) Expected Value Computation.

☆☆☆

MONEY AND CAPITAL MARKETS IN INDIA

4.1 Indian Financial System

Money is a claim on real resources and facilitates the allocation of real resources whichare going to decide, direct and foster the composition as well as the size of the basket of goods and services that an economy would be able to produce. These monetary resources which are claims on real resources (like machinery and equipment, fuel and power or man-power) are broadly referred to as *finance* and are required by individual households and the Government for buying income-generating assets; by firms for purchasing equipment and machines and factory-buildings and also for paying wages and buying raw materials etc. Trading firms require finance for purchase of goods they are dealing in or stocking in their warehouses. In the agricultural sector, funds are required for short-term, medium-term and long-term to meet the farmer's needs of working capital or of purchasing livestock, implements and agricultural machinery or for digging wells and buying additional land etc., respectively. The Government too, needs finance for buying goods and services and for making a number of investments which are planned under development programmes.

(A) The Structure of the Indian Financial System :

The term Financial System covers a wide range of institutions and individuals who are engaged in borrowing and lending or demanding and supplying of funds. The structure of this system refers to the form in which the whole architecture of the system stands. Obviously, the components of this architecture and their inter-linkages will have to be taken into account, a task which we are dealing within the next few pages. Initially, however, we shall try to look at the model of the system and its parts.

Once we understand that this system is concerned with activities connected with the give-and-take of finance, we would realise that there could be more than one angle from which we can view the system. One way of classifying the financial system would be as follows :

(1) Industrial Finance : This type of finance is required by industry and trade for meeting their short-term and long-term needs of funds. Obviously, they must include the needs of working capital as well as those for long-term investments.

(2) Agricultural Finance : Financial needs of agriculture are different both in terms of quantities as well as durations. The conditions governing them are also different. Agricultural finance is classified into short-term, medium-term and long-term finance. Such finance is required by agriculture and allied activities like animal husbandry, forestry, fisheries, poultry and so on.

(3) Development Finance : This type of finance is required by all sectors including agriculture and industries and is characterised by the long-term investment needs.

(4) Government Finance : The Government raises its resources through tax and non-tax revenue plus other sources of income. However, the Government also needs short-term funds for overcoming the problem of gaps in payments and receipts, since the latter tend to concentrate at the end of the financial year. Long-term funds, on the other hand, are raised through public borrowings for purposes of investment.

(5) External Sector Finance : Borrowings and lendings also arise in the external sector of the economy. These include import credit, export credit, loans for investments in foreign countries and financial needs of a multiplicity of activities requiring foreign exchange loans for education, travel, transport, insurance etc.

One way of looking at the structure is as shown in Fig. 4.1

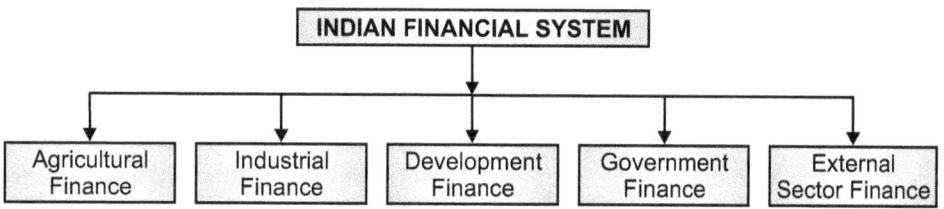

Fig. 4.1 : The Structure of the Indian Financial System – Classificatory View

An alternative and functionally more useful way to look at the structure is to look into the constituents of the Indian Financial System. This can be done basically from the supply and demand sides. In the various segments of the financial system, there are various institutions like banks and insurance companies which mobilise savings and supply them to the needy.

(a) As such, on the supply side, we have Banks, Insurance Companies, mutual funds, Non-banking companies and the Indigenous bankers, development banks and other institutions of the money and capital markets.

(b) On the Demand side, we have the borrowers like the Government, Corporate bodies, small-scale industries, trading firms and individual investors.

Figure 4.2 depicts this structure.

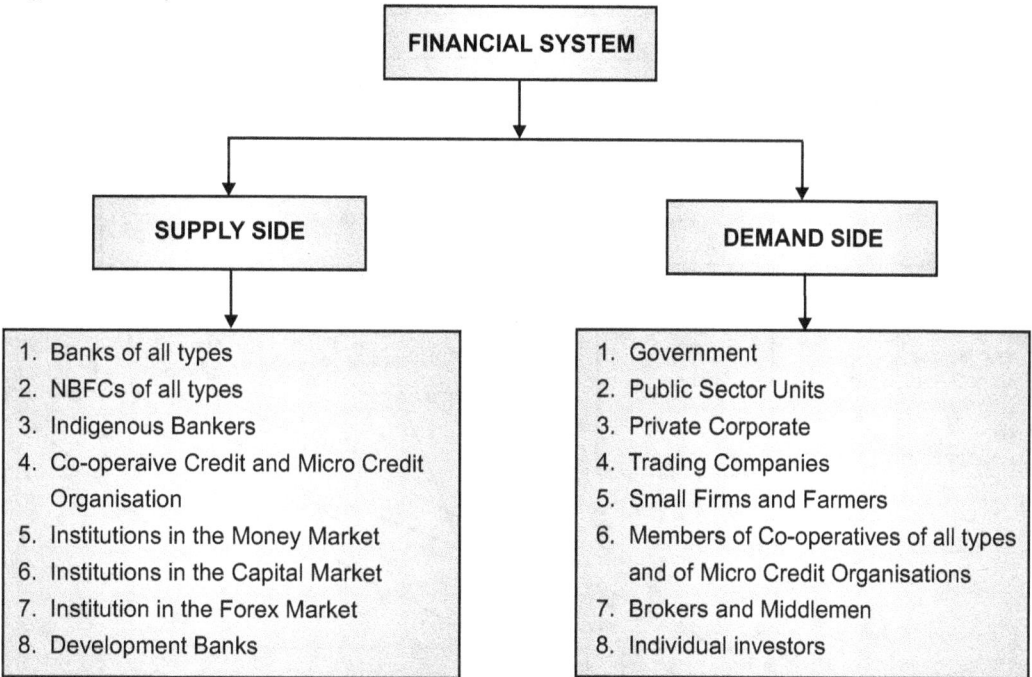

Fig. 4.2 : The Structure of the Financial System – Viewed as Financial Markets

(B) Constituents of the Indian Financial System :

All constituents of the financial system together make the structure of the system. However, for the purpose of our study of the financial markets, we have to take a narrower perspective as we want to take a closer look. Again, those who enter the markets as borrowers are not dealers in funds they have their own roles to play, as producers or traders or other functionaries. Therefore, for our present purpose, the subject-matter being financial institutions, we shall concentrate on those institutions only which are dealing in finance and credit instruments. These are the institutions which constitute the financial system proper.

As noted in the beginning, the monetary resources are claims on real resources. But money is also the most liquid asset and as such it meets the need for liquidity. Therefore, it becomes necessary to distinguish between money or funds needed for liquidity and funds needed for production/purchase of real resources i.e. capital. The former requirement is one of short-term while the latter is the long-term requirement. This is the basic difference between the money market and the capital market. Capital market is the market for medium and long-term borrowings and lendings; while the money market is for short-term borrowings and lendings. The financial system of any country must, therefore, meet all these requirements. As such, money and capital markets are the basic constituents of the Indian financial system. Fig. 4.3 gives a broad outline of these constituents.

The diagrammatic representation (Fig. 4.3) shows the constituents of the financial system which we are going to study in detail, in the present book. The subject-matter of our study is as depicted in bare outline in Fig. 4.3.

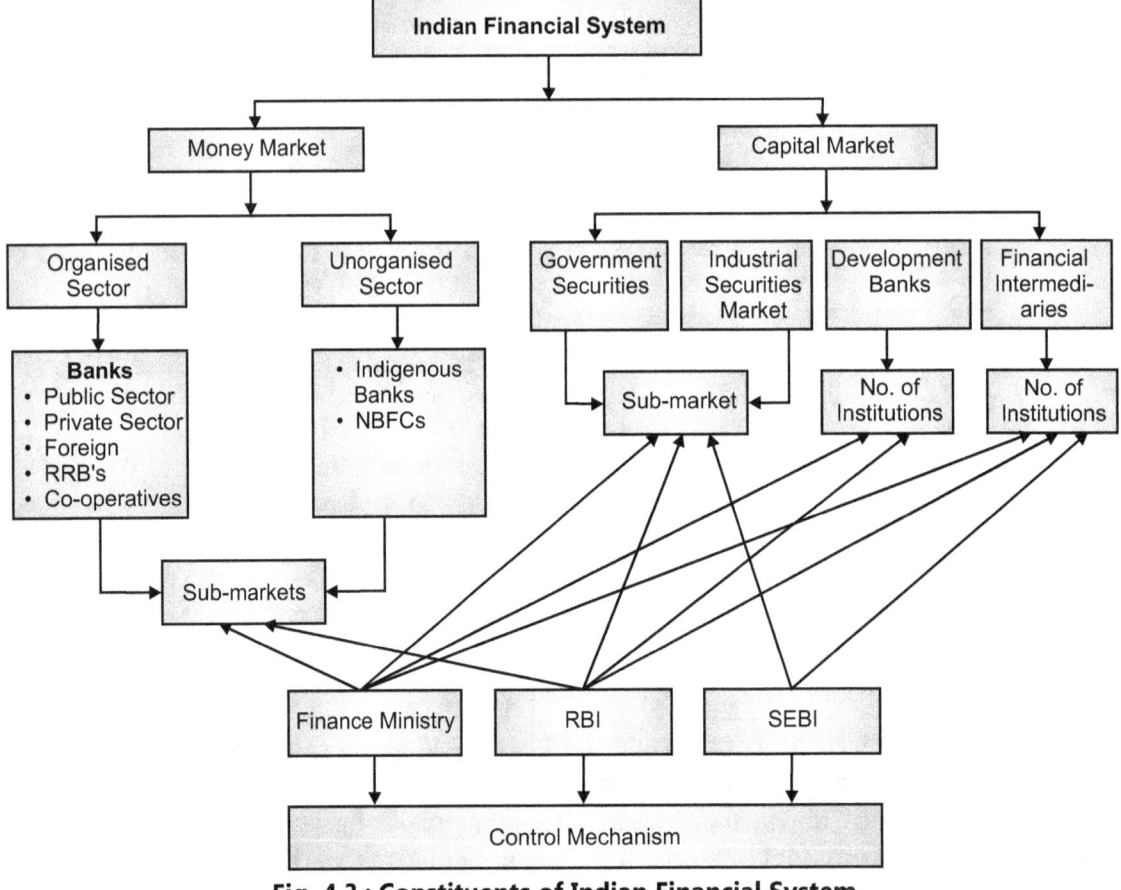

Fig. 4.3 : Constituents of Indian Financial System

(C) Role of the Financial System in Economic Development :

Financial markets in India, as in other countries, perform an important function of mobilisation of savings and channelising them into the most productive uses. Well developed money and Government securities markets help central banks to implement and effectively conduct monetary policy with the use of market-based instruments. Well developed financial markets are also required for creating a balanced financial system in which both financial markets and financial institutions play important roles. This point is indicated by the recent crises in East Asia, where lack of well developed money and capital markets was one of the major causes of crises. During times of financial stress and strain, there is likely to be a large demand for liquidity, which only deep and liquid markets can provide. Besides, it is necessary to have well developed markets to derive appropriate reference rates for pricing financial assets. Again, in a developing economy, capital formation is of crucial importance.

The immediate precondition of capital formation is investment. Investment comprises of private investment and Government investment. Since Government investment is determined by the deliberate decision of the Government we need not go into those details at this juncture. However, the reasons responsible for the low rate of capital formation can be discussed by taking into account the fact that capital formation depends upon savings, on the institutions mobilising these savings and on the investment of the savings. If these three stages of capital formation fail to operate properly, the rate of capital formation must remain low.

The savings which are made and mobilised are *supplied* for the formation of physical capital; while those who are engaged in the creation of this physical capital are the people who *demand* these savings. The entrepreneurs and the producers of capital goods, therefore, operate from the demand side while the individuals and institutions effecting and mobilising savings are on the supply side. Let us take a look at these general reasons for low capital formation from these two sides first.

Let us bear in mind that capital formation involves three steps : (i) saving, (ii) mobilising of savings, and (iii) investment of these savings. Difficulties on the supply side are concerned with step no. 1, i.e. saving, or the supply side. Difficulties or reasons from the demand side are associated with the third step, i.e., investment of savings. The major difficulties associated with the second step are concerned with underdeveloped money and capital markets.

In view of whatever we have said above, it should be possible to spell out the *role of the financial system* which consists of various financial markets. Since the financial system basically comprises of two parts : the Money Market and the Capital Market, both interlinked but having different functions to perform, it would be desirable to understand the role of both these markets separately and remember that together they perform the role of the financial system, as a whole.

The basic difference between the capital and the money market is that the former is a market for investible funds i.e. savings which can be made available (and are borrowed) for the building up of real or physical capital i.e. for purchase of machinery, for construction of factory buildings, for the construction of roads, bridges etc. (by the Government); while the latter (money market) is a market for liquidity i.e. cash or something close to cash. When people save, and make their savings available for investment through financial institutions, their savings get locked up for long periods. But if they need money for some reasons before their own investment can be converted back into money, they can turn to this market.

4.2 Role and Functions of Money Markets

(A) Meaning and Nature of a Money Market :

In the money market, the short-term surplus investible funds at the disposal of financial and other institutions and individuals are bid by the borrowers comprising institutions and individuals, and also by the Government. The money market, thus, meets the short-term requirements of borrowers and provides liquidity to the lenders.

Though we defined the money market as a 'Centre' for dealings in monetary assets, students of Economics are familiar with the term 'Market'. Though, in common language, market refers to a particular place, in Economics, it does not refer to a place. A market, in Economics, refers to a particular commodity and it emphasizes the establishment of contact between the buyers and the sellers of that commodity. In the same way, money market, too, does not refer to a particular locality. It refers to the whole of a region in which the buyers and sellers of 'Money' come into close contact with one another.

We must, however, hasten to steer clear of the misconception that is likely to surround the term 'Money' in this context. The commodity traded in the money market is not legal tender money in the form of currency notes and coins. The traded commodity is the rights to money and capital in the form of credit such as a bill of exchange.

Money market is, therefore, the market in which short-term funds are borrowed and lend. *Madden* and *Naddler* have defined money market as, *"A mechanism through which short-term funds are loaned and borrowed and through which a larger part of financial transactions of a particular country or of the world are cleared."*

This definition will serve the purpose of understanding the meaning of the term Money Market. In the first place, the 'Trade' in the money market refers to the activities of borrowing and lending. In case of money, its sale and purchase always mean lending and borrowing. Secondly, the transactions in the money market are limited to short-term funds only. Many writers do not think it necessary to make a distinction between short-term and long-term borrowings, and include only the former in the money market. They consider both short-term and long-term borrowings and loans as the function of the money market. But, as a matter of fact, short-term bills which form the major portion of the money market are as good as money in the sense that they can be readily converted into money. They are therefore, known as, near-money. Money being the most liquid form of assets, this test of liquidity (or easy convertibility into liquidity) becomes a confirmative test of what should be included in the Money Market. Since only the short-term claims to money can satisfy this test, long-term funds need to be excluded from the money market. The long-term borrowings and lendings, therefore, should form the capital market rather than the money market. Thirdly, the money market does not refer to any locality but it refers to the transactions of a whole country or even of the whole world. This characteristic needs to be emphasized because, in practice, we do use geographical names like London Money Market, New York Money Market or Bombay Money Market. The transactions in all these money market, however, are world-wide. The only thing is that these transactions are channeled through these centres. Finally, the borrowers at the money market are the traders, speculators, brokers and producers of various commodities as well as Government and other institutional borrowers. The lenders include commercial banks, insurance companies, other finance companies and the Central Bank of the country. The institutions enumerated here as lenders, may also borrow from one another; they especially borrow from the Central Bank.

(B) Scope and Operations of a Money Market :

Some writers do not distinguish capital market from the money market. But, by applying the test of liquidity, as we have seen, it is possible to separate the two. The distinction between the money market and the capital market can be made clear on the following counts :

(1) Market of Short-term Funds : Money market refers to the market of short-term funds. The short-term refers to a period which is, usually, ninety days but may extend to a maximum of hundred and eighty days. The capital market, on the other hand, refers to the market for long-term funds where the period of borrowing exceeds six months and may extend to twenty-five years or more.

(2) Dealing in Various Credit Instruments : The money market deals in credit instruments like bills of exchange, treasury bills, and short-term government bonds. The capital market, on the other hand, refers to long-term securities such as shares and debentures of business companies and industrial concerns; bonds and debentures of semi-government institutions like autonomous boards, corporations; etc., and long-term promissory notes and bonds of the Government. The capital market is actually of two types : The market for new capital in which stocks and shares of new companies are bought and sold, and the market for old capital which refers to the stock exchanges where stocks and shares of old companies are bought and sold.

(3) Central Position of Commercial Bank : In the money market, Commercial banks occupy the central position in the sense that the various constituents of the money market approach the commercial banks for accommodation. On the other hand, in a capital market, the commercial banks may enter as buyers of stock exchange securities, i.e. papers dealt with the capital market. They may do this for their own investments.

(4) Position of the Central Bank : The Central Bank occupies a key position in the money market. As a residual source of supply of funds, it occupies this position. The money market can obtain funds from the Central Bank in two ways: either by borrowings or by sale of securities.

(5) Organised Sector and Unorganised Sector : In India, the money market comprises of an organised sector and an unorganised sector. In the unorganised sector, we have the indigenous bankers and money-lenders. The line of demarcation between the money and the capital markets in this sector is blurred; because, hundis do not clearly show whether they represent genuine trade activities or not.

It must, however, be noted that though a line of demarcation between the money market and the capital market is drawn for purposes of analysis, they two have a close relationship. The close relationship between the money market and the capital market will be discussed, in detail, in the next chapter. However, we may remember, here, the following points :

(a) The capital market and especially, the old capital market seeks financial assistance from the money market, or depends upon the money market for its short-term financial needs.

(b) Many of the constituents of both the markets are the same, i.e. institutions dealing in the money market papers also deal in the capital market papers.

(C) Features of a Developed and Underdeveloped Money Market :

For a fuller understanding of the nature of the money market, it is necessary to describe the characteristic features of a Developed Money Market. In every country, some type of money market must be in existence but these markets may be in different stages of development. Once we enumerate the characteristics of a well-developed money market, it will be obvious that the absence of any one or more of these necessary features will render the relevant money market under-developed.

Features of a Developed Money Market :

These basic *characteristics or features of a Developed Money Market* are as listed below :

(1) Existence of a Well-Organised Commercial Banking System : As we have already noted, the Commercial banks occupy a pivotal position in the money market. They are the most important suppliers of credit to the various borrowers of a money market. Their investment policies and changes therein, obviously, have an important influence upon the flows of short-term funds. Similarly, as the Commercial banks are intimately connected with the Central Bank, they also serve as an important link between the Central Bank on the one hand and the various sub-markets of the money market on the other hand. The elasticity of the supply of short-term funds as well as the effectiveness of the regulation of credit by the Central Bank depend upon the existence of a well organised commercial banking system. If Banking is partly organised and partly unorganised as is, for example, in India, the smooth functioning of the money market is not possible. Such a money market, then, becomes an underdeveloped money market.

(2) Existence of Central Bank : The existence of a Central Bank is the second pre-requisite for the effective functioning of a money market. The existence, however, should not be a mere legal one; but it should be effective. In times of difficulty, the Central Bank is expected to come to the rescue of the Commercial banks and the money market as a whole. When there is a shortage of liquidity, the Central Bank can enable the money market to increase its liquidity by providing rediscounting facility to the constituents of the money market. This facility enables the constituents to convert their eligible bills into cash. Similarly, by its function, known as open market operations, the Central Bank can absorb surplus cash by selling securities in the market, and can increase liquidity by buying securities and rediscounting of bills and sale and purchase of securities, influences the flows of funds at the money market. In fact, the regulation of these flows is necessary and significant part of the functioning of the Central Bank. It is this role of the Central Bank that institutes it in the position of the leader of the money market.

(3) Adequate Supply of Proper Credit Instruments : A country may have a well-organised Commercial Banking system as well as a Central Bank equipped with the necessary powers of control and regulation, and still there may be no Developed Money Market worth the name. Such a state may arise if proper instruments of credit are not available in adequate quantities. An effective and smooth functioning of the money market, therefore, requires a continuous and sizeable supply of negotiable instruments of credit such as bills of exchange, treasury bills, short-term Government bonds, and so on. The demand for these papers comes from the dealers in these papers who borrow from the commercial banks and purchase these papers. Therefore, alongwith the availability of these credit instruments, the presence of dealers and brokers for these papers, is also a necessary condition. The competition among these brokers is the very life of the money market. The availability of an adequate amount of short-term assets, and the presence of dealers and brokers in these assets, therefore, becomes another necessary condition for the evolution of Developed Money Market.

(4) Existence of a Number of Sub-markets : Another condition for the evolution of a well-organised money market is the existence of a number of sub-markets. Each sub-market, as we have seen, is specialised in a particular type of short-term asset. Each sub-market differs from every other in respect of nature of the asset and period of its maturity. Many such sub-markets, if they are well-developed, provide a broad base for the money market. The London Money Market which is probably the most developed money market in the world contains a number of sub-markets like the Call Loan Market, the Commercial Bill Market, the Treasury Bill Market, the Foreign Exchange Market etc. The larger the number of such sub-markets, the broader and more developed will be the structure of the money market.

In connection with the existence of a number of sub-markets, it must be emphasized that the mere existence of the sub-markets is not enough. These sub-markets should consist of a large number of dealers, with an effective competition among themselves. These dealers should have an access to adequate funds for dealing in the respective assets of the sub-markets. Similarly, all these sub-markets should not be isolated or independent but should be intimately related to each other to form an integrated structure of the money market. This leads to a free flow of funds from one sub-market to another and, thus, enables equalisation of interest rates being established in different segments of the money market. The comparability of various rates of interest in the money market and the influence of changes in one sub-market upon the rates prevailing in every other sub-market, are important characteristics of a Well-Developed Money Market.

In the absence of all the characteristics of the sub-markets, the money market will be underdeveloped. Isolation of the sub-markets, loose connection amongst them or lack of any connection between interest rates prevailing in different sub-markets would, therefore, be the characteristics of an Underdeveloped Money Market.

(5) Availability of Funds : The extent and magnitude of dealings in the various sub-markets are directly dependent on the availability of funds for financing the dealings. Obviously, therefore, ample funds become a condition for the smooth functioning of the money market. Usually, these funds come from within the same country, but, in the most developed money markets like the London and New York Money Markets, funds are attracted from all over the world.

(6) Other Factors : The evolution of a developed money market depends on a number of other factors not directly connected with the money market. Thus, the development of internal trade and commerce leads to an increase in the volume of internal bills of exchange, and these bills are important credit instruments of the money market. A growth of international trade, in the same way helps the money market by; augmenting the supply of international bills of exchange. Industrial development increases the supply of stocks and causes the emergence of a Developed Stock Market. Since Stock Brokers are active in the money market, industrial development indirectly helps the development of money market. Besides these factors, political stability, a sense of a security regarding business and property, and the economic stability are other factors which contribute to the development of the money market.

All these characteristics of a Developed Money Market, if found together, make a full developed money market. Such money market are, however, few and far between the London Money Market can be cited as an example of a fully developed money market. All the characteristics may not be found together, but if most of them are present, the money market can be called a fairly, developed money market. It follows, therefore that, an absence of some of these characteristics will render the money market under-developed.

Features of an Underdeveloped Money Market :

The characteristics of a Developed Money Market, we noted so far, will underline the association between development of the money market and the development of the Economy.

A Developed Money Market is to be found only in an advanced economy. Therefore, the features of the Developed Money Market, enumerated in the preceding paragraphs, are the features of a money market in an advanced economy. While describing these features, we have noted that an absence of these features will make the money market underdeveloped. Such an underdeveloped money market is to be found in an underdeveloped economy. It will, therefore, be superfluous to describe, in detail, the characteristic features of a money market in a developing economy. However, for clarity of understanding, it will be desirable to summarise the special features of a money market in a developing economy. They are as under :

(1) Loosely Organised Banking System : In developing economies, the modern banking sector suffers from a number of short-comings. In the first instance, its coverage is limited to certain areas only. The number of unbanked areas, in other words, is very large. Secondly, the attitudes of the Commercial banks in developing economies are traditional, cautious, and therefore, they lack the initiative and inventiveness that are expected of them. Thirdly, there may be different types of banks working independently, without any connections among themselves. For instance, the Joint Stock banks, Foreign Exchange banks Co-operative banks may be, individually, well-developed. But, at the same time, each type of banks may limit its field of activities to some function in the money market. Since there is no connection between any two banks, the influence on the money market remains imperfect.

(2) Existence of an Unorganised Sector : Many times, there exists an unorganised sector associated with the money market. The Indigenous bankers in India are an example of this type. There is a large number of Individual bankers and money-lenders each participating in short-term credit. But none of them is, in any way, connected with any other banker or the Central Bank of the country.

(3) Lack of Proper Credit Instruments : In a developing economy, since trade and commerce are not organised on modern lines, the supply of credit instruments is both inadequate and heterogeneous. As the volume of credit instruments is the direct result of growth of trade and commerce, it is limited in a developing economy. There are fewer bills of exchange, finance bills and other short-term paper, as compared to an advanced economy. The heterogeneity, on the other hand, refers to the multiplicity of types of bills. The practices, periods, rates of interest etc. that govern the bills are different. Hence, it becomes difficult to speak of a single Bill Market in an under-developed money market.

(4) Multiplicity of Rates of Interest : If the sub-markets are closely related to one another, the interest rates tend to be comparable in various sub-markets. In an under-developed economy, on the other hand, the sub-markets are not related and so, there are wide variations in rates charged at various markets. For example, the Central Banking Enquiry Committee (1929) describes the state of affairs in India, at that time, in the following words: "The fact that a call rate of 3/4 %, a hundi rate of 3 %, a Bank Rate of 4 %, a bazaar rate of small traders of 6.3/8 %, and a Calcutta Bazaar rate for bills of small traders of 10%, can exist simultaneously, indicate an extraordinary sluggishness of the movement of credit between various markets". This quotation so aptly describes the characteristic that it needs no further comments.

(5) Inadequate Funds : Another feature of the money market in a developing economy is its lack of resources. For one thing, the lack of resources is the result of a low level of savings which characterise the developing economy. Secondly, whatever savings are generated, find their way into traditional channels of investment like gold, land, money-lending and so on. Thirdly, because many of the institutions of the money market are new and yet to be firmly established, these do not command the confidence of the people.

(6)   Limited Development of Sub-markets : A look at the sub-markets which constitute the London or the New York Money Market, discussed in a subsequent section, will enable the readers to understand the multiplicity of sub-markets in a Developed Money Market. In contrast to such money markets, the money markets in developing economies have a smaller number of sub-markets. Further, whatever sub-markets are in existence, are not fully developed. The Bill market does not have an adequate supply of bills. It is not closely connected with other sub-markets. Discount houses are conspicuous by their absence. Brokers are limited and mostly guided by cautious outlooks. The Commercial banks are extra anxious about their liquidity. In this way, under-developed sub-markets become a feature of a money market in a developing economy.

(D) Role and Functions of Money Market :

In a modern economy, the money market occupies a position of great importance. The process of modernisation has gone through the stages of fundamental changes in commerce and industry. The money market has gradually evolved to the position of well-developed and integrated market along with the evolution of commerce and industry. The development of commerce and industry on one hand and the development of the money market, on the other hand, have therefore, interdependence in the sense that the development of the one has influenced and helped the development of the other. Since we are examining the importance of the money market, we shall concentrate upon how a money market influences the functioning of the economy in general, and commerce and industry in particular.

The functions of a developed money market can be summarised as follows :

(1)   Finance for Industry and Commerce : The money market plays an important role in providing finance to trade and industry. The finance bills, bills of exchange and other instruments of credit are of great help to industries in meeting their requirements of working capital. Similarly, the rates of interest prevailing at the money market influence the long-term rates prevailing at the Capital Market. This interdependence between the money market and the capital market must be borne in mind while judging the importance of the money market in the development of industries. The development of the capital market is vital for the development of industry but the former depends upon the existence of a well-organised money market. This is how the money market and the capital market together, add to the economic development of a country.

The provision of finance to trade and commerce through the money market is too obvious to need a detailed explanation. Internal trade-especially the wholesale trade and international trade are largely based on a system of credit purchases which are made possible by bills of exchange. The emergence and spread of bills of exchange, in turn, depends upon the existence of well-developed Discount markets, Acceptance Houses, and Rediscounting facilities provided by the money market.

(2) Short-term Investment Opportunities for Banks and other Financial Institutions : Commercial banks raise their resources in various ways; but the most important item on the side of their liabilities is deposits from the public. Taking into account the commitment of the bankers to pay back the deposits in accordance with the terms that go with the nature of the deposits, it becomes necessary for these banks to maintain adequate amounts of cash balances with themselves. For this reason, short-term investments attain special importance from the point of view of Commercial banks. The Call Loan market and the Bill Market provide such an opportunity to the Commercial banks. Thus, the money market helps the Commercial banks to employ their funds in short-term Near-money assets without foregoing liquidity altogether. In fact, these very assets constitute the second line of defence of the banks and enable the bankers to reconcile liquidity with profitability. The same is true of other financial institutions as well. If they need opportunities for short-term investments, such opportunities are provided by the money market.

(3) Central Bank's Functioning More Effective : The money market is of great help to the Central Bank in making its (Central Bank's) functioning more effective. This is due to a number of reasons. In the first place, the state of the money market and the short-term rates of interest prevailing at the money market serve as a barometer of the Monetary and Banking conditions in the country. This enables the Central Bank to formulate a proper Monetary policy. Secondly, for effecting controls over credit and money flows, it is enough to control the most sensitive sub-markets when there exists a well-integrated money market. The effect of the Bank's control would then spread to other sub-markets and, thus, the task of the Central Banks becomes easier. Though it is true that the Central Bank can function even in the absence of a money market, its functioning is more smooth when there exists a well-organised money market.

(4) Money Market and the Government : The money market helps the Government in two ways : (i) By selling Treasury bill, the Government can raise short-term funds. In the absence of a money market, the Government will have to borrow from the Central Bank, or, it will have to print additional currency notes. Either of these methods causes a rise in prices.

Raising resources by the sale of treasury bills is, therefore, a better alternative. This is one way in which the money market helps the Government. (ii) Even for a long-term borrowings of the Government, the money market is helpful. The short-term rates of interest at the money market have their influence on long-term rates at the capital market. The conditions at the capital market should be favourable to the Government when it wants to enter the capital market for long-term borrowings. By influencing conditions at the money market, it is possible to make the conditions at the capital market favourable through the rates of interest.

(5) Short-term Deficits and Surpluses : Various players in the financial system are demanding and supplying short-term funds. In the absence of well-developed money market, there would arise a mismatch between demand and supply. Similarly, there would arise market imperfections, in the sense that different rates of interest may prevail at different sections/segments of the economy. This is an indication of imperfections in terms of lack of mobility of funds, ignorance of market conditions or bottle-necks in terms of legal or other barriers. Money market provides an equilibrating mechanism for levelling out the short-term surpluses and deficits by removing market imperfections.

(6) Competitive Price : The users of short-term funds have a right to get those funds at a realistic and fair price. Money market creates an access to short-term funds for the users of these funds. This ensures competitive rates of interest which are realistic and reasonable.

4.3 Composition of Money Market

The organised part of the Indian Money Market initially consists of the four institutions or components, viz., (A) the Call Money Market; (B) the Bill Market; (C) the Collateral Loan Market; and (D) the Treasury Bill Market. Let us see some more details about these components of the Indian Money Market.

(A) The Call Money Market :

This is the most important and sensitive part of the money market. It can also be called 'The Inter-bank call money market'. In this market, the banks borrow and lend money to each other. It operates in Mumbai, Kolkata and, to some extent, in Chennai. Whenever a bank is short of cash, it borrows from another bank having surplus cash.

The functioning of this market is smooth. The lending and borrowing in this market is done without any security. This enables the banks to replenish their cash or liquid money as and when required, without touching their real assets. The borrowings are normally for a few days and no collateral security is insisted.

Other activities which form a part and parcel of the call money market are the lendings and borrowings of brokers and dealers in shares. Whenever they required accommodation for a short period, they step into the call money market. Large business houses and financiers also lend their surplus money in the call money market, either directly or through agents. All those who invest their surplus money in this market can call their money back in the shortest possible time. In fact, that is why it is called as the "call money market".

The State Bank of India does not participate in this market. But the volume of transactions in this market is fairly large and varies from season to season, but does not exceed ₹ 70-75 crores. The roles of the different banks, participating in this market as borrowers or lenders, change according to their liquidity position and requirement of cash. Similarly, the number of banks participating in this market changes. It has changed through time also. For example, before 1956, mainly foreign exchange banks used to borrow from or lend to this market. The reason was that their assets were comparatively more liquid and could be readily called back. But now, all banks have started participating in this market.

Similarly, the rates of interest prevalent in this market before 1960 hardly ever rose above the Bank Rate because banks could borrow without any restrictions from the Reserve Bank. But after that, as restrictions were imposed by the Reserve Bank on the borrowings of commercial banks, the range of variations of these rates continuously widened. They are very low in the off season, but very high during the busy season. In the slack season, that is between May and October, it may be even less than one percent; but during the busy season, i.e., during November-April it may be as high as 15 per cent per annum. After 1960, the funds of money have started flowing more freely within the same money market and even within different money markets in India.

(B) The Bill Market :

A bill market is a market in which short term bills are sold and purchased. These short-term bills are, normally, for a period of three months and are of three types :

(1) Bills of exchange or trade bills,

(2) Promissory notes, and

(3) Treasury bills.

All these three types of bills are promises to pay the specified amount on a particular day. These can be sold or purchased in the discount market. This discount market consists of commercial banks and special agencies performing the business of discounting bills only. These agencies are known as discount houses and are in existence in most of the developed money markets. These bills are of special importance in the money market as commercial banks, with extra liquid cash, can invest their extra cash in this market, which otherwise, would have remained idle.

The investment in these bills does not impair the liquidity of the commercial banks as these bills can be disposed of easily or the Central Bank of the country can rediscount them. Thus, these bills enable commercial banks to earn profit without any risk. But, unfortunately, there was practically no such Bill market in India till 1950-51.

The main reasons for the non-development of the money market in India may be mentioned as follows :

(a) The necessity to keep large amounts of cash due to the high liquidity preference of the people;

(b) The preference given by the trading community to borrowing rather than rediscounting bills;

(c)   The improper or defective drafting of the bazaar hundies;

(d)   The system of advancing cash credit by banks;

(e)   The preference for cash transactions;

(f)   The absence of warehousing facilities;

(g)   The high stamp duty on such transactions, etc.

But perhaps, the most important reason for the non-development of the bill market in India was the practice of most of the foreign exchange banks, to dispose of the bills in the London money market when necessary, and holding them till maturity if they could afford to do so.

(1) The Bill Market Scheme of 1952 : In January 1952, the Reserve Bank of India introduced a scheme known as the Bill Market Scheme. Under this Scheme, the Reserve Bank agreed to advance loans to the commercial banks, as and when required, against their promissory notes, supported by the approved usance bills of their customers. Before that, if a commercial bank was in need of cash in the busy season, the bank had to sell some of the government securities held by the commercial bank. Now, the bank could lend to its customers on the basis of securities provided by them, pass on the same security to the Reserve Bank and get an advance against that.

This scheme was introduced initially for a period of 4 years on an experimental basis, and was restricted to the scheduled banks only, having total deposits of ₹ 10 crores or more. Similarly, the minimum value of one bill was to be ₹ 1 lakh and the bank was to advance a minimum of ₹ 35 lakhs. This Scheme became popular and subsequently, several modifications were made in the Scheme so as to make it more advantageous to small banks also. In 1957, the Scheme was extended to export bills also. Originally, the Scheme was applicable to the Bombay and Kolkata branches of the Reserve Bank. Later on, it was extended to Madras, Kanpur, Delhi, Bangalore and Nagpur. Further, the minimum amounts of an advance was also reduced gradually, and in 1961, it was ₹ 1 lakh, and the amount of one single usance bill, to be lodged as security, was reduced to ₹ 5,000 from the entire burden of the stamp duty on such transactions.

Inspite of all these attempts, one has to accept that this Scheme, though called the Bill Market Scheme, did not bring into existence an organised bill market, in the sense that not the type which is functioning in other developed countries. In a real Bill market, there are a number of discount houses ready to discount trade bills. Actually, they compete with each other. That was not the case in India. The Reserve Bank was the only institution purchasing bills. No features of a real Bill market were found in India, and the Reserve Bank continued to be the lender of the last resort.

(2) The Bill Market Scheme of 1970 : Subsequent trends in the development of Banking in India prompted the Reserve Bank of India to introduce a New Bill Market Scheme, in November 1970, with a view to develop a genuine Bill market in the country. In April 1971, the Reserve Bank enlarged the scope of the New Bill Market Scheme to facilitate more widespread use of bills of exchange as an instrument of credit. This Scheme envisages putting into circulation short-term trading bills of exchange, relating to the sale of goods between first class parties. The Reserve Bank has defined the various categories of bill of exchange which are approved for discounting. Accommodation bills are not covered under this Scheme. The usance period of the bills is confined to 90 days only and for export bills upto a maximum of 180 days. Prior to this Scheme, the R.B.I. used to rediscount bills drawn on and accepted by buyers' banks only.

In order to make the Bill Market Scheme function successfully, some other measures such as commitment charges on cash credit, more stringent control on cash borrowings, etc., have been adopted by the commercial banks, at the instance of the R.B.I. The commercial banks have been instructed to make every possible effort to propagate this Scheme. It is too early to comment on the success or failure of this Scheme just now. Some time must pass till its results can be studied and evaluated.

On the face of it, the following defects could be observed in this scheme :

(a) This scheme makes possible the conversion of advances and loans given by the commercial banks into usance bills. Actually, such loans and advances are provided with refinance by the R.B.I. So, this is not an establishment of the Bill market as such.

(b) As it is expected to function today, the commercial banks will approach the R.B.I. for advances against bills discounted by them, only when their own funds are exhausted. This may happen only in an extremely busy season. So, this is an arrangement to meet seasonal credit stringencies.

(c) This Scheme has been extended to commercial banks which have obtained permission from the R.B.I., and thus, indigenous bankers have been excluded, and hence, its effect will be limited.

(d) The Scheme is actually a scheme of granting accommodation to the commercial banks against eligible usance bills. Similarly, it is not obligatory and the R.B.I. may refuse to accommodate any bank leading to a discriminatory approach on the part of the R.B.I.

(e) In addition to this, the critics point out that inspite of the concessions about the stamp duty, the transactions become costly for the banks. Similarly, this accommodation is available only in the case of trade bills and not available for agricultural transactions. This is a serious drawback which limits the utility of this Scheme.

(C) The Collateral Loan Market :

This forms an important part of the lending activities of a commercial bank. The banks lend money on the security of valuables like Government bonds, shares of limited companies, easily marketable industrial agricultural commodities, gold etc. These loans are usually made in the form of simple, loans cash credit or overdrafts.

These loans are usually made for a longer period, and strictly speaking, do not come within the purview of the money market. They are made against the securities mentioned above with a larger margin. In the case of gold and government securities, the margin is slightly less. But in the case of other types of securities, the margin between the loan and the value of the security varies between 30 and 50 per cent.

Overdraft and cash credit are very popular amongst Indian traders and are used on a large scale. As compared to the other sources of the supply of short-term finance, these two are simple and are within easy reach of traders and businessmen in India.

(D) The Treasury Bill Market :

Treasury bills are short-term Government securities normally maturing within a period of 90 days. These are sold by the Reserve Bank of India on behalf of the Government. These bills are also known as, gilt-edged securities, or, first class securities, and they command unquestioned acceptance in the money market.

Normally, these are purchased by the State Bank of India and other major banks, as and when sold by the R.B.I. In general, 90 to 95 per cent of these securities are held by big banks.

4.4 Money Market Instruments

Credit Instrument	Issued by	Maturity Period	Purpose Served
1. Commercial Bills	Individuals and Institutions	90 days	(i) Credit Sales / Purchases (ii) Borrowings and Lendings
2. Commercial Paper	Top-rates Companies	30 days to 1 year	(i) Investors (Banks) can use surplus funds. (ii) Borrowers get short-term loans
3. Certificates of Deposits	Banks	Minimum 15 days	(i) Liquidity to banks. (ii) Liquidity easy for depositors.
4. MMMF units	Mutual Funds	Minimum 15 days	(i) Individuals' participation in money market. (ii) Additional resources for Mutual Funds + Liquidity
5. Repos	Govt. through RBI	Minimum 3-4 days	(i) Guarantee for Govt. Securities (ii) Surplus Funds of Banks utilised.
6. Reverse Repos	RBI	Minimum 3-4 days	(i) Helping Primary dealers
7. Inter-bank Repos	Banks	Minimum 3-4 days	(i) PSU Bonds/Company bonds/debentures can be converted into liquidity.
8. Treasury Bills	Government	14 days 91 days 182 days 364 days	(i) Short-term requirements of Govts. (ii) Semi-liquid assets for banks
9. Dated Government Securities	Government	85 years to 10 years	(i) Meeting Govt. needs (ii) Flexible & suitable to investors. (iii) Used for Repos.

4.5 Recent Developments in Indian Money Market

Financial reforms in India began is the early 1990s. However, various segments of domestic financial markets, viz., money market, debt market and forex market underwent significant shifts mainly form the 1990s. Earlier, the Indian Money Market was characterised by paucity of instruments, lack of depth and distortion in the market micro structure. It mainly consisted of uncollateralised call market, treasury bills, commercial bills and participation certificates.

Following the recommendations of the Chakravarty Committee (1985), the Reserve Bank adopted a monetary targeting framework. At the same time, efforts were made to develop the money market following the recommendations of Vaghul Committee (1987). In this regard, important developments were : (i) setting up of the Discount and Finance House of India (DFHI) in 1988 to impart liquidity to money market instruments and help the development of secondary markets in such instruments; (ii) introduction of instruments such as certificate of deposits (CDs) in 1989 and commercial papers in 1990 and inter-bank participation certificates with and without risk in 1988 to increase the range of instruments; and (iii) freeing of call money rates by May 1989 to enable price discovery. However, the functioning of the market continued to be hindered by a number of structural rigidities such as skewed distribution of liquidity and the prevalence of administered deposit and lending rates of banks.

Recognising these rigidities, the pace of reforms in money market was accelerated. Following the recommendations of an Internal Working Group (1997) and the Narasimham Committee (1998), a comprehensive set of measures was undertaken by the Reserve Bank to develop the money market. These included : (i) withdrawal of interest rate ceilings in the money market; (ii) introduction of auctions in treasury bills; (iii) gradual move away from the cash credit system to a loan-based system. Maturities of other existing instruments such as CP and CDS were also gradually shortened to encourage wider participation. Most importantly, the *ad hoc* treasury bills were abolished in 1997 thereby putting a stop to automatic monetisation of fiscal deficit. This enhanced the instrument independence of the Reserve Bank (Table 4.1).

Table 4.1 : Major Developments in Money Market since the 1990s

1. Abolition of *ad hoc* treasury bills in April 1997.

2. Full fledged LAF in June 2000.

3. CBLO for corporate and non-bank participants introduced in 2003.

4. Minimum maturity of CPS shortened by October 2004.

5. Prudential limits on exposure of banks and PDs to call/notice market in April 2005.

6. Maturity of CDs gradually shortened by April 2005.

7. Transforamtion of call money market into a pure inter-bank market by August 2005.

8. Widening of collateral base by making state government securities (SDLs) eligible for LAF operations since April 2007.

9. Operationalisation of a screen-based negotiated system (NDS-CALL) for all dealings in the call/notice and the term money markets in September 2006. The reporting of all such transactions made compulsory through NDS-CALL in November 2012.

10. Repo in corporate bonds allowed in March 2010.

11. Operationalisation of a reporting platform for secondary market transactions in CPS and CDS in July 2010.

More importantly, efforts were made to transform the call money market into primarily an inter-bank market, while encouraging other market participants to migrate towards collateralised segments of the market, thereby increasing overall market stability and diversification. In order to facilitate the phasing out of corporate and the non-banks from the call money market, new instruments such as market repos and collateralised borrowing and lending obligations (CBLO) were introduced to provide them avenues for managing their short-term liquidity. Non-bank entities completely exited the call money market by August 2005. In order to minimise the default risk and ensure balanced development of various market segments, the Reserve Bank instituted prudential limits on exposure of banks and primary dealers (PDs) to the call/notice money market. In April, 2005 these limits were linked to capital funds (sum of Tier I and Tier II capital) for scheduled commercial banks.

In order to improve transparency and efficiency in the money market, reporting of all call/notice money market transactions through negotiated dealing system (NDS) within 15 minutes of conclusion of the transaction was made mandatory. Furthermore, a screen-based negotiated quote-driven system for all dealings in the call/notice and the term money markets (NDS-CALL), developed by the Clearing Corporation of India Limited (CCIL), was operationalised in September 2006 to ensure better price discovery.

Beginning in June 2000, the Reserve Bank introduced a full-fledged liquidity adjustment facility (LAF) and it was operated through overnight fixed rate repo and reverse repo from November 2004. This helped to develop interest rate as an important instrument of monetary transmission. It also provided greater flexibility to the Reserve Bank in determining both the quantum of liquidity as well as the rates by responding to the needs of the system on a daily basis.

4.6 Reserve Bank of India – Functions, Regulatory Role of R.B.I. w.r.t. Currency, Credit and Balance of Payment, Open Market Operations

(A) Evolution of the Reserve Bank of India :

The need for a Central Bank or an authority of a similar type was, perhaps, first felt by Warren Hastings as early as 1773. It did not, however, materialise until 1921, when the three Presidency Banks were amalgamated to form the Imperial Bank of India.

The Imperial Bank of India was, primarily, a commercial bank until the establishment of the Reserve Bank of India. It functioned as a Central Bank partially. At least, it functioned as a banker to the government.

In 1926, a Royal Commission on Indian Currency was appointed under the chairmanship of Sir Hilton Young and was popularly known as the Hilton Young Commission. This Commission recommended that the responsibility of issuing paper currency and performing the functions of the central bank should be unified and should be entrusted to one single authority. The Commission recommended the establishment of a central bank, to be named as "Reserve Bank" and both these functions were to be entrusted to it. Before that, the issuing of paper currency was the responsibility of the Central Government and the banking functions of a Government were performed by the Imperial Bank of India.

In compliance with the recommendations of the Hilton Young Commission, the Finance Minister introduced a bill in the Indian Legislative Assembly in January 1927. But, unfortunately, this bill was dropped owing to sharp differences of opinion on the constitution and composition of the Bank and its Board of Directors.

The question of establishing a separate Central or Reserve Bank of India was taken up again, as a result of the unanimous recommendations of the Central Banking Enquiry Committee to that effect in 1931. The second push to the idea of establishing the Reserve Bank, to function as the Central Bank, was the White Paper on Indian Constitutional Reforms in 1933. The establishment of the Reserve Bank was laid down as a precondition for the transfer of responsibility at the Centre from British to Indian hands. The Reserve Bank was to be free from political influence.

Subsequently, a fresh bill was introduced in the Indian Legislative Assembly, in September 1933 and was passed in due course and got the assent from the Governor General in March 1934. After completing the organisational preliminaries, the Reserve Bank was inaugurated on the 1st of April, 1935.

From 1935, the Reserve Bank of India started functioning as a Central Bank for undivided India and Burma. In 1937, Burma was separated but the Reserve Bank of India continued to function as the currency authority of Burma till June 1942. Even after the partition of the undivided India into dominions of India and Pakistan on 15th August, 1947, the RBI continued to function as a Central Bank and rendered central banking services to Pakistan till the end of June 1948. Thereafter, it is solely functioning as a Central Bank for India.

(B) Reasons for the Establishment of the Reserve Bank of India :

The need for establishing the Reserve Bank of India was being felt by the country mainly because of the following reasons :

(1) The Internal and External Stability of the Purchasing Power of the Rupee : The need for maintaining the internal and external value of the Indian rupee was felt right from the beginning of the 20th century. But it became more pressing especially after the end of the First World War. The value of money in any country fluctuates because of the internal as well as external disturbances. Internal disturbances like famines, floods, excessive rains, droughts, etc., were experienced by this country since ages. The external causes like trade cycles or depression in other countries also affect the purchasing power of the currency.

The internal value of the rupee can be maintained stable by the Reserve Bank of India, as the Bank was given the monopoly of issuing the currency. The value of money can be kept stable by adjusting the supply of money to the demand for money. The demand for money at any given point of time is determined by the level of transactions, the liquidity preference of the people, and the velocity of circulation of money. By keeping a close watch on these factors, the Reserve Bank of India can adjust the supply of money and, thus, can control excessive fluctuations in the internal value of money.

The external stability depends on the internal stability of the value of money. If the prices in India rise in relation to world prices, then, it will be beneficial for the foreign countries to sell their commodities in India, as they will fetch a higher price. At the same time, it will be disadvantageous for them to buy commodities in India. This will make the balance of trade for India, unfavourable. This may have various effects : There may be depression in India as there will be no demand or less demand for Indian commodities; or it may create difficulties in balancing the balance of payments; and so on. The Reserve Bank of India can maintain the stability of the external purchasing power of the rupee, by buying from or selling sterling or gold to the members of the public as the circumstances demand. The Reserve Bank of India can maintain the external value of the rupee by keeping sizeable stock of foreign exchange or gold and using it wisely to correct the imbalance as and when it occurs. Similarly, the RBI can follow a suitable credit policy.

(2) Following a Proper Credit Policy : In all modern economies, the Central Bank performs the function of chalking out and following a proper credit policy; A judicious and appropriate credit policy keeps the volume of currency and credit properly adjusted to the volume of business transactions in the country. If this is done, the stability of prices is maintained which keeps the internal value of money stable.

To enable the Central Bank to do this, it is armed with various weapons of credit control. By using these weapons of credit control, the Central Bank can keep the credit situation in the country under control. This had been necessary in India.

(3) Removing the Structural Instability of the Banking System : The banking system in India till 1935 did not have a proper base. There was keen competition amongst the banks and the big banks were always at an advantage in this race. Sudden demand for withdrawals of funds was enough to disturb the banks and it may have resulted in a financial crisis.

There were many reasons for this : For example, many banks had large amounts of liabilities and had conducted a large amount of business which could not be justified by their cash reserves. The exchange banks, too, were no exception to this rule.

In case there was a run on the banks, the only way to restore confidence was to pay-off cash to anybody who wanted to withdraw his deposit. This could be done if there was a co-ordinating authority and co-operation amongst the banks. As there was no Central Bank, there was no co-ordinating authority, and there was no co-operation amongst the banks. They were competing with each other.

Similarly, when there was a run on one bank, other banks also were afraid of a similar run and, hence, were reluctant to come to the help of the bank which was exposed to the run. It would spread like an epidemic because once the confidence in one bank was shaken, the depositors of other banks also started doubting the creditworthiness of their banks.

(4) Need for Protecting the Banking Business during the Period of Crisis : The need for a Central Bank was felt more as there was a need for protecting the banking business during the period of crisis. The organisation of a Central Bank would have allowed the banks to pool their reserves together and thus, ensure help in case of danger. The reserves, thus pooled together, would have been a sizeable amount and would have been very handy in meeting unforeseen difficulties in the field of banking. The single reserve system could have been more mobile and elastic. The transfer of funds to any bank would have been easy and banks could have borrowed easily from the Central Bank.

(5) Need for Establishing a Clearing House : With the development of commercial banking, the need for establishing a clearing house was felt. Such a clearing house should function under the supervision of the Central Bank. This makes transactions more easy, legal and smooth. The Central Bank also gets an idea of the financial resources of the different banks and also the level of transactions effected by every bank.

(6) Collection of Statistics : Various economic and other activities were being undertaken and were carried on in the country. It was necessary to have an agency that could collect the data and statistics available in the country. This would have been extremely useful in planning and controlling the economic activities in the country.

(7) Other Reasons : In addition to the functions mentioned above, providing agricultural credit, providing rediscount facilities, handling foreign exchange transactions, providing banking and finance facilities to internal trade, etc. were other functions which were to be performed by an institution which would not compete with the banks and other financial institutions in the country. For all these reasons, a need for establishing the Reserve Bank was long felt, and because of all these reasons, the decision to establish the Reserve Bank was finally taken.

The Annual Policy Statement for the year 2006-07 of Reserve Bank of India had indicated that amendments to the Reserve Bank of India Act, 1934 and the Banking Regulation Act, 1949 were under consideration in order to provide greater flexibility in the conduct of monetary policy and to strengthen the regulatory powers of the Reserve Bank. The Reserve Bank of India Act, 1934 was amended in June 2006 with a view to enhancing the Reserve Bank's operational flexibility and providing it with greater maneuverability in monetary management. The Reserve Bank of India (Amendment) Act, 2006 gives discretion to the Reserve Bank to decide the percentage of scheduled banks' demand and time liabilities to be maintained as CRR without any ceiling or floor. Consequent to the amendment, no interest will be paid on CRR balances so as to enhance the efficacy of the CRR, as payment of interest attenuates its effectiveness as an instrument of monetary policy. The revised definition of "repo" and "reverse repo" provided under the amendment would facilitate transactions of market participants/ banks in these instruments. The amendment also provides the Reserve Bank with the statutory backing for regulating the money market and also for regulating trading of over-the counter derivatives.

(C) Organisation and Management of Reserve Bank of India :

The Reserve Bank of India was originally started as a shareholders' bank. The share capital of the Bank was ₹ 5 crores, divided into shares of ₹ 100 each. These shares were fully paid-up shares. Out of this share-capital, shares worth ₹ 2.2 lakhs were allotted to and purchased by the then Central Government. The rest of the share-capital was entirely contributed by private shareholders. Shares worth ₹ 2.2 lakhs which were allotted to the Central Government were to be sold to the Directors of the Central Board of the Bank, at par, in order to enable them to fulfil the minimum share qualifications.

While allotting the shares, care was taken to see that the shares were not concentrated in a few hands. The entire country was divided into five different regions : viz, Mumbai, Kolkata, Chennai, Delhi and Rangoon (Burma). At every place, mentioned above, there was a separate office. The Rangoon office was closed in 1947. The value of the shares, originally allotted to the different offices was as follows :

(i)	Mumbai	:	₹ 140 lakhs;
(ii)	Kolkata	:	₹ 145 lakhs;
(iii)	Delhi	:	₹ 115 lakhs;
(iv)	Chennai	:	₹ 70 lakhs;
(v)	Rangoon	:	₹ 30 lakhs;
	Total	:	**₹ 500 lakhs**

Out of this, the shares on the Rangoon Register were transferred to the Chennai Register. The shares were alloted to the following persons or institutions :

(1) A person domiciled in India; or

(2) A British subject ordinarily residing in India; or

(3) A person domiciled in any part of the British Empire, the Government of which did not discriminate, in any way, against Indians; or

(4) A Company registered under Indian Companies Act; or

(5) A Company incorporated under a law of any part of the British Empire having a branch in India, the Government of which did not discriminate, in any way, against the Indians.

The shareholders were registered in the respective registers, maintained at the above mentioned four regional registers, depending on the residence of the shareholders.

In allotting the shares, the Central Board of the Bank allotted shares to those who had applied for five or more shares, in multiples of five. This was necessary to allot the shares evenly and avoid concentration of shares in a few hands. Every shareholder was entitled to one vote for every five shares held, subject to a maximum of ten votes. This meant that any shareholder having more than fifty shares was entitled to have ten votes only.

Inspite of all these precautions, the number of shareholders went on declining and the number of shareholders in Mumbai and Kolkata went on increasing continuously. This happened inspite of the limitations imposed by an amendment of Reserve Bank Act on the number of shares to be held by an individual to 200. The shares of the Reserve Bank of India were quoted at a very high premium, right from the beginning, and continued to rule high till the nationalisation of the Bank in 1949.

The Head Office of the Bank was in Mumbai but the Bank had its offices at Kolkata, Delhi, Chennai, Kanpur, Bangalore, Hyderabad, Jaipur, Lucknow, Nagpur, Patna and London. If necessary, the Bank was entitled to open more offices in India and, with the prior permission of the Government, outside India also.

(a) The Central Board of Directors : The general administration of the Bank was entrusted to the Central Board of Directors. The composition of the Central Board of Directors was to be as follows :

1. Governor	: 1	
2. Deputy of Governors	: 2	All these where to be appointed
3. Directors	: 4	by the Governor-General-in-Council
4. Government Officials	: 1	
5. Directors	: 8	Two each, for Mumbai, Delhi and Kolkata and, one each for Chennai and Rangoon to be elected by the share-holders from the respective registers

The Governor and the Deputy Governors were appointed for a period of five years and were entitled to the reappointed and hold office during the pleasure of the Governor-General-in-Council. The Directors were elected for a period of five years and were eligible for re-election. The remuneration of all those who were appointed by the Governor-General-in-Council was fixed by him and that of the elected Directors by the Central Board of Directors. The Deputy Governors and the Government officials were not entitled to vote.

In addition to this, there were Local Boards consisting of not more than 8 members. Out of these, 5 were elected by the shareholders of the respective regions and not more than 3 members were nominated by the Central Board of Directors.

All the shareholders who were holding shares for a period of six months prior to election, were entitled to vote. The elections of new members of the Board of Directors and those of the Local Boards were held three months prior to the retirement of the old members. As mentioned earlier, the outgoing members were eligible for re-election or re-nomination.

The following conditions were to be fulfilled by the persons who desired to become the members of the Central or Local Board of Directors by election or by nomination :

1. They must not be servants of the Central or State Governments.

2. They must not be, or must not have been, declared as insolvent or have suspended or refused payment to their creditors, or must have been compounded with the creditors.

3. They must not be employees of a bank or a director of any bank other than a Co-operative bank.

4. They must hold unencumbered shares of the Reserve Bank worth at least ₹ 5,000 each, after six months from the date of their nomination or election.

5. They must not be members of the Central or a Provincial Legislature.

Of course, the first and third conditions did not apply to the officer appointed by the Government.

The Central Board of Directors of the Reserve Bank of India was to meet six times every year. The Local Board was to advise the Central Board of Directors on such matters as were referred to it and performed such other duties delegated to it by the Central Board of Directors. Generally, the Committee of the Central Board used to meet more often, say, about 30 times during the period of the year, and used to conduct most of the routine work. The meeting of the shareholders was held, annually, within six weeks from the data on which the annual accounts of the Bank were closed. If necessary, an additional general meeting of the shareholders could be convened by the Central Board at any other time.

(b) The Ownership and Control of Reserve Bank after Independence : After attaining Independence, it was necessary to review the ownership and control of the Reserve Bank, in the new context. It was thought desirable to nationalise the Reserve Bank. This was just falling in line with the worldwide tendency to nationalise the Central Banks. Accordingly, an Act was passed in 1948 and the Reserve Bank was nationalised. This Act is known as the Reserve Bank (Transfer to Public Ownership) Act of 1948. By this Act, the entire share capital of the Reserve Bank was acquired by the Central Government. The shareholders were compensated at ₹ 118–10–0 per share of ₹ 100. From 1st January 1949, the Reserve Bank started functioning as a State-owned and controlled Bank.

(c) The Administration of the Reserve Bank : After nationalisation, the administration of the Reserve Bank was entrusted to a Board of Directors consisting of the following members :

1. **Governor**	:	1	Appointed by the Central Government under Section 8 (1)(a)
2. **Deputy Governors**	:	4	for a period of 5 years
3. **Directors**	:	4	Nominated by the Central Government one, each, from the Local Boards under Section 8 (1)(b)
4. **Directors**	:	10	Nominated by the Central Government, to represent difference interests under Section 8 (1)(c).
5. **Official of the Government**	:	1	Appointed by the Central Government, under Section 8 (1)(d).

In addition to this, there are four Local Boards for four regional areas of the country having head-quarters at Mumbai, New Delhi, Kolkata and Chennai. These Local Boards consist of five members each, nominated by the Central Government to represent regional and territorial interests and the interests of the indigenous bankers and Co-operative banks. All these members of the Local Boards are appointed for a period of *four* years and are entitled to being reappointed. These Local Boards are to elect the Chairman of the Board from amongst themselves.

The duties of the Local Boards are very limited. They are to advise the Central Board in respect of matters referred to them by the Central Board. They are also expected to perform any other functions, if and when delegated to them by the Central Board. These Local Boards are expected to act as a link between the Central Boards and the respective regions, and keep the Central Board informed about the financial and banking problems of the regions, if any.

(D) Functions of the Reserve Bank of India :

(1) Issue and Management of Currency :

The Central Bank of a country is always entrusted with the monopoly of issuing paper currency. This function is entrusted to and performed by the central bank almost from its origin; so much so that till the beginning of the twentieth century, the central bank was generally known as the bank of issue.

Historically speaking, the privilege of minting money and printing paper currency was enjoyed by the State of the country concerned. But, with the lapse of time and because of the bitter experiences of currency depreciation, this privilege has now been passed on to the central bank. The reasons for transferring this privilege to the central bank appear to be as follows :

(a) Every country found out that, in order to have wide circulation and acceptance, the paper currency issued in any country must be singularly uniform in all respects. This paper currency was also to be declared as 'legal tender money'. Of course, this could have been achieved by means of direct State-issue. But, history provided many examples of the depreciation of the State-issue and the consequent distrust of the public in government paper currency. So, most of the States considered it advisable to entrust this work to the central bank, and exercise an indirect control over currency-issue through the central bank.

(b) With economic development and prosperity, the amount of deposit money created by the commercial banks went on increasing continuously. This led to large-scale credit creation by the commercial banks. This made some sort of credit-control necessary. An expansion of credit, obviously, leads to an increased demand for paper currency. In such circumstances, the commercial banks must borrow from the central bank in order to fulfil the demand for currency arising out of their credit expansion. As the commercial banks themselves cannot issue paper currency, they have to approach the central bank. As the central bank is entrusted with the sole right of issuing paper currency, it can exercise a better control on the expansion of credit by the commercial bank.

(c) The monopoly of note issue, with the support of the State, gives a special prestige to the notes issued by the central bank. This has proved to be of great value, especially in critical conditions.

(d) The issue of notes is many times a valuable source of profit. It appeared to be more advantageous to concentrate the privilege of note-issue in the central bank, and share the profits, instead of directly issuing the notes.

(e) The central bank is a non-political body and is in a position to regulate and control the issue of currency more scrupulously, without being influenced by any political ideology.

(f) If the note-issue is done by the State, in case of a budgetary deficit, the government may be tempted to inflate the currency and bridge the deficit gap. This is very detrimental to the stability of the entire economy.

Nowadays, because of the reasons mentioned above, the monopoly of note-issue is mostly vested in the central bank of the respective countries. But, even today, it is true that the government of the country can interfere with the function of note-issue. An increase or decrease in currency can be brought about by the government through the central bank, if the government so desires.

Reserve Bank as Banker of the Government :

The Reserve Bank is charged with the duty of acting as a banker to the Government under Sections 20, 21 and 21 A of the Reserve Bank of India Act. The Bank is entrusted with the *Banking Business* of the Government free of charge. In other words, the Reserve Bank is to the Government what any other bank is to ordinary citizens as customers of such a (commercial or co-operative) bank.

Banking Business :

The RBI, therefore,

(i)   accepts money on account of the Government,

(ii) makes payments on behalf of the Government,

(iii) carries out exchange remittance of the Government,

(iv) manages public debt and the issue of new loans and treasury bills, and

(v)   performs all other banking operations as an agent and representative of the Government.

In respect of all these banking functions, the RBI has to act as a banker to all the State Government as well.

Further, where the RBI has no office, it is under obligation to appoint the State Bank of India as its agent and the SBI and its associates with their network of branches can provide the necessary services of receiving and paying money on behalf of the Union and the State Governments.

(2) Banker's Bank :

The central bank has, now, become the custodian of cash reserves of the commercial banks in every country. This function also has been acquired by the central bank by a process of evolution. When the central bank became the bank of issue and the bank of the government, many commercial banks started keeping some balance with the bank, permanently. This helped the commercial banks to settle inter-bank claims, to make payments to the governments or any others banks, etc. What was first done as a matter of convenience is, now, being done as a legal requirement.

This became necessary when the central bank of the country was entrusted with the work of controlling credit creation in the country. In India and in the U.S.A., every bank has to keep a fixed percentage of its deposits, as a permanent deposit with the central bank. In England, the commercial banks keep 3 to 4% of their deposits with the Bank of England. Thus, now, the practice of keeping a certain percentage of the total deposits of commercial banks as a permanent deposit with the central bank is being universally followed.

This method of pooling all the reserves with the central bank is called the System of Centralised Cash Reserves.

Following are the main advantages of the Centralised Cash Reserve System :

(i)   It serves as a basis for a large and more elastic credit structure.

(ii) It generates and strengthens the confidence of the public in the banking system.

(iii) As the cash reserves are pooled together with the central bank, it is possible to utilise them in the best possible manner.

(iv) In case of a sudden run on any bank, the cash reserve can be easily and quickly mobilised to rescue the bank in trouble.

(v)   The central bank, if necessary, can impose quick and easy control on the credit system in the country by increasing the reserve ratio.

Because of all these advantages, most of the banks have adopted this system.

Reserve Bank as Banker's Bank :

Under the Reserve Bank of India Act, banks included in the second schedule of the Act i.e., the scheduled banks are eligible for financial facilities and in return they bear certain obligations to the Reserve Bank. They have to submit weekly statements and have to maintain reserves as specified in the Act. The non-scheduled banks also have to maintain reserves. The Reserve Bank of India, for certain purposes, does observe certain distinction between various categories of banks. However, the Reserve Bank acts as a banker to all the banks – Scheduled and Non-scheduled, Commercial, Co-operative and Regional Rural Banks.

(a) Assistance to Banks through Rediscount Facilities :

(i)   Under Section 17(2)(A), the RBI is empowered to purchase, sale or re-discount Bills of Exchange and promissory notes drawn and payable in India and arising out of *bonafide* commercial or trade transaction bearing two or more good signatures, one of which has to be that of a scheduled or state co-operative bank, and maturing within 90 days from the date of such purchase or rediscount.

(ii) Section 17(2)(b) empowers the RBI to purchase, sell or rediscount Bills of Exchange and Promissory notes drawn and payable in India [as in 1 above] and drawn and issued for the purpose of financing seasonal agricultural operations or the marketing of crops and maturing within 15 months from the date of purchase / rediscount.

(iii) The RBI is empowered under Section 17(2)(c) to purchase, sell or rediscount Bills of exchange and Promissory notes issued or drawn for the purpose of holding or trading in securities of the Central Government or State Government and maturing within 90 days.

(iv) In respect of Bills of exchange drawn outside India but in a country which is a member of the IMF and the bill has a maturity below 90 days, the RBI under Section 17 (3)(b) can purchase, sell or rediscount such bills.

(b) Financial Assistance to Banks in the form of Advances :

(i) Section 17(4)(a) authorises the Reserve Banks to make loans and advances to scheduled banks, State Co-operative banks etc., repayable on demand or expiry of fixed periods not exceeding 90 days against the security of stocks, funds etc. These securities must be readily marketable and must be selected by the RBI, on merits, for advances.

(ii) The RBI can make similar advances against Gold, Silver and documents of title to gold and silver, under Section 17(4)(b).

(iii) Section 17(4)(c) relates to the powers of the RBI to make loans and advances against the security of bills of exchange guaranteed by the State Government.

(iv) Section 17(4)(d) authorises the RBI to make loans and advances for a period upto 90 days against security of promissory notes of scheduled or state co-operative banks supported by documents of titles to goods.

(c) For Financing Exports :

(i) Section 17 (3 – A) inserted in 1962 empowers the Reserve Banks to make loans and advances to any scheduled bank against the promissory note of the latter repayable on demand or on the expiry of the fixed period not exceeding 180 days.

(ii) A new sub-section 3 (B) was inserted by an Amendment in 1974. This empowers the RBI to make loans and advances upto 180 days against scheduled commercial bank's promissory notes on declaration that the transactions are *bonafide* or the financing is for agricultural operations.

(3) Lender of Last Resort and Central Clearance :

The central banks perform the functions of rediscounting the first class bills already discounted by the commercial banks. This is why it is referred to as a bank of discount. Similarly, it acts as a lender of last resort when it rediscounts the first class bills or securities presented for rediscounting by the ordinary commercial banks.

When any commercial bank, holding first class securities or bills, is in need of liquid cash and is not in a position to get it from any other source, the bank approaches the central bank. This is known as seeking accommodation. When any commercial bank seeks accommodation, the central bank is supposed to provide it. This accommodation is provided and the cash is made available to the commercial bank by rediscounting the bills already discounted by the commercial banks. The rate of interest charged on such re-discounting is known as 'Bank Rate'. As the commercial banks approach the central bank when they are not able to sell their bills to any other bank, and as a last resort, the central banks function as a lender of the last resort. Thus, while performing the function of rediscounting, it also performs the function of providing accommodation, and functions as a lender of last resort. So these two functions are performed simultaneously by the central bank.

The central bank also functions as the bank of clearance. This function can be easily performed by the central bank as it holds the cash reserves of various banks. This makes it easy for the central bank to settle inter-bank indebtedness. The central bank, normally, set up speedy and economical machinery for clearing of drafts and settlement of internal accounts of the banks. The claims of various commercial banks against each other are settled by simple transfers of money in their respective accounts maintained by them with the central bank. If the commercial banks find that their reserves have fallen below the prescribed limit, they can immediately replenish these either by remitting the required amount in cash or by rediscounting bills.

Where there are separate clearing houses, the central bank supervises the functioning of these and, in case of necessity, completes the clearing function. Otherwise, the central bank itself acts as a clearing house. Thus, the central bank reduces the expenses, delay and risk involved in collection and clearing of cheques, and economises on time.

(4) Supervision of the Banking System :

For healthy growth of banking system, regulation and supervision are required. To regulate means to control, to govern, to provide direction, and to supervise means to oversee the performance of the individual banks in terms of prescribed norms, procedures, legal framework etc. Without supervision all regulatory measures will be futile. Supervision is ensuring compliance with regulatory requirement. Supervision is conducted through either on-site inspection under which the inspectors from the authorities scrutinise the books and other documents of the banks or off-site surveillance under which reports are called from the supervised entities and scrutinised at the office of authorities. The collection of the data could be periodic or *ad hoc* depending upon the need. The information could be collected from auditors and other sources.

The soundness of the financing system of the country depends on the health of the banking system. The Board of Supervision (BFS) is entrusted supervision of the banks, financial institutions, NBFCs etc. A number of supervisory initiatives were taken by BFS to strengthen its oversight over the financial system in the light of the fast changing economic and financial landscape.

For placing better internal controls in the banks, it was considered that the time allowed for reconciliation of outstanding entries for making provisions be reduced from one year to six months. With a view to reducing the burden to examine the adequacy of provisions for pension, gratuity and other terminal benefits for bank employees in the light of a recent revision by LIC in the premium rates was also brought out. It has also been decided to allow banks to disclose their provision for NPAs not reported in the previous year separately, if these did not reflect the performance of the present management, after due assessment by an independent auditor appointed by the Reserve Bank. Banks are also asked to disclose the total amount of loan assets subjected to restructuring under Corporate Debt Restructuring (CDR) and amount of sub-standard assets subjected to CDR. In the notes of account, the banks are required to disclose the total investment made in equity shares, debentures, convertible bonds, mutual funds and aggregate advances against shares.

The supervision of commercial banks and financial institutions is vested in the Reserve Bank in terms of the provisions of the Banking Regulation Act, 1949 and the Reserve Bank of India Act, 1934. This task is carried out by the Department of Banking Supervision (DBS) under the guidance of the BFS. The basic objective of supervision of banks is to assess the solvency, liquidity and operational health of banks. The onsite inspection of banks referred to as Annual Financial Inspection (AFI) is conducted annually (except in the case of State Bank of India in which case it is done once in two years). For this purpose, the unit of inspection is the Head Office (HO) of the bank. A team of Inspecting Officers from the Reserve Bank led by the Principal Inspecting Officer (PIO) visits the bank and conducts the inspection based on the internationally adopted CAMEL (Capital Adequacy, Asset Quality, Management, Earnings, Liquidity) model, modified as CAMELS (S for Systems and Control) to suit the needs of the Indian banking system. The focus of the AFI in recent years has been on supervisory issues relating to securitisation, business continuity plan, disclosure requirements and compliance with other existing guidelines.

(5) Custodian of Foreign Exchange Reserves :

The regulation and management of foreign exchange is a very important function involving policy decisions and policy implementation by various Government departments. In respect of the Reserve Bank of India, the *Exchange Control Department* was constituted in 1939. It is this department which acts as the custodian of foreign exchange, as well as the regulator of foreign exchange. It deals with the work relating to the control of foreign transactions in exchange, bullion and securities. The financial provisions of the Foreign Exchange Regulation Act need the R.B.I's participation in implementation on a big scale. The Central Government has authorised the R.B.I. to deal in foreign exchange, gold coin and bullion. The Reserve Bank has, in turn, licensed certain commercial banks, known as Authorised Dealers, to deal in foreign exchange. Each authorised dealer has to submit to the R.B.I. everyday a statement and the relevant application forms. Besides, there is a group of licensed dealers known as authorised money changers whose business is buying and selling foreign currency notes and coins.

Under regulations, five categories of remittances are distinguished, *viz.* (i) payment of imports, (ii) petty private remittance, (iii) travelling expenses, (iv) other trade purposes, and (v) capital transfers. Different rules are made applicable to different categories because of the problems associated with each one of them. Investment of foreign capital and their repatriation require prior permission of the Bank. From time to time, rules and regulations are framed relating to foreign investments in India, foreign currency accounts in India, exchange entitlement scheme and such other incentives to exporters, and various NRI accounts which are also operated by the Indian commercial banks. All such matters need to be handled by one single authority in a co-ordinated manner and under an expert's supervision. Logically therefore, the function is delegated to the *Exchange Control Department* of the Reserve Bank of India.

(6) Collection and Furnishing of Credit Information :

While performing its routine central banking functions, the reserve bank comes to receive a lot of data that could be useful for analysing and interpreting the behaviour of a number of micro-economic variables. Such information can be compiled, processed, handled and interpreted by the economic/statistics departments.

The Economic Department of the Reserve Bank :

(a) Conducts research in problems of economic policy, mainly monetary, banking, fiscal and those related to agricultural credit, International trade etc. and advises the government on the basis of this research.

(b) It also conducts periodical and *ad hoc* surveys in banking, rural credit, foreign assets, liabilities etc.

(c) It carries out research assignment referred to it by the planning commission.

(d) This department is directly responsible for publishing the results of Research studies and bringing out Reserve Bank of India Bulletin and other publications for the dissemination of information.

(e) It conducts the Bank's press relations.

(f) This department maintains a liaison with IMF, IBRD, ECAFE, and other international bodies as well as central banks of other countries of the world.

(g) On behalf of the Reserve Bank, this department participates in discussions with government officials, international agencies, etc., and it represents the RBI at conferences, committees and other meeting and discussions.

The Statistics Department of the Reserve Bank of India is entrusted with the following functions :

(a) It processes the data on money and banking and brings out periodical and *adhoc* publications on Banking, Monetary and Corporate Statistics.

(b) The index numbers of prices and yields of securities, stocks etc. are constructed by this department.

(c) It prepares and publishes studies on the finances of joint stock companies in India.

(d) It conducts technical studies and services / monitors the movement of Index numbers of various prices and productions. For this purpose it employs statistical and econometric techniques.

(e) It organises machine tabulation, computer programming and system analysis of the banking and exchange control statistics and other data.

(f) Finally, it provides statistical support to programmes of other departments where the applications of statistical techniques is required.

The 1962 amendment of the RBI Act has empowered the Reserve Bank to collect credit information from banking companies and to furnish such informations in a consolidated form to any banking company applying for it. Credit information includes – (a) Information regarding loans and advances granted by a bank, (b) The nature of security, (c) The guarantee, etc. However, this information is to be treated as confidential and it is to be used for the smooth functioning of the banks only.

(7) Agricultural Finance :

The R.B.I., under the Reserve Bank of India Act, is charged with the responsibility (Sec. 54) of making its resources available to agriculture. Under section 54, the Bank has to maintain the Agricultural Credit Department. This department has been assigned the following functions :

(a) To maintain an expert staff to study all questions of agricultural credit and be available for consultation by the Central and State Governments, provincial (State level) co-operative banks and other banking organisations.

(b) To co-ordinate the operations of the Bank in connection with agricultural credit with those of provincial co-operative banks and other institutions in the supply of agricultural credit.

4.7 Role and Functions of Capital Markets

(A) Meaning and Nature of a Capital Market :

In the words of **G. H. Peters,** "*In its widest possible sense the capital market could be defined as being the market, or collection of interrelated markets, in which potential borrowers are brought into contact with potential lenders*". But, thus defined the Capital Market includes the Money Market, the New Issue market, Discount market and so on as specialised sub-divisions of a single market in loans. This definition, therefore, precludes the possibility of distinguishing the money market from the capital market.

Frequently, therefore, the term 'Capital Market' is used to connote markets in permanent long-term or medium-term loans. The term 'Capital Market' indicates it is a market which deals with capital. Capital here refers to long term funds. The capital market has nothing to do with capital goods, but it is concerned with the raising of money capital. It can be said that the capital market is a market where transactions of borrowing and lending of long-term funds take place.

The capital market is concerned with supply of long-term capital and medium term capital. The capital market is a series of channel through which savings of the community are made available for industrial and commercial enterprises and public authorities.

"*Capital markets are complex institutions and mechanism whereby intermediate term funds (loans upto 10 years maturity) and long term funds (longer maturity loans and corporate stock) are pooled and made available to business, government and individuals and where instruments that are already outstanding are transferred.*"   **– H.E. Dougall**

Capital market provides long-term and medium-term loans. In the capital market, funds are invested in corporate securities. The development of capital market depends upon the availability of savings, proper organisation of intermediary institutions to bring the investor and business ability together for mutual interests, regulation of investments etc. However, in many underdeveloped and developed countries (also) the capital markets are underdeveloped. It is essential to make special efforts to develop capital markets in such countries.

(B) Characteristics of a Capital Market :

The above definition highlights certain features which can be enumerated for the sake of clarity, as under :

(1) Dealing in Long-term Funds : Traditionally, the money market has been described as the market for short-term debt, with a year or less to maturity. The capital market on the other hand, has been described as dealing in long-term funds : both debt and equity. Obviously, these traditional designations have a category of intermediate-term or medium-term money represented by debt with maturity ranging from I to 5 or 10 years. The above definition includes transactions involving such debts in the concept of capital market activity.

(2) Raising of Productive Capital : Capital markets are markets wherefrom productive capital is raised and made available for industrial purposes. Because these deal with instruments representing longer-term funds, the capital markets involve capital in the economic sense. Funds raised through debt instrument by business and individuals are invested in fixed assets and inventories. Of course, not all the funds will be necessarily used for this purpose. Thus, the funds raised through Government bonds and through corporate shares may be, and actually are, used for a variety of expenditures and types of assets.

(3) Long-term Money : Though the transactions in the capital market involve the raising of productive capital, they have nothing to do with capital goods. Involvement of capital, in the economic sense, referred to above, is only through the money capital which is the concern of the capital market. The commodity that is dealt within the capital market is long-term money, i.e. money which is either lent for long periods or is invested more or less permanently.

(4) Instruments : Since capital market refers to all the institutions and mechanisms of raising medium-term and long-term funds, it embraces all the instruments of a permanent form such as shares and stocks, bonds and debentures, and all the institutions dealing in these instruments.

(5) Character : Like the money market, the capital market too can be local, regional, national or international.

(C) Inter-relationships of the Money and Capital Market :

In the preceding section, we noted the definition and the general character of the capital market. Inspite of the difficulties involved in drawing a line of distinction between the two, we have noted that the money market refers to the short-term funds while the capital market refers to medium and long-term funds. The instruments used for transactions in the money market are bills of exchange, finance bills of individuals, and treasury bills which are finance bills issued by the State. The Instruments of capital market are stocks, shares, bonds, debentures, and so on. The money market meets mainly the credit requirements of traders; while the capital market supplies money capital to producers whose investments means commitment of funds to capital assets. The set-up of institutions engaged in transactions of the money market is different from the institutions of the capital market.

Inspite of all these distinctions the capital and money markets are not independent. The Interrelations between the two can be summarised as under:

(1) Suppliers of Funds : Suppliers of funds may choose to direct them to either the capital market or to the money market or both. Though some institutions specialise in supplying funds to one or the other market; by and large, the individuals as well as institutional suppliers enjoy the freedom of choice between the two. Their choice will depend upon their investment policies, in the first instance. A policy of short-term investments will guide the suppliers to the money market; while those who are in search of longer term investment opportunities will turn towards the capital market. The choice will also depend upon the rate of return to capital. A comparison of rates between the two markets will determine the choice. The fact, therefore, remains that the freedom of choice between the two, serves as a link between the two markets.

(2) Users of Funds : The users of funds also have a choice : They can obtain the funds they need either from the capital market or from the money market. For example, a firm which needs funds for additional inventory may raise these by selling Commercial paper at the money market. It can also negotiate a short-term debt from a commercial bank. Alternatively, the firm can turn to the capital market and raise funds by selling stocks or issuing bonds for its working capital requirements. The demand for funds, therefore, can switch over from either one to the other market.

(3) Flow of Funds : Between the two markets, funds usually flow back and forth. For example, the Government may decide to refinance its maturing treasury bills by issuing treasury bonds. Since bills belong to the money market and bonds to the capital market, this causes a diversion of funds from the money market to the capital market. Similarly, to take another example, the proceeds of a maturing mortgage may be used by a bank for making a short-term loan to a business firm. In this case, funds flow from the capital market to the money market.

(4) Dependence of Capital Market on Money Market for Finance : Old capital market, i.e. that part of capital market which deals in stocks and shares of old companies, largely depends upon the money market for finance. The brokers usually depend upon call loans.

(5) Common Institutions and Facilities : Some institutions and facilities are common for both; that is, they serve both the markets. For example, dealers in short-term securities also buy and sell long-term bonds; or commercial banks make both intermediate and short-term loans.

(6) Yields : Finally, the yields in the long-term and short-term markets are interrelated. A rise in short-term lending rate is accompanied or followed by a rise in the long-term rate of interest. However, two features in this regard need a special attention : First, money market rates are more sensitive in the sense that a slight change in the demand or supply conditions is immediately reflected in changes in the rate of interest. The long-term rates are not so sensitive. Secondly, geographical differences in short-term rates are negligible; but in long-term rates, they can be wider. All the same, the two are interrelated, and the rise in the rate indicates stringency of funds in the money market which has its repercussions in the capital market.

(D) Role and Functions of Capital Markets :

(1) Capital Formation : The Indian Capital Market is in the stage of evolving into a sound market; but there are limitations which we noted. A number of policy initiatives for reform have been introduced which we will note a little later. First let us understand the *functions* or the *importance* of the Capital market in a developing country.

The economic strength of any nation can be measured by the value of its accumulated wealth and by the rate at which this wealth grows through savings and investments. The wealth of a nation includes natural and man-made raw materials, all structures, equipments, inventories, land, precious metals like gold and silver, and net foreign assets. The first four can be labelled capital goods. The creation of capital goods is the result of allocation of income to what we call investment. Investment represents allocation of income for future production rather than present consumption.

Students of economics know that in the strict economic sense, capital means capital goods. By capital goods, we mean the stock of means of production which covers buildings, equipment and inventories. Economic capital does not include claims to assets; it consists of the assets themselves, The problem, however, becomes difficult when we try to distinguish durable consumer goods from capital assets. Thus, even passenger buses are excluded from capital assets on the ground that they yield immediate satisfaction. But residential buildings are sometimes somewhat arbitrarily, included in capital assets because they command a great value and more so, because they can be thought to produce a service.

Capital goods are owned by individuals, business firms and the Government. Individuals own residential houses; business firms own fixed assets, machinery and equipment, and inventories; while the Government owns public utilities.

By, capital formation, we mean the growth in the stock of these Economic capital goods. For the obvious difficulty of measuring this stock in physical terms, it is measured in terms of money and in relation to Gross National Product. Net capital formation, is the addition to the stock of capital goods less depreciation of those goods already on hand. If we ignore depreciation and take into account the total production of all capital goods in a year, it becomes 'Gross capital formation'. Because it is the gross investment that must be financed, mainly in the capital market, gross investment is more significant in the study of the capital market .

Capital Formation and the Capital Markets :

The development of the capital market as a catalyst of capital formation is a concomitant of modernisation of various economic institutions. In primitive societies, the people who save and the people who used capital were largely the same. Some exchange, of course, did occur between capital goods and consumer goods through barter. The problem of financing was, therefore, ruled out. In a modern, capitalistic economy, however, credit instruments and claims to money are necessary for two reasons : in the first place, they facilitate specialisation and division of labour; and secondly, they enable the transfer of savings to those who want to invest in capital goods. Without money and capital markets, capital formation will be impossible. Some units in the economy generate savings, and the money value of these savings is to be channelled to those, who use these savings. This task requires extensive institutional machinery. It is true that some direct investments take place - for instance, a firm uses its profits for expansion of its plant. But most of the savings employed by the investors are collected and redistributed through the capital markets. This is how the process of capital formation becomes possible due to the existence of capital markets. The great growth in the industrial power of modern communities, as pointed out by Livington, has been accomplished by an increase in specialisation, which in turn has been "dependent on the provision of means and facilities for effecting payments in general and on the provision of facilities for effecting those particular payments by which capital is transferred from the control of one party to another".

There is no such thing as a market for capital in the sense of economic capital goods themselves. But there is a market or a group of markets for the instruments that represent either title to, or claims to capital and to the other resources owned by the individuals or the business units or the Government. Capital, in Economics, denotes assets which are of a durable character. But the term capital, in practice, is also used to represent the money value of the credit instruments as well. The money value of real assets can also be termed as capital. Thus, all the instruments which act as claims to capital become capital *by proxy*.

(2) An Intermediary between Savers and Investors : In the preceding paragraph, we saw the meaning of Investment from economic point of view. Investment, i.e. creation of real capital, is a function which is performed by the entrepreneurs. For this function, they require funds on a long-term basis; these funds have got to be collected from people who have accumulated them out of surpluses of their incomes over their current consumption expenses. Thus, we get two classes of societies which are relevant to the process of capital formation. There is a class of investors or the entrepreneurs who are undertaking investments by building up real capital; and there is a class of people who are accumulating savings. These two classes are required to be brought together by some third agency. The capital market acts as such a third agency which is above the Banking and Non-banking intermediaries. Those who have got savings, hand over their savings to the banks and other financial institutions in the form of term deposits. These deposits constitute the supply of funds available for long-term investments in the capital market. On the demand side, we have all the entrepreneurs, big and small. These two sides are given an opportunity of coming together by the capital market.

(3) Mobility of Capital : Without the help of capital market, the mobility of capital remains limited. Geographically, people would make capital available only at the local level. But when capital market enters the scene with all its constituents like the Stock Market, Commercial Banks, Development Banks, etc., the geographical mobility of capital increases. As a result, anybody who has some savings to invest can invest anywhere in the country, or even outside the country, through the capital market.

Industrywise mobility of capital is also important. If people desire to switch their investments from one industry to another, such a facility must be readily available. This is made available by the capital market. People can sell their shares and stocks and buy different ones through the capital market. This facilitates mobility of capital from one industry to another industry.

(4) Economic Dynamism : In a modern dynamic world, the economy is required to be dynamic, when old order changes giving place to a new, availability of capital must also change accordingly. Inventions and innovations effect changes in the pattern of capital requirements of various industries. New companies enter the capital market with new public issues. Old stocks are required to be liquidated. These functions are the functions of the new and old stock markets which are a constituent of the capital market.

(5) Economic Development : In a developing economy, capital market has to function as an inevitable catalyst of development. In a developing economy, capital is basically shy. With the development of capital market, capital becomes bold in the sense that it starts undertaking risks of various types. In course of economic development, new avenues of investment are required to be opened-up. People must respond to these new challenges. Capital market provides such opportunities to the people. With growing incomes of people, additional resources are generated in areas where these never existed before. For example, the rural areas in India never served as sources of funds until the nineteen-sixties or seventies. But now, even in rural areas, savings are being generated on a significant scale. For mopping up these savings and channelising them towards capital formation. Capital market acts as an effective instrument. This is why the institutions of a capital market are expected to provide a network of branches throughout the country.

4.8 Composition of Capital Market

The organisation of a capital market consists of mechanisms and institutions, or the various intermediaries responsible for the transfer of funds from those who save to those who require them for investment. These intermediaries bring together the borrowers and the investors, that is, companies that issue capital and the persons desirous of purchasing capital so issued. As we have send in our definition of the capital market, these intermediaries also deal in existing financial instruments. In, the preceding section, we noted all such financial instruments and saw that they can be classed together as securities.

According to our definition, all the mechanisms and institutions or intermediaries, for short, which bring together the suppliers of capital and those who demand them, comprise a capital market. All these would, therefore, be the constituents of the capital market.
It is customary (and convenient too) to divide the capital market into two sub-markets : the market in existing securities (or old capital market) and the new issue market (or new capital market). Let us therefore, discuss the constituents of the capital market along the lines of this dichotomy. But, first, let us get a clear idea regarding the structure of capital market.

(A) Structure of Capital Market :

The structure of capital market consists of : (i) lenders section, (ii) borrowers section, (iii) the credit instruments and (iv) sub-markets.

The lenders section consists of commercial banks, savings and loan associations, stock exchanges, insurance companies, mortgage banks and so on.

The borrowers section mainly consists of corporate enterprises, Government and Semi-Government undertakings which require funds for various development purposes. In other words, corporate enterprises, Government and semi-Government undertakings are the main participants in the capital market as borrowers.

The main credit instruments of a capital market are : Bonds, debentures, equities, shares and stocks.

There are various sub-markets in the capital market. The sub-markets of a capital market consists of (1) mortgage markets, (2) corporate stock markets, (3) government bond market, (4) stock exchange market and (5) new issue market. The flow of investment is tackled by the stock exchange and it is supplemented by issue houses, underwriting houses and shareholders.

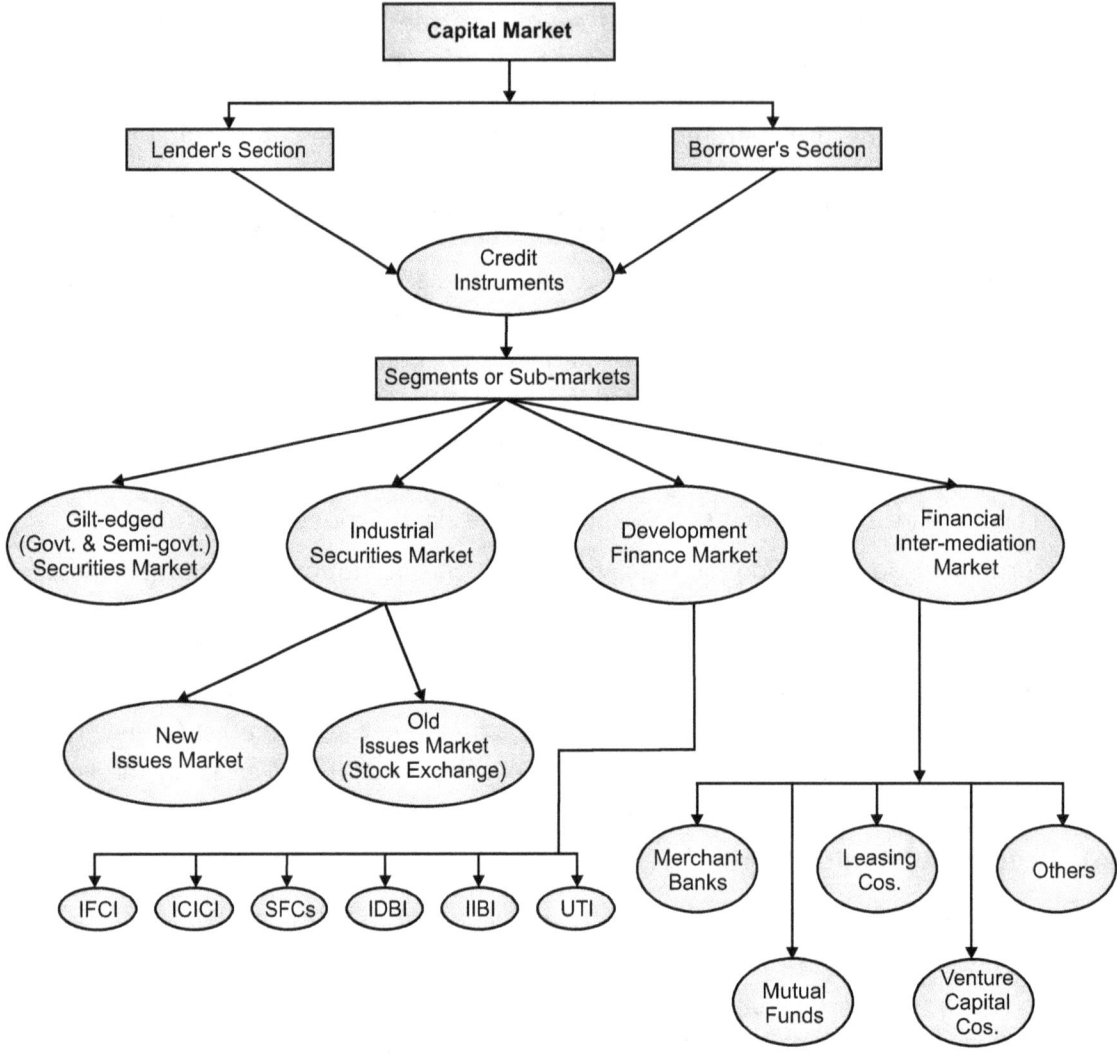

Fig. 4.4 : Structure of the Indian Capital Market

(B) The Market in Existing Securities (Old Issue Market) :

A security, whether issued by a company, a local authority, or the government, is, in itself, an illliquid asset. This means that the issuer does not undertake to repay the capital value to the holder immediately. Repayment in cases of bonds and debentures is made only when they reach their maturity. In cases of shares, the problem of repayment does not arise at all. It is here that the role of the market in existing securities becomes relevant. This is a market role of the market in existing securities becomes relevant. This is a market where a potential holder can obtain securities without waiting for new issue to where a potential holder can obtain securities without waiting for new issue to appear, and the holders of securities can sell their securities if they want cash or if they want a rearrangement of their investments.

In this market, the following agencies normally operate :

(1) The Stock Exchange : The stock exchange provides an organised market for the purchase and sale of existing securities. Though we speak of a stock exchange, there are, in fact, numerous stock exchanges in a country. As noted above, the holders want to arrange their investment portfolios from time to time. Similarly, some of the holders may be in need of cash. Some people who might have accumulated surplus funds may want to invest these. The needs of all these people can be met by the stock exchange. Through the stock exchange, shares, stocks, bonds and debentures can be bought and sold. Hence, in a modern capitalist economy, the stock exchange has become an important institution. In fact, we can say that the stock exchange is the most important constituent of the capital market. They act as the 'weather cock' of the economic climate of the country. The stock exchanges serve as a mirror of the investors confidence in the financial position of the economy. The stock exchanges stimulate capital formation. These ensure a constant flow of capital into industrial stream. On account of these services provided by the stock exchange, its importance has been recognised by every country. In a country like India, which has undertaken development programmes, the stock exchanges have to play a very crucial role in mobilising and channelising these instruments into investments.

During the period of Second World War, there were seven stock exchanges in India. However, the speculative gains during the war time led to the establishment of several stock exchanges in India. With the existence of too many stock exchanges with a wide diversity in the rules and regulations with respect to membership and trading and the postwar crash compelled the Government of India to enact. The Securities Contract (Regulation) Act in 1956 came into force in February 1957. With the provision in the Act, only eight stock exchanges had been given licence to operate in the country. The recognised eight stock exchanges in India were :

(a) Mumbai Stock Exchange   (b) Kolkata Stock Exchange

(c) Chennai Stock Exchange   (d) Ahmedabad Stock Exchange

(e) Delhi Stock Exchange   (f) Hyderabad Stock Exchange

(g) Indore Stock Exchange   (h) Bangalore Stock Exchange

Now the number of stock exchanges is twenty-three, including the NSE and OTCE, and includes centres like Cochi, Kanpur, Pune, Ludhiana, Guahati, Kanara, Magadh, Jaipur, Bhubaneshwar, Saurashtra, Vadodara and Coimbatore.

Functions of Stock Exchanges :

These stock exchanges in India perform the following functions. They are :

(a) To promote facilities for sale and purchase of securities;

(b) To provide a continuous market for all types of securities;

(c) To provide facilities of evaluating the income-yielding worth of securities,

(d) To provide guarantee about the integrity and honesty on the part of businessmen by listing only those securities which are reliable and which are issued in accordance with the rules laid down by the stock exchanges,

(e) To help mobilise the surplus funds of individuals, business firms and corporations for investment into more productive fields, and,

(f) To serve to bring about the even distribution of funds, geographically as well as among different types of industries.

(2) Stock Brokers : The stock brokers provide the link between the market and the public. They are authorised broker-members of the stock exchange. They act as intermediaries on behalf of their clients, charging a commission for their services. In other words, people who want to buy or sell securities have to place their orders with a broker who is a member of the stock exchange. This they can do by opening an account with a broker.

(3) The Jobbers : Jobbers are important constituents of a British stock exchange. Unlike the brokers who carry out their client's instructions, jobbers deal as 'principals', trading on their own account. They purchase securities from the brokers; they sell to brokers, and, technically, 'own' the securities which may be in their possession at any given time.

The transactions take place in the following way : A stock broker with a sale or purchase order from his client approaches a jobber dealing in that type of security which is to be bought or sold, on the floor of the exchange. The jobber quotes two prices : the higher at which he would sell and the lower at which he would buy. If the broker agrees with the quotation, the deal is made. The difference between the two prices is the jobber's profit. The task of the jobbers is very difficult as he should be able to read the market trends and he must weigh the market demand and supply pressures. This is why the jobbers, usually specialise in a small segment of the stock market.

(C) The New Issue Market :

The stock exchange, as we saw above, provides an organised market for the sale and purchase of existing securities. Every day the securities of various companies or of the Government may be traded. But this does not mean that every day, additional finance is made available to the Government or to the companies. Raising of new money capital is, therefore, the task of the New Issue Market.

Any joint-stock company wants its securities to be freely dealt in by the stock exchange. This secures marketability and attracts individual as well as institutional investors. But, for availing of the facility, a company has to apply to the Stock Exchange Council for dealings to be allowed-or getting its securities listed in the officially-traded securities of the exchange. For getting the securities listed, the company has to fulfil, satisfactorily, a number of conditions.

Let us know the constituents of the New Market and their working.

(1) Issuing Houses : Issuing Houses of the United Kingdom are specialised agencies for promotion of new enterprises. Raising of capital requires a reputation which a new company may not have. Unless the new company wins the confidence of the investing public, its shares are not likely to be subscribed.

Besides, floatation of capital involves many technicalities and legal provisions. An Issuing House provides these services. On the basis of the prospectus, potential buyers apply to the Issuing House which performs the function of allotment of shares to various applicants. Sometimes, the issue is over subscribed and the Issuing House makes a proportional allotment to each subscriber. Full payment is made, sometimes, after the date of issue.

Thus, even if a company is new, the Issuing House is reputed and it becomes easy to collect funds through a Issue House. Besides, all the technicalities can be completed satisfactorily. All this is done by the Issue Houses against a commission.

In case of Government securities, however, the Central Bank of the country shoulders the responsibility of issuing and so the services of the Issue Houses are not required.

The function of the Issuing Houses is a promotional one. In the U.S.A. this function is performed by the *Investment Banks*. In some countries, including U.K., this type of service is provided by the Commercial banks.

(2) Underwriters : It is also possible that the issue is under-subscribed. i.e. the issued capital is not fully sold. The new company, under such conditions, will not only be greatly disappointed but will be handicapped. It will not be able to proceed with its plans. To avoid this, the company, directly or through the Issuing Houses where they exist, may arrange for its issues to be underwritten. Sometimes, the Issuing Houses themselves do the underwriting business. But, usually, underwriting is done as an independent function, by institutions that specialise in this function. Underwriters have an obligation to take-up any parts of the issue that have not found other purchasers. Thus, for example, if a company employs the services of an underwriter and issues shares worth ₹ 10 lakhs, but can sell shares worth ₹ 5 lakhs only, then the underwriter will have to buy the remaining shares and pay ₹ 5 lakhs to the company.

In many countries where independent underwriting institutions do not exist, the function is performed by the banks or other financial institutions. Development banks are an important category of such institutions doing this business.

Underwriting, obviously, involves a risk and those who perform this function are rewarded by a commission. The function is an important one, as it paves the way for the launching of new enterprises

(3) Stock Brokers : Stock brokers function in this segment of the capital market as well. Especially, the individual buyers of securities employ the services of brokers.

(4) Financial Institutions : The agencies which we discussed so far, perform the function of bringing together the buyers and sellers of securities. The new enterprises and the Government are the major sellers of securities in the New Issue market. But, for subscribing to these, enough funds should be available. Some other intermediaries should be there who collect the savings of the individual savers and direct them to the capital market. This function is performed by a number of financial institutions who have collected investible funds and who are in search of investment opportunities. Since these institutions are varied, we shall discuss them, in detail, under a separate section which follows :

(a) Commercial Banks : The second important constituent of the Indian capital market are the Indian Joint Stock Banks or the Commercial banks. The Commercial banks in India were the product of the British Commercial banking model. The concept of Term-loan runs counter to this model. That is, a Commercial bank with its liabilities payable on demand, should carry the bulk of assets in self-liquidating short-term paper or in the paper which is readily saleable. Thus, the Commercial banks in India restricted their activities to only short-term lending during the pre-independence period.

However, after independence, particularly after Nationalisation of 14 Commercial banks, the Commercial banks are taking active interest and increasingly participating in term-lending through subscribing substantially to the shares and debentures of special financial institutions. The Commercial banks have also taken lead in setting up Venture Capital companies, Leasing companies, Mutual Funds etc. to mobilise savings for investment in industrial securities.

The Commercial banks in India purchase old securities as well as new securities appearing in the capital market. The Commercial banks also perform the underwriting function. The Commercial banks also serve as a link between the capital market and the money market in India. Thus, the Indian Commercial banks have come to play a very crucial and important role in the Indian Capital market.

(b) Specialised Financial Institutions : The most remarkable feature of the development of the Indian capital market, during the post-independence period is the establishment of several specialised financial institutions. We mention below such specialised financial institutions :

(i)   The Industrial Finance Corporation of India (IFCI).

(ii)   The State Financial Corporations (SFCs).

(iii)   The Industrial Credit and Investment Corporation of India (ICICI).

(iv)   The Industrial Development Bank of India (IDBI).

(v)   The Industrial Investment Bank of India (IIBI).

(vi)   The Unit Trust of India (UTI).

Each of these specialised financial institutions serves a specific requirement of capital in the industrial economy of India. These specialised financial institutions have, together, served to fill up the wide gaps that existed in the institutional structure of Indian Capital Market.

(5) Specialised Financial Intermediaries : In Western countries, we come across Specialised Financial Intermediaries to "promote", "issue", "underwrite" and "distribute" securities. In the Indian Capital Market, such Specialised Financial Intermediaries were conspicuous by their absence.

However, the Government of India has, now, taken a lead in setting up new Financial Intermediaries. We mention here below some of the important financial intermediaries :

(a) **Risk Capital And Technology Corporation Ltd. :** This Corporation provides assistance in the form of technology finance and risk capital.

(b) **Technology Development and Information Company of India Ltd. :** Whenever new technology ventures are undertaken, this Company assists in the form of 'project finance'.

(c) **Leasing and Hire-Purchase Companies :** Such leasing and Hire-purchase companies assist small and medium sized enterprises to acquire plant, equipment and infrastructure development.

(d) **Mutual Funds set up by Commercial Banks :** Mutual Funds developed by Commercial banks mobilise savings of the public and utilise the funds so collected in the capital market.

The institutions, mentioned above are of recent origin and are in the stage of development. These institutions are playing and are bound to play an important role in the Indian Capital Market. Some more institutions have emerged on the scene these few examples are only illustrative.

4.8.1 Recent Developments in Indian Capital Market

(1) New Measures of Risk Management System in Indian Capital Market : Every shareholder or investor wants to protect his investment and promote it as his source of earning. So, my always concentration is on new measures the Risk Management System of SEBI which is the controller of Indian Capital Market. SEBI did several steps in this regards.

(a) Price Volatility : It is the relative rate at which the price of a security moves up and down. But this technique of profit maximisation which is used by bad guys for wrong purposes. They buys shares at very cheap rates and sell when overpriced. Because, they get idea of trend of next price of shares with invalid source instead of using mathematical formula which is given below.

Using a simplification of the formulas above it is possible to estimate annualised volatility based soley on approximate observations. Suppose you notice that a market price index, which has a current value near 10,000, has moved about 100 points a day, on average, for many days. This would constitute a 1% daily movement, up or down. Volatility is often viewed as a negative term in the market that represents uncertainty and risk. Higher volatility brings worry to the investors as they watch the value of their portfolios move wildly and decrease in value. To reduce price volatility and stability in the prices of stock market. A major reform undertaken by SEBI was the introduction of derivatives products : Index futures, Index options, Stock options and Stock futures.

(b) Current Breakers : This is another recent development in Indian Capital Market. We all know an excessive speculation is always risky for every investor. For reducing it, SEBI has introduced place circuit breakers.

A circuit breaker is the system which stops to trade in stock market when prices move after a specific level. For example, if a stock is at ₹ 100 and circuit breaker is fixed at 5%, then stock trading will stop if it hit of ₹ 95 or ₹ 105. There are mainly two types of circuit breakers. One is index wise circuit breakers and other is stock wise circuit breakers.

The index-based market-wide circuit breaker system applies at 3 stages of the index movement, either way viz. at 10%, 15% and 20%. These circuit breakers when triggered bring about a co-ordinated trading halt in all equity and equity derivative markets nation-wide. The market-wide circuit breakers are triggered by movement of either the BSE Sensex or the NSE S&P CNX Nifty, whichever is breached earlier. In case of a 10% movement of either of these indices, there would be a one-hour market halt if the movement takes place before 1 : 00 p.m. In case the movement takes place at or after 1 : 00 p.m. but before 2 : 30 p.m. there would be trading halt for ½ hour. In case movement takes place at or after 2 : 30 p.m. there will be no trading halt at the 10% level and market shall continue trading. In case if the market hits 10% before 1 : 00 p.m. then as explained there would be a one hour halt in trading and after resumption of trade in case if the market hits 15% in either index, then there shall be a two-hour halt. If the 15% trigger is reached on or after 1 : 00 p.m. but before 2 : 00 p.m., there shall be a one-hour halt. If the 15% trigger is reached on or after 2 : 00 p.m. the trading shall halt for the remaining part of the day.

(c) Intraday Trading Limit : Intraday Trading, also know as 'Day Trading', is the system where you take a position on a stock and release that position before the end of that days' trading session. Thereby making a profit for yourself in that buy-sell or sell-buy exercise. All in one day.

(d) Mark to Market Margin : MTM margin is imposed to cover loss that a member may incur, in case the transaction is closed out at a closing price different form a price at which the transaction has been entered.

It is just collection in cash for all futures contracts and adjusted against the available Liquid Networth for option positions. In the case of futures Contracts MTM may be considered as Mark to Market Settlement.

(2) Investigations : If any company law or SEBI Act's rules regarding Indian capital market are violated, its investigation is done by SEBI. This is the 1st of cases resulted in compounding in the prosecution filed by SEBI (As on 30th June 2010).

(3) Investor Awareness Campaign : For making Indian Capital Market more secure for Indian and foreign Investors, SEBI has started investors awareness campaign. For this, SEBI has made his official site's sub domain at http://investor.sebi.gov.in/.

Under this campaign, Workshishops/Seminars Conducted by Investor Associations recognised by SEBI. There the following things are included :

(a) Do not enter into securities transactions with unregistered intermediaries.

(b) Do not get carried away by advertisements promising unrealistic gains and windfall profits.

(c) Do not invest based on market rumours or unconfirmed or unauthentic news. Be aware that advice through television or print media does not mean that it is the opinion of the channel or publisher.

(4) Ban on Inside Trading : Insider trading is the trading of a corporation's stock or other securities (e.g. bonds or stock options) by individuals with potential access to non-public information about the company. In most counties, trading by corporate insiders such as officers, key employees, directors. To ban on inside trading, SEBI has made (Prohibition of Insider Trading) Regulations, 1992.

(5) Trading Cycle under T + 2 : 'T' represents the trade day. 'T + 2' implies the settlement on the 2th trading day. SEBI has reduced the settlement cycle upto T + 2 and in future, it may be T + 1 settlement cycle. But SEBI accepted shorter settlement cycles will mean more pressure on trade processing systems so that funds/ securities are ready for pay-in/pay-out on the next day.

4.8.2 Modern Instruments of Indian Capital Market

(1) External Commercial Borrowings (ECB) : ECB is emerging as an important segment of diversified sources for finance for Indian corporates. External Commercial Borrowings (ECBs) are defined to include commercial bank loans, buyers' credit, suppliers' credit, securitised instruments such as Floating Rate Notes and Fixed Rate Bonds etc. credit from official export credit agencies and commercial borrowings from the private sector windows of multilateral financial institutions such as Internal Finance Corporation, Asian Development Bank, etc.

Purpose of External Commercial Borrowings :

ECBs are being permitted by Government as a source of finance for medium corporate for expansion of existing capacity as well as for fresh investment. ECBs are supposed to utilised for meeting foreign exchange cost of capital goods and services and also project related rupee expenditure.

(2) American Depository Receipts (ADRs) : It is a tradable instrument, equivalent to a fixed number of shares, which is floated on overseas market. ADR issues can be made at four levels on the preference of the company. The norms for each level differ and are based on the specific criteria to be satisfied by the issuer.

Levels of ADRs :

(a) Level - I : The ADRs is the most basic route under which the company issues depository receipts which are traded on the OTC exchanges abroad. Under this programme, the company gives a mandate to a depository which provides information about the company to investment institutions, brokers, equity analysts and other investors. The company executives interact with the investors and analysts to provide the relevant particulars about the company. Once the investors are convinced, the investors place their orders through an overseas investment banker who contacts an Indian broker. The local broker purchases the shares on behalf of the depository, which in turn issues ADRs against these shares in a pre-determined ratio. The ADRs so issued are traded on the OTC exchange overseas.

(b) Level - II : In Level - II ADR programming, listing of ADR is manadatory. The company proposing a Level - II ADR issue has to conform to US accounting practices and SEc norms and satisfy certain financial and listing criteria. A non - US Company should have at least 5000 shareholders and a market value of public shares of at least $ 100 million.

(c) Level – III : In Level - III ADR programme, or the non-sponsored level is for companies which have already made ADR issues and the ADRs are listed on one of the US exchanges. This issue is targeted at American investors.

(d) Level - IV : In Level - IV ADR programme, or the Restricted Area ADR programme, is same as the level - III route. Under this issue, the ADRs are offered only to qualified institutional buyers. Reliance Industries and Grasim Industries Ltd. has adopted this route for raising resources.

(3) Global Depository Receipts (GDRs) : Global Depository Receipt (GDR) is a negotiable instrument and is created when an investor purchases shares of a foreign company in the domestic stock market and the same is deposited with a custodian of a depository. The depository issues receipts regarding such shares and such receipts represent a depository receipt. A GDR can be traded publicly and is issued by the depository banks in terms of deposit agreement entered into with the issuer company.

The concept of GDR was originated in the Western Capital Markets. Originally GDRs were designated on instruments which enabled investors in USA to trade in securities which were not listed in stock exchanges in the USA in the form of American Depository Receipts (ADRs) till 1983. The market for ADRs was largely investor driven and the depository banks were permitted to issue ADRs to investors even without the consent of the company. However, in 1983 the Securities Exchange Commission (SEC) made it mandatory for the companies to provide for certain information for issue of ADRs.

Advantages of GDRs :

(a) The GDRs offer to the issuer company that the issue proceeds are collected in foreign currency and the same can be utilised for meeting the foreign exchange component of purchase cost, repayment of foreign currency loans, meeting overseas commitments for some other purposes.

(b) GDR is denominated in US dollars with the equity shares underlying each GDR is denominated in rupees, there is no exchange risk for the issuer.

(c) A GDR also gives an option to the holder to convert the same into underlying shares and holds equity shares of the company instead of GDRs.

(d) An investor who wants to cancel his GDRs can cancel it by advising the depositor who un-issued such a receipt in lieu of the shares held by the custodian. It can be cancelled after 45 days. The depositor instructs the custodian regarding the cancellation of GDR and to release the corresponding shares in the market, collect the sale proceeds and remit the same abroad.

(e) A holder of GDRs does not have any voting right and so the company does not have the fear of losing management control.

4.9 Stock Exchanges in India

The stock exchanges which impart liquidity to the capital, already issued are the most important part of the capital market. These serve as trading centres for stocks, shares and bonds which have large local and national following. They bring the buyers and sellers of securities together quickly and effectively.

Common Characteristics :

Though there are differences in the characteristics of stock exchanges, their *common characteristics* can be, summarised as follows :

(1) These are voluntary associations regulated by law, which provide facilities to members to transact business and regulate their operations.

(2) These are managed by a governing body consisting of elected members. It regulates by using wide disciplinary powers, the dealings of the members which take place on the floor of the exchange.

(3) Membership rules are very strict. This is due to the responsibilities and standards expected of the members.

The transactions in stock exchange are limited to securities which are included in the official list of the exchange. Such securities are known as 'Listed Securities' and these are subjected to rigid rules. Listing of securities is preceded by the fulfilment of various conditions. The company applying for getting its securities listed has to furnish, in the beginning as well as regularly afterwards, the information regarding its own financial affairs. Adequate number of share certificates, in proper forms, are required to be printed. Manipulation of ownership is controlled by the exchange. Similarly, all changes in the assets and capital position of the company are required to be reported to the stock exchange.

Working / Operating Mechanism of Stock Exchanges :

The *working* of typical *stock exchange transactions* can be summarised in the following steps :

(1) Since only the members can transact business in a stock exchange, outsiders, interested in buying or selling securities, have to do so through a member broker. Everybody who is not a member has to open an account with a member-broker. Then, he places his orders with broker. There are many types of orders, each having a definite meaning.

(2) The orders are then executed by brokers or their representatives. The bargain appears in the exchanges. Daily Official List indicating the number and price of securities traded on that day.

(3) Transactions are then reported to the clients, and contract notes are sent to them by the brokers.

(4) Finally, the transactions are settled. In the case of ready delivery transactions, payment is to be made immediately or within seven days after the transfer of securities. In case of forward deals, transactions are settled once in a month at the Bombay Stock Exchange or once in a fortnight at the London Stock Exchange.

Control of Stock Exchanges :

Because the stock exchange occupies an important position in the capital market, it is subjected to legal controls by the government. Only the recognised stock exchanges are allowed to function. Recognition rests on (1) whether the rules and bye-laws of the stock exchange, ensure protection to depositors, and guarantee fair dealings; (2) whether the functioning is in the interest of trade and also in the interest of the public; and (3) whether the exchange is willing to abide by the rules imposed by the government.

The Government control the activities of the stock exchange by elaborate legal provisions. The major objective of such controls is to restrict speculation in to safeguard the interest of genuine investors. They also aim at creating conditions favourable for a healthy growth of the capital market.

National Stock Exchange (NSE) :

The IDBI and other All India Financial Institutions in Mumbai jointly came forward to establish the National Stock Exchange in November 1992. The paid-up equity capital of the NSE was ₹ 25 crores. After getting recognition from the Government during the same year, the NSE started operations in Wholesale Debt Market in June 1994 and those in Equity Trading in November 1994. The Wholesale Debt Market primarily aimed at catering to the money market needs of banks and other financial institutions with a view to encouraging high value transactions of the bonds issued by the Public Sector Undertakings, units issued by the UTI, Treasury Bills and Government Securities issued by the Government and of call money transactions. The important characteristic of the NSE is that there is no trading floor of the exchange and the trading, though in large volumes, is over the telephone and other telecommunication in India. Trading is done on the computer with the help of PC Terminals in the offices of the brokers. Alongwith this money market segment, there is a capital market segment also which is operated on computer based trading. The settlement is on T + 7 basis for equity trading.

Advantages of the National Exchange of India (NSE) :

The advantages claimed for the working of the NSE are :

(1) The issue of securities becomes prompt and easy;

(2) The investors get a direct confirmation from the screen;

(3) Being a screen-based trading with national network, transparency is guaranteed;

(4) Both the time and the money spent on sales and purchases are reduced to the minimum, making the equity trading cost-effective;

(5) The investment counters can be spread throughout the country under the electronic network of the NSE;

(6) With the setting up of the Central Depositories, the book entry of deals and the mobilisation of certificates becomes easy; and

(7) A large number of companies are already listed on the NSE and an important feature is that trading in their securities is continuing simultaneously with those in the principal and Regional Stock Exchanges.

Operations of the NSE :

The NSE functions in the capital market segment of the country where corporate equity shares are traded on a weekly settlements basis, since November 1994. As noted earlier, it has no trading floor. Each trading member has a computer in his office, anywhere in India and is connected to the Central Computer System of NSE through leased lines or Very Small Aperture Terminals (VSATs), for an interim period, to be followed   by a satellite link. The members for debt market would be different from those in the equity market and the same members are not allowed to operate in both the markets. This is because the NSE operates two segments :

One, the debt market which is a part of the money market, and, two, the equity market which is the part of the capital market. Operations in both these segments are maintained separately. The post-trade services are also automated.

For confirmed traders, the settling bank would arrange for payment and clearance and depository for effective transfers by electronic book entry system. Today several banks are providing the depository facility for NSE.

(1) The Central Depository System : The system of multiple depositories has been accepted by the Government and SEBI was asked to formulate the guidelines for their operations. These depositories keep the physical custody of share certificates leading to immobilisation of shares to be followed later by dematerialisation and complete book entry system of trading in future.

Dematerialisation requires that the statement given by the depository is treated as evidence of the ownership of the shares. This method was being operated for the financial institutions, banks and mutual funds in the beginning and was, subsequently, extended to corporate bodies and individuals later on. The depository transfers securities between the participants through electronic book entries while the settling bank effects the transfer of funds.

(2) Listing and Settlement Systems : All medium and large-sized companies with a paid up equity capital of ₹ 10 crores and above are eligible to be listed on regular Stock Exchanges and can be listed on the NSE. Some of them may be listed and traded on the regular Stock Exchanges as well. Formalities of listing observed by the NSE are the same and a listing agreement is entered into with the company, as in case of a regular exchange and needs to the approved by the Government and SEBI.

The trading period on any day varies for the debt segment and the equity segment. So far as the capital market operations are concerned, the trading is done in equity shares, convertible debentures as well as non-convertible debentures. The trading network can spread all over the country, depending upon the availability of the electronic link through the satellite. A rolling settlement system operates in NSE with the settlement period of T + 7. What this means is that transactions on a given day (T) will be settled seven days later (T + 7). On that day, funds and securities are exchanged by passing the debit and credit entries electronically.

4.10 Role of SEBI

In April 1988, the Government established the Securities and Exchange Board of India (SEBI). Initially, the SEBI had no statutory powers. The Government had assigned certain preliminary functions to SEBI. These functions included (a) Collection of information regarding the capital market in general and the stock market in particular and advice the Government on the conditions and policy matters regarding the capital market; (b) Licensing of merchant banks, mutual funds etc. and regulation thereof; (c) Preparation of legal drafts in connection with both the regulatory and the developmental functions of SEBI; and (d) Carrying out such other functions entrusted to it by the Government.

(A) The Need for Setting up the SEBI :

The history of the stock markets in India dates back to 1875 when the Bombay Stock Exchange was established as a voluntary non -profit-making association of brokers. This was followed by the establishment of similar stock exchange at Ahmedabad in 1894. The stock exchanges in India thus, have a history of 125 years. However, during this period a number of defects and shortcomings crept into the functioning of the stock exchanges. We have already noted these shortcomings of the Indian capital market in general. Here we have to take note of specific drawbacks of the Indian stock exchanges.

(1) With the onset of economic reforms, the first phase of which can be said to have started in 1984, involved opening up of the economy. This necessitated the entry of foreign companies made easy with facilities for the issue of shares in India as well as outside. This was a much wider and broad-based task for which the Indian stock exchanges needed to be properly prepared. Such a preparation involved development of the stock markets as well as regulation of the activities in the stock markets.

(2) With the imminent privatisation, it had become necessary to attract private capital to the industrial field. But as we noted earlier, Indian capital has been proverbially shy. It was, therefore, necessary to instill confidence in the minds of the individual investors. This required some mechanism protecting their interests.

(3) The linking up of the Indian economy with the global economy presupposed the acceptance of universal standards and norms with which the Indian stock exchanges were not familiar. The enforcement of these norms was the responsibility of some body for which SEBI was best suited.

(4) The development of a balanced capital market had been a long-felt need. For this purpose, some special agency which could denote full time to the development of capital market was needed. The SEBI was expected to perform this function.

(5) A number of efforts are required for raising the level of capital formation and the establishment of SEBI was one such measure. This is because availability of a large number of shares and the guarantee of safe investment were the pre-requisites for such a development of the capital market.

(6) The rate of economic growth in India had reached a satisfactory level indicating that the propensity to save must be rising. In fact, with the spread of the benefits of development over a wide area and a diverse cross section of the society, the need to mop up small savings and channelise them into the industrial sector was necessary. This would serve to broad - base the industrial investment. This, in turn, required proper regulation and control of the market.

(7) By far, the most important need of SEBI sprang from the need to control various mal-practices for which the Indian stock markets have become notorious. Some examples of such malpractices could be given :

Malpractices in the Primary Market :

(i) The existence of too many self-styled investment advisors and consultants, (ii) The existence of what is known as the Grey Market, i.e., charging unofficial premiums on new issues, (iii) The practice of manipulating prices before floating a new issue, (iv) Delays involved in the despatch of letters of allotment, refund orders or share certificates, and (v) Delay in the listing of shares and the starting of open trading of shares.

Malpractices in the Secondary Market :

(i) Secrecy or lack of transparency in the trading operations as well as prices charged to clients, (ii) Either delay in passing contract notes or not passing contract notes at all, (iii) Delays in both delivery of shares and making of payments, (iv) The practice of allotting odd lots of shares to the share holders and refusal of the companies to stop this practice, (v) Insider trading by agents of companies or brokers, (vi) Rigging and manipulating stock prices, and (vii) The bids to take over and thereby to destablise the management.

(B) Objectives of SEBI :

As mentioned earlier, the SEBI was assigned with both regulatory as well as developmental functions. In view of these functions, the following objectives of SEBI can be stated :

(1) Protecting the Interest of the Investors : *To protect the interests of the investors so that the flows of savings into the Capital Market are stabilised.* With this objective in view, the SEBI began by collecting the grievances of the investors and seeking their redressal by referring them to the companies concerned, licensing of merchant banks and evolving guidelines for merchant banks as well as other financial intermediaries like the mutual funds. For this purpose the SEBI was given the necessary legislative back-up by the Government. It was also expected that the SEBI should act as a watch dog for the capital market. The Act passed in 1992 entitled the Securities and Exchange Board of India Act, 1992, contains provisions empowering the SEBI to protect the interests of the investors.

(2) Ensuring Fair Practices : *To ensure fair practices by the issuers of the securities,* i.e., the companies so as to minimise the costs of raising resources. With this in view, the SEBI has been given wide powers to call for information from the companies, to effect an audit of accounts, to impose fines, penalties etc. on erring companies and to play down the procedure for issue of shares and also to modify the procedure, from time to time, if the changing circumstances so demanded.

(3) Efficiency : *To promote efficient services by brokers, merchant bankers and other intermediaries* so as to make them more competitive and professional. For this purpose, various provisions in chapter V of the Act have been made which concerned the registration of Stock Brokers, Sub-brokers, Transfer agents etc. The members of recognised Stock Exchanges and their authorised brokers and sub-brokers operating as on 21-2-1992 were made to register with the SEBI immediately after the passing of the act.

(C) Powers, Functions and Role of SEBI :

Under the provisions of the Act, the SEBI can promulgate orders and regulations. Accordingly, initial regulations orders issued by SEBI related to registration, licensing, code of conduct, inspection of books of accounts etc. These powers were exercised by SEBI under section 12 of the SEBI Act. The SEBI started with issuing guidelines for merchant bankers, Mutual funds, portfolio managers and subsequently extended its guidelines to all intermediaries including brokers, sub-brokers, underwriters, registrars, collecting bankers, debenture trustees, and so on.

Under the Securities Contracts (Regulation) Act, 1956, the Government possessed powers to control the Stock Exchanges and their members. These powers were gradually delegated to the SEBI. For example by an amendment passed in 1995, the SEBI has been entrusted with penal powers and more extensive coverage. SEBI now wields powers to use its discretion in respect of permitting options and futures. Provisions regarding listing agreements and penal powers in cases of Default now vest with the SEBI. The SEBI has also got powers to regulate the capital market operations of the companies. Powers to grant recognition to Stock Exchanges, inspection and audit of Stock Exchanges and stock brokers' membership etc. including the recognition of Attached Trading Floors have been given to the SEBI . Venture capital funds are also brought under SEBI's control. Similar guidelines are given for mutual funds. In fact, SEBI's power extends to initiating civil and criminal proceedings against those who violate SEBI regulations.

The most note-worthy feature of the powers of SEBI is that they are being modified and extended according to changing circumstances in the financial markets. In a subsequent section, we are going to discuss reforms in the capital market in greater detail, where references to the widening of the scope of powers of SEBI will be made at appropriate places.

Chapter IV of the SEBI Act enumerates the powers and functions of SEBI. The functions of SEBI as given in this chapter can be summarised as follows.

Functions / Role and Powers of SEBI :

(1) To act as an apex institution for development and regulating of securities market.

(2) To register stock exchanges and to regulate trading on them. Co-ordinate, integrate and monitor the working of stock exchange and to establish new stock exchanges.

(3) To register, monitor, co-ordinate and regulate the activities pertaining to the issue and trading of securities.

(4) To grant permission for issue of securities and to formulate guidelines for issue and listing of securities.

(5) To define and enforce disclosure requirements on issue of securities both at the time of issue and at regular intervals after listing either in its own or in consultation with professional bodies like the Institute of Chartered Accountants, Institute of Cost and Works Accountants of India and Institute of Company Secretaries of India.

(6) To check insider trading and excessive speculation and to control practices not in the interest of investors.

(7) To monitor and regulate the functioning of mutual funds and investment companies.

(8) To regulate takeover deals, mergers and amalgamation.

(9) To conduct inspection, to order special audit of books of brokers, jobbers, merchant bankers, underwriters, investment advisors, to call for evidence and to institute civil and criminal proceedings were required.

(10) To conduct investment research and analysis to build up the data bank in the working of public limited companies and to help in setting of national information system.

Powers of SEBI :

In order to carry out the above functions effectively and efficiently, SEBI has been given various powers which were previously vested with the Central Government. These include :

(1) Power to call for periodical returns from stock exchanges.

(2) Power to call upon the stock exchange or any member of the stock exchange to furnish the relevant information.

(3) Power to appoint any person to make inquiries into the affairs of the stock exchange.

(4) Power to amend bye laws of stock exchange.

(5) Power to compel a public company to list its shares in any stock exchange.

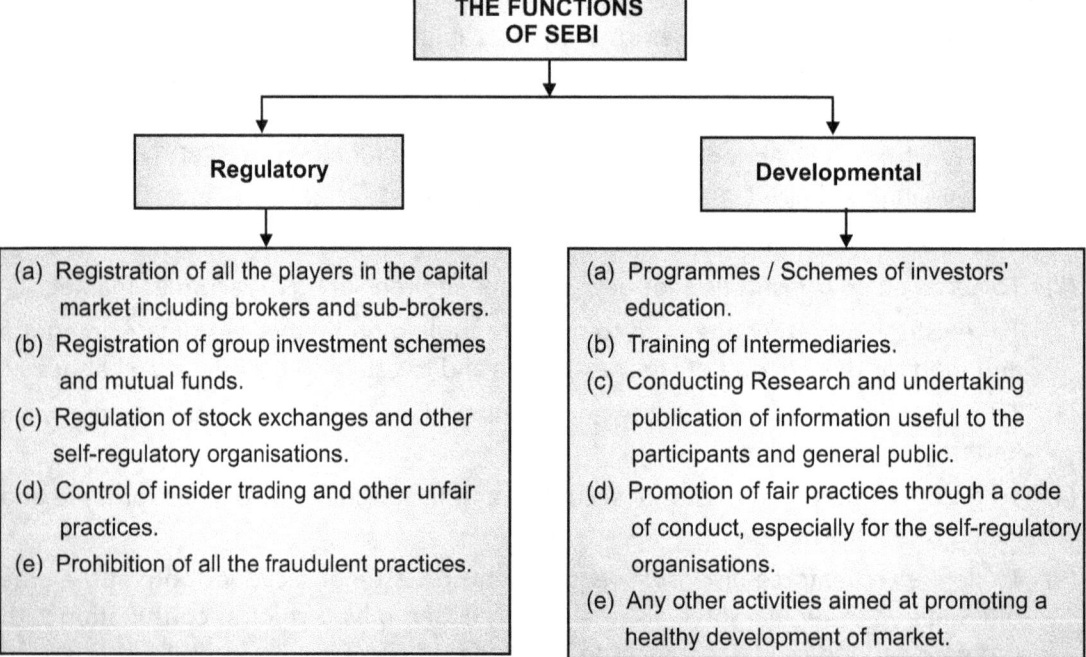

Fig. 4.5 : Functions of SEBI in Outline

The regulatory and the developmental functions listed above are illustrative. As noted earlier, these functions also go on increasing in accordance with the requirements of changing times. For example, with the launching of the OTCEI or with the extension of the facilities of ECS or with the establishment of depositories, requisite promotional steps and provision of necessary guidelines were undertaken by the SEBI.

4.11 Understanding of Stock Market Quotations

Stock Market Quotes refers to the prices of stocks traded in Stock Exchange.

Stock Market Quotes of Major Nifty Companies (As on 24-07-2013) Price Quotes on

Name of the Company	Open	High	Low	Close	P.E. Ratio	Volume
1. ACC	1241.90	1242.25	1211.05	1230.55	17.16	249 K
2. Ambuja Cement	194.00	194.10	186.60	191.20	20.05	3395 K
3. Axis Bank	1172.85	1172.85	1120.00	1125.15	9.71	2958 K
4. Bajaj Auto	1962.00	2010.00	1954.50	2001.80	18.91	278 K
5. Bharati Airtel	327.00	339.00	327.00	337.40	59.27	4354 K
6. BHEL	164.80	166.15	161.10	163.10	6.04	3718 K
7. BPCL	351.00	357.00	345.70	348.05	9.52	1151 K
8. Cairn India	300.10	311.75	300.10	308.60	4.89	1530 K
9. Hindalco	104.45	105.05	101.60	103.25	11.63	3803 K
10. HUL	718.00	725.00	705.25	709.45	40.71	3485 K
11. ICICI Bank	972.00	972.00	942.75	951.80	13.19	4640 K
12. Reliance Industries Ltd.	908.00	916.90	895.15	909.35	13.46	3152 K
13. SBI	1820.00	1827.00	1786.35	1801.25	6.88	2628 K
14. Tata Motors	298.00	300.95	294.70	297.30	9.67	4796 K
15. TCS	1748.50	1792.00	1745.00	1782.80	24.18	1091 K

Source : Financial Press 25-07-2013

Explanation of the Terms :

(1) **Open :** It is the open price of the share in the stock exchange.

(2) **High :** It shows the day's highest price of the stock.

(3) **Low :** It shows the day's lowest price of the stock.

(4) **Close :** It is the closing price of the share in the stock exchange.

(5) **P.E. Ratio :** It indicates the price-earning ratio of the company.

(6) **Volume :** It shows the total number of shares traded in the stock exchange.

Questions for Discussion

1. Explain the Role and Functions of Money Market.

2. Describe the Composition of Money Market.

3. State the Various Money Market Instruments.

4. Explain the Functions and Regulatory Role of RBI w.r.t. Currency, Credit and Balance of Payment.

5. Explain the Role and Functions of Capital Market.

6. Explain the Composition of Capital Market.

7. Describe the Role of SEBI.

8. Write short notes on :

    (A) Indian Financial System.

    (B) Scope and Operations of Money Market.

    (C) Features of Developed Money Market.

    (D) Characteristics of a Capital Market.

    (E) Stock Exchanges in India.

    (F) National Stock Exchange (NSE).

    (G) Need for Setting-up of SEBI.

Lets go with...

CHAPTER

5

PUBLIC FINANCE INFRASTRUCTURE

5.1 Meaning of Public Finance

Public finance is an important constituent of macro-economics, as the money-raising and money-spending activities of a modern government have a significant influence on the functioning of the economy. The functions of a modern government have become complex, and the resources available to these governments are diverse. In fact, both functions as well as resources of a modern government have undergone a great deal of change during the last few decades. It is this element of dynamism in public finance which calls for our closer examination.

Definitions of Public Finance :

(1) In the words of **Hugh Dalton**, *"It (Public Finance) is concerned with the income and expenditure of public authorities and with the adjustment of the one to the other, adjustment not necessarily to equality but to whatever arithmetical relationship in given conditions is best".*

(2) Another authority on public finance viz.; **Prof. Philip Taylor,** defines public finance in the following words : *"Public finance deals with the finances of the public as an organised group under the institution of Government. It thus deals only with the finances of Government. The finances of Government include the raising and disbursement of funds. Public finance is concerned with the operation of the fiscal or public treasury".*

Nature of Public Finance :

(1) **Public Authorities or Government :** The concern of public finance is the operation of the public as an organised group. For example, the expenditure of the Government on supplying safe drinking water is necessitated by the fact that people of a locality or a region live together as a group. The concern of public finance relates to all public authorities, in the sense that the local Government (in Municipal Council or a Village Panchayat or a Zilla Parishad) the State level Government as well as the federal or the Union Government are all public authorities and their activities are studied by public finance. In other words, public finance seeks to lay down the principles that govern the money-raising and money-spending activities of public authorities, at all levels from the local to the central.

(2) **A Fiscal Science :** Since public finance seek to lay down the principles underlying the fiscal activities of public authorities, it can legitimately claim to be termed as a science concerning the operations of the public treasury. As a science it has to formulate certain basic principles, laws and theories underlying the fiscal operations.

It has to follow certain logic or a discipline of reasoning and it also has to accept the responsibility of predicting the outcomes of fiscal operations. For example, public finance must undertake the responsibility of forecasting the effects of a particular tax or the entire tax system, on the economy as a whole or on different sectors of the economy taken separately. Similar exercises regarding predictions have got to be made regarding public spending and public borrowing.

(3) **Raising and Disbursement of Funds :** The funds raised by the Government can take various forms like direct taxation, indirect taxation, market borrowings, foreign loans, etc. Each one of these sources of funds have different policy implications and different consequences upon the economy. In the same way the disbursement of funds can be classified into current and capital expenditures, developmental and non-developmental expenditures, economic and social expenditures, productive and unproductive expenditures so on. Dichotomies like these in classification are relevant because each of these pairs implies different effects on aggregate production, distribution of income, etc.

(4) **Budgetary Policy :** Each public authority has to prepare a budget and get it sanctioned from the relevant legislative authority. Normally, the budget is balanced, in-so-far as the state or the local level authorities are concerned. However, whether the budget should be a balanced one, or a surplus one, or a deficit one depends upon the need of the economy and taking into account the effects of each of these types of the budget, the decision regarding the national budget has to be taken.

(5) Fiscal Problems : The operations of the public treasury can entail certain fall-outs in terms of unintended or undesirable effects. For example, the imposition of a tax on bank transactions may lead to certain favourable and certain adverse effects, some of which might be unintended and some might be undesirable. Such and several other fiscal problems are studied in public finance.

(6) Fiscal Policies : After taking into account the effects of each of the operations of the public treasury, it is possible, and indeed desirable, that these operations are used for bringing about the desired results and for discouraging undesirable activities of the people.

5.2 Familiarity with Important Terms / Agencies / Approaches / Practices related to National Income (Such as GDP, PPP, Growth Rate)

(A) Meaning and Definitions of National Income :

National income is the flow of goods and services which become available to a nation during a year. In common, national income means the total value of goods and services produced annually in a country.

National income is a macro economic concept. It is expressed and counted in money terms for one year.

In India, since 1955, the responsibility for the calculation of national income rests with the Central Statistical Organisation (CSO).

Definitions of National Income :

(a) **Marshall :** *"The labour and capital of a country acting on its natural resources, produce annually a certain net aggregate of commodities, material and immaterial including services of all kinds. This is true net annual national income."*

(b) **Pigou :** *"National Income is that part of objective income of the community including of course income derived from abroad which can be measured in money."*

(c) ***Fisher :*** *"The national income consists solely of the services as received by ultimate consumers, whether from their material or from their human environment."*

(d) **National Income Committee (1948) :** *"A national income estimate measures the volume of commodities and services turned out during a given period counted without duplication."*

(B) Importance of National Income Analysis :

National Income statistics are important for economic analysis and for framing economic policies. It appears that this realisation has grown particularly in the last thirty to forty years.

(1) National Income : *A Mirror of Economy :* The estimates of national income reflect the structure of economy, importance of the various sectors of economy as well as of the share of each sector and the factors of production like land, labour. They also reflect economic activities in various regions of the concerned country, etc. It can, therefore, be said that national income data are just a mirror of the country's economy.

(2) Level of Living of the People : One can get an idea of the standard of living of the people of a country from the statistical data concerning its national income. We have seen this in the context of Per-Capita-Income.

(3) Knowing the Trends of the Economic Activity : If national income statistics relating to a considerably long period in succession, are available, the trends taking stock of the economic activities can be judged. For example, these statistics help knowing the annual rate of growth of the national income, or, the trends of consumption, saving and investment. Similarly, these statistics are useful in finding out the causes of the decrease, instead of increase, in the national income, or of growth of production in a particular sector getting stagnated.

(4) Helpful in Framing Economic Policies : The statistical data relating to national income estimates make one understand the trends of the distribution of people's consumption-expenditure, saving and investment. Various policies can be framed on the basis of this data. For example, government can take measures like evolving schemes to promote popular savings, offering income-tax relief, etc. if it feels that the propensity to save on the part of the people is falling short of expectations. Also, by observing the actual levels of investment taking place in various sectors of the economy, government can act in giving appropriate direction to these investments. To illustrate, for motivating investment in the field of agriculture, banks in India give loans at low rates of interest.

(5) Judging Price-Trends : The data relating to money as also real income gives an idea about the trends of prices. In keeping with these trends, anti-inflationary or anti-deflationary programmes can be taken up.

(6) Providing a Basis for Economic Planning : The national income data are basic to economic planning. The position of each sector in a economy, and the trends in its development can be understood from these data. On the basis of this information, developmental targets for each of the sectors of economy can be fixed.

(7) Intra-National and Inter-National Comparison : The per capita income data enables to compare between the economic condition of various regions of a country. Likewise, on the basis of this data, the stages of economic development of different countries can be compared in various ways.

(C) National Income Accounting :

At the outset, it is necessary to explain the concept, 'Income'.

Man participates in the process of production, and gets income, as a return for this participation. But one who organises this work of production may be someone else, i.e., other person. Many individuals work for such 'others' and earn their livelihood. Someone works in an office while some others in a factory; some other person works at someone else's house as a house-maid while some other person works in a shop as a salesman. In each of these various examples, we have used the wording 'works'. What does this mean ? It means when a man works for another man or others, he sells his labour, i.e. his physical capacity to work. When a person earns income by selling merely his labour (and when no capital of any type whatsoever is not owned by this person), his income is of the nature of 'wages' or 'salary'. Wages and salaries, as reward for physical or intellectual types of work, are taken together for measurement. For the reward for labour, we are going to use the term '*Wages*'.

Those who hold money, can lend it do others. This money may be lent to an individual professional, trader, etc.; or it may be lent to an institution-a bank, company, government, etc. Such amounts lent earn the lender an interest. And '*Interest*' is an alternative source of earning income.

The third source of earning income is '*Rent*'. Rent is earned by an owner of one or more assets by making available one's land, plot, open space, building or its part, or even vehicles, furniture, etc., on rental basis, to tenants related to land or other of the above assets, from rural or urban areas.

Sometimes, a person undertakes, on his own enterprise or in partnership or alongwith the shareholders of his company, to enter a business activity and run a firm. If he does not have money, he borrows it and purchases or gets on rental basis, space for location, building, etc. He also, obtains raw material, installs machines, employs workers, and undertakes the process of production. Finally he also manages the marketing of his product. The income received by such a person is of the fourth type or source, and is called '*Profit*'. Profit is found out as follows :

Profit = VGO – (INP + FP)

In this equation, VGO means Value of Gross Output, INP means Value of All Inputs, and FP means Factor Payments. That is

Profit = Value of Gross Output – (Value of All Inputs + Factor Payments)

The value of Gross Output means the amount of the total sale-proceeds obtained after selling the goods or output. We get this value of gross output by multiplying the units produced by the per unit market price. By finding out the value of the raw-materials and auxiliary goods (like coal, fuel, electricity, etc.) on the basis of the market price, we get the Value of All Inputs. Factor Payments means the wages paid to all the workers plus rent for land, building etc., plus interest on the borrowed capital. Thus, Wages, Interest, Rent, and Profit are the four types of income, which are now considered and accepted by all over the world. Out of these, the first type, i.e. 'wages' are referred to as 'income from labour' while the remaining three types ('rent', 'interest', and 'profit') are referred to as 'income from assets' (or, in modern times, as 'income from capital').

According to the definition by **Dr. Alfred Marshall,** "Labour and capital (factor of production) of a country, acting on its natural resources (the basic factor of production), produce, annually, a certain 'net' aggregate of commodities, material and immaterial, including services of all kinds. The limiting word 'net' is needed to provide for using up of raw materials, and half-finished commodities and for wearing out and depreciation of plant which is involved in production, all such waste must, of course, be deducted from the gross produce before the true or net income can be found. And net income due on account of foreign investments must be added in. This is true net annual income or revenue of the country or national dividend".

This definition given by Dr. Marshall is accepted by all as a simple and yet all- inclusive definition. In computing income of a country, as this definition tells us, it is necessary to compute net income. For example, when the value of cloth is computed, the value of yarn and cotton should not be counted separately. Just as material goods are included in national income, immaterial or intangible goods like goodwill also are included in the income of the country. Also, many people like doctors, lawyers, professors, architects and other professionals, artists like singers, dancers, and priests, etc. are providing several services which cannot be shown in tangible, i.e. physical form.

Dr. Marshall's definition asks us to include such and all other services in national income. Moreover, the net addition to capital also is computed in income; but it is necessary to deduct depreciation to provide for replacement and maintain, intact, the original capital.

The intermediate goods used to produce final, i.e., finished goods, semi-finished goods like yarn, steel sheets or tanned leather that is circulating capital, should be excluded from the total gross output. Also, depreciation, i.e. loss of fixed capital due to wear and tear, should be excluded. The expenditure on these two types of capital is related to the perishing of goods in the process of production. And, therefore, unless it is excluded, we cannot know Net Income.

Taking into consideration the above discussion and following its essential points we can show, in the form of the following equation, how National Income (Y) can be arrived at :

$$Y = VGO - INP$$

Here, VGO means Value of Gross Output and INP means the value of Intermediate Products used during the period of production i.e. of Inputs.

For the purpose of the functional distribution of National Income, the four factors that have to be taken into account are : wages, interest, rent, and profit which are the sources of income to the people. It is practicable to treat 'Mixed Income' as the fifth factor. Theoretically, however, there are only four types of Income. But, in practice, there arises a problem in the case of the people who are engaged in self-employment, i.e., individual profession : farmers, artisans, those who run cottage and small industries, doctors, pleaders, artists petty shop-keepers and the like who provide many other services to society. All these people themselves work; use their own residential or other type of place; contribute, to some extent, their own capital; and organise their own business. Of course their income includes elements of all the four types of income, i.e., wage, rent, interest, and profit. In practice, it is impossible to separate these four types and hence, it is desirable to include their net sums in national income, as 'mixed income'.

If the value of all the goods used as inputs (INP) is deducted from gross output (VGO), we get the income of the four factors of production-labour, land, capital, and enterprise-*viz.* wages, rent, interest, interest and profit, and the mixed income. By adding these types of incomes earned in all the sectors of the economy as rewards to the factors of production, we get *Net Domestic Product* (NDP) at *Factor Cost*. Adding to this NDP, the net income received by the factors in foreign countries (abroad), we get *Net National Product* (NNP) at *Factor Cost*. The NNP at Factor cost itself is called *'National Income'*.

(D) Basic Concepts in National Income :

To understand the various forms of national product or Income, let us start with Net Domestic Product at Factor Cost :

(1) Net Domestic Product at Factor Cost [NDP (FC)] :

$$\text{NDP (FC)} = \text{Wages} + \text{Interest} + \text{Rent} + \text{Profit} + \text{Mixed Income}$$

(2) Net Domestic Product at Market Prices [NDP(MP)] :

$$\text{NDP (MP)} = \text{NDP (FC)} + \text{INT} - \text{S}$$

Where INT denotes Indirect Taxes and S is subsidy.

The taxes on goods (commodities) are called 'Indirect Taxes'. Their examples are : Excise Duty, Sales Tax etc. As, due to these taxes the market price of the good increases, this amount is included in the original price. Inversely, 'Subsidy' is the amount paid by the Government to assist the producer in meeting the cost of his production. Subsidy on chemical fertilisers is one of such examples. The market prices of the goods decrease because of this subsidy. And hence, subsidy is deducted in this calculation.

(3) Net National Product at Market Prices [NNP (MP)] :

$$\text{NNP (MP)} = \text{NDP (MP)} + \text{NFI}$$

Where, NFI stands for Net Foreign Income.

In an open economy, citizens of the country can earn income from abroad. Similarly, foreign nationals earn some income in our country but this income goes out of the country. For example, dividend received by foreign shareholders, interest on foreign loans, or rent for accommodation of the Embassy, etc. are the ways through which our income goes out of the country. Likewise, income from abroad-by way of dividend, interest, royalty, tariff, etc. comes into our country. By deducting these two, we get Net Foreign Income (NFI). This net amount is arrived at by deducting the income going out of our country from the income coming into our country. By adding this amount of Net Foreign Income to Net Domestic Product at Market Prices, we get Net National Product at Market Prices' [NNP (MP)].

(4) Gross National Product at Market Prices [GNP (MP)] :

$$\text{GNP (MP)} = \text{NNP (MP)} + \text{D}$$

Where, D is Depreciation.

Lastly, when the loss of Fixed Capital or Depreciation is added to the Net National Product at Market Prices, we get 'Gross National Product at Market Prices' [GNP (MP)].

From these four equations, equations of other concepts relating to the computation of National Income, or of the other forms of National Income, or of the other forms of National Products can be framed. Such equations are given below :

(5) Gross Domestic Product at Market Prices [GDP (MP)] :

$$GDP \ (MP) \ = \ C + I + G + (X - M)$$

Where,   C = Consumption Expenditure,

I = Domestic Private Investment,

G = Government Consumption and Investment Expenditure, and

X – M = Export – Import.

(6) Gross National Product at Factor Cost [GNP (FC)] :

$$GNP \ (FC) \ = \ GNP \ (MP) - INT$$

It should be remembered that here (as also later), Indirect Taxes (INT) are considered in their 'net' form, i.e. deducting Subsidy (S) from the total amount of Indirect Taxes (INT).

(7) Gross Domestic Product at Factor Cost [GDP (FC)] :

$$GDP \ (FC) \ = \ GNP \ (FC) - NFI$$

(8) Net National Product at Factor Cost [NNP (FC)] :

$$NNP \ (FC) \ = \ GNP \ (FC) - D$$

Thus, National Income or National Product is expressed or computed in eight different forms. These forms can easily be remembered. But for that, these forms should be classified, and it should be understood how one form is arrived at from the other.

Fig. 5.1 clarifies this.

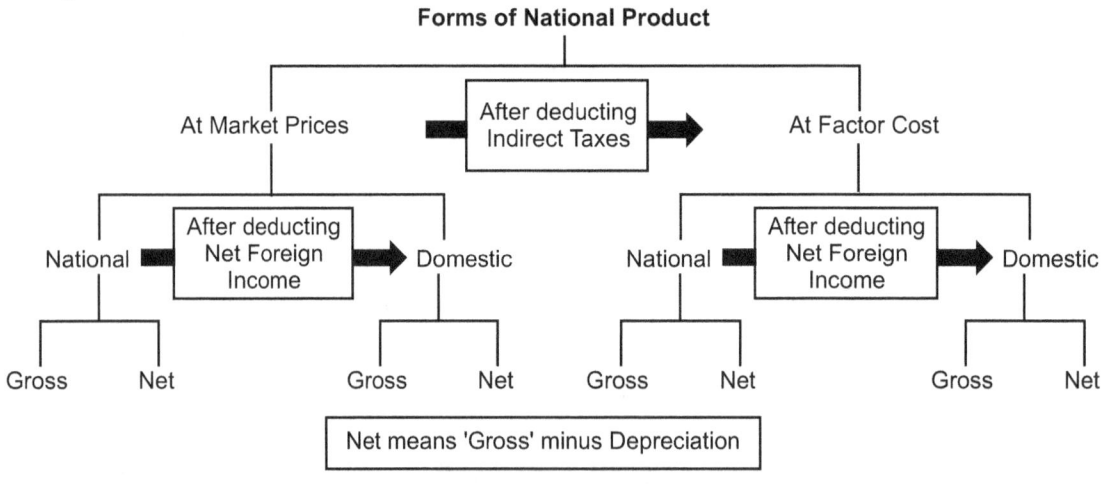

Fig. 5.1 : Concepts in National Income Estimation

These forms can also be shown in a different way. Fig. 5.2 shows these. It will be easier to follow the inter-relationship between the eight forms of National Product because of their presentation in equations.

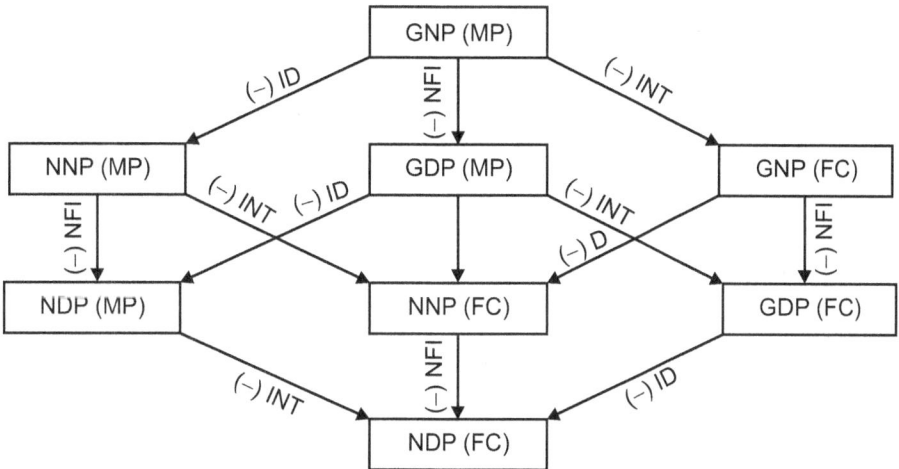

Fig. 5.2 : Inter-relationship between Various Forms of National Product

GNP = Gross National Product	FC	= At Factor Cost
NNP = Net National Product	D	= Depreciation
GDP = Gross Domestic Product	INT	= Indirect Net Taxes
NDP = Net Domestic Product	NFI	= Net Factor Income from Abroad
MP = At Market Prices		

(E) GDP, PPP, Growth Rate :

(a) GDP at Market Price and GDP at Factor Cost : Gross domestic product at market price is the gross market value of all final goods and services produced within the domestic territory of a country during a period of one year.

Symbolically, $GDP_{(MP)} = C + I + G + (X – M)$.

Gross Domestic Product at Factor Cost : Gross domestic product at factor cost refers to the gross money value of all final goods and services produced within the domestic territory of a country during a period of one year.

Symbolically, $GDP_{(FC)} = GDP_{(MP)} – $ **Indirect Taxes + Subsidies.**

(b) PPP : Purchasing Power Parity (PPP) is an economic concept and a technique used to determine the relative value of currencies estimating the amount of adjustment needed on the exchange rate between countries in order for the exchange to be equivalent to (or on par with) each currency's purchasing power.

It asks for how much money would be needed to purchase the same goods and services in two countries, and used to calculate an implicit foreign exchange rate. Using PPP rate, an amount of money thus has the same purchasing power in different countries.

The rate of exchange represents the ratio of purchasing powers of two currencies only in respect of internationally traded commodities. PPP, however, takes into account all (domestically + globally) traded commodities traded against a currency. Therefore, PPP is a realistic measure of the value of that currency.

(c) Growth Rate : 'Growth rate' refers to the rate of increase in the value of goods and services produced by an economy during a year.

Growth rate is the amount of increase that a specific variation has gained within a specific period and context.

The rate of economic growth means the rate at which the national income increases annually. When calculated at constant prices, it measures the real rate of growth.

(F) Personal Income (P.I.) :

P.I. is the sum of all incomes actually received by all individuals or households during a given year.

Thus,   **P.I. = N.I. – Social security contributions – Corporate Income taxes – Undistributed Corporate Profits + Transfer payments**

(G) Disposable Personal Income (D.P.I.) :

After we deduct personal taxes like income tax and personal property taxes from Personal Income, we obtain D.P.I.

Thus,   **D.P.I. = P.I. – Personal taxes**

5.3 Foreign Trade (Such as GATT, WTO) and Union Budget

Consequent upon the Uruguay Round Agreement, GATT was converted from a provisional agreement into a formal international organisation. This organisation is called World Trade Organisation which became functional with effect from 1st January, 1995. The general council of WTO is incharge of its regular business while a ministerial conference meeting alteast once every two years gives direction to the working of WTO.

(A) Difference between GATT and WTO :

With the formation of WTO, the old system of GATT has come to an end. It would therefore, be educative to find out the extent to which and the respects in which the new system of WTO differs from the old one called GATT.

(1) Wider Coverage : In the old system, there was GATT as the agreement between contracting parties; and GATT was the organisation facilitating administration related to the agreement. With the establishment of WTO, the organisation of GATT ceased to exist. But *the GATT as the agreement dealing with trade in goods continues to exist*, though in an amended form. Under WTO, two more agreements *viz.* General Agreement on Trade in Services (GATS) and General Agreement on Trade Related Aspects of Intellectual Property Rights (TRIPS) have come into existence. The old text is now called *GATT-1947* and the new version is called *GATT-1994.* The WTO is thus GATT + much more.

(2) Provisional Vs. Permanent : GATT was *ad hoc* and Provisional. It had no provisions for creating an organisation. The WTO and its agreement, on the other hand, are permanent. The latter as an international organisation, has a legal basis because the member nations have verified the WTO agreements. Moreover, these agreements themselves describe how the WTO shall function.

(3) Legal Status : GATT was an agreement among signatories who were legally the contracting parties. The general agreement therefore, was a legal text. As against this, the WTO is an international organisation formed by and comprising of member nations.

(4) Possibility of Contravention : The old GATT system allowed the existing domestic legislation to continue even if it went against   a provision of the general agreement and the country concerned was a signatory to the GATT. The WTO, on the other hand, does not allow such a contradiction in the provisions of the WTO agreement clause and the existing law of any member country.

(5) More powers to WTO : The WTO yields wider powers and more functions than the GATT. It plays an important role in the economic affairs of the world. By accepting the Uruguay Round Provisions, a nation can become a member of WTO. Again, the system of settling disputes in the WTO is faster and automatic compared to the earlier system.

(B) The Principles and the Functions of WTO :

This latest international organisation has been based on certain basic principles and is assigned specific functions.

(1) Principles of WTO : The following are the fundamental principles on which the trading system of WTO is based.

(a) Non-discrimination : This principle implies that –

- All trading partners shall be granted the most favoured nation treatment i.e. no discrimination is made except in cases of regional trade agreements; and
- Foreign goods, capital, services, trade marks, and patents are given the same treatment as is given to their national or domestic counterparts.

(b) Freedom of Trade : The most important and ultimate objective of WTO is progressive liberalisation of trade so that there remain no barriers in the free flows of goods and services internationally.

(c) Stability and Predictability : The WTO are committed not to create or raise trade barriers arbitrarily. This provision aims at imparting stability and predictability to the trading system.

(d) Fair Competition : The WTO system of trade, it is claimed, aims at creating open, fair and undistorted competition. The rules regarding equal treatment to all trading partners as well as those regarding dumping and subsidies are framed to ensure fair conditions of trade.

(e) Case of Developing Countries : In respect of developing countries, especially the least developed, are given more time to adjust and are given special privileges.

(2) Functions of WTO :

(a) Facilitating the implementation, administration and operation for the furthering of the objectives of multilateral trade agreements and providing the framework for such implementation and operation.

(b) Providing a forum for negotiations among the members concerning their multilateral trade relations.

(c) Administering the 'Understanding on Rules and Procedures Governing the Settlement of Disputes'.

(d) Administering the Trade Review Mechanism.

(e) Achieving greater global economic policy co-ordination in co-operation with such agencies as IMF, IBRD etc.

The general Council of the WTO is assigned the following functions :

(i) To supervise the operations of revised agreements relating to goods, services and TRIPs.

(ii) To act as the Dispute Settlement Body.

(iii) To serve as a Trade Review Mechanism.

(iv) To establish the three councils for goods, services and TRIPs as its own subsidiaries.

(C) The Agreements covered by WTO :

As referred to earlier, the WTO agreements are three in number and they are

(1) General Agreement on Tariffs and Trade (GATT).

(2) General Agreement on Trade in Services (GATS).

(3) General Agreement on Trade Related Aspects of Intellectual Property Rights (TRIPs).

These agreements start with broad principles enunciated in the GATTs, and TRIPs. They are followed by extra agreements and annexure dealing with special requirements of specific sectors like agriculture or textiles etc. as noted in the earlier section. Besides, there are detailed and lengthy schedules of commitments made by individual countries allowing specific foreign product or services and access to their markets. In addition there are two groups of agreements *viz.* Agreement on Trade Policy Reviews and plurilateral agreements not signed by all the members.

(D) Enforcing Liberalisation of Trade :

The WTO stands for liberalisation of international trade in goods and services. Implications of this measure for various sectors are as follows :

(1) Trade in Manufacturers : Major liberalisation in this respect includes :

(a) commitment not to exceed a particular level of tariffs,

(b) reduction in tariff rates, and

(c) expansion of duty-free access.

However, so far, the gains accruing to developing countries have been more. This is because developing countries whose exports are mainly labour-intensive have not been accorded enough tariffs-cut. The cuts given are below average. Besides, the non-tariff restrictions are to be phased out by 2005.

(2) Agricultural Trade : Important aspects of liberalisation in this respect include :

(a) Tariffication, i.e., use of tariffs instead of quotas and other non-tariff barriers;

(b) Industrial countries should reduce tariff by an average of 36%;

(c) Developing countries can indicate maximum ceiling tariff bindings (e.g. India has indicated 100% on primary products); and

(d) Regarding subsidies, separate provisions are made to effect their withdrawal in cases where they become discriminatory or otherwise.

(3) Trade in Services (GATS) : The liberalisation provisions in respect of services include :

(a) No discrimination between national and foreign services to be made;

(b) All countries are basically obliged to foster freedom of trade in services including financial services, tele-communications, transport, audio-visuals, tourism and professional services as well as movement of workers;

(c) Transparency requirement is obligatory so that every member country should publish all its relevant laws and regulations pertaining to services, including agreements related to trade in services.

(4) Dispute Settlement : A multi-lateral system of settling disputes has been provided for. No member country therefore, can take unilateral action and every country has to abide by the agreed procedures and to respect the judgements. First stage is one of mutual discussion; second is mediation and finally there would be proceedings like a tribunal.

(E) WTO and Developing Countries :

It is important to remember that 80% of the member countries of WTO are developing countries or Under Developed Countires (UDCs). Under the GATT system these countries were given certain privileges and concessions. The WTO also has provisions to deal with the special needs of the UDCs. These are as follows :

(1) Special Provisions in WTO Agreements : The WTO Agreements provide the following main features to the UDCs :

(a) The liberalisation obligation is lower in respect of the developing countries.

(b) These countries have been given extra time to fulfil their commitments.

(c) The Agreement has a special section dealing with provisions on the concept of non-reciprocity in trade negotiations between the industrial countries and the UDCs. For example, the developing countries are not expected to give matching offers to the developed countries, while finalising trade concessions.

(d) Special and differential treatment given to the UDCs entitles them to concessions which are not available to developed countries. A section entitled 'Economic Integration' contains some preferential treatment for the UDCs.

(e) To augment the areas of opportunities for developing countries in trading, there are provisions giving special access like those in respect of textiles, services and technical barriers to trade.

(f) When the developed countries adopt some domestic or international measures like anti-dumping or safeguards against technical barriers, they are required to safeguard the interests of the developing countries.

(g) There are also provisions which require the developed countries to support the developing countries in establishing plant and animal health standards, assisting them to establish a tele-communications network, and so on.

(2) Committee on Trade and Development : There is a special committee on Trade and Development which oversees the special aspects of WTO Agreements related to developing countries. Among areas receiving priority are : Low provisions favouring developing countries are implemented, what guidelines are furnished for technical co-operation, how the participation of the UDCs in the trading system can be enhanced and what is the position of the least developed countries in the whole system.

Member countries are expected to bring to the notice of the WTO, special programmes involving trade concessions for products of the UDCs, and regional arrangements also as finalised among the developing countries. The Trade and Development Committee has handled notifications of the Generalised System of Preferences (GSP) programmes, (in which developed countries lower their trade barriers preferentially for the products from the UDCs) preferential arrangements among developing countries like those in cases of Southern Common Market in Latin America or that in Southern Africa and AFTA (ASEAN Free Trade Area).

Besides, the sub-committee on the Least Developed Countries reports to the Trade and Development Committee. The work of the former relates to –

(a) ways of integrating the least developed countries into the multi-lateral trading system; and

(b) exploring extension of technical co-operation to them.

Technical co-operation is an area devoted entirely to helping the UDCs. This involves helping build-up institutions and train the staff.

(F) An Assessment of WTO Arrangements :

The Uruguay Round was so complex, comprehensive and controversial that the negotiations needed to complete the round, took as many as seven years. The success or failure of the WTO, like all other international organisations, will depend upon how the set of agreements is translated into practice.

Various estimates of gain from the UR agreements have been made but most of the gains will accrue to the developed countries; while some least developed countries which are importers of food are expected to be losers. According to some estimates, the increasing real income for the European Union will be roughly 1.6% of the GDP, for the US it will be 0.2% and for Japan it is likely to be 0.9% of GDP. The gains for some other countries as a percentage of GDP are estimated to be China : 2.5%, India : 0.5%, South Africa : 0.6%, and Brazil : 0.3%. In absolute terms however, the US would be the largest beneficiary with a gain between $ 28 and $ 67 billion; while all the developing countries constituting 80% of WTO member countries might gain between $ 36 and $ 78 billions.

As has always happened, the developing countries in general are getting little out of the Uruguay round. The Wall Street Journal has said that the US and the EC are getting best pieces of the World trade pie, the developing countries are getting the crumbs. As already noted, some concessions are given to the developing countries. But the experience so far is discouraging. While the liberalisation of agricultural trade and a hike in agricultural prices would benefit agriculturist exporters in the LDCs, the high food prices due to cuts in subsidies would adversely affect food importer countries.

One of the major areas of disappointment is the trade in textiles. Textiles happen to be an important item of export for many developing countries. The existing restrictions on imports of textile in developed countries are going to be reduced in phases extending over ten years. This is too long a period according to many LDCs.

Developing countries are also worried about trade in services. But because of the differences of opinion, the final picture has not yet been clear. One of the achievements of the UR is that the rules and regulations have become more transparent making trade harassment more difficult.

Similarly, the machinery for the settlement of disputes and the provision for arbitration are the new rays of hope for the developing world.

(G) Union Budget :

Union budget refers to the annual financial statement of the estimated receipts and expenditure of the central government.

Meaning of Government / Union Budget :

According to **Gladstone,** "*Budgets are not merely matters of arithmetic, but in a thousand ways to go to the root of prosperity of individuals and relation of classes and the strength of kingdom*".

A budget maps out the process of acquiring scarce resources for government use or for use under government direction. It is not a balance sheet of the whole economy because it does not present a complete picture of the financial condition of the country. From government budget, we know about the receipts and expenditures of a government for the year under reference. In no way it gives us a picture of the financial condition of the country. In other words, a government budget is a financial plan covering outlays and receipts of the government.

Government budget serves several objectives :

(1) Budgeting is a means of policy implementation. The budget is a guide for management and budgetary procedures are instruments of administrative control.

(2) The budget document may be a source of information to the public on past activities, current decisions and future prospects.

(3) The budget is a means of legal control. In other words, at each stage of budget formulation and execution, questions can be raised. The stress on legal control implies that, government budgeting prevents the abuse of power or improper use of public funds.

To sum up the features of government budget :

(a) **It is a tool of accountability :** It states the purpose of expenditures and is presented in the form that will be useful for legislative action.

(b) **It is a tool of management :** The budget specifies directly or implicitly the cost, time and nature of expected results.

(c) **It is an instrument of economic policy :** Budgeting has variety of functions. For instance, it indicates the determination of natural growth and investment goals. It promotes macro-economic balance in the economy. It is a vehicle of reducing economic inequalities.

(H) Components of Government / Union Budget :

The major two components of government budget are the expenditure and revenue.

(1) Government Revenue : We study all those sources from which the government derives its revenues. Taxation is the major source of revenue to the government. The income of government through all sources is called public revenue. It includes income from taxes, prices of goods and services supplied by public enterprises, revenue from the administrative activities such as fees, fines, gifts, grants etc.

(2) Government Expenditure : It includes the ways and means of allocation and resulting effects of public expenditure. It is well-said by **Findlay Shirras,** "the finance department must, in special degree, prove to be an unsleeping guardian of the public purse."

Public expenditure is that expenditure which is incurred by the public authorities say, central, state and local governments, either for promoting economic and social welfare of the citizens or for protecting them or satisfying their collective needs in the economy.

(3) Government Debt : Government needs loans to meet certain situations created by war, famine, floods or other natural calamities. When the governmental expenditure exceeds governmental income, deficit is created in the budget and the government borrows from the public. It also borrows to promote the economic development of the country. The government may borrow from banks, business organisations, business houses, individuals and also from foreign countries.

Thus, a government budget is a financial plan covering outlays (expenditure) and receipts of the government. One should not mistake government budget as a balance sheet of the whole economy as it does not present a complete picture of the financial condition of the country. From government budget we cannot get a picture of the total assets and liabilities of the country but, we can only know about the receipts and expenditures of the government for the year under reference. It shows us whether the expenditure and receipts are in balance (Balanced budget) or expenditure is more than receipts (Deficit budget) or expenditure is less than receipts (surplus budget).

(I) Types of Government / Union Budget :

(1) Balanced Budget : In classical approach, a budget is essentially a balanced budget i.e. balance of revenues and expenditures. This view was based on the analogy of behaviour expected of an individual that, he must not exceed the expenditure more than his income. As Adam Smith states that, what is true of every private family is true to the economy. That is, government must spend according to its income.   Exceptions can be only during situations of emergencies such as wars.

This principle of balanced budget was stated by **Bastable** as, "under normal conditions there ought to be a balance between these sides of financial activity.   Outlay (expenditure) should not exceed income". The limitations of the balanced budget became a key operating factor for politicians and civil servants.

Different economists supported the principle of balanced budget. The French economist, **J. B. Say** was of the opinion that, wasteful public expenditure leads to budget deficits.

Hugh Dalton raises three preliminary questions relating to a balanced budget. They are :

(a) What should be included in "expenditure" ? Here Dalton states that in a balanced budget the new capital expenditure is financed not by loan or by taxation.

(b) What should be included in revenue ? Dalton suggested excluding all receipts which are in the nature of capital. In other words, a budget is balanced if during the accounting period there is no increase in the net public debt.

(c) What length of time should be taken as the accounting period ?

A year is the usual accounting period as Dalton states it.

When a budget is a balanced budget ? On this question no unanimous opinion exists. According to one view, a balanced budget means equality between income and expenditure without any funded debt. This is really an ideal condition which is seldom realised. Governments generally carry considerable long-term debt.

Another view is under a balanced budget, current expenditures are to be covered by current revenues, while capital expenditures are to be financed by borrowing without unbalancing the budget.

The classical approach of balanced budget was based on the assumption that full employment is the normal condition. This approach further, does not accept the prevention of unemployment through budgetary action.

(2) Budget Surplus : The principle of sound government finance in the classical system, loses its glamour, when widespread involuntary unemployment exists. Keynes, Beveridge, Dalton etc. maintain that a budget policy should aim at attaining and maintaining full employment.

According to Hansen, "if one adopts whole heartedly the principle that government financial operations should be regarded as instrument of economic and public policy, the concept of a balanced budget can play no role in the determination of that policy".

In Keynesian terms, "Budgets have come to be linked with management of the economy, in turn bringing a greater consideration of the effects of expenditures on the economy". This role of the budget is quite comprehensive.

Surplus in the budget occurs when the government revenues exceed expenditures. The policy of surplus budget is followed to control inflationary pressures within the economy. It may be through : (a) increase in taxation, (b) reduction in government expenditure; (c) or both.

This will reduce income and aggregate demand. During inflationary or Boom period, government must follow surplus budget. It can be by increasing the taxes. This would increase the revenue of the government but reduce the purchasing power of the people and consequently the fall in aggregate demand. On the other hand, government reduces its expenditure on public works and other infrastructure. Thus, the revenue with the government is in excess of its expenditure. This is surplus budget. A current surplus is a positive indicator and helps to impose discipline on current spending and encourages investment indirectly.

(3) Deficit Budget : In Keynesian terms, budget deficits are viewed as positive instruments to raise aggregate income to stimulate all sectors to spend more.

Deficit budgeting is an important method of overcoming depression. When government expenditures exceed its receipts, it is deficit budgeting. Deficit budget may be secured by reduction in taxes and not reducing government spending. Reduction in taxes tends to leave larger disposable income (purchasing power) in the hands of the people and thus encourage consumption expenditure. This would lead to increase in aggregate demand, output, income and employment.

However, reduction in taxes may not lead necessarily always to increase in aggregate demand if the tax relief given is saved and not spent on consumption. Businessman may not also invest more if the business expectations are low. Thus, to safeguard against such eventualities government should follow (alongwith reduction in taxes) increased government spending. Its multiplying effect will be high and thus increase consumption and investment expenditures in the economy.

The role of budget in a developing economy is much different from that an industrialised economy.

In developed countries, budgetary measures can minimise the cyclical influence through maintenance of aggregate demand and full employment. However, in developing countries, unemployment is not cyclical but chronic in nature, reflecting structural bottlenecks of the economy. Therefore, through deficit budget when government injects more purchasing power it only increases imports and raises the price level in the economy.

But, the fact is that, more than monetary policy, budgetary policy is important due to the presence of non-monetised sector in developing countries. Further, public sector has a dominant role in the economy. Thus, budgets play a more positive role in developing economies.

A budget that has intentions of forgetting inflation, public debt and encourage private sector, need not necessarily be balanced, it may be a deficit, but it should be "prudent".

To conclude, balanced budget laws are very hard to implement as it does not correspond to the economic definition of government surplus or deficit. In other words, it is difficult to define 'budget balance'. The more functional budgets are either surplus budgets or deficit budgets.

5.3.1 Revenue Account, Capital Account, Revenue and Capital Budget, Fiscal Deficit, Plan and Non-plan Expenditure

(1) Revenue Account : Taxation is the major source of revenue to the government. The income of government through all sources is called public revenue. It includes income from taxes, prices of goods and services supplied by public enterprises, revenue from the administrative activities such as fees, fines, gifts, grants etc.

(2) Capital Account : Capital account is one of the two primary components of the balance of payments; the other being the current account. Capital account reflects net change in national ownership of assets.

A surplus is the capital account means money is flowing into the country. Whereas, a deficit in the capital account means money is flowing out of the county.

Capital Account = Foreign Direct Investment (FDI) (+) Portfolio Investment (+) Other Investment (+) Reserve Account

(3) Revenue and Capital Budget : The budget of any government (or any other organisation is an estimate, for a certain future period, of receipts and expenditures. The budget of the Government of India is a document of such estimates and contains three sets of figures. For example, the budget for the year 2014-15 would contain : (i) Actuals i.e. accounts for the year 2012-13, (ii) Budgeted and revised figures for the current year 2013-14; and (iii) Budget estimates for next year 2014-15.

Revenue and Capital Budgets :

The budge is divided in two parts :

(a) Revenue or Current Budget : Current receipts and payments are included in the *Revenue Budget*. These receipts and payments are recurrent i.e. arise every year.

(i) Revenue Receipts : Revenue Receipts are divided into two parts :

- **Tax Revenue :** Revenue or proceeds from Union Taxes such as Income Tax, Corporation Tax, Wealth Tax, Estate Duty and Taxes on Commodities like Central Excise Duties, Service Tax, Customs Duties. Yields of some of these taxes are shared with states, and by deducting states' share, net tax-revenue is also shown in the budget.

- **Non-tax Revenue :** Receipts other than tax yields are shown as non-tax revenue i.e. income from other sources. They are : (i) Interest Receipts, (ii) Dividends and Profits of government enterprises, and (iii) Fiscal and other services like grants form external sources, fees, fines, gifts etc.

(ii) Revenue or Current Expenditure : Revenue expenditure is recurring expenditure that has to be met out of current or revenue receipts. It includes :

- Expenditure on general administration including internal law and order (police), judiciary, defence, collection of taxes etc.,

- Social and community services like education, medical and public health, labour welfare, child and mother care, food security, and

- Economic services like roads, bridges, trade and transport, agriculture, industries etc.

(b) Capital Budget : This part of the budget contains receipts and payments arising from investments in terms of physical capital goods.

(i) Capital Receipts : Capital receipts are receipts on the capital account. They include :

- Net recoveries of loans and advances given to State Governments and Union Territories and PSUs earlier for a fixed period and currently due for repayment,

- Net market borrowings,

- Net small savings collections, and

- Other capital receipts like provident funds, PPF collections, special deposits like SCSS-2004 etc.

(ii) Capital Expenditure : Capital expenditure of the Government of India consists of plan and non-plan expenditure financed out of capital receipts. These items of expenditure are :

- Loans to States and Union Territories for funding plan projects and also loans to foreign countries,
- Capital expenditure on economic development,
- Capital expenditure on social and community development,
- Capital expenditure on defence and border security, and
- Capital expenditure on general services.

(4) Fiscal Deficit : The Chakravarthy Committee pointed cut the inherent weaknesses of narrowly defining Deficit Financing as Budgetary Deficit and recommended a change in the concept. The Government accepted the recommendations of Chakravarthy Committee, dropped the conventional concept of deficit financing. With effect from 1997-98, the Government of India started calculating the real deficit of fiscal operations (or deficit financing) as defined by the Chakravarthy Committee. This third concept of deficit is termed as *'Fiscal Deficit'*. Thus,

> **Fiscal Deficit = Revenue Receipts + Capital Receipts (only recoveries of loans and other receipts) – Total Expenditure**

OR

> **Fiscal Deficit = Budget Deficit + Government's Market Borrowings and Other Liabilities.**

(5) Revenue Deficit : Right from the launching of the First Five Year Plan (1950-51), the Government of India recognised two types of deficits only : Revenue Deficit and Overall Budgetary Deficit. Both these concepts are very simple to understand.

The budget is classified into 'Revenue Budget' and 'Capital Budget'. Revenue budget comprises of the current receipts and current payments. Current (or revenue) receipts refer to the tax and non-tax revenue of the Government. Current payments, on the other hand, refer to the total plan and non-plan revenue expenditure of the government. Thus,

Revenue Deficit = Revenue Receipts – Revenue Expenditure

It is noteworthy that from 1951 to 1975, the policy of the Government of India was to generate revenue surplus so that the surplus could be used for financing the Five Year Plans. This policy was adopted on the recommendation of the Taxation Enquiry Commission (Krishnammachari Commission). It was like saving by individuals from current incomes, to be used for purchase of assets. This meant the effort was to widen tax-base and keep public expenditure under control. But (unfortunately) subsequent years witnessed growing revenue deficits mainly due to increasing non-plan expenditure i.e. expenditure on general administration, defence, interest payments and subsidies etc. despite remarkable increase in tax-revenue.

(6) Overall Budgetary Deficit : Overall budgetary deficit, also called 'Budget Deficit' implies excess of total expenditure over that receipts. In other words,

Budget Deficit = Total Receipts i.e. Revenue Receipts + Capital Receipts – Total Expenditure i.e. Revenue Expenditure + Capital Expenditure.

This amount was treated by the Government as 'Deficit Financing' since it represented borrowing from the RBI which meant printing and injecting additional currency into the economy. This concept of equating Budget Deficit with deficit financing was criticised by **Prof B.R. Shenoy,** way back in 1954-55. His objection was to exclude government borrowing from the market or raising funds from other sources like National Small Savings Schemes, Post Office Savings Deposits, Provident Fund etc. which were, in fact, other liabilities of the Government. It was only the Report of the Committee appointed by the Reserve Bank of India to review the working of the India Monetary System under the chairmanship of **Prof. Sukhoonoy Chakravarthy** in 1982 was accepted by the RBI that the various concepts of 'Deficit' were clearly defined. This enabled the Government of RBI as well as public to understand and analyse the impact of budget deficits on total money supply and effects of changes in money flows on various sectors of the economy.

(7) Plan and Non-plan Expenditure : Before 1987-88, the expenditure proposed in the budget (and actually incurred during previous year) was classified into : (a) development expenditure, (b) defence expenditure, and (c) other expenditure. With effect from the budget 1987-88, the Government of India adopted a new classification, viz., non-plan expenditure and plan expenditure.

(a) Plan Expenditure : Plan expenditure of the Union Government can be classified in two parts :

(i) Expenditure incurred on central plans like on schemes of agriculture and rural development, irrigation and flood control, energy, industry and minerals, transport and communication, science and technology, environment and social services.

(ii) Central Assistance to plans prepared by the states and finalised by mutual discussion between the Planning Commission and the chief minister and other representatives of the state concerned. Allotments are duly approved and then disbursed.

(b) Non-plan Expenditure : Non-plan expenditure is further classified into revenue expenditure and capital expenditure.

(i) ***Revenue Expenditure*** *:* Revenue expenditure financed from revenue account includes interest payments, defence expenditure on revenue account, all subsidies like food supplied through PDS (or under food security when it becomes operational), fertilisers, debt relief to farmers, postal and other general services, pensions and salaries of government and aided educational, health, social, broadcasting etc. service providers' staff. The areas funded by the Government of India through match grants, full grants, conditional grants etc. include social services, economic services (power, communications, science and technology, besides agriculture, industry, transport etc.).

(ii) ***Capital Expenditure and Non-plan*** *:* Capital expenditure and non-plan includes defence (building, purchase of equipment, missiles, vehicles etc. and infrastructure like roads etc.), loans to public sector enterprises, loans to states and loans to foreign countries.

5.4 Understanding of Summarised Budget for the Current Financial Year

The Union Budget of India, referred to as the Annual Financial Statement in Article 112 of the Constitution of India, is the annual budget of the Republic of India, presented each year on last working day of February by the Finance Minister of India in Parliament.

The Union Budget of India for the Financial Year 2013-14 was presented by the Finance Minister **Mr. P. Chidambaram** on 1st March, 2013 in the Parliament.

Prominent Features of Budget, 2013-14 :

(1) Non change in slabs and rate for personal income tax.

(2) Tax credit of ₹ 2,000 to be provided to every person having income of upto ₹ 5 lakhs. This will benefit 1.8 crore people.

(3) 5 to 10 per cent surcharge on domestic companies whose taxable income exceeds ₹ 10 crore.

(4) Commodities transaction tax levied on non-agricultural commodities futures contract at 0.01 per cent.

(5) Modified GAAR norms to be introduced form April 1, 2016.

(6) No change in peak rate of customs duty on non-agricultural products.

(7) Direct Tax Code (DTC) bill to be introduced in current financial session.

(8) No change in basic custom duty rate of 10 per cent and service tax rate of 12 per cent.

(9) Import duty on rich bran oil cake withdrawn.

(10) Import duty raised from 75 to 100 per cent on luxury vehicles.

(11) Duty free limit on gold raised to ₹ 50,000 in case of male and ₹ 1,00,000 in case of female.

(12) No countervailing duty on ships and vessels.

(13) Specific excise duty on cigarettes and cigars raised by 18 per cent.

(14) Service tax to be levied on all A/c Restaurants.

(15) Education cess to continue at 3 per cent.

(16) TDS of one per cent on value of properties above ₹ 50 lakhs agriculture land exempted.

(17) Fiscal deficit will be 5.2 per cent in current year and 4.8 per cent in next fiscal.

(18) Plan expenditure pegged at ₹ 5,55,322 crores for 2013-14.

(19) Non-plan expenditure pegged at ₹ 11,09,975 crores for 2013-14.

(20) ₹ 86,741 crores capital expenditure to Defence.

(21) ₹ 532 crores to make post offices part of core banking.

(22) ₹ 5,87,082 crores to be transferred to states under share of taxes and non-plan grants in 2013-14.

(23) FIIs will be allowed to participate in exchange traded currency derivatives.

(24) Total budget expenditure is ₹ 16,65,297 crores and plan expenditure is ₹ 5,55,322 crores.

Questions for Discussion

1. State the Importance of National Income Analysis.

2. Explain the Following Concept : (A) GDP, (B) PPP, (C) Growth Rate.

3. Explain the Principles and Functions of WTO.

4. Explain the Following Concepts :

    (A) Revenue Account, (B) Capital Account, (C) Revenue Deficit, (D) Fiscal Deficit, (E) Plan and Non-plan Expenditure,

5. Write short notes on :

    (A) Public Finance.

    (B) Basic Concepts of National Income.

    (D) Budget for the Current Financial Year.

www.ingramcontent.com/pod-product-compliance
Lightning Source LLC
Chambersburg PA
CBHW080904020726
47502CB00008B/2343